About the Author

Mark Robson was born in Wanstead, Essex, in 1966, and was raised, for the most part, near Carmarthen in West Wales. In 1982, he gained a scholarship to join the Royal Air Force as a pilot and he is currently serving at RAF Brize Norton, Oxfordshire. His first book *'The Forging of the Sword'* was largely written during tours of duty in the Falkland Islands. The long quiet hours maintaining the constant vigil of the Quick Reaction Alert Force proved to be an ideal breeding ground for flights of fantasy, mainly because the wet and windy weather of the Falkland Islands prevented flights of anything else! Subsequent books have been inspired by the wave of encouragement by readers. Mark now lives in the Midlands and is married with two children.

By this author:

The Darkweaver Legacy

Book 1:	The Forging of the Sword	*ISBN 0953819000*
Book 2:	Trail of the Huntress	*ISBN 0953819019*
Book 3:	First Sword	*ISBN 0953819027*
Book 4:	The Chosen One	*ISBN 0953819035*

The Imperial Series

Book 1:	Imperial Spy	*ISBN 141690185X*
Book 2:	Imperial Assassin*	*ISBN 1416901868*
Book 3:	Imperial Traitor*	*ISBN (978)1847380352*

Imperial Spy

Femke, a gifted and resourceful young spy, is entrusted with a vital foreign mission by the Emperor. It appears a simple task, but nothing is straightforward when your enemies are one step ahead of you. Framed for two murders while visiting the neighbouring King's court, Femke finds herself isolated in an alien country. As the authorities hunt her down for the murders, her arch-enemy, Shalidar, is closing in for his revenge...

*Publication dates
Imperial Assassin - published Nov 2006
Imperial Traitor - published May 2007

For up to date information on future releases see:

www.markrobsonauthor.com

THE FORGING OF THE SWORD

Mark Robson

SWORD PUBLISHING

THE FORGING OF THE SWORD
ISBN: 0-9538190-0-0

First published in the United Kingdom by Sword Publishing

First Edition published 2000
Reprinted 2001
Revised and reprinted 2002
Reprinted 2003
Reprinted 2004
Reprinted 2005
Reprinted 2006

Published by Sword Publishing,
9 Wheat Close, Daventry, Northants, NN11 0FX.
www.swordpublishing.co.uk
info@swordpublishing.co.uk

Printed and bound in Great Britain by Technographic, Kiln Farm,
East End Green, Brightlingsea, Colchester, Essex, CO7 0SX.

For my wife, Sarah,
who insisted that it would be a good idea if the hero had a mobile phone, but had the grace to accept that this story was mine to tell –
and for my parents, real and inherited, who have always been there when it mattered.

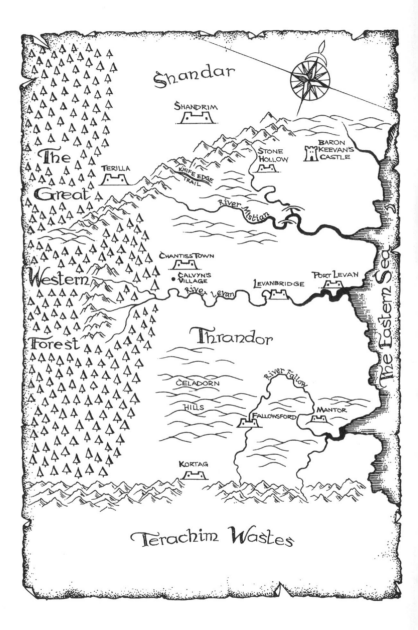

PROLOGUE

Demarr stumbled, bone weary. The end of another day of hard walking over the forbidding terrain of the Terachim wastes was drawing near. The attack came without warning, a huge shape lunging out of the rapidly lengthening shadows. It was the loose rock that saved him in that initial instant. Even as Demarr stumbled he sensed the movement in his peripheral vision and rolled into the mis-step, drawing his sword as he fell. The creature's jaws snapped closed on empty air a split second behind him.

Adrenalin slammed into his system as Demarr rolled into a fighting crouch, all tiredness forgotten and survival instincts taking over. 'Whatever the beast is, it's big and it's damned fast,' he thought.

The low cliffs loomed unnaturally large in the half-light of dusk as the sun, sinking blood red into the desert, played its daily game with the shadows. Out of a large crack in the cliff face the massive head arrowed down on its long, heavily scaled neck. Demarr dived to the right, again narrowly escaping death as the vicious tooth clashed terrifyingly close by.

'What the hell is that thing?' he thought, as he scrambled for cover into a line of rocks.

Shrugging off his pack, Demarr ventured a glance around the large rock behind which he had taken refuge. At first he could see nothing, the inky black fissure cloaking the creature in darkness. Then, with a slight clatter of disturbed stone, the attacker stepped jerkily out

7

into the open.

'Great Tarmin! It's a firedrake,' he breathed, stunned by the reality of his situation. Firedrakes had been thought extinct for generations, and in some quarters had begun to be regarded as legendary creatures created by the over-active minds of minstrels intent on making their sagas more entertaining. Yet here was a firedrake, larger than he had ever imagined possible and infinitely more dangerous.

The firedrake stuttered forwards a few more steps, its head and long neck swaying slowly from side to side and its elongated scaly body partially emerging from its lair. Demarr squinted as he peered into the half-light, his thoughts racing as he weighed up his options. There was nowhere to run, and to attack would be suicidal. He ducked back down behind the rock and his hand came to rest on an egg-sized stone. Stalling for time, he grasped the pebble and flicked it out low and hard to his right. The diversionary projectile clattered noisily to rest at the base of the cliff some thirty yards away, yielding an instantaneous result. The firedrake's head snapped round like lightning to face the rattling sound of the settling stone, and the huge creature's body lurched slightly in the same direction.

There was a slight pause as the firedrake seemed to assess the situation, a silhouetted statue of terror against the cliff. Suddenly, bursting into motion, the beast charged along the base of the cliff to the impact point of the thrown pebble, its head arching forward in a blur of speed to find... nothing. It stopped, momentarily confused, its head scanning constantly from left to right and its eyes probing the dusky shadows for signs of movement.

A crack of stone sounded in the darkness and a huge boulder smashed into the firedrake's shoulder. Screaming in pain, the beast reared its head as a gigantic section of the cliff began to collapse towards it. The rumble of falling rock drew Demarr to sneak a quick glance from his hiding place. It seemed like the whole rock face was in motion and time seemed to stand still as the semi-darkness was filled with crashing rocks, tumbling as if in slow motion. He crouched, frozen in place by the incredible scene unfolding before him, until a boulder the size of a beer barrel bounded past nearby, bringing him back to his senses.

The air filled with choking dust as Demarr flattened himself behind the ever-dwindling security of his defensive barrier of rock. The avalanche seemed to continue crashing around him for an age as he lay with his arms curled protectively over his head. An apparent eternity later, silence settled like a blanket. He could not believe his luck. First the firedrake, then an avalanche, and he was not only still alive but also unharmed.

Quickly and silently he opened his pack and pulled out an old shirt. Tearing a wide band from the back of the garment, he folded the resulting strip of material in half and bound it around his lower face to form a filter against the dust. Placing the remainder of the shirt back into his pack, he cautiously peered into the dust-filled darkness. Demarr's eyes streamed with grit-induced tears. He could make out nothing. Shouldering his pack and holding his sword warily in front of him, Demarr turned to retrace his steps towards the firedrake's lair. He reasoned that no other living creature would share such a retreat, so with the beast buried under the rockfall it made sense to make use of the shelter for the night, providing that the avalanche had not blocked the entrance.

Demarr stepped carefully through the treacherous boulders and had taken no more than a dozen paces when there, no more than six feet in front of him, was the head of the firedrake. The creature's eyes were unfocused and its double eyelids were fluttering seemingly at random. Without hesitation Demarr leapt forward, driving the point of his sword with all of his might into the nearest eye. The already stunned firedrake lashed out automatically at this new source of pain, catching Demarr squarely in the chest with the side of its head. The force of the blow lifted him off his feet, hurling him several yards through the air to land flat on his backpack. Demarr's head snapped back and connected hard with the ground, bringing instant unconsciousness. Consequently he saw and heard nothing of the screeching, thrashing death throes of the firedrake as he lay unmoving long into the night.

When he came to, Demarr was aware of nothing but a blinding headache and the bitter cold of the desert night. It was black as pitch, the stars obscured by a curtain of high cloud. All he could think of was getting warm and finding something, anything, to stop his violent shivering. Struggling out of the shoulder straps of his backpack, he fumbled the ties open and pulled out his blanket. Cocooning himself in it, he immediately plunged back into the oblivion of sleep.

The sun crept its way up over the bleak horizon, bringing warmth back to the rock-strewn scene of carnage. The raucous cries of feeding vultures dragged Demarr slowly to an awareness of his surroundings and of the pain in his head. Slowly he pushed himself up to a sitting position, only to retch violently and immediately lie back down.

'Concussion,' he thought. 'I must rest, but not here. It's not safe.' The events of the previous night flooded back. Carefully, he sat up again. This time his stomach did not betray him and he surveyed the scene around him, wide eyed with wonder.

'How the hell did I get away with that?' he muttered to himself, awed by the devastation of the avalanche and the size of the dead beast only yards away.

Lifting himself slowly to his feet, Demarr draped his blanket around his shoulders and, dragging his pack, threaded his way to the huge black cave entrance. Once there he paused briefly and sifted through his pack for his tinder, flint and small remaining piece of candle. Finding them, he ventured on into the darkness, determined not to waste his precious resources unless absolutely necessary.

The floor of the cave was even, making progress easy. The solid rock surface underfoot soon gave way to a sandy dust layer that was dry and soft to walk on. Surprisingly, the cave was not very deep and Demarr reached the furthest wall long before losing sight of the entrance.

'Time for a quick look around,' he thought, fumbling briefly with his flint as he lit the candle. Shadows leapt around the cave, dancing about in the flickering light. A small casket sitting against the back wall immediately caught his attention.

'Well, well! What have we here?' he whispered to himself, kneeling down to examine his find. The lid was not locked so, with hands that were trembling with a mixture of fatigue and excitement, he unclipped the ornate hasp and carefully lifted the lid. It opened easily, as if the hinges had been kept perfectly oiled. Inside, cradled on a bed of dark silk, gleamed a beautiful silver talisman.

'At last my fortunes are changing,' he breathed.

CHAPTER 1

Trapping the recently landed speckler with his left hand, Calvyn deftly rapped the fish hard on the head with a lump of wood. Placing it alongside the other four laid out on the bank, he surveyed his catch with a slight smile. He would be popular at home tonight. Five good sized specklers made an excellent catch, and by his reckoning it was only just past midday.

Low cloud scudded across a leaden grey sky as a few more drops of rain plopped into the still water of the slowly flowing river pool. The unsettled weather appeared wracked with indecision. It had been spitting with rain on and off since dawn but could not seem to make up its mind whether to rain properly or not. Despite the overcast skies, the mild spring temperature had encouraged Calvyn to ignore the overcast skies and strike out for the River Levan on his rest day to try to entice the succulent speckled torpedoes onto his hook.

Fishing had been a passion for Calvyn since his father had given him his first pole for his seventh birthday. However, now that he was fourteen and starting to develop his adult strength, tasks like chopping logs for the fire or working in the village fields occupied more and more of his time. Not that he was unhappy – far from it. Calvyn enjoyed the work that he was given and savoured the company of the adults that worked alongside him. The conversations of the grown-ups fascinated him, and though he would generally remain quiet, he would listen for hours as he worked, soaking in information like a sponge and storing it away in his busy head.

'Well my beauties,' he said, addressing the line of dead fish, 'consider yourselves invited to dinner this evening. If we leave now we should have plenty of time to get cleaned, dressed and suitably warmed up.' His smile widened further as he remembered the first time he had seen Joran, his father, making this little speech. He had stood wide-eyed as Joran had solemnly picked up the recently deceased fish fresh from the river and, holding it in front of his face, had formally invited it to dinner. Then he had held the fish's mouth to his ear briefly and had turned to Calvyn, his face serious.

'He says he'd be delighted to join us for a meal,' Joran said, with that deadpan expression which he was so good at.

'Really?' the young Calvyn had replied in amazement. Then Joran had laughed, put down the fish and picked up his son in a big hug. 'Yes, son. Really,' he chuckled.

Today Joran had been too busy to go fishing, so Calvyn had gone to the river alone. He had enjoyed the time of quiet and the chance to daydream to his heart's content. He had imagined that he was a dashing adventurer dressed in shining armour, rescuing princesses and riding a great white stallion. His mind soared as he fought imaginary monsters and duelled with evil knights, overcoming all odds and becoming a great hero. However, despite the freedom he had missed his father. Joran's little dry witticisms and light-hearted humour always made him great fun to spend time with.

'Dad's really going to wish he'd come with me today,' Calvyn thought as he packed the fish into his satchel-like bag and, ducking his head through the strap, swung it onto his back. He carefully fastened his hook into the butt of his pole, slanted the rod against his shoulder and set off through the trees towards the road.

The walk back to the village would take the best part of an hour from this far downstream, but Calvyn liked to fish the bigger pools where the large specklers lurked under overhanging trees so he did not consider the distance a significant inconvenience. If he felt lazy he could always start fishing at the point where the River Levan wended its way closest to the village, a mere fifteen minute stroll from home. However, when he did, somehow he always seemed to be drawn downstream, and would find himself further from home than he initially intended.

A fine mist of drizzle started to fall as Calvyn left the protective shelter of the thin bank of woodland lining the riverbank. The tiny pervasive droplets of water rapidly penetrated his clothes, leaving him soaked to the skin. His fair hair darkened as it became plastered against his head. Droplets of water ran down from his forehead, forming drips at the end of his nose, which in turn were blown against his mouth and lower face, causing him to lick his lips with ever-increasing frequency.

Calvyn began to look forward to getting home and pictured in his mind the big log fire in the living room. He imagined stripping out of his sopping wet garments and the feel of the fresh warm clothes against his skin. His imagination pictured a mug of steaming broth warming his hands and a seat in the comfortable chair by the fire. In his mind's eye, he recounted to his parents the tale of how he had ensnared his catch. Inevitably, he chuckled to himself, he would add a little more size and weight with each retelling of the elusive fish that got away.

He could almost hear his mother, Elenor, giving him the standard lecture for being mad enough to stray so far from home when the weather had been teetering on the brink of rain all day. Despite her worry she invariably relented very quickly, and Calvyn felt that she berated him more out of a sense of duty these days than because she really meant it. He knew that she understood the lure of the riverbank, and appreciated his need to get out of the house on his rest days.

As he thought about life at home, it dawned on Calvyn just how fortunate he was to have such a good team in his parents. They were always ready to help and they took a keen interest in his hobbies and pastimes. Both also worked extremely hard to make their life as a family in the little community of farmers as comfortable and happy as they could. Their small cottage was warm and homely, and their garden was always neat and blooming with flowers. Joran had a way of making life fun, no matter what they were doing. He always had a laugh and a joke, even whilst instructing Calvyn in a new skill or carrying out the most boring of chores. There did not seem to be anything about maintaining the cottage and garden or working on the farmland that Joran did not know. Even if he was not an expert at something, he always knew enough to get jobs done, and would invariably raise a laugh or two whilst he did it.

Elenor maintained a much more sober front and had always controlled the discipline during his childhood, as Joran with his happy-go-lucky nature and relaxed attitude towards life tended to make light of Calvyn's occasional misdemeanours. Calvyn knew that she actually had a very sharp wit, but could only recall a handful of times that she had displayed it openly. Elenor took her wifely and motherly duties most seriously, and developed very effective methods to stop Calvyn from straying too far from her house rules. She was also an excellent cook and her kitchen was perpetually filled with the smells of her baking. She seemed to have a sixth sense that knew exactly which herb or spice would heighten the effect of the meal, and precisely when to add it to produce the perfect strength of flavour.

Just thinking about his mother's cooking started Calvyn's stomach rumbling. He picked up his pace a bit as he started to think of some of the amazing meals that Elenor had produced with the fish that he had caught in the past. His mind and stomach now focused, caused him to stride forward with a renewed sense of purpose as his hunger dominated his thoughts. He had brought a couple of bread rolls with him, snatched hastily from the kitchen as he had crept out of the house in the early hours of the morning, but he had eaten those a couple of hours ago. Now the combination of the fresh air and the walking was building his appetite up rapidly towards what his father often described as a teenage feeding frenzy.

The road to the village came into sight as he topped a slight rise, and as if that view inspired the elements against him, the wind hit him with its full driving force as he marched onwards into the blowing rain. Minutes later he stepped through the sparse hedgerow and onto the road.

'You couldn't give an old man a hand could you?'

Startled, Calvyn looked up to see a slender figure wrapped in a long dark cloak, iron grey hair hanging lank and dripping water from the sides of his otherwise bald head. Twinkling blue eyes watched Calvyn's reaction, and the old man's weather beaten face displayed a gentle amusement.

'Sorry to surprise you but I saw you come down the field there, and when you turned to head in my direction I thought that you might be able to help me out of a spot of bother. It's my cart, you see. It's stuck in a pothole.'

Calvyn had been head down, mind elsewhere and barely conscious of more than putting one foot in front of the other. He had completely failed to notice the canvas-topped wagon and its owner only a few yards away. Being naturally wary of contact with strangers, warnings from his parents bombarded Calvyn from the past. However, this old man looked harmless enough, and his genuine smile and obvious predicament settled the boy's conscience.

'By all means, Sir,' Calvyn replied politely, and unslinging his satchel he propped his fishing pole against a nearby tree and placed the bag down beside it.

'Thank you, young man. I've been stuck here for about half an hour, but it seems like days in this foul weather. With two of us we should be able to shift it without too many difficulties.'

The old man turned and walked to the dappled grey horse that stood patiently in front of the wagon, flicking its ears at the rain. 'There, there, girl, we'll soon have you on the move again, you'll see,' he said, patting the horse on the side of the neck. Fishing out a treat from somewhere inside his cloak, he held it in his cupped hand to the horse's mouth. The horse snuffled briefly and its lips gently accepted the proffered offering.

'We've tried rocking free... er, I am sorry, I haven't asked your name.'

'I'm Calvyn,' confided the young man. 'I come from the village about a mile and a half down the road.'

'Well met, Calvyn. My name is Perdimonn,' the old man replied, extending his hand in greeting. They shook hands briefly. 'My good friend here is Steady,' he continued, patting the horse's neck again. 'It's not much of a name but when I first got her I seemed to be yelling it at her so often that it kind of stuck. Now it actually describes her quite well, so in the long run it's not worked out so badly.'

Walking back from the horse and around the side of the wagon, Perdimonn beckoned for Calvyn to join him. The old man gestured down at the wheel which was stuck up to its axle in a deep hole filled with muddy water. Side by side they surveyed the predicament for a few moments. A sudden gust of wind bearing larger droplets of rain dimpled the surface of the muddy puddles into choppy wavelets.

'Well, Calvyn, as I said we tried rocking the wagon free, but Steady isn't easy to co-ordinate and tends to live up to her name. What do you think? Have you got any ideas?'

Calvyn looked thoughtfully at the problem and wondered what his father would do in the same situation. No doubt Joran would come up with something simple and effective. Something like...

'We could try to lever the wheel up, but we would need a big lever,' he answered, voicing his thoughts with a tentative tone.

'Good for you, lad,' Perdimonn said, looking pleased. 'That was my solution too. Unfortunately I'm not heavy

17

enough to make any impression on the wagon loaded as it is, but if we both put our weight to it, then Steady should be able to pull the wagon free. I have a piece of wood we can use as a lever. Just a minute and I'll bring it out.'

Sheltering behind the wagon and still looking at the half submerged wheel, Calvyn wondered to himself whether this rescue operation would work. A minute or so later, Perdimonn reappeared with a long sturdy piece of wood which looked ideal for the task. Together, the two of them worked the lever into the pothole under the rear of the wheel. Initially, they made little headway until, leaning around the side of the wagon Perdimonn shouted into the swirling wind, 'Ho, Steady!' He clicked his tongue loudly against the roof of his mouth twice and turning back to Calvyn flashed him a quick grin as Steady began to pull. The wagon lurched forward slightly as Steady leaned forward, and Calvyn jammed the lever down into the mud beneath the wheel, lodging it in place.

'Whoa, Steady!' yelled Perdimonn, and the wagon settled back against the lever. 'Well, the moment of truth, lad. Are you ready?'

'I guess so,' smiled Calvyn. He enjoyed a good challenge, and this was starting to become fun despite the rain. 'Let's go for it.'

Perdimonn chuckled at the grinning face of the young man, dripping wet but shining with enthusiasm. 'Right then, as soon as Steady starts her pull we both put our weight onto the lever, all right?'

'Sure,' Calvyn replied, positioning himself at the end of the beam and giving Perdimonn a thumbs up signal to indicate his readiness.

'Forward, Steady!' bellowed Perdimonn at the top of his voice. As the horse strained to move, Calvyn and the old man threw their weight onto the lever which creaked alarmingly under the strain. The wheel crept up about halfway out of the pothole before stopping, the opposing forces deadlocked for several seconds. 'Still too heavy,' Perdimonn grunted, doubled over the beam. 'Whoa,

Steady!' The wheel sank back into the hole with a muddy squelch and they both took their weight off the straining lever.

Perdimonn stood, frowning slightly as he looked at the offending wheel. 'It looks like we will have to do this the hard way after all,' he muttered to himself. Taking a deep breath, he sighed heavily and turned to Calvyn with a wry smile. 'Well, my boy, let's try that again. This time though, I'll lighten the load of the wagon whilst you lever the wheel.'

Calvyn shrugged noncommittally and nodded. He could not see any way that the old man could effectively make any significant difference to the weight on the sunken wheel without unloading the contents of the wagon onto the roadside. He was even more puzzled when Perdimonn disappeared behind the opposite side of the wagon muttering something unintelligible under his breath. He leant back against the wagon and sheltered from the rain, preparing himself for at least a short wait. The wind carried Perdimonn's soft words to Calvyn's ears, but although he could hear some of them quite clearly, they made no sense to him at all. The man appeared to be speaking gibberish.

It could only have been about a minute before Perdimonn shouted from behind the wagon, 'Are you ready, Calvyn?' Surprised, Calvyn jumped back into position and stood, poised to throw his weight onto the lever.

'Ready when you are,' he yelled back.

The muttering resumed briefly. Then Perdimonn's voice raised again. 'Forward, Steady!'

Hurling himself up onto the lever, Calvyn had no time to react when, in one unchecked movement, the wheel eased straight out of the pothole. The astonished Calvyn landed flat on his face on the muddy road, the lever under his stomach knocking all the breath from his lungs. He looked down the road and found that the wagon moving away had left Perdimonn directly in his line of sight. For an instant he could see the old man standing with his arms stretched out horizontally towards where the wagon had been, palms up and fingers splayed. His long dark cloak billowed in the wind and his lips were still forming words that held no meaning to Calvyn. A drop of splashed mud dripped into his left eye, causing him to screw up his face and blink rapidly, all focus momentarily lost. Calvyn raised his hand to wipe the offending dirt clear but stopped, realising that his hands were probably even filthier. Blinking furiously and still gasping for breath, he rolled onto his back and sat up. Perdimonn stopped his strange monologue and Calvyn heard the footsteps of the old man as he approached.

'Take it easy and get your breath back, young Calvyn. That was quite a fall you took there. Here, use my cloak to wipe that mud out of your eyes.'

Calvyn felt the old man's hand grasp his wrist and soft material was placed in his hand. He dabbed and wiped gently at his stinging left eye. It was still watering a lot but he could now open it long enough to focus on the old man's face, which was studying him with some concern.

'Are you all right?' Perdimonn asked.

Nodding, Calvyn replied in gasps. 'Nothing broken... just give me a... second or two... I'll be fine.'

'Slow down. Breathe deep and slow. That's right. Now then, let's get you up out of that wet mud or you'll catch your death of cold and I'll catch an earful from your parents!'

Perdimonn helped him upright and stepped back a pace. Calvyn controlled his breathing and glanced up at Perdimonn to find him looking back with a slightly sheepish expression on his face. He certainly appeared embarrassed for some reason, which only added to Calvyn's confusion.

'Well, your wagon's free but I don't understand how it came out so easily with only my weight on the lever. Are you a Sorcerer or something?' The question was out before Calvyn could censor it, and he gulped quietly as his mind raced.

'The "or something" is more accurate,' Perdimonn answered, looking away. 'We can talk about it on the way to your village. I appear to be heading in your direction and you certainly deserve a lift for your help. Come on, grab your pole and bag and join me on the driver's bench. I've got some dry blankets in the back. You'll feel the chill, sitting in this weather after all that hard work.'

Calvyn mentally kicked himself for his tactless question as he gathered his belongings and clambered up onto the wide seat at the front of the wagon beside Perdimonn. The old man was kneeling on the bench, leaning into the enclosed body of the wagon and rummaging around. When he turned round he brought out a thick grey blanket with him and handed it to the muddy and bedraggled young man.

'I know that it doesn't feel that cold right now, but being so wet, and with this wind, believe me you will be glad of it before we get you home.'

Calvyn thanked him and bundled himself up in a warm wrapping whilst Perdimonn picked up the reins and with another double click of his tongue, started the wagon moving on along the road towards the village. The road was really little more than a track, and the going was very slow as Steady clopped along at a careful walking pace. Steering as best he could on the narrow lane, Perdimonn meticulously avoided the larger puddles and obvious potholes. He certainly did not want a repeat performance of his earlier predicament. The rain was now getting heavier, the fine misty drizzle giving way to larger raindrops swirling in the squalling winds.

'By Tarmin! What on earth possessed me to come here in springtime?' Perdimonn exclaimed. Looking across at Calvyn with a grin he continued, 'Does it never stop raining in this godforsaken country?'

Relieved that the awkward quiet had been broken, Calvyn tentatively smiled back. 'Oh yes, normally the weather isn't too bad at this time of year. Besides, the spring rains are good for the crops.'

'Spoken like a true farmer,' Perdimonn chuckled. 'I

suppose I should be glad that I am not up in the Vortaff Mountains, or I might be buried up to my neck in snow by now.'

'Have you really seen the Vortaff Mountains?' Calvyn asked, amazed. 'I've never been further than Chantiss Town and that's only about ten miles east of the Baron's Manor. My father took me there last year when the main crop was taken to market.'

'Oh yes, I've been through the Vortaffs a few times on my travels. I've been on the road for... well a long time now. I wouldn't have it any other way. Steady and I have seen a lot of things together over the years.' Perdimonn paused briefly, his eyes suddenly distant and his mind obviously elsewhere. 'Mmm the mountains,' he murmured softly to himself. Then, snapping out of his reverie, he turned his head towards Calvyn and continued, 'Before I get lost in stories of far-off places, I owe you an apology, young man.'

Calvyn looked across into Perdimonn's twinkling blue eyes, and for some strange reason that he could not quite fathom found himself holding his breath in anticipation. However, despite his sudden rush of adrenalin, the expectant young man was certainly not prepared for the revelation that was about to change his whole perception of life.

'Just between us lad, I used a little magic to lighten the wagon. I'm sorry that I didn't warn you first. I can assure you that what I did certainly wasn't sorcery. That works in a different way entirely, and I'm not entirely sure that sorcery could be used for such a purpose. I must admit that I hadn't used that particular spell for such a long time that I'd forgotten just how effective it could be,' the old man said, turning his eyes back to the road.

'Magic!' the astonished Calvyn gasped, eyes as round as saucers. 'I thought that was just make believe, you know, for stories and poetry.'

'Make believe? Far from it. Why there's even a Magicians' Academy in Terilla where many go to study the arcane arts. Many Magicians and even a few Grand Magicians have earned their robes there over the years.' Perdimonn glanced across at the wide eyed boy again and smiled. 'So what made you think that magic wasn't real?'

'Well, my parents, I suppose,' he replied. 'They used to tell me the old tales, of course. There were Sorcerers and dragons, heroes and princesses, but I was always left with the impression that they were only stories.'

'Most of them probably were just fiction, or at least largely so,' said Perdimonn, returning his concentration to the winding road. 'Magic, as you have just witnessed, is real, but as people are usually afraid of what they cannot understand, we had better keep this as our little secret. What do you say, young Calvyn? Can you keep a secret?'

'Yes, Sir, you can trust me,' Calvyn replied quickly.

The boy's mind raced as fantasies surfaced, flashing through his head in a jumbled mass of heroic deeds. Snapshot images of Magicians pouring lightning bolts from their fingers, turning dragons to stone and wielding various famous magical objects fired through his imagination in rapid succession. He tried placing his own face into some of the pictures but somehow they did not seem quite right. Instead, he voiced the question to Perdimonn that burned hotter than any other.

'Can anyone learn magic?'

'Fancy yourself as a Grand Magician, do you? But then what young lad of your age doesn't, eh?' Perdimonn bantered, momentarily locking eyes with Calvyn. For an instant it seemed to Calvyn that the old man looked directly into his mind, those incredible blue eyes laying all his fantasies bare. Though it lasted only for a second, he felt the hairs on the back of his neck stand on end and a shiver ran down his spine. The moment passed and Perdimonn looked forward at the road again.

'Anyone can learn the theory of magic, but the ability to become a magician lies all in the application, and that depends on the individual. Much of my knowledge is allied to the healing arts, but I've mastered the odd spell or two from the other disciplines over the years.'

'So you didn't go to the Academy then?' asked Calvyn.

'What? Oh, the Academy at Terilla. No. I sometimes regret not having at least tried to gain entry, but Terilla is in Shandar and I never much cared for the Shandese. Besides, you need a respected sponsor to be accepted there, which I never had, and I'm far too old to think about trying now. The knowledge that I've gained of the arcane arts has been mainly self-taught from books. It was perhaps not the ideal way to learn but effective enough for my needs.'

Both fell silent as they each became absorbed in their thoughts, one reliving times gone by, going over past decisions and regrets, the other imagining a future filled with adventure and magic.

The rain began to ease again to a fine drizzle as the horse and wagon wended its way along the muddy lane towards the small collection of dwellings that made up Calvyn's home village. The gently rolling countryside thereabouts was divided into a patchwork of fields by high hedges, often thickly strewn with large trees, making it virtually impossible to see more than one or two fields ahead. The occasional copse of trees and small stands of woodland bore witness to the fact that the entire area had once been part of the Great Western Forest. However, the forest borders now stood some twenty miles distant, as over the years a succession of Barons had given their farmers the work of claiming the land for crop production and profit.

The lane itself was almost entirely tree lined and bright green with fresh new spring leaves. Blossom bloomed in the occasional cherry and apple trees, and also in many of the hedgerows. Despite the rain, bird song filled the air with its constant melody, but the occupants of the wagon remained all but oblivious to their surroundings as their thoughts and dreams carried them both to lands strange and distant.

Steady blew hard through her nostrils, her head coming up sharply. After a couple more prancing steps she came to an abrupt halt, her eyes rolling in alarm.

'What is it, girl?' Perdimonn asked as Steady remained stationary, sniffing at the air and occasionally stamping one foreleg in irritation.

'It's probably just a bonfire or something,' Calvyn said, surfacing back to reality and turning to Perdimonn. 'The village is just around that next bend.'

'No, something is wrong here,' the old man replied, his voice dropping in volume to a bare whisper and his face looking rather worried. 'Steady isn't spooked that easily. Let's keep moving, but stay on the lookout for trouble. If Steady smells something in the air then we ought to at least be cautious. I've come to rely on the old girl a lot over the years, and she's kept me out of trouble many times. I'm not going to start ignoring her warnings now.'

Tapping Steady with the reins and talking gently to her, Perdimonn coaxed the horse into a slow walk. Alert and aware of Steady's continued uneasiness they continued around the last stretch of lane to the village. Again the horse came to an agitated standstill, prancing and blowing shuddering snorts through her nose. The man and boy could only sit, stunned in silent shock as they gazed, frozen in disbelief at the stark scene of death spread before them.

CHAPTER 2

Perdimonn settled himself onto the driver's seat with a sigh of relief, and watched as Calvyn bounced around with even more than his usual energy and enthusiasm, making the final preparations for them to get back on the road. The young man was almost bursting with excitement, and obviously high on the anticipation of this evening's promised lesson. Perdimonn was beginning to regret telling Calvyn of his intention to commence the boy's practical instruction in elementary magic that evening, as the exercise would require mental calm and focus. However, as they moved along the lanes at Steady's slow plodding pace, the old Magician sensed Calvyn calming his excitement.

It had been two years since the murder of Calvyn's parents, and the time had softened his grief. The boy's initial bouts of weeping had eventually given way to an inconsolable silence and finally, after several weeks, Perdimonn had managed to begin drawing him out of his mourning and back to the reality of the present. Even now, two years on, Calvyn still suffered the occasional intense nightmare about the slaughter of his family and friends. Sometimes the memories of the three days that Perdimonn and he had spent burying the people of his village would surface as dark dreams, the images so vivid that he would wake with tears running down his cheeks. However, the passage of time was gradually dulling the sharp edge of the pain.

There had been survivors of course, mainly women

and children who had run or hidden successfully from the raiders, but those who had defended their homes had all been killed without mercy. Sadly Calvyn's parents were amongst these, as were all those with whom he would have claimed a close relationship. Gradually over that first day, people had surfaced from their hiding places and returned from wherever they had run to. Cautiously they had gathered to count their losses and their dead, and to begin the mourning.

The old man had stayed in the village with Calvyn through those few days and helped as best as his old bones would allow. Calvyn, for his part, kept the secret of Perdimonn's magical abilities and indeed said very little to anyone during those painful days and nights. Perdimonn had watched sadly as the village people struggled to find some form of normality and routine to ease the pain and begin to move on. With so few men left it was certain to be a long time before life would return to anywhere near normal. Several of the village women had offered to take Calvyn into their households but he had refused them all in turn, claiming that he wanted to make a life for himself elsewhere and to try to leave his grief behind him.

On the fourth day, Calvyn had approached Perdimonn and asked to join him on his travels. The old man had been reluctant but Calvyn's quiet persistence had won through and Perdimonn had agreed that Calvyn could travel with him to Chantiss Town. The old man planned to trade there for a week or two before moving on and the boy would have time to change his mind before getting too far from home.

Perdimonn had realised straight away that Calvyn would need to focus on something other than his loss. Therefore, after what he deemed to be an appropriate time of grief he had dangled the lure of magic to catch the young man's attention, and then with relentless patience, Perdimonn had carefully reeled him in.

Calvyn was not completely blinded by his grief, and even in the depths of his sorrow he analysed what

Perdimonn was doing and considered what ulterior motives the old man might have to teach a recently orphaned teenager the secrets of magic. With subtle care he studied Perdimonn's facial expressions and words over those first few weeks together, trying to detect a hint of anything other than kind concern. There was nothing to find. He gradually realised that life had just dealt him one of those bitter-sweet coincidences, which gave with one hand and took away with the other. Once convinced of this, Calvyn embraced the old man's offer of tutelage with open arms and an intensity that allowed him to bury his loss deep within his heart.

To begin with, Calvyn had needed to learn to read. In his village, where farming was the main concern, reading and writing were discouraged. Some farmers, by necessity, had learned some basic skills such as carpentry and weaving, and old Korvan had also done an apprenticeship as a blacksmith in his youth. The villagers had therefore been largely self-sufficient. It was generally understood that there was no need to learn to read and write when hard physical graft and clean living embodied the goal of every good farmer.

Perdimonn quickly realised that Calvyn had only the vaguest notion of the geography of the Kingdom of Thrandor and its neighbouring lands. Moreover, whilst the boy knew many of the ballads and sagas sung by the minstrels, his knowledge of factual history was virtually non-existent. With this in mind, Perdimonn tutored Calvyn daily in the skills of reading and writing, and as the boy progressed, gave him history books to practise with. Perdimonn and Calvyn sat and studied maps together, and Calvyn never ceased to be amazed at the extent to which his new found friend and mentor had travelled.

The first few months were a testing time for the old traveller. Perdimonn had been on his own for many years. He was used to wandering alone as free as a bird, plying his services and wares where he willed. The sudden burden of responsibility weighed heavily on his shoulders. He was sorely tempted to leave Calvyn at the orphanage in Chantiss Town, or with the local Baron who would have been bound by law to feed and clothe him. How ever, he found that he just could not bring himself to be that callous. 'Besides,' he thought, 'the boy would be good company on the road and a welcome helping hand with some of the heavier chores that had begun to get harder over the previous few years. Time would tell whether the boy would stick out his childhood dreams of learning the art of magic, and in the meantime he would be a useful extra pair of hands.'

For his part, Calvyn was grateful to the old man for his support, and after getting over his initial wariness he dived into his set tasks and studies with a wholehearted dedication. Even whilst chopping firewood or fetching water he recited the alphabet or pictured the written words in his mind to match the objects around him.

Two years had seen Calvyn grow several inches in height and begin to fill out his more adult frame with muscle. His sharp mind had progressed his education far faster than Perdimonn had initially believed possible. He could now read and write fluently in Common and had recently started to learn the Runic language in which all magical texts were written. Tonight's lesson, though, was to be both momentous and different. It would be the culmination of two years of frustration as Calvyn was to learn how to cast his first spell.

Many of the exercises that he had been cajoled into learning had seemed utterly pointless to the impatient young man.

'Why do I need to learn how to read and write in Common if all spells are written in runes?' he had asked one night, after wading through a particularly dry text that described, in seemingly endless detail, the Peace Treaty of Kortag.

'Trust me, Calvyn,' Perdimonn had replied with a patient smile. 'It's a necessary part of your education. You must learn to walk before you try to run or the results may be catastrophic.'

Calvyn had sighed heavily in resignation at the task ahead. He rose and walked across to the wagon, carefully packed the book into the purpose built case and strode back to the campfire, deep in thought. Perdimonn had watched him, quietly amused by the lad's frustration. He could remember the times when he too had been roiled to the core by what he felt was the snail's pace of instruction and progress in his own education. With hindsight it was perfectly clear why it had to be done this way. The unprepared mind would not achieve the clarity of vision, the purity of thought or the focus of concentration required to master even the simplest of magic spells. However, he had been forced to admit to himself that the boy showed incredible potential. He was extremely quick to learn, always cutting through to the point of the lesson and displaying the commitment and tenacity to achieve, in a fraction of the time, what it had taken Perdimonn years to learn.

What had surprised Perdimonn more than anything else was Calvyn's progression in the meditation exercises that would be so crucial to his abilities at working with magic. After about six months of reading and writing lessons, the young man was really beginning to become irritating with his constant requests to start learning the practical side of magic and how to cast spells.

'Believe me, Calvyn, you are not ready to start with that yet,' he had said, his patience starting to wear a little thin. 'You don't just learn a few words and launch into a magical spell. It doesn't work that way. Your training has only just begun, and if you are serious about pursuing a path of magic as a career you have many, many lessons to learn. Patience is required in large quantities I'm afraid. Soon you will come to realise that the learning will never end, and the size of the task that you have undertaken will become more apparent. Perhaps, though, it is time to introduce some variety into your lessons. Maybe that will show you some indication of just how far you have to go.'

Perdimonn's eyes had gone distant for a moment, and

he paused for a few seconds before his focus snapped back and locked on to Calvyn's face. Despite his suitably chastened appearance, Perdimonn could not fail to note the rebellious glint in the young man's eye that spoke volumes of his lack of appreciation of just what was involved in his chosen vocation. A slow smile spread over Perdimonn's face.

'This exercise will be more to your liking I think,' the old man had said, moving his point of focus into the dancing flames of the fire. 'It is an exercise of the mind. You will need to master this and many others like it before you start trying to perform any serious spells.'

Calvyn had perked up markedly at this, his eyes sparkling with excitement in the flickering firelight.

'Now, close your eyes. Not too tight, that's it,' Perdimonn had instructed, watching the young man intently as he complied with the directives. 'Now try to completely clear your mind of all thoughts. I want you to picture nothing in your mind but whiteness. Pure whiteness. Let your mind's eye see nothing but a blanket of pure white that obscures all else. When you have achieved that picture, let me know.' Falling silent, he had watched the boy's eyes flicker under his eyelids as he tried to achieve the simple picture.

Calvyn had sat with his eyes closed, thinking that the request was ridiculously easy. However, no matter how hard he tried to focus on whiteness, other pictures and thoughts had continually intruded. After the best part of an hour he had conceded defeat and retired to bed wearing a very thoughtful expression.

Each night over the next two weeks, Calvyn had struggled with this meditation after his literature lesson in the evening. Time after time he would manage to picture the whiteness spreading out across his mind's eye, only to have a blob of red or blue or some other colour appear and spread in opposition. Mentally exhausted he had fallen into bed each night dreaming of whiteness being invaded by armies of coloured shapes. Finally, after about a fortnight, the pure white vision had

31

solidified in his mind: a wall of whiteness with no chink of colour to be found.

'I have the whiteness, Perdimonn. What comes next?' he had asked quietly, having maintained it in a stable state for a couple of minutes.

Startled out of his own meditation, Perdimonn had answered gently, 'Just hold the picture for as long as you can.'

Muttering a spell under his breath, the old man looked into Calvyn's mind to read his thoughts. Sure enough, the boy's mind had been filled with a blanket of dazzling white. Astonished, Perdimonn had withdrawn to massage his temples briefly and sit silently observing the quiescent face of his pupil.

'Enough, Calvyn, open your eyes and relax,' he had said after a few minutes, continuing after a short pause, 'That was good work tonight. Well done. Tomorrow we will move onto something a little more challenging.'

'Either I was dull or this boy is incredible!' Perdimonn had thought to himself as he remembered the long months of concentration that he had taken to achieve the balanced picture that had taken Calvyn just two short weeks.

Today, once more the old man found himself reviewing Calvyn's meteoric progress as he worked. The day was following a standard pattern as they set up shop in the little village on the banks of the River Mistian. Since Calvyn had started travelling with Perdimonn, trading odds and ends had become almost as profitable as the selling of his healing potions and ointments. The young man had developed a knack for bartering and had turned the wagon into a regular tinker's trove of oddments. Initially the old healer had been a little annoyed, but he soon realised that people were often far more interested in looking through the boy's collection of bric-a-brac than they were in specifically looking for miracle cures. Many who browsed through Calvyn's collection departed with items from Perdimonn's, so he held his peace.

Their stall had been set up and the villagers had

gradually filtered out from their homes and traded with a mixture of barter and coin. The wagon was then reloaded, and after a leisurely meal they had continued on their wandering journey. Making use of the meditative exercises that he had spent months perfecting, Calvyn suppressed the boiling miasma of thoughts that had bubbled through his mind all day long. Realising that he would have to be mentally focused for this special lesson for which he had waited so long, he worked on one of his favourite meditations whilst rumbling through the countryside.

Carefully he reconstructed in his mind the image that he had been mentally building over the previous few months. The outline started as a silhouette of a knight on his great charger, black against a light grey background. First came the backdrop of a castle. Proud battlements with pennants fluttering from the towers stood against a deep blue sky punctuated only by the occasional puffy fair weather clouds, snowy white in the afternoon sun. Next Calvyn added a moat with the drawbridge lowered and the tips of the portcullis just visible within the top of the archway that framed the solitary entrance.

The horse became a glistening chestnut brown, rearing its defiant challenge to any pretender to its master's might. The knight, encased in silver armour, had a bright red plume on his helmet and a colourful coat of arms emblazoned on shield and tabard. The powerful figure sat tall with his lance butt holstered vertically down, its point towering high in the air. The shadows and details of wind-stirred grass rippling in the breeze, all became a part of the mental discipline to produce clarity of vision.

The picture embodied all that Calvyn thought of as noble and inspiring. It was full of details from the adventure stories which his father had told him before he went to sleep at night, the perfect hero out to save the righteous from evil monsters and villains. Today, however, the vision served a far greater purpose than that of a daydream. It worked as a focus to calm his mind and channel his thoughts in a precise, disciplined exercise of mental control.

Perdimonn and Calvyn pitched their tents late that afternoon within a small copse of trees, a little way off the road. The wagon was safely parked nearby at the edge of the trees, and Steady was tied on a long reign to a stake that Calvyn had driven into the ground in the adjacent field. Calvyn prepared a small firepit and gathered wood enough to feed a small fire for several hours before he walked to a nearby stream to draw water. When he returned, Perdimonn had all but finished preparing their evening meal. Dusk was settling in as the two travellers, having finished their supper, prepared to begin their nightly study time together.

Calvyn felt another surge of excitement flow through him, but he smothered it quickly and forced himself to sit quietly awaiting his lesson, and completely at peace with the world around him. The occasional call of a night bird punctuated the rapidly thickening darkness with its mournful hooting cry as he patiently sat watching the old man.

Perdimonn too sat waiting. Testing his pupil's patience, he sat pretending to be engrossed in deep meditation. As time crept onward and the full darkness of night became complete, he realised that this was yet another test which Calvyn would not fail. It became obvious that the boy would sit there, still and silent, all night if necessary. Pride swelled in Perdimonn as he reached this conclusion and he spent the next minute or two collecting his thoughts before looking up at Calvyn.

'Pick up one of the straighter sticks from the firewood pile and study it closely, Calvyn. We will start your instruction with a light spell and I want you to have an object from which the light can emanate. Also, you will need to memorise this set of runes,' Perdimonn said, handing across a small piece of parchment with a single line of the strange characters printed on it in clear script.

Calvyn set to his tasks. He carefully studied the stick

in the light of the fire until he was sure that he could picture every slight angle, knot and twist in the piece of wood. Then he turned his attention to the runes. They were all symbols that he had seen before, and the appropriate sounds seemed to ring in his mind as his eyes ran along the line of the spell. He went over the runes again and again until they burned vividly in his mind.

'I think I'm ready,' he said eventually, looking across at Perdimonn expectantly.

'Well let us see what you have learned then, shall we?' the old man replied with a slow smile of encouragement. 'Firstly, hold the stick out in front of you with one end vertically up in the air.'

'Like this?'

'That's fine. Now take a good look at how it appears in the light of the fire, and when you are ready, close your eyes and try to keep the image of the stick firmly in your mind.'

Everything suddenly seemed to click into place in Calvyn's mind, interlocking like the pieces of a familiar puzzle. Suddenly he knew what was coming next. It was as if he had known for a long time. The pieces had been there all along, but until now he had not fitted them together to complete the conundrum. With his eyes closed and the image of the stick locked firmly in his mind he signalled to Perdimonn with his spare hand for him to continue the instructions.

'The spell is a simple one, but just pronouncing the runes will not cause it to work. You must see the runes in your mind's image creating the effect that you desire. For this spell, as you speak each set of runes, you must see them flowing into the tip of the stick. Make them the pearly white of the light that you wish to create. Flow them into the stick, making the tip glow brighter with every rune until it is glowing white enough to fill our campsite with its light. Keep repeating the spell to hold the light stable, and under no circumstances should you open your eyes until I tell you to do so.'

Calvyn began. Softly he enunciated the strange syllables that the runes represented, his mind picturing the glowing symbols melting into the tip of the stick. In his mind's eye the stick began to give off a soft white light, almost ethereal in nature. Gradually the intensity of the light continued to grow ever stronger. He reached the end of the spell and, without pausing, he recommenced with the first set of runes.

'Very good, Calvyn. Don't stop,' the old man said softly. 'When I give you the word I want you to open your eyes. However, I want you to continue with the spell and try to keep the vision of the runes entering the stick even with your eyes open. Give me a "thumbs up" if you understand and are ready.'

Still muttering the syllables in continuous sequence, Calvyn signalled his readiness.

'All right, open your eyes.'

For an instant after Calvyn opened his eyes he viewed their campsite, bathed in the beautiful soft incandescence emanating from the glowing white stick in his hand. With an abruptness that was momentarily blinding, his concentration wavered and the light died away instantaneously to nothing, leaving only the flickering orange light of the campfire.

'That was pretty darned good for a first attempt, Calvyn. Well done,' Perdimonn said, grinning from ear to ear, the pride shining in his eyes.

'But I lost it almost immediately after I opened my eyes,' he replied, disappointment colouring his tone with the sound of implied failure.

'It's very difficult to keep the picture solid with your eyes open. There's an additional part to the spell which will stabilise the effect that you created, making the light remain even if you were to stop speaking, but it is quite complex, and the counter spell to cancel the light is equally so. You should understand that if you failed to learn the counter spell, the stick would glow for all eternity which would be a little ostentatious even for a branch from a decorated midwinter feast tree, let alone this piece of Ash!'

They both chuckled a little before Perdimonn continued, 'We will progress to the more complex spells in good time, but for today you have made a good beginning, and certainly should not be disheartened with your performance.'

'Perdimonn?'

'Yes?'

'Surely if stabilising spells are difficult, then trapping the effects of magical spells within the elixirs, potions and ointments that you produce must be even more so. Why can't you just cure people of their illnesses directly? It would certainly be less complicated and time consuming.'

'You are right of course,' Perdimonn replied, his face suddenly becoming very serious, 'but think back to before you met me. Do you think that anyone from your village would have let a crazy old man who claimed to be a Magician try to magic away their problems? I don't think so. People are very suspicious of things which they do not understand. They are quite happy to use physical things that they can touch and appreciate, like medicinal ointments. However, if we were to tell them that the cures were magical, their superstitions would fill them with doubts, and they probably would not have anything to do with us. Besides, it goes deeper than that. The practice of magic in Thrandor has been outlawed for the best part of two centuries now. Magic is not welcomed in this kingdom.'

'But what about the Magician's Academy at Terilla that you told me about? That must lend credibility to magic, so why do people not believe in it? And how can you ban something which people don't even believe exists?' Calvyn asked, confused by the apparent discrepancy.

'If you remember, I told you that Terilla is in Shandar where Magicians are respected and the practice of all the arcane arts is much more widely accepted. Also, the ban on magic has been in force for so long that people have become used to life without it. Combine this with the fact that most true Magicians do not involve themselves too closely with the affairs of normal folk, tending to keep their studies to themselves, and you can see how magic has fallen into the realms of mythology. There are many charlatans, of course, who use sleight of hand and illusions to amuse and beguile people with their skills. However, no true Magician would stoop to that unless it suited their purpose to disguise some other agenda within the trivial tricks of street artists.'

The relative location of Terilla and even Shandar, apart from being somewhere to the north, were somewhat hazy in Calvyn's memory of world geography, so he let that go. Instead, he directed his questions at the points which he perceived to be more critical.

'But why would magic be outlawed, Perdimonn? Surely Magicians have a great deal to offer people. Look at your healing powers for example.

'Unfortunately, not all magic is beneficial to mankind, and the vast majority of people are not as trusting as you are, my young friend,' he said, shaking his head slightly. 'Indeed, people are quite right not to trust us blindly, as Magicians can equally well use their power to do harm as they can to do good. You must have heard tales of Derrigan Darkweaver and his attempt to take over this land by use of his dark powers of magic. Not all of those tales are fictional. It took the entire Brotherhood of Magicians to foil his plans. The final confrontation was so awesome that it is not surprising that the Saga of the Downfall of Derrigan is dismissed by most as pure fantasy. Believe me when I tell you that it was anything but fantasy. It's hardly surprising that the King outlawed the use of magic in Thrandor after the Derrigan disaster. People distrust all things supernatural, and though I am loath to say it, they probably have good cause to do so. Take my advice in this. As you develop your control of magic, be sure to keep your abilities secret or you will only invite trouble for yourself.'

CHAPTER 3

The two travellers broke camp shortly after dawn. Packing the wagon had become a fine art, with both partners knowing exactly who put what where, and in which sequence. Consequently it was not long before they were underway and enjoying the fine spring morning.

It was a wonderful day to be on the road. The weather was sunny and relatively warm for the time of day, and the profusion of spring flowers lining the country hedgerows scented the air with their distinctive fragrances. Drinking in the sights and smells of the beautiful rolling countryside, Calvyn noticed that in a few places the flowers were just beginning to die back, heralding the imminent arrival of summer.

Before long they began to pass small caravans of merchant wagons carrying their wares to market and to the wharves of the various ports along the coast.

'Good morning. What news from the south, my friends?' called a passing merchant, bringing his wagon to a halt.

'Not much of any significance. Where are you bound, good Sir?' Perdimonn replied, checking Steady to a stop alongside the merchant with a gentle pull on the reins.

'Port Levan to off-load this winter wool.'

'As far as we have heard, the roads in that direction should be free of trouble. The only real disruptions that we've had news of are the occasional raids on smaller villages by the remnants of Demarr's rebels, but those have all been well to the west of your route.'

The merchant's eyebrows raised in surprise. 'Have the King's troops still not wiped those vermin out? I would have thought that having caught Demarr and banished him into the wastelands, his followers would have seen sense and given up their tired excuse for a rebellion. What's it been? Two? Two and a half years now since Demarr was banished?'

'Two and a half,' Calvyn interjected, his face flat and his voice carrying a bitter edge. A lump had come to his throat as unwanted and unforgettable memories were dredged back to the surface.

'The King should have hung that son of a bitch when he had the chance. Maybe that would have been more of a deterrent to those crazy rebels of his,' said the merchant with feeling. 'I know that he was an Earl and claimed a royal bloodline, but I still think that the King was soft not to have had him executed.'

'That would only have sparked even greater trouble,' disagreed Perdimonn with a slight shake of his head. 'As a martyr, Demarr would quite likely have been the instigator of a full-blown civil war. This way the other nobles who are somewhat less than patriotic have not got an excuse to get involved. The King's decision to banish the traitor was a wise one I think. Thankfully, due to his wisdom it is only the odd pocket of renegades who are causing trouble, and not an entire army of them.'

'Well you may be right, my friend, but it still feels wrong that he should be allowed to go free after all the trouble that he caused, even if it is freedom only to roam the Terachim wastes. Hopefully one of the Terachites will do us all a favour and ensure that he suffers a terminally unfriendly welcome.' The merchant gave a nasty sounding little chuckle. 'Thanks for the information. You'll find the road to the north is in fairly good condition for this time of year. The locals appear to have carried out some reasonable repairs to it recently so we've had an uneventful couple of days travelling. Take care and may all your ventures be profitable,' he said, and with a wave and a smile he gave his horse a gentle tap with the reins and moved away.

Calvyn sat quietly, lost once again in thoughts of vengeance as they moved slowly northward. He had discovered that Demarr's rebels had claimed responsibility for the savage attack on his home village shortly after beginning his travels with Perdimonn. Apparently the killings had been in retribution for the local Baron's part in the capture of Demarr. The village had been a soft target, having no weapons to speak of and no apparent need for any defences or fortifications. However, the rebels knew all too well how much the losses would mean to a man like Baron Anton.

The Baron had always been a staunch supporter of the Crown, and was amongst the King's most loyal and trusted nobles. He often attended court at the King's palace in Mantor and it was widely known that he had been a close personal friend of the King since they had undergone their training at arms together as young men. It had been during one of his visits to the palace that the attempted assassination of the King had occurred.

Demarr and a hand-picked group of his men had quietly killed many of the palace guards during the middle of the night and had gathered in one of the anterooms before moving on to the royal sleeping quarters. Meanwhile, Baron Anton had been having difficulty getting to sleep. He had gone out for a late night stroll attempting to induce tiredness, and had stumbled across one of the dead guards by pure chance. Realising the implications instantly, Anton had quickly and quietly roused his own men from their barracks in the eastern wing of the palace and had hastened them to the royal quarters with all possible speed.

They arrived in the nick of time to catch Demarr and his men poised to enter the King's bedchamber. A short, ugly fight had ensued. Demarr's men had not only been taken by surprise, they were also outnumbered. The resulting rout was inevitable and concluded with most of Demarr's companions dead or severely injured, and the traitor himself captured.

Inevitably, the King had been most grateful to Anton for his timely rescue. After the trial and subsequent banishment of Demarr, the King had offered the lands of the traitor to Anton as reward for his services. To everyone's surprise the Baron had refused the gift.

'The land and people that I have in my care at present are enough responsibility for one man, and I doubt that I could effectively supervise the estates of the former Earl Demarr in addition to my own, your Majesty. I thank you for your generosity, but I must decline your kind offer. It is enough to me that I have helped to maintain order in Thrandor, and to keep the rightful King on the throne,' the Baron had replied.

Nothing that the King had said would change Anton's mind, and he had remained adamant in his refusal of any gift. Eventually the King had conceded defeat with a laugh and said, 'Anton my friend, I cannot argue your logic, but your sons may not approve of your decision in years to come.'

'My sons will have their work cut out looking after the estates that they are already due to inherit, your Majesty. Please do not seek to burden them with more. Excess is the path to ruination, and I would spare them that.'

'It shall be as you say, Anton. Let all here witness that I declare the lands of the traitorous Earl Demarr forfeit to the Crown. I will appoint an overseer in due course.'

Calvyn smouldered silently as he rehearsed for a thousandth time what he would like to do if he ever met the infamous Earl Demarr. His imagination, sharpened by his recent lessons in mental discipline, focused razor sharp images of himself facing down the traitor in a duel and eventually, after a titanic struggle, running the banished noble through with his sword. It never occurred to Calvyn once during these frequent flights of fantasy that not only did he not possess a sword, but that as he had never actually handled one, the odds of his lasting more than a few seconds with a renowned swordsman like Demarr were something in excess of astronomical. However, this time Perdimonn did not allow the imaginary battle to reach its unlikely conclusion.

'I did not begin teaching you mental focus techniques for you to indulge yourself in pointless destructive fantasies, young man,' he said in a stern voice. 'If you wish to continue your studies with me, then I suggest that you concentrate on something more constructive.'

'I'm sorry, Perdimonn. That conversation with the merchant just brought it all back so vividly that I couldn't help myself. I sometimes wish that Baron Anton had just left Demarr to his devices and not got involved. Then Mum and Dad and the others would all be alive and happily minding their own business.'

'Not necessarily, Calvyn. Ask yourself what would have happened to the kingdom if Demarr had succeeded in killing the King and claiming the throne for himself. What would the kingdom have been like as a place to live, under the rule of a man who gained the throne in such a manner? Place yourself in Baron Anton's position and ask yourself how you would have felt if you could have prevented those consequences but did not, simply because you did not want to get involved. There will always be "what ifs" in your life, Calvyn. However, it's important not to let "what might have been" rule your future.'

Gazing out over the beautiful green fields of the Mistian Vale, Calvyn thought through the admonition and wise words of Perdimonn. Slowly he began to realise that much of his anger had actually been directed at Baron Anton. His heart had unfairly convicted Anton of condemning his former village and family to destruction. He could rationally see that the Baron had acted with honour and saved the King from certain death at no small risk to himself. However, it still rankled in Calvyn's heart that due to such a noble act, someone had decided to respond by murdering first his family and friends, and subsequently many more innocent people.

The rest of the morning passed without further

incident as Calvyn turned his concentration to a new mental focus exercise. Perdimonn had set him the task of picturing a perfect black square on a pure white background. Once the picture was clear and perfect in form, he then had to start the square turning clockwise about a central axis and accelerate the rotating square until it was spinning as fast as he could possibly get it to go. Despite managing to get a vivid starting picture, he found it immensely difficult to spin the square in a steady acceleration whilst maintaining the integrity of the image. Time after time he tried and failed until, with a sigh, he gave up. Instead he massaged his temples and looked around at the picturesque scenery as the world rolled slowly by.

Shortly after midday they arrived at one of the small market towns dotted along the banks of the River Mistian. Perdimonn stopped the wagon outside one of the inns on the outskirts of town. A sign hung over the door of the Inn with a picture of a fox peering out of a hedge and the name "The Sly Fox" printed in bold letters underneath.

'It's time that we caught up on some news, Calvyn,' Perdimonn said, looking at the townsfolk moving around purposefully from building to building, intent on their business. The passers-by appeared largely unaware of each other, and were certainly not giving any attention to a couple of strangers in a tatty old wagon. However, that would all change when they set up their stall in the market place – it always did.

'Well, this is one house of information that you should certainly feel at home in,' Calvyn replied with a laugh, pointing up at the sign.

Handing the reins across to Calvyn, Perdimonn chuckled and stepped down from the driver's bench. Calvyn looked down at the old man who was grinning back up at him with a mischievous expression on his face.

'I'll see you at the market place shortly, Calvyn. Just follow this street around to the left and you can't miss it.'

'Don't drink too much, Perdimonn.'

'Me? Drink? Perish the thought!' Perdimonn replied with a bright twinkle in his eyes as he laughed. 'Don't worry, Calvyn, you won't have to come back and pour me into the wagon. I'll see you in the market place before you can set up the tables... well, maybe not quite that quick, but I promise that I'll not be long.'

'OK. I'll see you later,' Calvyn replied with a grin, and with a gentle flick of the reins, he set Steady off at a slow walk down the street as he watched Perdimonn disappear into the Inn.

The clatter of Steady's shod hooves on the cobblestones of the main street, and the juddering rattle of the wagon and its load sounded loud in Calvyn's ears as he made his way to the market place. As he rounded the left-hand bend he began to make out the familiar clamour of market traders above the racket of the bouncing wagon. A slight breeze carried a hint of the potpourri of scents that characterised the rural bazaars of Thrandor. Calvyn tasted the anticipatory flow of adrenaline in the back of his throat as the thrill of the wheeling and dealing captured his imagination once more. 'Trading is definitely fun,' he thought to himself. 'It's unpredictable sometimes, but definitely fun.'

As he arrived in the market square Calvyn paused at the edge, scanning the noisy throng for a suitable site. Spying a likely gap towards the end of one of the more central rows of stalls he parked the wagon at the edge of the square nearest to the potential site. Tying Steady to the purpose built railing, he fitted her with a nosebag of grain before setting out in search of the Market Master to pay the trading levy imposed by the local Baron.

Finding the Market Master was never a major problem as they were always located at the centre of the market. Each trader would pay his due before commencing any transactions or run the risk of being punished by the local militia. Invariably the Market Masters had non-uniformed informants that would wander through the stalls on the lookout for any illicit dealing. If the informants did not catch offenders, often the legitimate traders who had paid the tax would turn in any transgressors to the authorities. Illegal trading was not taken lightly, and the punishments were severe.

Calvyn made his way through the crowd to the Market Master's desk. The market was certainly far more extensive than any that he had been to for several months. 'This should be a good afternoon's trading,' he thought as he ducked between the stalls, and threaded his way through the milling groups of villagers and townsfolk. He arrived at the central desk to find the Market Master talking to a local trader.

'I'm sorry, Dergan, but there's nothing I can do,' the huge, barrel-chested man was saying. 'He's paid his dues and there's no law against low prices. I suggest that if you don't want to lose all your customers to him then you had better start cutting your losses and lowering your own prices. Life is tough. Now for goodness sake leave me to do the job I'm paid for and take your whinging elsewhere.'

The disgruntled trader turned and walked away with his head down and muttering to himself under his breath. Shaking his head in annoyance the Market Master turned with a frown to Calvyn who smiled back unperturbed by the big man's disgruntled manner.

'Don't tell me you've got a complaint, young smiler,' the Market Master grunted.

'Not at all, Sir. I merely wanted to pay the trading fee before setting up my stall,' Calvyn replied pleasantly.

'Well that's all right then.'

The official moved back behind his table and riffled through the box of parchments that sat at his right hand side. A single candle stood alight at the other end of the table, sheltered from the wind by an open-topped glass case. Pulling a single sheet from the box he seated himself on his wooden chair, and looked up expectantly at Calvyn.

'Name?'

'Calvyn.'

'How many days will you be trading?'

'Just for today,' Calvyn replied, peering to try and see what else the Market Master was likely to ask. However, the form appeared very simple and looked more like a receipt than a serious questionnaire.

'The cost for one day's trading is fourteen copper pennies,' the big man said, looking up at Calvyn and extending his hand for the money.

'Sir, if the price of a day's trading is fourteen copper pennies, then surely as it's past midday the price should now be seven.'

'The time of day is irrelevant. The price is fourteen copper pennies.'

'Sir, I appreciate that you are a busy man and I don't want to trouble you unduly, but I'm only a poor tinker, and fourteen copper pennies is more than I would probably make in one afternoon. I don't want to waste your time but if you cannot lower the price to at least eight copper pennies, then I will have to move on, and I am sure that your Baron would rather some revenue than none at all.'

The Market Master looked Calvyn up and down, noting his shabby clothing. The boy kept his expression a picture of innocence as the big man locked him eye to eye. Calvyn held his breath as the staring match extended uncomfortably. Suddenly, without another word, the Market Master picked up his quill and signed the form. Having done this he then produced a small block of wax and held it briefly over the candle. The softened end of the wax was then pressed onto the bottom of the form, and the large ring on his right hand was used to imprint the wax with his Master's insignia.

'That will be eight copper pennies please,' the Market Master said, looking up at Calvyn with an ambiguous smile.

'Certainly, Sir,' Calvyn replied, maintaining his straight face as he counted out the money. 'Thank you for your patience and understanding.'

'Enough of your impudence, young man,' the Market

Master growled with mock ferocity. He held the parchment up as if to tear it in two. 'Take this and go before I change my mind and have you run out of town as a troublemaker.'

Calvyn did not need telling twice. He took the sheet that authorised him to trade, and with a quick wave of thanks he departed, blending quickly into the crowd. For all the official's gruff manner, a quick backward glance as the boy left caught a glimpse of the expression of amusement on the Market Master's face. 'Unpredictable, that one,' Calvyn thought to himself, as he slipped through the crowd back to the wagon.

A short while later, with the stall set up and the goods displayed to his satisfaction, Calvyn started to trade. He did not expect to see anything of Perdimonn for a little while yet, and he had set himself a personal goal to sell or trade as much as he could before the old man reappeared. Indeed, the initial rate of sales left Calvyn wondering whether he would have anything left by the time that Perdimonn caught up with him. Business was swift, and as the townsfolk had more ready cash to spend than most of the villagers that he normally traded with, he found his stock going down and his capital increasing rapidly.

It was during one of the brief lulls that a stranger appeared at his stall who obviously did not originate from this town, as his skin was swarthy and his shoulder length hair was jet black. The outlander was quite tall and lean, wearing rich clothing, delicately piped and embroidered in a way that only a skilled tailor could achieve, and his soft leather calf length boots had obviously not been cheap. Over his beautifully stitched tunic and fine hose flowed a full black cloak that was lined with a deep black fur, the like of which Calvyn had never seen. The whole ensemble dripped with money. Calvyn watched the foreigner as he made a pretence of inspecting some of the dwindling merchandise. However, his piercing brown eyes, deep set under his thick black eyebrows were seemingly never on the item which he was handling, and his thin lips seemed to be constantly pursed into a hard line.

As his own stock of items had gone down, Calvyn had set up a small display of Perdimonn's ointments and tonics to fill up the empty space. It was as the strange man picked up one of these that his head came up suddenly and he looked at Calvyn briefly with an intensity that was more than a little alarming. The moment passed as the man's face broke into a friendly smile that displayed perfect rows of white teeth.

'Tell me, young man, how much is this ointment?'

'Three copper pennies is the normal asking price, Sir,' Calvyn replied uneasily, still unable to shake the feeling that something about this man was not as it seemed.

'Surely not!' he exclaimed, 'Only three copper pennies for such a... potent remedy. Its value must be, well, a lot greater than that.'

Calvyn was really beginning to get worried now. What if the man called for the Market Master and accused him of dealing in items of magic? What if he was an informant? What was the penalty for working magic in this town anyway?

The stranger noticed the boy's agitation and made a signal with his hand for him to calm down. He carefully placed the pot of ointment back on the table and started looking more carefully at some of the other objects for sale. As he was inspecting the various items he spoke again, but this time his voice dropped to a virtual murmur.

'I'm sure that you have good reason for selling things at such unexpectedly low prices, lad, but I'm really not that interested in them. However, I might be interested in purchasing any old books that you might have, especially if they have any inscriptions like these in them.'

The man pulled out a small black bound notebook from an inside pocket of his tunic and opened it at a random page. He turned the book to Calvyn to allow him to see the script on the open pages. Sure enough, the pages were covered in magical runes. Calvyn ran his eyes over the characters and determined that what he was looking at was part of a protection spell. Protection against what he could not tell, but the runes were definitely arranged in a sequence for some form of defence or barrier.

'I'm afraid that I don't have anything like that at all, Sir,' Calvyn said, keeping his face as blank and uncomprehending as he possibly could. 'The only books that I have for sale are these three here, and these are all written in Common. I've never seen anything quite like that book of yours. What language is it written in? Shandese perhaps?'

'Not exactly,' the stranger replied, looking intently at Calvyn with his dark eyes. He paused, seemingly unsure of what to say next. He put the notebook back into his tunic and picked up one of the three books that Calvyn had indicated. He flicked through a couple of pages and shook his head. 'No. These are not what I am looking for, but if you do see anything like my book, I implore you, don't sell it until I have had a chance to make you an offer. I would most certainly offer you a good price.'

'How would I find you, Sir, if I should come into possession of such a book?'

'Oh, we will meet again, my young friend. Have no fear, we will meet again.'

'Found any good bargains then, Selkor?'

The dark skinned stranger turned to find Perdimonn regarding him with the coldest, hardest expression that Calvyn had yet seen on the old man's face.

'Most certainly, exalted Perdimonn,' Selkor replied with a slight bow, 'the boy seems to be virtually giving things away. However, I have no real need for any of the items on display, and I am sure that your young apprentice would not try to deliberately conceal anything that I might wish to purchase. Incidentally, his appreciation for the written form is really quite good, but I've always found that the real proof is in the practical. I see that you haven't been neglecting his academic education. That's good, but really Perdimonn I ask you, 'The Peace Treaty of Kortag'? There's education, and there is education.'

The whole time that he had been talking, Selkor had been backing away subtly from Perdimonn who was still concentrating intently on staring him out. Calvyn watched in fascination as the old man proceeded to launch a scornful verbal riposte without so much as raising his voice one decibel above its normal volume.

'You never did possess any real appreciation for true learning, Selkor. The only thing that you ever craved was knowledge that you felt would increase your power. It is amazing to me that you haven't managed to destroy yourself yet, I could always give you a hand if you're foolish enough to stay around long enough.'

Perdimonn raised his hand slightly and Selkor flinched visibly, the colour draining from his face as he looked on the deadly serious face of the old man.

'You wouldn't dare!' Selkor gasped. Then he rallied a little and continued with slightly more conviction, 'No, you wouldn't dare, and definitely not here. Your threats mean nothing here, old man. It's forbidden. You know that as well as I do, so save yourself the trouble of wasting your empty words. Waste your hollow posturing on your young student here if you will, but your time is nearly over, Perdimonn, and my strength grows daily. You are weakening, old man, and when the time is right I will take from you that which I desire. There will be no escape.'

'You dare to tell me what I can or cannot do? Well, Selkor, you must have increased your skill significantly if you feel that you are ready to throw such things in my face, even if it is in public where you believe yourself safe. Perhaps you would like to reconsider your position?'

Perdimonn's voice was scathing and filled with an authority and power that Calvyn had not heard before. The young man was transfixed by the unexpected confrontation. Although Calvyn could see that Perdimonn and Selkor were obviously adversaries of old, it did not seem feasible to him that Perdimonn could have enemies. The old man had always been the soul of kindness to everyone that he met. This was a side of the Magician that Calvyn would never have believed possible if he had not witnessed it with his own eyes. What was more, Selkor appeared genuinely shaken by the old man's wrath and even showed signs of being afraid.

'Just what do you think that you could do with several hundred witnesses who would testify to the local authorities in an instant if you were to try anything, shall we say, exotic?' Selkor asked mockingly; 'Prison would suit you old man. The solitude and diet would no doubt aid your contemplation of death.'

'Oh, I shouldn't worry yourself too much about the people, Selkor. What they cannot see won't hurt them,' Perdimonn replied with a confident smile.

The old man made a sudden horizontal sweeping gesture with his hand, and everything in the square stopped moving. The silence hung, almost deafening in its completeness. Everything and everyone, except Perdimonn, Selkor and Calvyn, had instantaneously frozen. It was as if everything had turned to stone. Birds hung motionless in the sky, defying the very laws of gravity. Clouds towered unmoving as the wind died mid-gust, and the numerous people around the market place appeared as so many statues, remarkable in their detail as they posed, a frozen model of life in the town square.

'What have you done?' Selkor cried out in panic.

'Just given us a little time to finish our discussion without fear of undue interruption,' smiled Perdimonn. 'Well, eternity in fact. You see, time appears to have stopped for some reason. My goodness, Selkor, are you all right? You appear a little distraught. Would you perhaps be just a trifle regretful of some of your recent words? I hear that eating words can turn one's stomach. Maybe you should try to say sweeter things in future so that they don't taste so bitter when you're forced to swallow them.'

'It's... it's impossible!' Selkor stammered, his eyes wild

as he looked around frantically. 'No one has the power to stop time.'

'I think that you have got a lot of reconsidering to do Selkor. Would you like to do it here under my gentle tutelage? Or perhaps we could go back to our lives, and you could run away and consider the implications of this little lesson in your own time, providing of course that you take your contemplations elsewhere and don't annoy me with your presence anymore. The choice is yours, Selkor.'

Calvyn, who had been no less astounded by this turn of events than the unfortunate Selkor, watched the conflicting emotions play across the stranger's face. Anger, incredulity and fear vied for dominance as Selkor struggled to come to terms with his predicament. In frustration he raised his hand with the intention of venting his anger on the table.

'Stop!' shouted Perdimonn, causing Selkor to freeze in mid-swing. 'Don't be stupid, Selkor. Even with your limited capacity for thought you should be able to comprehend the implications of disturbing the continuity of events in this instant of time. If you break anything or change anything significantly it could prevent me from ever being able to restart time again. Is that to be your decision? Do you wish to remain in this instant of time with me for eternity?'

The question echoed around the square, its implications all too apparent. Selkor lowered his hand slowly to his side.

'No, Perdimonn. That would be the closest scenario to a living hell that I could possibly imagine,' he replied, his head dropping slightly in resignation. 'You win. I'll leave quietly – for today at least. However, we will meet again, old man. I cannot deny my destiny any more than you can deny yours.'

Selkor's dark eyes smouldered under his arched black eyebrows, and his lips were pulled together in a tight line of suppressed anger. Calvyn found it very hard to imagine this furious looking character departing quietly, and was about to say as much when Perdimonn, who was also watching Selkor closely, made up his mind.

'Very well, Selkor. Believe me, I will hold you to that promise. You had better try to stand as exactly as you can to where you were at the moment that I stopped time. You wouldn't want to be accused of being a Magician because you disappeared and reappeared somewhere else in the blink of an eye now, would you?' Perdimonn asked with a taunting edge to his voice.

'Ha, ha, Perdimonn. Very funny I'm sure,' muttered Selkor sarcastically.

'What was that?'

'Nothing, nothing. I'm ready when you are, old man.'

'Ready, Calvyn?'

'I'm fine.'

The old Magician repeated his sweeping gesture of before and the square burst back into life. The market continued its noisy bustling business, the people completely unaware of the events that had been transpiring within their midst. Both Calvyn and Selkor found themselves looking around almost in shock at the sudden resumption of life.

'Well, so long, Selkor. Thank you for looking us up. It has been a pleasure doing business with you,' said Perdimonn in a slightly louder voice than normal. 'It's such a shame that you have to be moving on so quickly, but I have no doubt that we will be seeing you again some time.'

'Count on it,' said Selkor, through a forced smile.

'Just don't forget that despite your age, time isn't always on your side,' Perdimonn added pointedly.

The richly dressed stranger whirled and pushed his way past several people, ignoring their angry complaints as he stormed away.

CHAPTER 4

Calvyn and Perdimonn watched the ripples of irritation spread outwards from the passage of Selkor as he barged his way through the crowd and out of the square. Dark looks and angry mutterings of 'Blasted foreigners!' and various other more blasphemous remarks rode on the waves of his wake. Perdimonn turned to regard Calvyn, who was still intently observing the dramatic withdrawal of the enigmatic stranger.

'Accept cash only from now on, Calvyn. We need to acquire enough capital to buy a couple of reasonably fleet-footed horses. Steady is an excellent beast for pulling a wagon, but she won't be much use to us now that we're in a hurry.'

'Cash is just about all that I've been getting all afternoon, Perdimonn. My stock is at an all time low, and I was considering closing down the stall temporarily to go and buy more merchandise for future trading. I also sold a fair number of your potions and ointments, so we can leave quickly without any problems.'

'Excellent. See if you can dispose of the remaining stock in short order. If necessary, sell the it to one of the market dealers. I know that you won't get full value for it that way, but we don't have time for any prolonged negotiations. We are getting out of here as fast as we can, and I definitely do not want to be trailing a wagonload of unnecessary junk behind me when we go. Is there anything in the wagon that you particularly want to keep?'

'Only my fishing pole and my flute,' said Calvyn, naming his only two remaining personal effects from his childhood home.

'The flute is no problem, but I'm afraid that you'll have to leave the fishing pole, Calvyn. It would be awkward to carry on horseback and would only slow us down. I'm sorry.'

'If I have to, then I suppose I'd better sell that too,' Calvyn said sadly. 'I take it that you are going to explain this unusual haste later?'

Perdimonn nodded, and with a slight shrug and an apologetic little smile he strode off to the wagon to organise for its immediate disposal. Calvyn watched him go, and then glanced briefly in the direction in which Selkor had departed. However, he had no time to ponder the events of the last few minutes as potential customers were already lining the frontage of his stall. Forcing a smile and welcoming the people as warmly as he could, Calvyn launched back into his role as a fast talking salesman.

Later that evening, camped in a wood several miles north of the market town, Calvyn stacked a large pile of firewood within easy reach of their small campfire, and sat down heavily with a huge sigh of relief at finally being able to rest. It had been a hectic afternoon's trading, and by dusk the two travellers had not only sold virtually everything they owned, but they had purchased two fine horses and some lightweight camping gear similar to that used by the King's own cavalry. Despite his initial protestations about Steady being too slow, Perdimonn found that he just could not bring himself to sell her. Instead they fitted her with light packs and loaded her with sufficient provisions to last them a week of hard travelling. Then, trailing Steady behind them, Calvyn and Perdimonn had ridden out of town shortly after nightfall.

It had been a long time since Calvyn had last ridden a horse, and although they had not ridden very far or very fast, he was certainly feeling a bit stiff. Trotting would definitely require a lot of practice if he was to feel truly comfortable. It had not been until they had come to mount up that Perdimonn had finally thought to ask him whether he had ridden before. Tempted though he was to pretend that he had never been on a horse in his life, Calvyn had decided that it was probably not a good time for practical jokes. Instead, he had just given Perdimonn an amused nod at the slight note of panic in the old man's voice, and swinging into the saddle, had led the way out of the stables at a gentle walk. Riding steadily for about an hour and a half, the two riders had pushed northwards along the road until Perdimonn had called for them to halt and make camp for the night.

Now, sitting by the flickering campfire and gently massaging his stiffening back and legs, Calvyn began to reflect on the day's remarkable events. Looking across at Perdimonn, who was gazing into the sprightly dancing flames, obviously lost deep in thought, the young man decided that the time had come for an explanation.

'I'm sure that you have a perfectly good reason for this sudden change of pace, Perdimonn, but I don't understand what spooked you into this frenetic departure today. In the last two years you have never spoken so much as a harsh word to anyone. Suddenly you frighten this Selkor character off with one of the most astounding magical feats that I have ever heard of, and then you run like a startled hare! Excuse me if I missed something along the way somewhere, but I fail to understand what you could possibly be afraid of.'

'If you thought about it logically, Calvyn, I'm sure that it would come to you in time. However, you are right, I should explain my actions. After all, it's only fair that having trusted me, you should be entrusted with my fullest confidence,' Perdimonn replied, and he looked across the fire and deep into Calvyn's eyes.

'Do not be deceived by Selkor's retreat. I merely surprised him with a trick that he neither expected nor fully understood. It's given him cause to be cautious, but not to give up.'

Perdimonn suddenly laughed, long and loud, leaving Calvyn even more confused.

'What is there to laugh about if he's going to come after us?' Calvyn asked eventually, as he began to get frustrated by the lack of forthcoming information.

'Selkor's going to take a week to figure out the stunt I pulled back there, and when he does work it out, he'll take another week to calm down from the temper tantrum he'll throw when he realises that he's been tricked,' Perdimonn said, grinning away to himself as he imagined what would be going through his adversary's mind.

'Tricked?'

'Just think about it for a moment, Calvyn. How would you describe time?'

'Well, it's a measurement of how long it takes things to happen I suppose,' Calvyn replied thoughtfully.

'Yes, a measurement or scale. Those are good enough descriptions for illustrating what I did. Let me ask you another question. If time is the way we judge how quickly things happen, and I had by some miracle managed to stop time from moving forward, what measured my conversation with Selkor whilst time had stopped?'

'I'm not sure that I even followed the entire question, Perdimonn. However, I gather from the way you phrased it that you didn't stop time, therefore... no. You've beaten me, I'm too tired for riddles.'

'You disappoint me, Calvyn, but you were on the right track. Nothing that I know of could stop the flow of time, and when he stops to really think about it, Selkor will undoubtedly reach the same conclusion. Actually, I altered the scale of time that was acting on just the three of us. I changed the time scale to one that was thousands of times faster than normal, which made everything around us appear to stop. In fact, if you had scrutinised certain things you would have observed them moving at an infinitesimally slow rate. You may have noticed that I didn't keep us in that state for very long.

To remain at that pace for a long period of time would almost certainly prove fatal. As it was, the experience was highly dangerous and almost ended in disaster.'

'Dangerous? How was it dangerous? It seems unlikely that anything was going to leap out and grab us whilst we were moving at that speed,' Calvyn said, throwing another couple of sticks onto the fire.

'No, the danger was more that you might have jumped out and grabbed someone or something else,' Perdimonn replied. 'Imagine what would have happened if I had allowed Selkor to strike that table with his hand. Time was actually still moving at its usual measured beat, but we were moving thousands of times faster than normal. The table would have smashed to smithereens in ultra slow motion, but there would have been nothing slow motion about what would have happened to Selkor's hand. He's nuisance enough as it is, without giving him cause for a personal vendetta.'

'That's still the part which puzzles me more than anything else,' Calvyn said, watching the old man carefully as he quickly continued with his train of thought. 'Just why are you afraid of him, and what does he want from you? I mean, is there something about your past that I should be aware of? Are you a renegade magician or something?'

'No! No, nothing like that. I do have something that Selkor would dearly love to get his hands on – the key to a source of power. Selkor has always craved access to such a source, but he is not interested in gaining the power for the well-being of the people of Thrandor or Shandar, or anywhere else for that matter. Far from it. His whole existence seems to be focused on drawing more and more magical energy to himself for his own ends. Quite what those ends are, only he truly knows. One thing is certain though; no desire that manifests itself in such a selfish way can lead to any good. Although he himself is not intrinsically evil, and may even truly believe himself pure and his cause just, I fear that great evil could result if he succeeds in his quest for power.'

Calvyn sat quietly for a while and tried to assimilate all the happenings of the day into some semblance of order. He sensed the truth in Perdimonn's words about Selkor, but wished that he could hear the other side of the story. Too many things still did not make any sense. One thing in particular suddenly struck him as being very peculiar. It defied everything that he had learnt about magic and spells. Looking back across at Perdimonn he found the old man watching him expectantly.

'How did you manage to move us to the other time scale without pronouncing any spells, Perdimonn?' the boy asked eventually, studying the Magician's face for his reaction.

Perdimonn merely smiled and replied, 'I wondered when you would get around to that. It took you a lot longer than I expected.'

'I had quite a few other things to think about. For some reason they seemed more pressing at the time,' Calvyn said, returning the grin which Perdimonn seemed to infect people with so easily.

'Well, with spells that you are not familiar with, or particularly difficult spells, or with any spells at all whilst you are learning, it is far easier to make the spell work by speaking the runes aloud. The focus of the sound helps to solidify the image of the runes and the result of the spell. The critical aspect of the spell is "seeing" the runes working the magic. The pronouncing of the runes need not be verbal, it can be mental, but don't be in too much of a hurry to try this for yourself, as it requires lots of practice and a clarity of focus that you have yet to achieve.'

Perdimonn paused slightly to let his words sink in. 'As it happens,' he continued, 'I have been rehearsing that spell for several years now against the chance that Selkor might catch up with me. The result justified the practice, but I have few other defences that could do much to slow that persistent Shandese dog down. He will be cautious about following us too closely until he realises what I did, and that distance will have to be enough of a lead to allow us to escape entirely. If it is not, then I may not be able to prevent him from gaining what he seeks. Selkor is a powerful Magician, and a deadly man to have as an opponent of any kind.'

'But what about this source of power that you have? If it's as great as you intimate, why can't you use it against him?'

'Well, Calvyn, the power that I have access to could indeed be called great, but not in the way that you, or even Selkor, would deem so. He just will not accept that. The power cannot be used as a destructive force. To do so would defile its very source, and possibly destroy it forever. There are several other similar sources of power to be found in this land, Calvyn, and Warders were originally set to guard their Keys. All of the Warders were chosen for their dedication to life and their abhorrence of violence, therefore I could no less harm Selkor deliberately than I could harm any living creature. If I could trap Selkor without doing him any harm then I would do so. Indeed, I played on the fact that Selkor would realise this when I tricked him into thinking that I could trap him forever in an instant of time. He was so sure of himself, thinking that I wouldn't violate the Magician's Law that forbids a public challenge, that he was completely unprepared for my removing the people from the equation. Still, enough self-congratulation, I think. Let's get some sleep – we've got a long day's ride ahead tomorrow, and I'm not entirely sure where to head for.'

'Are there any more of these Magicians' Laws that I should know about? You haven't mentioned anything about this public challenge thing before,' complained Calvyn, disgruntled that he had not been getting the full facts.

'Oh yes, lots of them! But let's face it, Calvyn, with one light spell in your repertoire, were you seriously expecting to publicly challenge another Magician?'

'No, I suppose not,' grumbled Calvyn, 'but it would

have been nice to know about it anyway.'

'Let me worry about what you need to know, and when, Calvyn. Believe me, there are many things that you are not yet ready for. When the time comes, you will learn what you need to know one way or another. Now, catch some sleep while you can, and no more questions for tonight.'

Perdimonn got up, stretched, and yawning, he wandered his way over to his improvised shelter and crawled in. Calvyn sat thoughtfully for a few moments watching the old man retire, wondering just how much more there was to this kind old Magician that he did not know about. What else was hidden behind that friendly exterior facade? A Warder of some great power? What power? Who had appointed him? How had he been chosen? The questions rolled through his mind like waves crashing on the beach, in an endless pounding cycle with no obvious resolution in sight. With one last rub at his aching thighs, Calvyn too retreated to his blanket and the welcoming arms of sleep, only to toss and turn in the surf of his questions as they manifested themselves in ever-changing dreams, never settling into any theme or pattern.

For the next few days the two travellers pushed their horses hard, avoiding towns and villages and often cutting across countryside rather than risking contact with other wayfarers. Calvyn's evening lessons were kept short, and concentrated on developing the basic skills of magic and learning simple spells. Calvyn progressed rapidly, mastering spells for lighting fires, healing straightforward wounds, creating simple illusions and also perfecting his light spell.

As the two pressed ever further north and westward, a faint purple haze on the skyline heralded the nearest heights of the Vortaff Mountains. The countryside gradually became more sparsely populated, and the hillsides and hedgerows displayed increasing amounts of heather and gorse.

Despite pressing so far out from the normal beaten

tracks of the trade routes and the civilisation of the lowlands, Calvyn noticed that Perdimonn was becoming increasingly edgy and agitated. Some of the precautions that they were taking to cover their tracks seemed excessive, almost to the point of paranoia. Perdimonn would often lay false trails and use magic to obliterate even the faintest hints of their actual paths. However, nothing seemed to quell the old man's uneasiness, until even the horses became skittish and nervous, obviously affected by his disquiet.

Calvyn found it difficult to believe that anyone could possibly follow them in light of the exotic precautions that Perdimonn was taking to hide any signs of their passage. Despite all the decoys and camouflage Perdimonn was using, the old man, who was normally such a cheerful individual, full of infectious laughter and bright smiles, was definitely not himself. The new Perdimonn was distinctly unnerving, and Calvyn found himself starting to look over his shoulder with increasing regularity for some sign of pursuit.

It had been nearly a week since the encounter with Selkor when Calvyn finally challenged Perdimonn's anxiety. They had stopped to water the horses at a small spring and Calvyn had heaved a huge sigh of relief for the brief respite.

'Come on, Perdimonn, surely you can't still believe that Selkor is following us. How could anyone possibly track a trail that just isn't there?'

'To be honest, Calvyn, I don't know how he's doing it, but he is tracking us. More to the point, he is slowly catching us up.'

'How do you know?' queried Calvyn, full of scepticism. 'You can't have seen him or he would be on top of us by now. What makes you so sure that he hasn't given up the chase and gone elsewhere?'

'Calvyn, you have only just begun to touch the edges of what is possible with magic. As you develop your knowledge of spells you will learn that the combinations of the magical runes are boundless, therefore the possibilities are also without limit. There is only one major restriction – your power source. For the sort of everyday spells that you are learning at present you draw the energy from everything around you. The birds, the trees, sunlight, running water, the blowing wind. Everything contributes in a general sort of way towards the effect that you shape with your magic. In time you will undoubtedly develop spells of your own that I could never dream of. This is purely because your mind works differently from mine, and will integrate elements of spells in combinations and concepts unique to your own way of thinking. You ask me how I know that we are being followed – watch the water of this pool, Calvyn, and you'll understand.'

Calvyn looked into the pool of water. It was shallow and clear, and the surface was as smooth as glass. The sun was at their backs, which reduced the reflections on the surface to a minimum and made the stones and water plants at the bottom of the pool clearly visible. Perdimonn began to murmur the phrases of a spell, and immediately the water appeared to film over with a milky white layer that spread until the pond was completely covered. With startling abruptness, the surface of the pool crystallised into a moving picture, causing Calvyn to draw back slightly, like a cat that had seen its reflection in the mirror for the first time. The imagery was so clear and precise in every detail that Calvyn felt he could just step into the vision and he would be there.

Disturbingly, the picture showed Selkor on a huge black horse, his long dark cape billowing behind him as he rode up one of the country lanes that Calvyn distinctly remembered riding along only the day before. The Magician had tied his dark hair back in a single ponytail which revealed his face, stern and full of determined concentration. His thick black eyebrows were drawn together in what was almost a scowl as he focused with single-minded absorption on the road ahead. Quite what he was looking for Calvyn had no idea, but it was clear that he was definitely hot on their trail.

As Calvyn watched in fascination, Selkor's eyes widened unexpectedly as if in surprise, and then narrowed almost to slits as he reined his horse to a dead stop. Sitting up tall in the saddle, he seemed to bring his menacing stare to bear on Calvyn, looking right out of the picture at him. Slowly, the Magician lifted his right arm and extended his finger towards the transfixed observer, his lips moving as he began to initiate a spell.

With a final, almost shouted syllable of power, Perdimonn wiped the image from the surface of the water. Calvyn, his almost hypnotic link to the image broken, staggered back a couple of steps and sat down with a squelch on the sodden grassy bank.

'By the beard of Tarmin!' exclaimed Perdimonn. 'How the devil did he do that?'

Reaching down, he gave the somewhat dazed Calvyn a hand back onto his feet, and then stamped off in annoyance to where the horses stood drinking. The young man remained where he was for a few seconds, rubbing at his eyes and shaking his head before looking up and following Perdimonn. The old Magician was patting Steady and muttering to himself.

'What happened, Perdimonn?' Calvyn asked hesitantly.

'To be honest, lad, I haven't a clue. As I said before, he is a powerful magician, but I don't know how he's following us, and I have absolutely no idea how he detected us looking at him. It's no good. We'll have to split up.'

'Split up?'

'Yes. It's me that he's after, not you. If you get in his way he won't hesitate to kill you in order to reach me, therefore, we must part our ways. Judging by his tracking abilities so far, I'm sure that he will continue to follow me and leave you alone, but be on your guard anyway, just in case.'

'I can't just leave you, Perdimonn. It wouldn't be right. I'm not afraid – I want to come with you.'

'I don't doubt your bravery, Calvyn, but I can't allow

65

you to come with me. It is time for you to start seeking your own destiny, for if I am not much mistaken, though our paths may cross at times, your future lies along a vastly different way from mine.'

Perdimonn's eyes and voice had gone distant, as if he was looking through time and space to see Calvyn's future. The hairs on the back of Calvyn's neck prickled up on end as he sensed the premonition in Perdimonn's voice. The look on Perdimonn's face was almost like the sort of trance that Calvyn had seen the old fortune tellers fake in the market places around central Thrandor, except that this had the ring of authenticity that broached no argument or disbelief.

'There is no recourse but to part our ways, I'm afraid,' Perdimonn stated, his eyes snapping back into focus on the somewhat shaken young man. 'You must leave me to face Selkor alone. You have no choice in this, Calvyn. I'm sorry. Believe me, I never had any intentions of leaving you alone like this, but I've been given no choice.'

'I'll be careful, Perdimonn. I can look after myself, thanks to you. But where will you go? Where should I go for that matter?'

'Well, I think I'll head for the Knife Edge Pass. Selkor is not that comfortable in the mountains and that should give me enough of an advantage over him, should I need one. As for you, I suggest that you take both your horse and Steady eastwards towards the border towns. By going that way you should avoid any possibility of encountering Selkor. Also, the town of Stonehollow is only about a day and a half away, which will allow you to replenish your supplies. You may as well take all the money as I'm not going to need any where I'm bound.'

'But what about the other side of the Pass? Surely you will need money when you get there,' insisted Calvyn, unwilling to leave Perdimonn both alone and penniless.

'The coins of Thrandor would be all but useless there, Calvyn. Don't worry, I am not without resources in Shandar. I will take a few days food and one of the water canteens. Believe me, I know what I'm doing and I can look after myself. This way will prove better for both of us. Besides, I may be forced to resort to more drastic measures in order to shake Selkor off, and if I do, then I would rather not have to worry about your safety at the same time. Come on, let's repack as quickly as possible. The race is on and we've no time to waste.'

Leading the horses a little way from the boggy ground around the spring, the two companions ransacked the saddlebags and repacked them to suit the two separate journeys. Calvyn was more than a little embarrassed to end up with most of the valuable items of equipment and all of the money, but Perdimonn insisted firmly that he wanted to travel light and fast. Calvyn did manage to persuade the old man to take almost all of the remaining travel rations, pointing out that the Magician would probably not have the option of diverting into a farmhouse to buy food.

Finally, about a half-hour later, the horses were all loaded and ready to go and the two unlikely companions faced each other to say their goodbyes. Calvyn found tears welling in his eyes as he struggled for appropriate words of thanks to say to the man who had given him so much over the past two years. It just did not feel right to abandon him in his hour of peril, and Calvyn was not at all comfortable with the circumstances of this parting.

The old man stood, and that infectious and endearing smile spread slowly across his face as he looked into the guilt-torn eyes of his young apprentice.

'Calvyn,' Perdimonn said, gently but firmly, 'this is not your conflict. If I am not much mistaken you will have many struggles of your own to face over the next few years, so please, leave this one for me.'

Pride filled the old Magician as he briefly enfolded Calvyn in a farewell hug.

'Remember, keep practising hard, but always in secret,' advised Perdimonn. 'You will find power to work magic in all things, but try never to use spells aggressively, even against evil. In the end that path will only lead you to evil yourself. If you try to bind magic into an object – beware! Some substances like silver will accept magic like a sponge soaks up water, but iron and steel require great power and skill to make the binding hold. Here... I have a final gift for you.'

The old man pulled out from an inner pocket a small, leather bound book. The cover was a deep earthen brown, etched with gold. He handed it to Calvyn almost reverently.

'This is my grimoire. Look after it and use it wisely. It contains virtually every spell that I have ever learned, but it will only release them to you at a rate that you will be able to cope with. I have also laid spells of protection on the book so that no one will be able to steal it from you, and water or fire will not easily damage it. If anyone should happen to see you reading it, all that they will see is an old battered storybook. However, the protection has limits, and another Magician could break through the protection spells and take the book from you by force.'

'I can think of nothing to say but thank you,' stammered Calvyn, completely flummoxed and overawed by the generosity of the gift. A single tear rolled down each of his cheeks. 'Are you sure that you won't need this for your business with Selkor?'

'Yes, I'm sure. There is nothing in there which would be of any use that I do not already know by heart,' replied Perdimonn confidently. 'Be aware that you too should not look to it as a font of all knowledge. Eventually you will write your own, and I would encourage you to begin sooner rather than later.'

'I will do my best not to let you down, Perdimonn.'

'I'm sure that you will, lad. Now, get on your way or we'll have that blasted Selkor joining in with our goodbyes. Take care, and safe journey.'

'You too. I look forward to hearing the tale of ho w you lost Selkor in the mountains.'

'And I look forward to telling it,' laughed back the old Magician, and clasping Calvyn's hand briefly in a final gesture of farewell, Perdimonn turned, mounted his horse, and rode off at a steady canter.

Calvyn remained where he was, clutching the precious book close to his chest. Emotions cascaded through the young man like a flood as he watched his mentor ride off towards the mountains: guilt, sadness, a profound sense of loss and helplessness that he had not felt since the death of his parents. He stood, torn between obedience to Perdimonn's advice and the desire to help the old man in some way. Unfortunately, he could find no inspiration on how to detain or delay Selkor one iota from his pursuit. Therefore, reluctantly, he turned to the two patiently waiting horses and swung himself up into his saddle.

'Well, old girl,' Calvyn said, looking down at Steady who was attached to his horse by a long leash, 'you've done well to keep up with us these past few days. You'll probably be pleased to know that we won't be pushing quite so hard from now on. Let's see if we can't make your old Master proud, shall we?'

Steady nickered and raised her head in what looked almost like a nod of agreement, causing Calvyn to give a brief bark of laughter. Then with a final glance of regret towards the mountains, he turned his horse and set out eastward.

CHAPTER 5

'What news of the Manticlaar, Ramiff?'

The servant bowed low before his Master and shifted his eyes around the luxurious interior of the vast pavilion, unwilling to meet the impassive gaze of the First Maharl.

'Not good, Chosen One,' Ramiff stammered, his hands clasped in front of him and his fingers unconsciously clenching and unclenching in sweaty, nervous anticipation of his Master's wrath. 'They have refused to join us.'

'Then they will die,' the First Maharl stated flatly. 'Prepare the warriors. We ride tonight.'

'Yes, Chosen One,' Ramiff replied, relieved that he was not to bear the brunt of his Master's anger. He bowed low once more and retreated through the entrance of the huge tented area that was the First Maharl's demesne. As he left, Ramiff pondered how his Master would have reacted if he had been given the full message from the leader of the Manticlaar Clan. Words like, "white skinned infidel" did not sit well with the First Maharl, and he doubted that the Chosen One would have granted a swift death to the sender of such insults.

Demarr sat cross legged on a fine silk covered cushion, atop the raised platform that allowed him to look down on his servants even whilst seated. Stone-faced, he watched Ramiff withdraw. 'A good man,' he thought to himself, as his personal aide disappeared through the exit. 'In the old days we might even have been friends.'

Looking back now, it was difficult to see how he had possibly hoped to take over Thrandor using friendship and trust to inspire his followers. The only way to power was to lead with an iron fist: punish those who failed him and kill those who defied him. In his naiveté and ignorance he had sought the throne of Thrandor in order to right what he had seen as the injustice of the reigning king. Now he saw clearly. Power was the only true objective – power, and possibly to a lesser degree, revenge.

To think that he had skulked along the northern edge of the wastelands for the first six months of his banishment. He had not dared to stray too far from the Terachim Mountains for fear of running out of water. Food had been scarce, and his sole ambition had been to find somewhere that would offer enough resources to be able to survive in even a modicum of comfort. Well, all that had certainly changed after his encounter with the firedrake, he mused.

From the moment that he had placed the talisman around his neck, he had known that his path stretched out into the uncharted wastelands. Instinct had appeared to guide him from one source of water to another, leading him ever deeper into unknown territory. Small creatures seemed to cross his path as if by request, for him to slaughter and consume, and the extreme heat of the desert sun and the freezing cold of night no longer troubled him. All the niggling doubts, and feelings of remorse had left him. What remained was a cool, calculating and self assured shell, burning with an inner anger towards those who had thwarted his bid for power.

'Next time, next time, next time,' rang in Demarr's ears for day after day, as his hunger for power and his desire for revenge had grown ever stronger.

'The time is here,' whispered Demarr to himself, his eyes alight with a cold fire. 'At last, the waiting is over and the action can begin.'

The First Maharl climbed to his feet and straightened

his pure white thobe. Whilst the Terachites normally wore the one piece, loose-fitting garment without any belt or accoutrements, Demarr was not a born Terachite and found it more comfortable to cinch the thobe at the waist with a thin band of leather. Permanently around his neck was the silver talisman that would invariably be worn outside of his garment, resting squarely in the centre of his chest. Often his fingers would unconsciously seek it out as he was thinking, his fingertips gently rubbing at the strange, unreadable symbols engraved on both sides.

The power of the talisman had only become truly undeniable to Demarr during his first encounter with the Terachites. Strolling up to the encampment in the depths of the Terachim Wastelands early one morning, Demarr had startled the guards, tired at the end of a long watch. It was unheard of for a soft-skin to survive this far from his precious "civilisation," and even more incredible that he should appear both healthy and apparently unconcerned at the weapons that the guards had immediately levelled at him.

'Stay where you are, infidel,' one unfortunate guard had snapped as Demarr had reached the outskirts of the camp.

'It is always wiser to find out who you are speaking to before insulting them,' Demarr had stated, and without breaking stride walked right up to the threatening guard.

The former Earl had been incredulous at what he was saying and doing, but seemed to have little control over his actions. It had been as if he were watching a play from inside one of the actors taking part, and he could only spectate as the scene reached what he perceived would prove a bloody and fatal conclusion to his role. However, the biggest surprise, both for Demarr, and more especially for the luckless guard, had been yet to come.

As Demarr closed in on the sentry, the Terachite had drawn back his curved sabre in preparation to strike, paused, and then in a 'matter of fact' tone said, 'Too close, soft-skin.'

Demarr's body had not flinched as the weapon sliced towards him. However, the talisman had flared into life, spewing lightning-like gouts of flame that totally consumed the guard in fire, reducing him to ashes in an instant. The sabre had dropped harmlessly to the floor and the remaining guards had backed away, mouths open wide in stunned shock. Focusing on the talisman, one of the guards shook his head slightly as if shaking scales from his eyes. Pointing at the still glowing medallion, he had started yelling at the top of his voice.

'The Chosen One. It's the Chosen One. He's here. He's here.'

A crowd of two hundred or so formed rapidly, the Terachites teeming from all corners of the encampment to investigate the source of the commotion raised by the guards. A buzz of excitement had thrummed through the rapidly developing throng. Despite pressure from the late arrivals pushing for a better view, the crowd line had held several paces back from the calm foreigner, who wore the brightly radiating symbol of power and an incredible air of nonchalance at his situation.

Demarr had raised his right hand for silence, and those nearest to him had drawn back slightly, obviously terrified of being struck down by the fire that had consumed the guard only moments earlier. The crowd had settled into an uneasy silence.

'Who is the leader here?' demanded Demarr in a loud, clear voice.

A tall nomad of middle years had pushed through to the front of the mass of people, and stepped forward to face Demarr.

'I am Marmel, First Maharl of the Adrel.'

'Wrong answer,' Demarr had snarled. 'You,' he barked, pointing at Ramiff. 'Kill him. Now.'

Without hesitation, Ramiff had whipped out his sabre and plunged it through the chest of the First Maharl. Marmel had been so astounded that he did not have time to react in any way. He fell, dead without uttering a sound.

Demarr had felt a wave of profound satisfaction wash through him as he watched the execution. This was power, and it felt good. He had nodded his approval to Ramiff, and once again posed his question to the crowd.

'Who is the leader here?'

'The Chosen One,' Ramiff had called back, supported more hesitantly by one or two of the crowd.

Placing the palm of his left hand behind the talisman, Demarr had lifted it slightly from his chest and shouted the question a third time.

Who is the leader here?'

'THE CHOSEN ONE,' the congregation had roared back as one.

'And who am I?'

'THE CHOSEN ONE, THE CHOSEN ONE,' they had chanted, repeating it over and over until he raised his hands for silence.

'That's right. I am the Chosen One, and you are my chosen people. Together we will make nations tremble at the name of the Adrel.'

The crowd had roared with approval, stamping their feet and taking up the chant again.

That day had been a start but tonight, nearly two years on, would see the true beginning of the rise of the Adrel, thought Demarr as he placed his black and silver-banded gutrah on his head. When he had arrived, the Adrel had been a mere two hundred strong. Now, having subsumed half a dozen other small tribes, he had better than a thousand warriors at his command. It was time to show the major tribes that he meant business.

*   *   *   *   *

'Excuse me, Sir, but do you know of anyone hereabouts who's offering work?'

The merchant looked Calvyn up and down with an air of disdain before deigning to reply. 'And what sort of work would that be? Have you any great skills that I should be aware of before I make my answer?'

Calvyn thought about that for a moment.

'Well, sir, I've had no formal training in any trade, but I've worked a farm with my father and I've made my way as a market stall trader for the last two years.'

'Judging by the state of your clothes, your way is about all that you have made,' mocked the merchant. 'Have you any skill with a sword or bow?'

'No Sir. Well... that is, I don't know really. I've never used either,' Calvyn replied honestly.

'Then I'm afraid that you are of no use to me, nor any other of my Guild,' the merchant stated flatly. 'What we do need desperately at the moment are trained fighters to help guard our caravans from those damned Shandese raiding parties. They seem to be everywhere, and are wreaking havoc on all the northern trade routes. If you want my advice then you should do yourself a favour, boy – get some military training. There's always work for a trained soldier.'

'Where would I go to get such training?' asked Calvyn dubiously.

'Oh, any of the local lords. They all have their own little private armies,' directed the merchant dismissively, making a casual shooing gesture with his hand before returning to his own private reverie of woe and lost profits.

Calvyn walked back across the street to where he had tied the horses. Since he had parted with Perdimonn three days before, Calvyn had given a lot of thought to his future. Much as he had enjoyed travelling around the villages and towns of central Thrandor with the old man, he had never stopped anywhere for long enough to make any friends. Already, the open road seemed lonely without Perdimonn's company, and the thought of re-entering the life of a tinker on his own was demoralising. At the moment he was, financially, quite well placed. However, he was aware that if he didn't start doing something to earn a living fairly soon, the money would quickly disappear.

The thought of military life did not much appeal to

Calvyn. Everything that he had heard about it – the poor standard of food, the long, boring sentry duties, the hours of drill and the barrack room quarters all represented an anathema to the boy who had enjoyed such a free lifestyle. Unfortunately, the story had been the same in each village and town that he had passed through. Nobody was hiring anyone unless they had served an apprenticeship in a recognised trade, or was a trained fighter. His options appeared limited.

Trying to think positively, Calvyn reflected that although becoming a foot soldier in a private army was hardly going to make him the all-conquering knight of his childhood dreams, it would give him a grounding in a highly sought trade. Furthermore, learning to defend himself with a sword or other weapon would certainly not be an unwelcome skill in these parts. From what he had heard, most of the lords only required two years of service in exchange for the training that a new Recruit would receive. Therefore, he could be trained, have served his time in the army, and be free to travel again at the age of only eighteen – nineteen at the outside. Viewed in those terms it did not seem such a bad idea.

Even though he had reluctantly resigned himself to the necessity of undertaking training as a soldier, Calvyn found himself unwilling to stop searching for alternative employment, though his enquiries for work were now interspersed with queries on the reputations of the more local northern lords. The information that he gathered indicated that two nobles in particular had good names, both for being honourable men and for having highly trained troops.

The first, Lord Valdeer, had the closest training fort, being only a day's ride southwest. However, Calvyn's decision to apply to the second, Baron Keevan, stemmed from the fact that the Baron's recruiters had only left town the previous day. This meant that a new batch of Recruits would be likely to begin their training imminently. As Calvyn saw no real profit in delaying the inevitable, he continued eastwards for the next two days in search of the Baron's castle.

It did not prove difficult to find the sprawling complex that was the Baron's training camp. Calvyn decided that 'castle' was perhaps a slightly grandiose title for the walled area that enclosed the buildings that made up the encampment. It was probably only called a castle because Keevan was a Baron, he decided, as he rode up to the gate in the twelve foot high outer wall that encircled the entire site. A sentry on the guard tower, which stood to the right of the solid-looking wooden gates, ordered Calvyn to halt and identify himself and his business.

'I am Calvyn, son of Joran,' he shouted back. 'I wish to join the army of Baron Keevan.'

'In that case, you've come to the right place.'

Turning and looking down behind him, the guard called for the gates to be opened. On entering, Calvyn was met by a lanky young soldier with short cropped hair so ginger in colour that it could almost have been described as orange. The Private grinned up at him with such a friendly smile that many of his pre-conceptions and worries dissolved like vapour dispersing into thin air.

'Can you dismount please?' the young man asked. 'I'm afraid that only the Baron and his captains are allowed to ride inside the Castle.'

'Certainly,' Calvyn replied, complying immediately.

'I'm Jez,' the young soldier stated, extending his hand in greeting.

'Calvyn,' Calvyn offered, matching Jez's smile. They shook hands like old friends, and Calvyn thought to himself with a wry inward grin that if everyone was as welcoming as Jez, he might not want to leave after only two years.

'It's good to meet you, Calvyn. I'll take you to see Sergeant Dren as soon as we've got your horses stabled. He's sure going to be pleased to see you. Rumour is that he's despairing of finding enough Recruits to start the next course on time... This really is a superb looking horse,' chattered the young Private, who had been leading

Calvyn and the horses across an open courtyard. Suddenly the ginger haired soldier glanced around furtively in all directions. 'It's not stolen, is it?' he added in a worried half whisper.

Calvyn stifled a laugh with a choked cough.

'No. I promise you, Jez, that both this mare and my old friend Steady here, are mine. This one I bought only about ten days ago from a market town in the Mistian Vale, and Steady here was given to me by an old friend.'

'Phew,' breathed Jez with an exaggerated gesture of relief. 'Sorry to question your honour, but if you don't mind my saying so, you seem quite young to own two horses – unless you come from a wealthy family. Looking at your clothes though...'

'Yes, I see your point,' Calvyn said, glancing down at his well worn clothing. 'I nearly bought some new clothes on my way here, but I figured that if I was going to spend most of the next couple of years wearing a uniform, why bother?'

'It would've been a bit of a waste of money under the circumstances I suppose,' Jez conceded.

They reached the stables and turned the horses over to the stable hand. Calvyn surreptitiously retrieved his money pouch from one of the saddlebags and, unnoticed, slipped it into an inside pocket of his tunic. No matter how friendly these people appeared to be, he was not about to start trusting them with his entire worldly goods within minutes of arriving.

Sergeant Dren proved to be a stocky, hard-faced individual whose arms and face bore scars that spoke volumes of his experience. His blocky frame and square jaw gave an appearance of granite-like solidity. Not a man to be trifled with, Calvyn surmised as they approached the Sergeant's desk.

'Yes?' Dren questioned, looking up from the report that he had been reading, and inspecting them both with a glance that made Calvyn all too aware of his shabby clothing, and caused him to question his decision not to buy at least a new tunic and hose.

'This is Calvyn, Sergeant. He wants to join us,' Jez stated formally.

'He does, does he? Very good, Private. Dismissed.'

Calvyn glanced back at Jez in time to note that the young soldier had been standing smartly to attention. The Private whirled in an immaculately precise turn, and marched smartly out of the office. Having watched Jez depart, Calvyn returned his attention to Sergeant Dren who was regarding him with a non-committal expression.

'So, why do you want to join the army, son?' the burly man asked, maintaining his face and voice completely deadpan.

'It's an honourable profession, Sir, and well trained fighters are seldom without work. I came here because I heard you were the best.'

The corner of Dren's mouth twitched slightly in amusement at Calvyn's compliment.

'Ever been in a fight?'

'No, Sir.'

'Can you handle a sword?'

'No, Sir.'

'Bow?'

'No, Sir.'

Dren's eyebrows raised slightly in surprise, and his eyes narrowed fractionally as he viewed Calvyn with renewed interest.

'Are you sure that you don't have any other reasons for joining us, young man? Trouble with the authorities? Run away from home?'

'No, Sir. Well... nothing like that anyway. My family are all dead, killed by Demarr's rebels. I'd like to be able to defend myself so that I don't suffer a similar fate. My plan was to get trained, serve the minimum two years, and then return to travelling – perhaps as a guard for a mercantile company.'

The Sergeant barked a quick 'Ha!' of amusement, and smiled a brief flash of acceptance at the last admission.

'Well, you're honest at least,' Dren grunted, satisfied for the moment with Calvyn's answers. 'Most of the lads, and even some of the lasses that we normally get here, arrive professing their undying loyalty to army life without any idea of what they're letting themselves in for. Just be careful what you say around here about Demarr though, and even about that band of hotheads that have named their terrorist group after him. For many in these parts, Demarr is the hero who tried to seize power so that he could restore order to the north. So if you've got any thoughts of vengeance, I suggest that you keep them to yourself. We do not tolerate brawls around here. We train professional soldiers, not street ruffians. Do you understand?'

'Yes, Sir,' affirmed Calvyn, determined not to upset this fearsome looking man.

Sergeant Dren allowed his voice to drop to not much more than a conspiratorial whisper.

'If it means anything to you, I personally think that what Demarr did was completely wrong, and he deserved everything that he got – and more. The Baron is also totally loyal to the crown, but I couldn't vouch for all of his captains.'

'This Estate has an honourable name with all the local communities,' Calvyn agreed.

'That doesn't always mean what you might think,' Dren replied cryptically. 'Anyway,' he continued at his normal booming volume, 'I'll have your Draft Papers drawn up. The next training course is due to start the day after tomorrow. Until then you will be assigned chores. You will be expected to leave all valuables with the Quartermaster. We try to avoid any problems of thievery around here by removing the temptation.'

'Excuse me, Sir, but what should I do about my horses?'

'Horses? You have more than one?' Dren asked in surprise.

'Two,' Calvyn informed the Sergeant. 'One is a superb thoroughbred mare, and the other is a carthorse. Much as I would like to keep them both, I doubt that I could afford to pay the livery costs for long.'

'If the mare is as good as you say, the Baron or one of his captains may wish to purchase her from you, but the carthorse...'

'I don't really want to part with the carthorse if I can at all avoid it. The Baron is welcome to buy the mare, but Steady and I have been together a while, and I'd rather not lose her if I can avoid it.'

'The livery isn't cheap,' countered Dren.

'Then I'll pay it as long as I can. Something may come up.'

'OK. If you're that set on keeping the beast then we may be able to sort something out. A friend of mine owns a farm not far from here, and he may agree to stable her in exchange for her services,' suggested the Sergeant.

'That would be great,' enthused Calvyn.

'Hey! I only said *may* agree. Don't get your hopes up too high. I'll ask for you, but can't promise anything. Now then, Recruit, get yourself around to the Quartermaster's store with your gear and get it inventoried. You'll find the door around the back of the far end of the stables. I'll send someone around to meet you there and give you a quick guided tour before lunch.'

Calvyn thanked the Sergeant for his kindness, and made his way back to where the horses had been stabled. The same stable hand showed him where his saddlebags had been hung up, and gave him a hand to lug them around the corner to the door that led into the Quartermaster's domain. A fussy old man with Segeant rank markings on his uniform met him at the counter inside, and insisted on emptying every last item from the bags. The assistant noted each of Calvyn's belongings on a list and carefully stored them in a large box that was then clearly marked with his name in big letters on the top.

The Quartermaster had refused Calvyn's request to keep his old flute to play in his spare time, saying that he would disturb his fellow Recruits with the noise. Calvyn was informed in no uncertain terms that he would have very little free time whilst he was a Recruit, but that he could come and sign the flute out on his rest days if he wished.

Somehow, the pernickety old storeman had completely missed Perdimonn's grimoire. Calvyn had managed to tuck it away inside his tunic unnoticed as he had brought out his money pouch to be added to the inventory. Calvyn had quietly chuckled to himself afterwards, and had then fallen to wondering for the hundredth time what had become of the old Magician. A shiver ran down his spine every time he thought about Selkor pointing at him out of the vision in the pond, and he found himself nervously looking around, as if expecting to find the dark stranger bearing down on him.

Jez had arrived at the Quartermaster's store just as Calvyn had signed over his belongings for safekeeping.

'Sergeant Dren ordered me to come and give you a quick tour of the castle and get you settled into your barrack room before lunch,' informed the cheerful Private, with that same friendly grin that he had displayed when Calvyn had first arrived. 'We've got just over half an hour to the lunch call, so if you're all done here we should have time to get around most places.'

Calvyn thanked the Quartermaster, and followed the lanky figure out of the dimly lit storeroom into the bright sunlight. Squinting, and shading his eyes with his hand, Calvyn looked around. As he had entered the outer gates in the north wall earlier, he had found himself facing the stables which had looked to be large enough to house at least twenty horses comfortably. There was a large tack room at the right hand end of the row of stalls, which provided storage room for saddles, reins and other accessories. Outside, a waist high, sturdy looking railing set several yards in front of the stalls, ran parallel to and virtually the full length of the stables. The Quartermaster's store was behind the tack store, the building sharing the thick, central stone wall with the back of the stables.

Standing outside the south-facing door of the Quartermaster's domain, Calvyn found his gaze drawn up towards the large stone buttresses and castellated walls of the Baron's keep which towered up directly in front of him.

'Impressive, isn't it?' grinned Jez. 'I'm afraid that's one place that's not included in the tour. The only way you'll get in there is if you make it to Sergeant. According to Dren, you get invited to eat with the captains at the Baron's table on your promotion night. Come on, let's go this way first.'

Jez led Calvyn to the left and showed him the armoury, which was next door to the Quartermaster's store and also backed onto the stables. The building which housed these three sections, together with the Baron's keep, comprised the only two freestanding structures within the castle. All the other rooms and buildings had been constructed against the outer defensive wall of the huge, rectangular fortified area. The outer wall was crenellated along its entire length and had seven watchtowers: one located at each corner; one halfway down the long southern wall; and two on the north wall, situated either side of the gates. Turning left around the corner of the armoury, Calvyn found himself facing Sergeant Dren's office. Jez explained that Dren was the Recruiting Sergeant this year, and was responsible for enlisting fifty to sixty fresh faces for each of the two training courses that would be run during the year. Each course normally took between four and five months, depending on when the Training Sergeant decided that the Recruits were ready to assume their posts as Privates.

'Dren was my Training Sergeant last year, and he was a complete bastard,' chuckled Jez in a low voice as they walked towards the Sergeant's office. 'The Sergeants all take it in turns to do the different senior posts, switching around about once a year. To be honest they're a pretty hard-bitten lot, and there's not a lot to choose between them when it comes down to it.'

To their right, as they walked next to the side wall of the armoury and stables, was the weapons training area.

The floor of the area was sandy, and several groups of soldiers were engaged in mock combat with wooden weapons. Calvyn wanted to stop and watch, but Jez ushered him on.

'You'll get a gut-full of that before you're through, and you'll want to find your way around before lunch,' explained the lanky Private. 'Look, next door to Dren is the archives room. If you can write then you may be seconded to help out the Archivist at harvest time. The door after that is the Training Sergeant's Office. I hear that you've got Sergeant Brett... bad luck!'

'Bad luck? Why?' queried Calvyn, who was still feeling more than a little uneasy about the whole situation, and was wondering once more what he was doing here.

'Oh, I don't know. I'd have probably said the same of any of 'em laughed Jez easily. 'Got you worried for a moment there though – didn't I?'

Calvyn just smiled weakly and asked himself once more just what he was letting himself in for. However, for all of his warnings about how 'bad' the Sergeants were, Jez did not appear in the slightest bit unhappy now, so Calvyn decided not to take too many of Jez's comments at face value.

Jez stopped outside Dren's office and just pointed out the other places of interest around the eastern side of the castle.

'The last office down there on the left is the Paymaster's office. You don't get paid anything as a Recruit though, so don't get too excited. The long building against the east wall is the captains quarters, and beyond that are the targets for the short range archery area. The long range archery training is done outside the castle walls in a special area out to the east. Those buildings down against the south wall are the food storage area and the Carpenter's workshops. Also...' Jez stood up on tiptoes looking into the southeastern corner of the castle. '...No, you can't quite see them from here, but over there in the corner,' said Jez, pointing vaguely at the eastern end of the food stores, 'are the steps that lead down to the dungeons.'

'Dungeons?'

'Yes. It doesn't pay to get into trouble around here, believe me.'

'I do,' said Calvyn with conviction, wondering just how bad you would have to be to get thrown into an underground prison, and vowing to himself that he, personally, would never find out.

Turning around, Jez then led Calvyn back past the large gates, which once again stood closed. Entering the western half of the castle, the first building on the right proved to be the smithy. The two young men glanced in briefly to watch the Blacksmith hard at work.

'The Baron is extremely lucky to have Gerran, he's about the best smith there is,' declared Jez, fondly caressing the hilt of his sword. 'What that man doesn't know about working metal isn't worth knowing. He's a genius.'

Gerran looked the archetypal blacksmith to Calvyn, with his huge frame of a body, tree trunk arms and balding head. A ruddy face poured sweat as the giant of a man pounded a piece of glowing metal with an enormous hammer. However, as Calvyn knew nothing of the trade other than what it produced, he could only take Jez's word that the man was truly skilled.

There was a vast open stone paved area in the western side of the castle, which Calvyn discovered was the drill area. The stone slabs looked almost polished where they had been worn smooth by countless Recruits pounding up and down the parade ground in an endless quest for precision marching. A huge building that ran almost the entire length of the west wall turned out to be the main barracks. The ablutions block stood in the southwestern corner adjacent to the mess hall which stood against the South Wall next to the Surgeon's office. Finally, the Corporals' and Sergeants' quarters nestled in the northwestern corner, between the Smithy and the Main Barracks.

Jez led Calvyn across to one of several doors that led into the barracks.

'Dren told me to put you into room two. Apparently there should be one bed left in there. Let's go see, shall we?'

Opening the door to the sleeping quarters, Jez let out a snort of disgust. Calvyn failed to see anything to cause the Private any sense of outrage. The room, lined with ten beds either side, was spartan and clean. All of the beds except one were already made. The unmade bed, the furthest on the right hand side, had a precisely folded pile of linen together with a blanket, placed at the bed's end.

'Looks like that one's yours,' Jez suggested, pointing at the unmade bed. 'Take a tip from me and note how the bed-pack is made up – you'll be expected to reproduce it daily when you start your training. Recruits are not allowed to make their beds until their bed packs have been inspected at first light. It's a real pain.'

Looking around the room, the Private was shaking his head in obvious disapproval. 'And I hope that you know how to make a bed a bit better than the rest of these "greenies" do,' he snorted.

Calvyn said nothing. He didn't want to admit that he was probably greener than those so-called 'greenies'. The fact was that he had not made a bed for over two years, and indeed had only slept in one on a handful of occasions during that time. He certainly could not see anything wrong with the way that the other beds had been made, and definitely would not know how to improve on those efforts.

'Well, I'll just let you get your bed sorted and I'll see you in the mess hall for lunch,' Jez said, walking back to the door. 'The next bugle call that you hear will be the lunch call.'

With that, the friendly soldier departed, leaving Calvyn a bit bemused at what he was supposed to do with his bed that would make it better than the rest. He took a good look at the way the sheets and blanket had been folded to make the pile that, he deduced, was the bed pack. It was not complicated, he decided, but it was very precisely folded.

Having had a quick look around at how the other Recruits had made their beds, Calvyn decided that it probably would not matter how perfect, or otherwise, his bed was made for the first day. Providing that he learned quickly, and did not repeat his mistakes, Calvyn concluded that he should manage to prevent himself from landing in too much trouble.

Carefully smoothing down the blanket, and turning down the top sheet as precisely as he could, Calvyn just finished his work of art as the bugle sounded the call for lunch. The last meal that he had eaten had been supper the previous evening. Desperately worried that Baron Keevan's Training Course might have started before he arrived, and that he would have to go elsewhere for his training, Calvyn had skipped breakfast in his hurry to reach the castle as quickly as possible. Consequently, Calvyn's stomach answered the bugle call with a growl of its own, clearly ready to sample the gastronomic delights of army food. Rubbing his still gurgling stomach, he took one last look at his bed and walked briskly to the door and out onto the edge of the drill square.

A mass of young men and women swarmed from all corners of the castle towards the wide mess hall doors. Taking a deep breath, Calvyn strode into the crowd and into a new way of life.

CHAPTER 6

'Right, you 'orrible bunch of lowlifes. STAND STRAIGHT!' bellowed Sergeant Brett with the full gusto of his stentorian voice.

Calvyn stood in line with the rest of the Recruits, dressed in his newly issued light green uniform and brown boots. 'Greenies' in more ways than one, he reflected, as the Sergeant continued his maximum volume denigration of the entire company of newly enlisted men and women.

For the previous day and a half, Calvyn, together with the other new Recruits, had been assigned various menial chores as they had waited for their training to begin. Despite many of his fellow Recruits having been open and chatty, Calvyn had found himself remaining quiet for the most part, listening with interest to the blend of bragging, bravado and speculation.

Things had worked out pretty well on the whole. Sergeant Dren's farmer friend had been more than willing to look after Steady, and Captain Strexis had taken one look at Calvyn's thoroughbred mare, and decided to buy her on the spot. Calvyn certainly had no financial worries, and would continue to have none for some time, having added the price of the mare to the money that he had already lodged with the Quartermaster. Although he would not be earning any money for the next few months, it seemed that he would have little opportunity to spend anything either, so he would be able to concentrate on his training with no external worries other than what had become of Perdimonn.

The question of what had happened to the old Magician played on Calvyn's mind a lot. However, somehow he sensed that Perdimonn was still alive and well. How, he did not know, but his heart was certain that Selkor had not killed him... yet.

The first morning of training had offered a rude awakening to many of the Recruits. Reveille had blasted out at the first hint of daylight, followed seconds later by someone throwing the barrack room door open and banging what sounded like two saucepans together with a resounding metallic din.

'Get up, you sluggards!' yelled the mystery morning caller, and without pausing to observe the results had moved on to the next room to repeat the process.

'Welcome to the army, ladies and gentlemen,' groaned someone from the middle of the room, and was rewarded with a mixture of grunts, sniggers and a thrown pillow for his effort.

A short while later, washed, dressed and bed packs made, the entire intake of sixty-two Recruits had been herded across to the Quartermaster's store to be issued with their uniforms. Everyone was given two complete sets of clothing, a single pair of brown leather boots and a poncho of waxed, almost canvas-like material. The poncho had a drawstring to tighten the neck hole and a strange flap of material sewn just below the neck that served no obvious purpose whatsoever. Some of the clothes issued were new, but many had evidently been worn before. Olive green uniforms were the Baron's way of branding the trainees with their status until they had proved themselves worthy of the blue and black chequers of his regular troops. By recycling the greens through several successive sets of the Recruits, the Baron saved himself unnecessary expense.

All of the Recruits had been given the same admonition to take good care of their uniforms, as it was all that they would be given until they had finished their basic training. As each person had reached the counter, the Quartermaster had visually appraised the individual's size, walked down his rows of shelves pulling suitable sized garments onto one arm, and then dumped them onto the counter in front of the Recruit for him to change into. The Quartermaster's assistant had then taken the Recruits' personal clothing, added it to the inventory, and stored it with their other personal effects.

When his turn came, Calvyn once again managed to slip the grimoire past the Quartermaster's attention, this time by secreting it within his pile of spare uniform. This had seemed a good idea at the time but in retrospect, having got it back to the barrack room, Calvyn realised that he hadn't a clue where to hide it. In the end he decided to risk leaving the precious book under the mattress for the time being, at least until he could find a better hideaway for it.

'All those from barrack room one, form two ranks here,' bawled Brett, stabbing his finger downward at a point in front of him.

Twenty-one Recruits scrambled to comply.

'Barrack room two – here... three – here,' he continued, marching with meticulous precision to each of the points that he indicated. 'Come on! Snap to it.'

The ensuing melee gradually settled into some semblance of order.

'Right, you miserable looking bunch of bed-wetters,' Brett growled, his voice gradually building in that amazingly precise military crescendo, 'STAND STILL! Now I don't know where you boys and girls have all come from, and I don't really care. You're all mine now, and what I say is law. Do you understand?'

'Yes, Sergeant,' came the murmured reply from several of the Recruits.

'I can't hear you! I SAID DO YOU UNDERSTAND?' Brett boomed.

'YES, SERGEANT!' roared sixty-two voices in unison.

'Good! Over the next few months you will be transformed from the pathetic *rabble* that I see before me, into hard, professional soldiers that people will have no choice but to respect. The following are the people who will be largely responsible for that transformation. In charge of Squad One, Corporal Gan, Squad Two, Corporal Derra, and Squad Three, Corporal Beren. These fine soldiers will be your guides, tutors and most avid supporters whilst you work hard at your training. They will also be your judges, jury and executioners if you don't. Do you understand?'

'YES, SERGEANT!'

'Very good. Corporals, take over your squads.'

Snapping to attention, the three Corporals turned and marched to stand in front of their respective group of Recruits. Corporal Gan immediately got his group to turn to their left and move to the far northern end of the drill area. Corporal Beren similarly took Squad Three to the southern end. Corporal Derra however, just stood, quietly regarding Calvyn and the rest of Squad Two with her large brown eyes. Squad Two looked back.

Derra was certainly worthy of more than a cursory glance, Calvyn decided, as he contemplated the striking figure of the Corporal. Her slightly taller than average frame boasted not an ounce of fat, and her long, shapely legs appeared sleek and not overly muscled. Sharply angled, thickish eyebrows arched over her dark eyes, and her hair, cut so short that it was almost a stubble, accentuated the almost angular quality of her face into an air of harshness.

Without a word, Derra placed her hands behind her back, strolled across to the end of the rank, and began inspecting the Recruits one by one. The Corporal moved with the unconscious grace of a panther, smooth and silent. In the background, the other two Corporals had begun their high volume introduction to drill, but Derra continued to move steadily along the front rank, locking eyes with each Recruit in turn, her daunting gaze appearing to attempt to gauge their spirit in some way.

Calvyn bided his time, intrigued by the harsh-looking Corporal. Since leaving his village, he had not met many women other than those who had bought items from his stall, and certainly none that had held positions of any authority. The short wait was soon over. Derra stepped in front of him and regarded him with her impassive stare. Calvyn tried to smile slightly, but his lips refused to respond under the cold glare of Derra's glittering eyes. His breath seemed to freeze in his lungs as he held himself as stiffly straight as he could. Then she was gone, moving away to pierce her next victim with that dagger-like gaze. Calvyn exhaled slowly, trying not to make it too obvious that he had been holding his breath.

Derra completed her inspection of the squad and prowled back around to stand and face the twenty expectant trainees.

'Does anyone have any objections to being trained by a woman? If so tell me now,' asked Derra, her strong voice harbouring a soft, gravelly rasp that seemed to accentuate the volume.

Silence reigned.

'Excellent! Let's begin.'

'Sarcasm and mocking abuse must go with the territory,' thought Calvyn to himself as he joined the queue for breakfast an hour later. Time and again over the previous hour, Derra had insulted their intelligence, their parentage and their ability to comply with her simple instructions. However, Calvyn had to admit that the technique of instruction appeared effective, as the squad undoubtedly now performed the simple static manoeuvres in a far more fluid and precise fashion than when they had started an hour before.

'Great Tarmin's toes! What a ball-breaker, eh?' whispered a fellow squad member, rolling his eyes towards the Corporals' table. Calvyn vaguely recalled that the young man's name was Tyrrak, and that he had been one of the more outspoken of his barrack room occupants during the last few days.

'I think that the Corporals are all pretty much of the same mould,' Calvyn replied diplomatically.

'Boy, you must be half blind or something! That is one helluva woman. What's more, she'll probably chew us all up and spit us out without batting an eyelid. We're going to have a tough time of it over the next few months with that bitch running us to hell and back. The ones that I feel most sorry for, though, are the girls.'

'The girls?'

'You know, those three members of the opposite sex that sleep in our barrack room and stand out on parade with us,' Tyrrak replied, his voice dripping with sarcasm. 'Which girls did you think, for Tarmin's sake?'

'OK, I get the picture,' muttered Calvyn, mildly irritated by the Recruit's derisive tone. 'But why do you feel sorry for them?'

'Because Derra's going to kick seven shades of hell out of them to mould 'em in her own image, that's why.'

Calvyn thought about that for a moment. Tyrrak had a point, he decided, but Calvyn resolved to reserve judgement on Derra's treatment of the female Recruits until he had been around a little longer. However, he did look along the breakfast queue until he had picked out the three girls in question. The only one that he knew by name was Jenna, who slept in the bed opposite him. She had briefly introduced herself on the first night but, like himself, had remained quiet and out of the centre of attention ever since.

The subject of conversation on the Recruits' tables was inevitably about their designated instructors. Speculation ran riot, as hushed debates raged over who had gained and who had lost by getting which Corporal. Naturally, Derra was at the heart of many of the discussions as the mealtime character assassination groups got underway. However, for the most part, Squad Two remained silent about their Corporal, as if almost frightened that she might somehow be listening in.

After breakfast the squads reformed on the drill square and the shouting recommenced. Derra spent the first ten minutes revising all the static manoeuvres: attention, at ease, right turn, left turn, about turn and right dress, which Calvyn had been mildly amused to discover meant 'adjust your spacing' and had nothing to do with clothing whatsoever.

The demonstrations on how to march were finally given once Derra was satisfied with the static drill. Calvyn failed to see what the supposed difficulty was with marching. On the executive command "March" you stepped off with your left foot and pushed forward your right arm. Subsequently you walked, albeit swinging your arms a bit higher and straighter than usual, until someone yelled "Halt". The call to halt always came as the left foot hit the ground, and all that you had to do was to take one further step with the right and then bring the left foot in beside it. Easy!

Derra gave the full demonstration twice. Each time she showed the sequence in slow motion first, and then at the actual pace at which it should be carried out.

'Have you got all that?' she asked after the second demonstration.

'YES, CORPORAL,' blasted back the reply.

'Good. Squad, left, turn... Squad, by the left, quick-march.'

Calvyn was towards the rear of the squad as it moved off, and it was all that he could do to keep a straight face. Squad Two was a shambles! There seemed to be arms and legs going in all directions and timings.

'Left right left right left right left...' bawled Derra, working hard to rescue some semblance of order to the mishmash of shuffling arms and legs. 'Squad... halt! Squad, right, turn. That... was abysmal! Anyone would think that you had only learned to walk last week. If you don't get your act together better than that, you'll be here 'til midnight every night for the next fortnight practising. Understand?'

'YES, CORPORAL.'

'Right, let's try that again...'

Corporal Derra yelled and bellowed at them for a further hour with limited success. For the most part, Squad Two began to move more in unison. However, one poor Recruit in particular was having great difficulty. The young man was concentrating so hard on trying to keep in step and swing his arms, that his limbs would often move further and further out of synchronisation with one another. Eventually, his left arm and left leg were moving forward together whilst his right arm and leg were moving backward and vice versa. Calvyn agonised for the unfortunate Recruit as he progressed, tick-tock fashion, back and forth across the drill square.

At the end of the session, Squad Two was dismissed for a short break to visit the toilets prior to regrouping at the main gate for their first physical training lesson. Calvyn immediately took the opportunity to speak to his browbeaten roommate.

'Wow! Is Derra on your back or what?' Calvyn opened. 'Tell me about it.'

'Hey, no problem. We can sneak in a quick practice at lunchtime or this evening if you'd like. I'm sure that without the Corporal breathing down your neck you'll get the hang of it in no time.'

'Really? I'd really appreciate that. I just don't seem to be able to get it together at all.'

'Well, we're all in this together, so we'd better start looking out for one another, don't you think?'

'Sounds good to me. My name's Bek, and you are?'

'Calvyn,' he replied, and shook his counterpart's outstretched hand.

'Good to meet you, Calvyn, and thanks.'

'My pleasure, but it looks like we'd better get a move on. Derra's already over at the gate, and she's brewing a look that would curdle milk at half a mile.'

'Does she have any other kinds?' laughed Bek.

They made a quick dash to the toilets and reassembled with the rest of Squad Two at the main gate a couple of minutes later. Corporal Derra stood at the archway with one hand tapping her leg in annoyance as the last stragglers made their way across the drill square. Looking around the group with her baleful stare, Derra left Squad Two in no doubt that once again she was unhappy with them. However, when she finally began speaking, the Corporal began at such a normal, conversational volume that Calvyn momentarily thought that he had been mistaken in his diagnosis of her mood.

'OK, ladies and gentlemen, have you all had sufficient break time?'

Scattered murmurs and nods signalled the apprehensive affirmation that Squad Two was ready to move on.

'Good, I'm *so* glad that you're all happy and ready to continue with your training,' crooned Derra, her voice suddenly dripping with sarcasm. 'However, I just have one minor observation to make before we start the physical training session...'

'Here it comes,' thought Calvyn, mentally wincing as he prepared himself for the inevitable barrage to come.

'YOU ARE A RABBLE!' blasted the Corporal at maximum volume. 'Whenever you are outside you will march everywhere – to the lessons, to the mess hall, to the toilets – everywhere. I don't care if you're all together, or in tens, fives or on your own – if you are outside, and you are moving, you will march. I will not have my squad meandering around the castle like it's some sort of rest day entertainment camp. Have I made myself perfectly clear?'

'Yes, Corporal.'

'Good. Well don't just stand there – fall in!'

The Recruits scrambled to their places whilst Derra signalled to the guards to open the gates. Squad Two marched out of the castle and halted some twenty yards beyond the archway. Having organised the squad to double space themselves, Derra led the group through a sequence of static exercises designed to warm and stretch each of the main muscle groups. After about ten minutes of what was the Corporal's warm-up routine, Calvyn, together with many of the other squad members, were breathing hard and already tiring.

'I think... I must have... died last night... and gone to hell,' gasped someone to Calvyn's right through gritted teeth as Derra called for them to relax and listen in.

'OK, boys and girls, this is your first chance to show

me what you're made of. The next exercise will be a foot race from here, around that stand of woods out to the west and back around the south side of the castle, right around the walls and back here to the gate,' Derra announced, pointing out the simple route. 'In case any of you should get tempted to cut the back corner of the woods, I'd just like to point out that there is a profusion of razor thorn bushes growing in there. Any of you displaying razor thorn scratches on your return will wish you'd never been born. Understand?'

'Yes, Corporal.'

Good. The whole route is only about a mile and a half long, maybe two miles at the most, so none of you should struggle too much. OK, let's see you run. Ready... GO!'

The twenty members of Squad Two leapt forward and jostled for position as they ran across the open grassland towards the distant woods. Calvyn pushed himself hard to keep up with the leading bunch of six others that had almost immediately broken away from the rest. Panting hard, he managed to stay with the group all the way to the corner of the woods. However, as the leaders turned to run along the edge of the trees, the pace began to tell on Calvyn and he very slowly began to fall behind the front pack.

Gradually, Calvyn found his breathing settling into a more rhythmic pattern as, having resigned himself to not being able to keep up with the fastest group, his legs adjusted to a more comfortable cadence. Saliva constantly oozed into his mouth, causing him to swallow frequently. Each gulping action hurt his throat as his laboured, gasping inhalations brought a faint taste of blood to the back of his tongue. As he ran, Calvyn's vision became more and more tunnelled on the ground ahead of him, the peripherals greying to insignificance as his sole focus became to drive his legs, one in front of the other, in a pounding rhythm of gasping pain.

All of a sudden the woods were behind him and the west wall of the castle stood beckoning him on across the open ground. Calvyn became vaguely aware of voices shouting both encouragement and derision from the south-west guard tower, although who the voices were supporting or scorning held no relevance to him as he battled to keep running.

Despite the physical strain, and his narrowed focus of purpose, Calvyn was quite surprised to find a part of his mind wandering in a strangely analytical semi-daydream. His thoughts meandered through an assessment of the characters that he had met since arriving at Baron Keevan's Castle. There was the jovial Private, Jez, who had calmed Calvyn's fears and apprehension with his honest and good humoured welcome, and the solid Sergeant Dren, who had gone out of his way to be helpful in the matter of Calvyn's horses. Both had, in their own way, displayed friendship in an instant. Was this a trait of military life, or just a coincidence? It was probably a bit early to make sweeping generalisations Calvyn decided. Observe and analyse for now, and the patterns of behaviour would undoubtedly slot into place.

Brett and Derra fell into a different category. Hard, aloof and professional, they, together with Corporals Beren and Gan, could ill afford to show friendship to the Recruits during the early stages of their training. No, they would remain detached for some time yet, Calvyn deduced. Bearing that fact in mind should make the next few weeks a little easier to accept, whilst the Sergeant, and more particularly Corporal Derra, continued to stamp their authority on the Recruits with relentless, iron fisted handling.

As for the other Recruits, Calvyn was only just beginning to distinguish any characteristics, as it was early days. However, the cynical and sarcastic Tyrrak did not strike Calvyn as someone that he would ever welcome as a particularly close friend. The self-assured arrogance that the man portrayed set Calvyn's teeth on edge, but given a few weeks of basic training, Tyrrak might mellow, Calvyn reflected as he pounded on along the length of the south wall.

Bek, on the other hand, appeared open to overtures of

friendship, and was humble enough to accept an offer of help with a warmth and gratitude that was heartening. Calvyn felt sure that he had won an ally and friend in Bek, and looked forward to having a chance to build on that friendship over the next few days.

The only other character that he had made any sort of contact with was Jenna, and that was no more than an introductory 'hello'. However, Calvyn was quite surprised to find that his mind recalled a remarkably vivid picture of her as she had made that handshake of greeting. He found that he could still almost feel the touch of her hand against his and see the glint of humour in her gentle brown eyes. He pictured her slender frame, which was quite tall for a girl, and her straight brown hair, woven into the single plait that reached down to the centre of her back, and Calvyn found that he could almost see her, moving around the barrack room with an unconscious grace. Jenna, although attractive, was certainly not the most physically beautiful girl that he had ever seen. Indeed, there were at least a couple of other girls on his course alone who were both prettier and shapelier. However, Calvyn sensed a kindred spirit in the quiet young woman, and so he promised himself that he would at least try to get to know her better.

Turning the corner at the south-east guard tower, Calvyn became aware that he was slowly gaining on someone else who had dropped out of the leading pack. Although tempted to try to increase his pace again, Calvyn found that his body was unwilling to respond, and that his head was advising him to save himself for a final burst along the north wall. Grinding onward, Calvyn caught up with his fellow Recruit about two thirds of the way down the east wall. As Calvyn came up alongside the other runner, the man increased his pace to match Calvyn's and the two continued running side by side along the rest of the east wall until they turned the last corner to face the finishing straight down the north wall to the main gate.

Calvyn's adversary put on a sudden burst of speed as

they turned on to the home straight. Gritting his teeth, and sucking air hard into his lungs, Calvyn accelerated to stay tucked right up on the other Recruit's shoulder. Then Derra's rasping shouts filtered through to Calvyn's consciousness, and all thoughts of rhythm forgotten, he forced himself into a sprint. Lungs burning and muscles protesting, Calvyn overtook his now flagging competitor and pulled away from him. Glancing over his shoulder, Calvyn was just starting to ease up as he approached the gate, safe in the knowledge that his opponent was well and truly beaten, when the tall figure of Jenna slipped past him on the outside to steal his finishing position.

Calvyn was a bit annoyed with himself for easing up, and even more so for not realising that anyone else was close behind. As he stood doubled over and panting for breath, he raised his head to find Jenna, also breathing hard only a couple of paces away. Unable to speak, Calvyn just gave his best impression of a smile and waggled a raised index finger at her as if to tell her off.

Jenna flashed a smile back.

'Hands on hips and walk slowly up to the gate and back until all the others get here,' Derra ordered, and then returned to shouting at the next members of Squad Two to appear on the home straight.

Calvyn placed his hands on his hips and felt the muscles across his heaving chest and across his stomach tighten in protest. Once he had calmed his breathing down to a less frantic depth and pace, he found that a gentle walking pace actually helped to speed his body's recovery to normal.

A rivulet of sweat trickled down from the outside of Calvyn's eyebrow and ran down his cheek. Another slid down to hang at the end of his nose, causing him to stick out his lower lip and blow upward to get rid of it.

'Looks like you've sprung a leak or two,' jibed the quiet voiced Jenna, who had walked up alongside him looking for all the world as if she had just been out for a rest day stroll.

'Yes, I was fine while I was running, but I'm definitely

feeling a mite warm now that we've stopped,' replied Calvyn, raising a sleeve to wipe his suddenly dripping forehead.

'If that's what you sound like when you're fine, then I'd hate to hear you when you're struggling! You were blowing so hard that I thought you were about to explode!' laughed Jenna.

Calvyn laughed with her, shaking his head slightly as he racked his brains for a suitably quick reply.

'Well, at least it gave me a good excuse for not hearing you sneak up behind me.'

'You can hardly say that I snuck up on you whilst running in these,' she chuckled, pointing down at the thick, brown leather boots.

'Hmm, OK, you win on that one!'

'Of course! What did you expect?'

Calvyn shrugged and smiled, unsure of how to continue the conversation. As he glanced across at her the fact dawned on him that she had already completely recovered from the run, and was breathing completely normally. As he was still struggling to calm his lungs down to some semblance of their regular, unconscious rhythm, he started to suspect that perhaps she had not run the race to the best of her ability. Although he certainly did not want to get Jenna into any trouble, he was intrigued as to why she would deliberately choose to underachieve when she was obviously capable of doing somewhat better. Dropping his voice to a whisper, Calvyn asked her why she had not stayed with the front runners.

'One of the few advantages of being a girl is that the Privates and Corporals who are not involved with the training are more than willing to talk to you. There are of course many disadvantages as well. However, in this case I discovered that one of Derra's favourite forms of beasting her Recruits is with foot races. Not a foot race... foot races!'

'You mean we're going to have to do that again?' Calvyn gasped, incredulous.

'Shh... yes. Probably more than once if my information is correct,' affirmed Jenna.

Calvyn groaned quietly.

'I figured that I probably wasn't likely to be the fastest in the squad on the first race, but that if I held a bit of energy back, I would do better on the second or third. Derra tends to hit the best and the worst of her squads the hardest by all accounts, so if you stay fairly anonymous and don't bring yourself to her attention too much, you should get through with the minimum of hardship.'

'But don't you want to do the best that you can? Surely you won't improve if you don't stretch yourself?' Calvyn asked, still keeping his voice low.

'True, but why take abuse for something that you are already good at? As far as I'm concerned, I'm here to learn to be a soldier, not a runner. I can already run, but I don't know yet how to be a professional fighter. That's what I came here to learn.'

'Well, I beg to differ,' Calvyn replied. 'I've always been brought up to achieve the very best that I possibly can at everything that I do. I may not be brilliant at certain things, but that's certainly not for lack of trying.' He grinned at her suddenly. 'So you'd best keep an eye out over your shoulder next time, as I intend to get my revenge!'

They both laughed.

'Squad Two! Fall, *in*!' yelled Derra, from some twenty yards away. 'Come on... move it, move it!'

Squad Two leapt to obey, and quickly lined up in two ranks.

'Well, Recruits, I don't think that I need to tell you that based on that performance we'll be doing a lot of physical training over the next few weeks. However, to show you that I'm not all bad... the Recruits who came in first, second and third in the foot race, fall, *out*! Well done, you're going to take a break from running, but the rest of you obviously need more practice. When I give the word I want you to run the same route again. Ready... GO!'

With a collective groan, Squad Two, minus the three smug-looking winners of the first race, set off again towards the distant woods. The starting pace was noticeably slower than on the previous race, and Calvyn found that his natural running speed kept him up in the leading group without any major discomfort. The front pack that broke away this time was bigger. Ten Recruits in all, including Jenna, Bek and Calvyn, settled into a steady rhythm and quickly pulled away from the seven stragglers.

Once again Calvyn found his mind wandering as he ran. This time, however, Calvyn decided to direct his thoughts towards a more profitable end and to concentrate on the last mental focus exercise that Perdimonn had set him. Attempting to "see" the black square on the white background both with his eyes open, and whilst running, added another dimension of difficulty, but to Calvyn's surprise he obtained the superimposed image before he had reached the woods. Maintaining the picture, he started to make the black square slowly rotate about its centre point and accelerate in a steadily faster and faster spinning motion.

By the time he turned the corner to run along the back of the woods, Calvyn found himself running at the front of the pack alongside Jenna, the mental effort of accelerating the image of the square subconsciously causing him to run faster. Stumbling slightly as his intense concentration on the mental exercise completely overtook his focus on where he was going, the image dissolved in an instant.

A quick glance around at his fellow runners revealed that the front runners had reduced to a group of seven, and two of those appeared to be struggling to maintain the pace. Calvyn felt good. He was breathing quite hard, but in a controlled fashion. The mental control required to picture the spinning square had kept his mind off the physical effort of the running, and his body was automatically regulating his breathing at the optimum rate for the punishment that he was dealing it.

Concentrating again, he began to rebuild the image.

Faster and faster the black square spun, until the corners began to blur and the square appeared more like an eight-pointed star. Calvyn was totally absorbed in the discipline once more as Jenna accelerated in front of him, running through the picture in a sprint for the finish. Snapping back to reality, Calvyn gritted his teeth and forced his legs to accelerate and give chase to the slim figure of Jenna who was rapidly leaving him behind.

Another runner overtook Calvyn, and yet another as he battled to maintain his charge for home. With his subconscious rhythm broken and the race for the line on, Calvyn's breathing pattern rapidly degenerated to his gasping efforts of the first race. However, as he dropped into fourth place, resolve and determination welled up inside him, bringing a wave of adrenalin with it. Bounding forward with a last ditch burst of speed and energy, he lunged into third place just as he reached the line of the road from the main gate.

Falling to the floor, chest heaving and lungs gasping for breath, Calvyn rolled onto his back to find the hard face of Corporal Derra looking down at him.

'Good effort, Recruit,' she said, maintaining her voice completely devoid of any warmth or congratulations. It was a straight statement of fact, nothing more.

Calvyn, unable to reply or even acknowledge the compliment, fought to control his overextended respiratory system whilst Derra returned her attention to shouting at the next bunch of runners.

CHAPTER 7

Calvyn felt as if he had not eaten for a month. As he attacked the plate of food that he had collected from the service counter, he looked across at Jenna who had sat down in the place opposite and was poking suspiciously at her food with her fork.

'It may not be home cooking, but it's hot and there's plenty of it,' mumbled Calvyn through a mouthful of meat and gravy.

'What have they done to these greens?' asked Jenna of no one in particular. 'They look as if they've been boiled for a week!'

'The meat's all but cremated as well,' added Tyrrak, taking the empty seat next to Jenna.

'Well it certainly fills a gap – or in my case a cavern. I'm starving,' replied Calvyn, taking another large mouthful of vegetables and ignoring the criticisms of Jenna and Tyrrak. 'Just be thankful that the Baron doesn't expect us to train on minimal rations. I for one would not want to repeat that last session with my stomach screaming for food.'

'And I would rather not repeat that last session at all!' retorted Tyrrak with feeling.

'Oh come on, it wasn't that bad,' Jenna laughed, whilst tentatively trying a delicate portion of meat.

'Speak for yourself! It may be all right for you racing snakes, but that third run nearly killed me. My feet have got blisters on their blisters! I'll be lucky if I can still walk by tomorrow, let alone run.'

Murmurs of agreement were sounded by nearby Recruits.

Jenna grinned and conceded the point with a nod. 'I've got to admit that I'm a little footsore myself. These new boots are going to rub like crazy until we've broken them in a bit more, but I think that I'd rather have run with you the third time than stayed at the gate with Derra. At least I could have run at my own pace.'

Calvyn gave a wholehearted 'Mmm' of agreement through another mouthful of food.

'So what did Derra have you doing that could possibly have been worse than that blasted run?' asked Tyrrak sceptically.

'Static strength exercises by the dozen,' Calvyn interjected with a grimace. 'Derra had us pushing out sit-ups, press-ups and no end of other exercises by the score until the first runner rounded the final corner. I thought that I was hurting after the second run, but that was nothing compared with the beasting we took after you lot had pottered off towards the woods.'

'Yeah, Derra really caught us well and truly,' drawled Jenna. 'She's sorted out who the runners are and will undoubtedly pounce on us if she catches us deliberately trying not to make the top three places. She's bound to have noted who the slowest ones were as well. I wouldn't fancy being in their boots over the next few weeks either, as they'll almost certainly be in for some extra curricular physical training.'

'When?' scoffed Tyrrak. 'There's only so many hours in the day!'

'We'll see,' replied Jenna, unperturbed by his patronising tone. 'I'm sure that Corporal Derra will have something up her sleeve.' With that, Jenna turned her attention back to her plate, pushing the food around briefly with her fork before placing both her knife and fork on the plate with a sigh and pushing the plate away from her. Looking up again she caught Calvyn's eye, and seeing his plate was already empty she raised her eyebrows questioningly at him whilst indicating with her hand for him to help himself.

'You sure?'

Jenna nodded.

'Well as it's to help out a fellow member of Squad Two then I don't mind if I do,' Calvyn jibed with a grin, and swapped his empty plate for Jenna's virtually full one.

'I don't know how you can eat that glop. It's had all the taste cooked out of it,' Jenna said, watching Calvyn devour the food with a look that flickered between amazement and disgust.

'It's food, it's edible, and right now I'm hungry,' stated Calvyn in a matter-of-fact voice. 'Anyway, I thought that you wanted to be a soldier, not a chef. If you can't eat the food you won't last long at the rate Corporal Derra's pushing us.'

'Oh, I'll stick the pace. You can be sure of that.'

'Yes,' replied Calvyn, looking thoughtfully at the determined set of her face and the steel in her eyes, 'I think you will at that.'

Finishing the second plate of food, Calvyn heaved a sigh of contentment and pushed the empty plate forward slightly whilst leaning back in his chair. Glancing around the room he noted that people were already leaving in dribs and drabs. It seemed that the protocol was to take your plate and cutlery to a hatchway just beyond the service counter. Any waste food was then scraped into a waste container and the dirty cutlery and crockery were stacked for cleaning by the appropriate chore section.

As he looked around the mess hall, Calvyn caught Bek's eye and remembered his earlier promise to help him with his marching. Calvyn gave a sideways nod of his head towards the door, which Bek acknowledged and stood to leave. Making a polite withdrawal from the table, Calvyn took his dirty utensils to the appropriate hatch and met up with Bek.

'Shall we grab a little practice while we can then?' asked Calvyn.

'That would be great if you're sure it's still all right.

That was a pretty knackering morning and we're only half-way through day one.'

'Yes, let's go for it. Corporal Derra said that we had 'til the next bugle call. I've got no idea how long that gives us, but we should have time for a few goes up and down the barrack room.'

'The barrack room?'

'Yes, it should be at least a little more private there, so you won't need to worry about too many onlookers.'

'Sounds good to me.'

Calvyn and Bek made their way to the door where they paused.

'Derra said that we were to march everywhere, so we'd better fall in,' reminded Calvyn. 'I'll tell you what, you go in front and just walk as smartly as you can to the barrack room. I'll fall in behind you and match your step. Don't even think about swinging your arms, just walk. OK?'

'Sure.'

They set off along the edge of the square as Calvyn had suggested. However, within a very few paces Bek's arms were already beginning to lose synchronisation with his legs. Calvyn elected to remain silent and wait until they were in the sanctuary of the barrack room before trying to correct Bek's timing. Remaining in step as far as the dormitory proved a challenge, and Calvyn found himself looking down at his compatriot's feet for much of the short distance.

Arriving at the door they halted, and dismissed with a half turn to the right. On entering the room, Bek shook his head in despondence.

'Hey, don't give up before you start,' Calvyn encouraged the dispirited Bek. 'Come on, let's start from the other end of the room.'

'OK, but I just can't seem to get the hang of it for some reason.'

'I'm sure that it will come to you in time,' said Calvyn, subtly falling into step with Bek as they walked the length of the barrack room.

Reaching the other end of the room, Calvyn turned and faced Bek with a big smile.

'There, that wasn't so hard, was it?'

'What wasn't?'

'Well, we just marched successfully for the full length of the dorm, and you did it quite naturally. Now tell me – what was so difficult?'

'We did?'

'Yes. It probably wasn't quite smart enough to satisfy Derra though, so we'd better try it again don't you think?'

Bek just grinned back at Calvyn and nodded.

'OK. By the left, quick, march.'

Unfortunately, even buoyed up by Calvyn's encouragement, Bek's co-ordination went to pieces within seconds of moving off each time. The dormitory echoed with the squeaky sound of their new leather boots as they marched up and down the polished floor, and the minutes ticked by with little sign of progress until an idea flashed into Calvyn's mind.

'Have you ever been to a village dance, Bek?'

'Yes, lots of times. Why?'

'Have you got a favourite tune?'

'Yes, I suppose so. The musicians in my town used to play a really lively jig called "Dance of the Wood Sprites", but what has this got to do with marching?'

'Actually it's got everything to do with marching. Now, can you whistle or hum the tune for me?'

'I suppose so. It goes something like this...'

Bek started to whistle the catchy tune and Calvyn quickly recognised the melody. It was perfect. The tune was the sort that stuck in the mind, and despite all efforts to stop it, would constantly repeat itself over and over in the listener's head until they would do anything to break its cycle. Moreover, the music had the ideal rhythm to get Bek's arms moving of their own accord.

'Brilliant, Bek. Listen, this is what we're going to do. You and I are going to walk up and down the dorm and whistle your tune, OK?'

'What if someone comes in?'

'Then they'll probably have a good laugh at our expense. Trust me Bek. This will help.'

'I must be crazy! All right, let's get on with it.'

Whistling the jaunty tune the two young men walked up and down the barrack room. Calvyn exaggerated the beat of the music, and the rhythm worked its own magic. Bek, concentrating on whistling the melody, subconsciously began swinging his arms in time with the tune. Calvyn happened to be looking across at Bek when the realisation of the fact dawned on him. A grin spread across the young man's face that lit up his eyes as he beamed back at Calvyn.

'Excellent! You've got it. Now what you need to do is to try just humming the tune in the back of your throat and see if you can keep in step like that. You see, just between you and me, I don't think that Corporal Derra will appreciate a rendition of "Dance of the Wood Sprites" on her drill square.'

They both laughed and continued their practice until the bugle sounded a couple of minutes later. Bek turned to Calvyn with a look of gratitude, but Calvyn held his hand up to stop the words of thanks.

'You don't need to say it, Bek. You're welcome. I'm sure that you'll have opportunities to lend me a hand sometime. Let's make a pact to look out for each other, shall we?'

'Done,' agreed Bek, clasping Calvyn's outstretched hand.

'Come on, let's go give Derra a pleasant surprise, shall we?'

The two Recruits made their way outside to join the rapidly forming squads on the drill square. Derra, Gan and Beren appeared seconds later and the Recruits fell silent as the Corporals took their positions at the front of the squads. Then, without comment on what she saw there, Derra brought the Recruits to attention and began the afternoon drill session.

Calvyn was really pleased to see Bek keeping good time during the marching. If anything, Bek had a bit more of a lively swing to his gait than was strictly required, but if Derra noticed it, she chose not to comment. However, what was noticeable to Calvyn was that Bek was no longer being picked on, and Derra did not pull him out once during the entire session.

Squad Two was already beginning to move as a unit and Corporal Derra's shouting was directed towards improving that unity of movement. She would make them halt time after time in an attempt to refine the stuttering clatter of boots to a single loud thump as the final step of the halt was carried out. It would take time, thought Calvyn to himself, but it was already becoming obvious that with practice their precision would improve.

On completing the session, Squad Two were given a five minute break and ordered to report to the weapons training ground when those who needed to had visited the necessary. After being dismissed, Calvyn went straight over to Bek and gave him a friendly clout on the shoulder.

'So drill isn't so bad after all then?' Calvyn asked with a grin.

'Thanks to you. Let's hope the next session goes as well.'

'What, the next drill session? Or the weapons training?'

'Well, both actually... but more especially the weapons training. I'm looking forward to seeing how Corporal Derra fights. It should be a sight to behold.'

'Yes, her movements are so fluid,' agreed Calvyn. 'I imagine that she'll make us all look like bumbling idiots in comparison.'

'As I said, I look forward with interest to finding out,' said Bek with a wink.

They did not have long to wait. Squad Two quickly reformed and marched with new-found co-ordination across the drill square to pass between the Baron's keep and the Quartermaster's store towards the sandy floored weapons training area. As they passed the door of the armoury, Derra emerged carrying two short swords.

'Sharpen it up, Squad Two!' Derra growled. 'Left right left right. Come on, get it together. Just because you're not on the drill square is no excuse to get sloppy!'

Swinging their arms higher and straighter, Squad Two swung past the armoury and halted at the edge of the open area. Derra yelled for them to dismiss and got them all to sit in a wide semi-circle whilst she stood in the centre regarding them with her piercing stare.

'Well, boys and girls, this is probably what you've been waiting for all day... the chance to swing a weapon. If it isn't what you've been looking forward to, then you've chosen the wrong profession. We're going to begin with the short sword, and later in the week you'll be introduced to the longbow to begin archery classes. Has anyone here got any experience with a short sword?'

Calvyn glanced around the semi-circle and noted that over half of the Recruits had raised their hands. Derra looked around the group and acknowledged the response with a curt nod.

'Lower your hands. We'll find out shortly what you know, or what you think that you know. Firstly, however, for the benefit of those who have not used a blade like this...' Derra brandished one of the two swords and then held it out for all to be able to see clearly. '...take a good look. This... is an implement of death. Death for your enemies, or death for you. The difference is merely the skill with which you wield it.'

Derra walked slowly around the semi-circle, holding the blade in front of her.

'The short sword is very versatile. It can be used to good effect both in a solo fight with a single adversary, or in an infantry battle line with many people fighting side by side. I will teach you how to use this weapon effectively in either of those situations. Eventually, we will concentrate on the battle line scenario and teamwork rather than duelling, for obvious reasons. Teamwork, Recruits, teamwork – that is the secret of staying alive in a battle. You must learn to move in harmony with one another and to fight effectively as a unit, not just as a bunch of skilled duellers who happen to be in the same place at the same time and fighting on the same side. Anyone can get together a bunch of mercenaries to do that, but you – you will learn to be sword brothers and sisters. You will learn each other's strengths and weaknesses, and how to use them to best advantage. You will become strong and fit together. You will march together, eat together, sleep together and break wind together! You will learn respect for one another – respect and trust. For if you do not learn these things, then you will almost certainly die in your first serious conflict. Am I making myself clear?'

'Yes, Corporal.'

'Good. Now then, let's see what you budding soldiers know already, shall we? Who amongst you fancies swinging one of these blades at me in a friendly challenge?'

Five Recruits raised their hands. Looking around, Calvyn was not exactly astonished to see that the arrogant Tyrrak had his hand high in the air. However, to Calvyn's surprise, Bek too had raised his hand.

The four young men and one woman were ushered forward and told to form a queue to one side of the semi-circle. Derra explained that each fight was only to be fought to the first blood or to a call of 'yield' by the defeated party. The rest of the Recruits shuffled around to close the gaps in their line, and waited with tangible anticipation to see how their fellow Recruits would fare against the veteran Corporal.

First in line was the female Recruit.

'Tondi, isn't it?' asked Derra.

The tall blonde nodded and stepped forward.

'Well, Tondi, pick your weapon and defend yourself,' Derra challenged, holding out the two swords for her opponent to choose from.

Tondi carefully weighed each weapon in her right hand, and having given each blade a trial swing she made her decision, passed the rejected sword hilt first back to Derra, stepped back and adopted a balanced stance with her chosen sword held ready.

'Begin,' ordered Derra.

The Recruit cautiously edged forward and launched her first attack, probing Derra's defence for a weakness. The clanging of metal against metal rang out across the square and the sound fired the blood of the seated members of Squad Two who watched with barely concealed excitement.

'Don't hold back on your strokes,' growled Derra as she matched Tondi's swings with ease. 'And grip the hilt a little tighter. You wouldn't want to lose your weapon... like this.'

With an incredible turn of speed, Derra twisted her opponent's blade with her own and flicked it from Tondi's grasp. The blade tumbled through the air to land some yards away, and the unfortunate Tondi found Derra's sword point under her chin.

'I yield,' Tondi gasped, her face mirroring her astonishment at how easily she had found herself disarmed.

'Take a seat,' Derra replied, and gestured to the next of her challengers to step forward.

Tyrrak strolled out and picked up the sword from the sand. Wiping the blade free of dirt with his sleeve, and flicking at the hilt with his hand to remove any unwanted particles of grit, he then twirled the sword experimentally as he casually walked back towards Derra. On reaching a suitable starting distance from his opponent, Tyrrak adopted a classic dueller's stance. A slight smile flickered across Derra's face as she watched the arrogant swagger and the defiant pose.

'This should be good,' whispered the Recruit next to Calvyn. 'Tyrrak was the best swordsman in his home town.'

'According to Tyrrak, no doubt,' murmured back Calvyn. 'I'd wager on Derra over him any day.'

The first clash of blades brought all attention back to the two protagonists. This encounter was more furious than the last. Quick, flicking, slashing blows were exchanged in a flurry of stroke and counterstroke as the two combatants engaged in a swirling exchange that lasted a full twenty heartbeats. Leaping back from the encounter, Derra circled the posturing Recruit, beautifully balanced like a prowling panther.

'Not bad, Tyrrak, but you should be careful not to over-extend yourself. You leave your sword arm open to attack.'

Lunging back into the attack, Derra casually exchanged a few strokes that finished with a lightning-like flick that sliced through Tyrrak's sleeve and caused an immediate red stain of blood to appear through the green material. Derra stepped back and held up her sword in brief salute.

'Take a seat, Tyrrak. It's only a scratch, but it could just as easily have been a maiming blow.'

Looking down at the cut, nonplussed, Tyrrak's head dropped slightly as he turned and rejoined his fellow Squad Two members. Still unsure of how Derra had cut him so easily, he handed the sword on to the next challenger.

'Be careful, she's bloody quick,' he muttered as he passed the blade over.

The advice proved irrelevant to the next two Recruits who were also beaten in short order. Derra had not even broken a sweat as she faced Bek, who had retrieved the sword from where the previous Recruit had stuck it, point down in the ground in disgust at his ignominious defeat.

'Well, if it isn't Mr Unco-ordinated himself,' Derra smiled, gesturing for him to make his attack. 'Let's see what you can do with a blade, shall we?'

Bek moved forwards with the blade held awkwardly in front of him. It was a ludicrous sight, and Calvyn could hardly bear to watch as his new friend appeared to bumble forwards to begin his attack. However, Corporal Derra remained no less poised than she had for her previous opponents, and treated him with no less respect. Bek swung. Derra parried easily and gave a counterstroke that he barely deflected. Again Bek swung, and again Derra countered and tested his reflexes with several stinging response strokes. Somehow, Bek managed to just catch Derra's counter-attacks and narrowly avoid getting cut.

Derra stepped back and her eyes narrowed slightly.

'This is it, she'll take him now,' whispered the Recruit next to Calvyn.

To everyone's surprise, however, as Derra leapt in for the winning touch Bek shifted his grip on the hilt and met her driving attack with relative ease. Switching stance in an instant, he replied with dazzling speed and the two blades met in such a rapid sequence of impacts that Calvyn could not even follow the play of the strokes.

'Go on, Bek,' Calvyn called, the words out of his mouth before he could censor them.

The words acted like a sluice gate, and within seconds the entire squad was cheering him on. A general awareness around the castle focused all eyes on the duelling couple in the centre of the training ground. Guards on the watchtowers turned their attention from outside to in as the blindingly fast exchanges rang their steely echoes through the air.

'Come on, Bek, you can do it.'

Both combatants stepped back and began circling each other. Each of them had broken into a sweat, the beads standing out on their foreheads. Bek was breathing quite hard but seemed focused and balanced as he stalked his Corporal. Derra, on the other hand, was breathing normally and appeared unperturbed by her opponent's unexpected skill. The Corporal's harsh stare bored into Bek with an intensity that was frightening to watch. In turn, Bek watched Derra carefully for any sign of weakness or imbalance.

The members of Squad Two continued to cheer Bek on, willing him to get the winning cut in. Shouts for Derra started echoing down from about the walls too, the fight drawing more and more attention.

Bek darted in with a driving lunge – blocked – riposte – parried. Again the rapid exchange left no winner and the shouts of encouragement for both parties raised another level of decibels. Sergeant Brett emerged from his office to investigate the source of the disturbance, and faces could even be seen appearing at the narrow windows of the Baron's keep.

Another whistling series of blows and yet another. The sword blades sang again and again, still with no clear result. However, it was becoming obvious that Bek was tiring whilst Derra was still looking as strong and as agile as ever. The Corporal pressed home her attack with a vicious series of blows which Bek barely managed to stave off. He found himself backing up under the rain of strokes that Derra was dealing, and in desperation tried to turn the tables with a rapid counter offensive.

The mistake was a small one, but Derra was waiting for it. Just over-extending slightly, Bek found his blade deflected downwards whilst Derra's swept up and nicked his upper arm. It happened so fast that many of the Recruits had not even seen the finish, but Bek felt the sting and knew it was all over. He stepped back immediately and, raising the sword first in salute, he then reversed the blade and offered the hilt to the Corporal.

Derra returned the salute, and a ragged cheer sounded from various points around the castle walls. Taking the sword from him, the Corporal gave him a half smile.

'Not bad for a Recruit,' she said casually. 'Once we've got you fit, you'l make an interesting match. You almost had me fooled with that little play-act at the start too.'

'What gave me away?'

'Experience on my part. I got caught out by the same trick a few years ago, and your parries just became lucky enough to arouse my suspicions.'

Nodding in acknowledgement, Bek turned and walked back over to sit down next to Calvyn. The Corporal, still showing little sign of her recent exertion other than a fine sheen of sweat, resumed her place in front of the semi-circle of Recruits and once again regarded them all with her forbidding gaze.

Around the walls, the onlookers melted away, returning to their duties as if nothing unusual had just happened. Sergeant Brett too returned to his office, all interest in the class apparently gone.

'Well, boys and girls, some interesting points came from that little exercise. The most important perhaps is never to judge your opponent by their appearance. Treat anyone who holds a weapon with the same respect. Any one of them might just kill you if you don't.'

Calvyn glanced around at the other Recruits. All were listening with rapt attention. Derra had certainly won the respect of her students this afternoon,he mused.

'This afternoon's challenge proved that you all have something to learn here,' the Corporal continued. 'In order to fight effectively you must be fit. If young Bek here had been a little stronger or faster he might just have marked me, and he would not be the first to do so.'

Rolling up her sleeves, the Corporal revealed several nasty looking scars on her wrists and upper arms.

'In a moment I would like those of you that are bleeding to report to the medics to have those cuts dressed. However, take heed, you'll have to become a damn sight better warrior than I am if you're going to stay in the army for any length of time without gaining a collection of marks like these. As I don't want you to receive too many scars like mine unnecessarily, you will be using blunt wooden swords called torps until you have mastered the basic sword drills. Furthermore, you will wear padded jerkins and leather skullcaps. Those of you who prove to be proficient will help me to improve the standard of the others. There will be regular competitions to add a bit of friendly rivalry, both amongst you and between the squads. I expect you to win every inter-squad competition, because you are my squad, and my squad is always the best. Understand?'

'Yes, Corporal.'

'Excellent. For now, Bek will be known as First Sword in Squad Two. Any of you who wish to take that title from him will have to beat him in one of our weekly competitions.'

'Fat chance of that!' someone muttered.

'Maybe for a while,' Derra said, her sharp ears picking up the comment and her voice taking on a harsher tone again, 'but if someone here wants it badly enough then they will learn the skills required to beat him. Now... those of you with cuts that require attention report to the medics and return here when they've finished with you. The rest of you – follow me.'

Derra led the remainder of Squad Two over to a metal shuttered window in the side wall of the armoury. A tap on the shutter with the pommel of a sword brought an instant response, and the clanking of internal bolts being drawn was followed by the squeak of the shutters being opened outwards.

The two swords were handed in through the hatchway and solid looking lumps of wood were passed out to each of the Recruits. Calvyn hefted his wooden training sword and was surprised by its weight. The handle of the torp was bound with a strip of leather that offered a bit more purchase to the grip, but there was no hilt to save the fingers from a sliding blow. The weapon felt more like a club than a sword. 'You could really brain a guy with one of these,' Calvyn reflected with a grimace.

'Great Tarmin's Teeth!' swore Jenna as she joined Calvyn. 'How the devil are you supposed to fence with these blundering logs?'

'I was just thinking something similar,' Calvyn replied with a grin. 'However, I'm sure that we'll find out soon enough.'

Handing out four extra torps to be put to one side for Bek, Tyrrak and the others, Derra led Squad Two back out onto the weapons training area to begin their tuition.

'All right, Squad Two, form a line spread approximately two paces apart. Go! Come on! Move it! We haven't got all day.'

The Recruits spread out as directed.

'Listen in. I'm going to teach you basic sword drill by numbers, so if you value your delicate little hides then I suggest you pay close attention. This... is position number one.'

Demonstrating the position, Derra held it for a few seconds.

'Squad Two, adopt position one.'

The Recruits all did their best to adopt the appropriate stance and hold it whilst Derra walked along the line, adjusting each person's position until it was perfect. This process took some time, and when Derra finally got to Calvyn his arm was trembling uncontrollably with the effort of maintaining an approximation of the desired stance. The Corporal's eyes held his as he continued to grit his teeth and hold the torp in place.

'A little higher... there. Bend your arm a little more at the elbow. Good, that's it.'

Derra moved on to the last few Recruits. Having finished, she moved back out to the front centre of the line and took another general look down the line.'

'And... relax,' ordered Derra.

Several sighs of relief sounded out along the line.

'As you can see, the torp has been designed to strengthen the sword arm. By the time you've had a few weeks worth of training sessions you'll hardly notice the weight, and when you move onto a real sword you'll develop speed of movement more quickly.'

'Assuming that our arms don't drop off first,' muttered Jenna who stood to Calvyn's left.

Calvyn smiled slightly at that but made no comment of his own. Instead, he flexed and relaxed the muscles of his right arm in an attempt to stop them twitching uncontrollably.

'Ah, Tyrrak, good of you to join us. Here – have a torp,' Derra said, picking up a spare and tossing it over to him.

'Now this... is position two.'

CHAPTER 8

Dawn broke across the desert plains. Demarr walked through the lines of tents, seemingly oblivious to the bodies strewn throughout the encampment. A small group of Adrel warriors led by Ramiff came running up to him, each of them displaying evidence of their recent battle.

'It is done, Chosen One. All but the Maharl and a handful of the Manticlaar warriors are dead. The prisoners are being held next to the well.'

'Excellent, Ramiff. You and the rest of the warriors have done exceedingly well,' Demarr replied, his eyes alight like sapphires, gleaming in the morning sun. 'What were our losses?'

'Minimal, Chosen One. Only thirty-six dead and seventy or so wounded. Most of the injured will be able to fight again within the week.'

Demarr nodded, fingering his silver talisman absently as he considered the figures. They were better than he had counted on, but still not without consequence. Thirty-six dead, and more than double that number wounded, totalling nearly a tenth of his force – that was not a statistic that filled him with joy. However, the battle had not only been won, but the enemy had been utterly destroyed. Every man, woman and child, with the exception of the necessary prisoners, had been put to the sword. That would make the major clans sit up and take note. It had to.

'Take your men and get some rest, Ramiff. You will

need it before this day is out, I think. Just confirm that the guards are in place and the patrols are set up – I wouldn't want one of the other clans to upset our victory today with a sneak attack of their own.'

'The guards are in place, Chosen One, and I briefed the patrols myself. Everything has been done as you ordered.'

'Go then. Get your rest.'

Ramiff and the other warriors bowed low and backtracked away from the First Maharl.

A wave of exultation swept through Demarr. This was what leadership was all about. Battle and victory. Men willing to die for you. Crushing your enemies to dust. The power to say who lived and who died. However, even as his inner rejoicing reached its climax, other thoughts and feelings intruded.

'It's not enough! This is but the beginning. Revenge *will* be mine. I will *not* be denied my rightful place,' Demarr whispered to himself. 'If I have to wash the desert in blood then so be it, but I *will* have my army. Thrandor *will* fall. I *will* be king.'

His right hand clenched the silver talisman tightly in an instinctive reaction to his determination to conquer, and the sharp edges cut into the palm of his hand. Strength seemed to flow from the medallion through his arm and tingle through his body, filling him with a sense of vitality that he had never felt before. He relaxed his grip and opened his hand to view the wondrous object with renewed awe. Demarr watched in fascination as a droplet of blood trickled across his palm and dripped to the floor. The silver medallion never seemed to lose its beauty. Even smeared with his own blood as it was, it appeared faultless to the enraptured Demarr – the most fantastically crafted piece of jewellery ever created.

'I wonder what you mean,' he thought, wiping the medallion clean on his thobe and tracing the intricate inscriptions with his finger as he had many times before. 'Whatever it is, I thank your maker for the power that you give me.'

Demarr smiled as he reviewed how the power of the talisman had manifested itself once more during the battle. The guards along the northern sector of the Manticlaar camp had been silently dispatched and the Adrel soldiers had crept forward into position. Demarr had moved forward noiselessly to the very edge of the tented area. The plan was simple. The campsite was reasonably well lit with burning torches at regular intervals. As soon as the nearest groups saw the First Maharl and his group of warriors enter the first tents, they were to move in and begin a cascade along the whole of the northern side of the camp. Once the attack had begun, the object was to slaughter as many Manticlaar as possible before the alarm was raised and an organised defence could be co-ordinated.

As Demarr had plunged his sword through the first of his enemies a shock of pleasure had surged through him, almost sexual in its intensity. Each subsequent killing had brought with it a similar wave of joy, and the silver talisman had glowed progressively brighter with every death. By the time he had killed half a dozen, the Chosen One was surrounded by an eerie silver glow of power and all but the bravest Manticlaar warriors had fled before him.

The Manticlaar had actually rallied quite quickly under the circumstances. However, just as they had begun to start an organised counter attack, Adrel warriors had started to torch row after row of tents, many still housing women and children. Screams of terror and shouts of dismay bred confusion, and disarray waxed once more amongst the Manticlaar as many men ran to the aid of their families, only to be cut down in short order.

At this point, the main bulk of the Adrel, led by Ramiff who had been waiting silently to the south of the camp, charged into the fray and the battle turned into a massacre. The Manticlaar, despite beginning the evening with marginally superior numbers, stood no chance.

Demarr had waded through the opposition in a state verging on ecstasy, his aura of power projecting fear into the hearts of the enemy. His sword glinted as it danced its deadly path, wielded with indisputable skill but also appearing to have a life of its own as the silvery glow extended along its length. He had been an unstoppable force. Even his own men fighting alongside him did so with awe-struck faces, and where possible maintained a discreet distance.

'Chosen One.'

It was Ramiff, who had reappeared as if from nowhere.

'I thought I told you to go get some rest,' Demarr stated coldly, not pleased at being disobeyed.

'I was on my way to bed when the first patrol came back in, Chosen One.'

'Came back in? They were due to be out until midday, were they not?'

'That is true, Master, but they have captured two scouts. One is Nemda, the other is Dagali. The patrol leader decided to bring them in before resuming his sweep.'

'Nemda *and* Dagali! Good... indeed, that is excellent news Ramiff, and I thank you for alerting me so swiftly. Where are they being held?'

'At the well, Master, with the Manticlaar prisoners.'

'Better and better. Go now, Ramiff, and get your rest,' Demarr ordered, not unkindly.

Ramiff bowed once more and walked off in the general direction of the centre of the encampment. Demarr watched him go and contemplated his next move. The Nemda Clan was fairly small, probably five or six hundred strong at best. However, the Dagali was a major tribe. If he could convince them that he was the Chosen One, then he would have significant leverage against the other major tribes. With a little cunning and a few demonstrations of power, he could have them all in the palm of his hand within a few months. This was the opportunity that he had been waiting for, and he would not waste it.

Striding through the remains of the Manticlaar encampment, Demarr made his way to the well. An open area with a large firepit marked the vital water source. The embers of the fire were still glowing as he marched past it and up to where the prisoners were being held.

The guards snapped to attention as Demarr approached.

'As you were,' Demarr ordered. 'Is the water supply still pure?'

'Yes, Chosen One. We gave them no chance to poison it.'

'Good. Draw me a draft, would you?'

'Yes, Chosen One.'

The guard turned and lowered the small bucket down on its chain until it splashed into the water below. Demarr waited patiently, quietly regarding his prisoners who sat tied up nearby. The guard picked up a clean beaker, filled it from the bucket and offered it up to Demarr, who accepted it with a nod.

The Nemda and Dagali scouts were easy enough to distinguish from the Manticlaar as their gutras were braided with the colours of their respective clans. Demarr walked over to them and locked eyes with each in turn.

'So, what say you, Nemda? Do you acknowledge me as the Chosen One?'

'On what basis, Maharl? A victory in what history, even the history of the clans, will see as a minor skirmish?'

Demarr thought about that for a moment. The Nemda had a valid point. History may well record the events of the last few hours as a minor skirmish, he decided, but at this moment in time it would be widely regarded as a major battle and a shift in power. No, the scout was merely following directives from his superiors. The trick would be to switch the scout's allegiance so completely that he could be used as an effective tool to change his clan's thinking.

'I suppose that you are of a similar mind, Dagali?' Demarr asked with a slight smile.

'Well, you have won an impressive victory here,

Maharl, but that hardly qualifies you to be the Chosen One,' the Dagali scout tempered, all too aware of his precarious situation, 'although I remain open-minded on the issue, although if I find sufficient proof to support your claim then I would gladly be the first of the Dagali to welcome the Chosen One.'

'Proof! Ha! You sit there, my prisoner, and you have the audacity to demand proof before bending your knee to me!' exclaimed Demarr with a laugh that cut the air like a knife. 'By Tarmin, man, I admire your spirit, but your gall will get you into more trouble than you can handle one of these days.'

Demarr turned to the guard and beckoned to him.

'Untie these two men. They would have proof that I am the Chosen One, and I intend to give it to them.'

'At once, Chosen One,' the guard replied quickly.

The Dagali scout continued to look more amused than impressed by the Adrel Warriors' automatic use of that revered title, and the Nemda scout merely looked suspicious and wary at having been released. Demarr ignored their faces, as he now knew what he had to do and his heart leapt in anticipation.

The remaining captives had been watching the exchange with scarcely concealed interest, and now Demarr addressed them.

'You must know by now that you six are all that remain of the Manticlaar. All of your warriors, your women and even your children are dead.'

The seated prisoners nodded, the realisation of their situation causing their shoulders to slump in resignation and defeat.

'You. Maharl of the Manticlaar Clan,' directed Demarr, pointing at the leader of the vanquished clan. 'What did my last message to you say?'

'That you were the Chosen One foretold by the prophets of old, come to unite the clans in order to fight a holy war, and that if we did not join you then your army would annihilate us from the land.'

'And what was your reply?'

126

'We chose to ignore your claim, and have paid the price for our foolishness.'

'No!' snapped Demarr. 'You have not yet paid the full price. I said that I would exterminate the Manticlaar and I have no intentions of breaking that vow. You are going to be executed, and nothing that you say in the next few minutes will alter that fate. Therefore, you have nothing to gain from lying, or indeed from telling the truth. Nothing, that is, except possibly saving two other clans from making the same mistake that you did. I leave it up to you what you decide to tell these representatives of the Nemda and the Dagali.'

Demarr turned and stepped a few paces away. He gestured to the two scouts to feel free to question the Manticlaar, and seated himself cross-legged on the ground to sip at his beaker of water as he watched the Dagali open the questioning.

'Do you now accept this outsider to be the Chosen One?' the Dagali asked the Manticlaar Maharl.

'I have no doubt that he is who he claims to be. You would be wise to listen to him,' the defeated leader answered.

'What about you others? Do you agree with him?'

The Manticlaar men all nodded, and one spoke up.

'He has the powers foretold of old. I saw him glowing with holy power as he slew many of my clan brothers. We were fools to mock him.'

'Glowing? Is that all? It could have been a trick of the light.'

'No,' disagreed the Maharl of the Manticlaar, 'it was no trick of the light. This man truly possesses the Holy Power. I have no doubt that he will unite the clans.'

'You have no doubts! Well, that is hardly surprising under the circumstances. You underestimated an enemy so badly that you got your clan exterminated, and only then you say that you have no doubts. Forgive me if your assurances don't fill me with confidence,' spat the Nemda scout, obviously unconvinced by the profession of faith.

'I agree with you. I made a terrible misjudgement, but

my mistake was not to underestimate the strength of the Adrel, it was to doubt the power of their leader. Whatever you do, and it does not really concern me what you decide, consider this... if this man is not the Chosen One then the Dagali Clan should be able to crush the Adrel in open battle. However, the Nemda are not in a position of such strength and would at the very least suffer huge losses if the Adrel were to confront them. You, Nemda, are in no position to be confident.'

'Nemda warriors do not bend under mere threats by any passing pretender,' sneered the Nemda scout with an arrogant wave of his hand.

'Neither did the Manticlaar... but that is of the past now. Hear me out. If this man *is* the Chosen One and you choose as I did, to ignore his claim, do you honestly believe that the outcome of any conflict that you undertake with him will end any differently for you than it did for us here? Dagali – you may think yourself in a strong position. Your tribe is many times that of the Adrel in number, but ask yourself this – if this man truly is the Chosen One, will your superior numbers mean anything when he rides against you? We were strong, and not totally unprepared. Take a good look around you, and be thankful that you have been given a chance to avoid suffering the same fate.'

The two scouts were obviously still sceptical, but the Dagali looked thoughtful. Now was the perfect moment that Demarr had been waiting for and he seized it.

'Enough,' he interrupted. 'This is going nowhere. You two, stand back. The rest of you, stand.'

The two scouts stepped away from the Manticlaar prisoners as Demarr walked forward and stood a few paces in front of them. He stood for a few seconds, probing them with his piercing gaze, his fingers clasping the talisman tightly in his hand.

'Your new found faith in me is touching, but it will not avert your fate. I have sworn to destroy the Manticlaar and you are all that remain. Now receive your reward for defying me.'

Demarr suddenly flung his arms wide as if he were about to run forward and embrace them. From the amulet six simultaneous bolts of lightning-like flame burst forth and struck each of the Manticlaar warriors squarely in the middle of the chest. As one, the Manticlaar were hurled from their feet by the force of the blast and were all dead before they hit the ground.

The jaws of the Nemda and Dagali scouts hung slack as they looked at Demarr with new eyes. The Chosen One turned to face them and they both dropped hastily to one knee, heads bowed in respect. Fear ripped through them with every small move or gesture that Demarr's hands made, and the glowing medallion kept drawing their eyes upward in an almost hypnotic fashion.

'I take it that no further explanations or demonstrations will be necessary, gentlemen?' Demarr asked, his barely contained anger visible in his eyes.

'No... Chosen One,' the Dagali scout answered.

The Nemda scout could only shake his head, still in a state of shock.

'Good. Then go back to your people and give them my message. Join me or die. Do you think you can remember that? Or shall I write it down for you?'

'They will join you, Chosen One. I guarantee it with my life,' the Dagali scout promised.

'Yes, you do. See that you do not fail me,' Demarr growled. 'Give them horses and see that they are escorted out of the camp,' he ordered the guards, and then whirled and strode away into the lines of tents.

*   *   *   *   *

'Ouch! My goodness, that's painful now, but it's going to be agony by tomorrow,' exclaimed Jenna, looking down at the blister on her heel.

Calvyn looked across from where he had flumped down on his bed. Jenna sat at the end of her bunk with her right ankle across her left knee, gently prodding at her heel with an investigative finger. A wince of pain flashed across her face as she uncrossed her legs and placed her foot gingerly back down on the floor. Then, removing her other boot, she repeated the meticulous examination on her left foot.

There were groans and sharp intakes of breath sounding right down the barrack room as other Recruits nursed sore muscles and various blisters. Calvyn too ached in more places than he would have ever thought possible. Also, having taken the weight off his feet he could feel them throbbing inside his boots. Sharp points of pain, both on his heels and on his insteps, indicated to him that he hadn't escaped without blisters either.

'I'm going to be a virtual invalid tomorrow,' groaned Jenna with another wince as she stood up.

'We all are,' someone agreed from further down the room.

'Derra's going to waltz all over us in the morning,' Tyrrak grunted. 'She's going to be unbearable when we turn up on parade looking like a bunch of cripples.'

'Not if I can help it,' thought Calvyn to himself. An idea had come to mind. Some of Perdimonn's healing potions were stored with his other belongings in the Quartermaster's store. Unfortunately, the store would have long since been locked up for the night. Somehow he would have to find a way of getting hold of the appropriate ointment. He could picture the pot of ointment that Perdimonn had prepared for just such ailments. It had a local anaesthetic effect and prompted rapid skin regeneration. Perfect. But how to get it? There was no way that the Quartermaster would open up his store for a mere Recruit, and the guards on duty would not have access to a key.

What he needed was an alternative. Whilst he could probably have just healed everybody directly by use of magic, Perdimonn's words of caution in revealing his abilities kept springing back to mind. Direct healing would probably prove more trouble than it was worth. Perhaps the grimoire would release him the spell for making the ointment, he thought. After all, he had progressed further with his mental exercises today than ever before. Even if it would not release the spell to make the ointment, the grimoire might provide the answer that he needed. It was worth a try.

Calvyn waited until he was fairly sure that nobody was looking in his direction and began a cat-like stretch that disguised his hand reaching under the mattress for the magical book. Having found it with his hand, he rolled over and tucked the book inside his tunic in one slick motion.

With no one the wiser, Calvyn stood and walked the length of the barrack room to the door. Nobody said anything as he left, everyone either too preoccupied to wonder where he was going or assuming that he was simply going to the ablutions.

Calvyn closed the door quietly behind him, to prevent arousing unwanted attention from the guards patrolling the walls. The interior of the castle was annoyingly well lit with torches burning at regular intervals around the perimeter of the drill square. Some had been bracketed onto the walls whilst others burned in free standing purpose built torch stands, giving off enough flickering light to preclude any thoughts that Calvyn might have had of sneaking, unseen, across to the Quartermaster's store. Instead, he made his way along the outside of the barrack room towards the ablution block.

'What I need is a quiet spot out of sight, but with enough light to be able to read by,' thought Calvyn to himself as he approached the toilet block in the southwest corner of the castle.

Carefully scanning the walls to see if anyone was watching him, Calvyn continued past the ablutions to the very corner of the Castle. The steps up to the south west guard tower climbed to his right and the mess hall doors stood closed to his left. The low wall of the circular castle well stood in front of him, a torch bracketed onto the wall beside it.

'Come on Calvyn, wherever you're going, make it quick!' he thought, frantically looking around for a place

131

to hide. There was nowhere. However, if he sat in the corner between the mess hall and the outer wall it was unlikely that anyone would notice him unless they came to draw water from the well. Calvyn decided that it would have to do, and walked quickly around the well to the secluded corner.

Once seated, Calvyn looked around. He felt very exposed and vulnerable, but there seemed to be little option. It would have to be here and now, or not at all. He reached into his tunic and pulled out the grimoire. One last furtive glance around revealed no imminent danger of being caught, so Calvyn opened the cover and began to read.

As he scanned the pages, Calvyn discovered several new spells for healing various ailments, but nothing to make the ointment that he needed. Disappointed, Calvyn closed the book and sat in silence, staring into space as his mind reviewed the situation.

He could not make the ointment that he needed and there was no way to get to the pot in the Quartermaster's store. What was left? A spell of 'finding' would be of no use because the nearest ointment would undoubtedly be his own. However, what would happen if he changed the emphasis of the runes to make the thrust of the magic work towards 'bringing' rather than 'finding'? Calvyn had no idea what would happen if he adjusted the runes in that way, but suddenly the words of Perdimonn seemed to ring in his ears.

'... you have only just begun to touch the edges of what is possible with magic... in time you will undoubtedly develop spells of your own that I could never dream of. This is because your mind works differently from mine, and will integrate elements of spells in combinations and concepts unique to your own way of thinking... This is my grimoire... eventually you will write your own, and I would encourage you to begin sooner rather than later.'

Buoyed by the thought of Perdimonn's reassurance, Calvyn started drawing out the runes on the dusty floor with his finger, adjusting and readjusting the strange symbols until he was happy that the spell reflected his desired intention. Calvyn then committed the spell to memory until finally, when he was completely happy that he could picture the runes in a smooth, uninterrupted sequence, he was ready to begin.

Holding his hand out in front of him towards the well, Calvyn noted all the details – the flickering light of the torch, the pointed stonework of the low wall surrounding the well, the ablutions and barrack blocks, and the castellated wall that was silhouetted against the night sky. Several minutes later, having assured himself that he had got every last detail firmly fixed in his mind, Calvyn closed his eyes and began the spell.

The combination of the runes was quite tricky to enunciate, but the syllables seemed to flow effortlessly from his mouth in a string of sound that was barely louder than a whisper. Calvyn pictured each rune floating onto his hand and locking together into an intricate structure that gradually evolved into the pot of ointment. Somehow the spell had a feeling of 'rightness' about it that he had not felt when casting the spells that he had been taught by Perdimonn. However, the young apprentice did not allow his concentration to be affected by thoughts or feelings of any kind.

As Calvyn pronounced the last syllable of his mental image, the conglomeration of runes coalesced into a picture of the desired pot of medicinal cream. At the same time as his mental picture solidified there was an audible pop, like the sound of a cork being pulled from a bottle of wine, and Calvyn felt the weight of something in his hand.

For a second Calvyn hardly dared to open his eyes. Then his vulnerable situation drew him back to reality and he gazed, his heart pounding with excitement, at the sight of Perdimonn's pot of ointment in his still outstretched hand. Grasping the pot with his fingers, Calvyn clutched it to his chest, slightly frightened that it might fly away or disappear.

Satisfied that the pot was real, Calvyn quickly scrambled to his feet and tucked both the pot and the grimoire into the front of his tunic. Trying hard to look casual, Calvyn sauntered past the well and along the edge of the parade square towards the barrack room door. He was almost there when a voice boomed across the drill square.

'Hey, you! Recruit!'

Calvyn stopped dead, his heart pounding once more.

'Yes, you. What do you think you're doing?'

'I've just been to visit the toilets,' he answered, looking across the drill square to the figure standing outside the Corporals' accommodation block.

'That's no excuse for shambling about the place like a slob. March, damn you! You're in the army now.'

Relieved that his only perceived crime was his effort to make himself inconspicuous, Calvyn snapped to attention and smartly marched to the barrack room door. Once inside, with the door securely closed behind him, Calvyn heaved a sigh of relief.

'And where have you been skiving off to whilst we've all been slaving to get this place ready for tomorrow's inspection?' Tyrrak demanded, an edge of venom in his voice.

'Risking my neck to get something to soothe *your* blisters,' retorted Calvyn, his hackles immediately up at Tyrrak's accusing tone. 'Of course if you're not interested...'

Calvyn pulled the pot from inside his tunic, waved it under Tyrrak's nose and then walked off down the room to his bed.

'I'm sorry, Calvyn. It's just that I thought...'

'You thought that I'd sloped off to avoid having to bull the room for Derra's inspection tomorrow. Well I didn't, OK? I'll more than happily do my fair share, Tyrrak, but first I'm going to provide any of you who wants it with a healing salve for your blisters. Do you have you got any problems with that?'

'No, I...'

'Good. Then if you want some of this, I suggest that you keep watch at the door whilst I see to some of the others. I would hate to have gone to all this trouble only to get the stuff confiscated.'

Crestfallen, Tyrrak did as Calvyn asked and kept watch for any sign of unwanted visitors. Calvyn worked his way down the room, applying sparing amounts of the salve to everyone's blisters. Although he could just as easily have passed the ointment around, he decided that many of the others were unlikely to appreciate the value or potency of the medicine, and it would probably prove less wasteful if he did it himself.

Once he had seen to everyone else, Calvyn got someone to replace Tyrrak as the lookout and tended to his feet as well. That done, Calvyn sat on his bed and began to remove his own boots. Stepping across from where she had been busily buffing the floor by her bed with a soft cloth, Jenna approached Calvyn with a smile.

'Here, let me help you with those. If your muscles ache as much as mine do, then you could probably do with a hand.'

'Thanks,' replied Calvyn with a grateful nod. 'How's it going?'

'What? The cleaning?'

Calvyn nodded as Jenna pulled off the first boot.

'Oh, OK I suppose. It's difficult to know what's acceptable around here yet. I've no doubt that Derra will leave us with very few illusions for long though.'

'You can say that again,' chuckled Calvyn as the second boot came off too.

'This stuff is amazingly good. I don't think that I've ever come across anything quite like it before,' Jenna said, sniffing at the ointment before dipping a fingertip in and smearing it onto Calvyn's left heel. 'So where did you get it from?'

'Ask me no questions and I'll tell you no lies,' replied Calvyn with a wink.

'As you wish. I'm just astounded at how quickly the anaesthetic properties take effect and more than a little intrigued to see whether it heals as well as it numbs.'

'Oh, I think that you'll find that it heals pretty quickly.'

'I wonder what the active ingredients are. My mother taught me a little herb-lore when I was a young girl. This has virtually no scent and no lumps or visibly identifiable herbs. It really is most unusual.'

'Don't worry about it, Jenna. Let's just be thankful that it works and worry about the more pressing problem of where to hide it now that we've got it.'

'The room inspection!'

'Exactly.'

'Yes, I see your point,' affirmed Jenna thoughtfully as she looked around the spartan barrack room for a less than obvious hiding place. 'Derra will probably go through this place like a deranged boar. What's more, she almost certainly knows where all the possible contraband hidey-holes are. What will you do?'

'The only thing that works in our favour this time is that Derra may think that we haven't been here long enough to gather anything worth her while searching for. Providing that we secure the pot out of immediate sight it should be fine for this time around,' answered Calvyn, vaguely aware that a general interest was being taken in the conversation.'

'There's a loose stone in the wall down here behind my bed,' offered one of the Recruits who slept a couple of beds down from Calvyn. 'If we can hollow out a bit of space behind it, we should be able to fit the pot inside the wall.'

'That would be ideal,' agreed Calvyn. 'Can I have a look... sorry I don't remember your name?'

'It's Matim, and sure you can,' Matim replied, gesturing for Calvyn to lend him a hand with the bed.

Calvyn and Jenna helped their fellow Recruit to pull his bed away from the wall, but having done so, Calvyn could not see any sign of a loose stone.

'Here,' Matim said with a grin, and reaching down he wobbled a large stone from side to side. 'Doesn't look loose at all, does it?'

'How on earth did you find that?' asked Jenna in amazement.

'Pure luck. I was told by one of the Privates when I first arrived that one of the places the Corporals look for dust on their room inspections is on this ridge behind the bed head,' explained Matim, pointing at the thin ledge of wood that was a part of the bed frame. 'So anyway, when I was allocated my bed I pulled it out to take a look at what he had meant. As I crouched down, I put my hand against the wall for balance and felt the stone that I was leaning on move slightly.'

'Well, it looks like chance has served us well. Let's have a go at getting it out of the wall, shall we?' suggested Calvyn.

'No problem, but I think that we'd better keep a lookout posted, just in case.'

'Good point.'

'I'll do it,' offered Jenna, and trotted down to keep watch through the partially shuttered window by the door.

As soon as Jenna gave a thumbs up signal for the boys to begin, they started rocking the stone back and forth to try and work it free from the wall. Gradually they succeeded in easing the rock out from its resting place, and having removed it, crouched down to peer into the hole.

'Brilliant! The inner layer of the wall is just loose rubble!' exclaimed Calvyn, jubilant at their success.

'That's good, but what can we do with the stones that we take out? We can hardly lose them on the drill square. It's immaculate out there. We're going to end up with the same problem that we had with the pot – finding a place to hide them,' pointed out Matim.

'No problem. We just throw them over the wall.'

'What if a guard hears them land, or catches us throwing them over?'

'Hmm. You're right,' conceded Calvyn. 'That would prove a little embarrassing! Never mind, let's just create a space, hide the pot, and worry about disposing of the rubble afterwards, shall we?'

Matim inclined his head in a gesture of agreement to Calvyn's suggestion, and started pulling the loose bits of rock out onto the floor. The requisite space was created in no more than a minute. Once Calvyn was satisfied that the pot would fit into the cavity, he placed the container of salve into the hideaway and began working the original loose rock back into place.

'Any ideas?' Matim asked, pointing at the small pile of rubble.

'Might I suggest a solution?' offered Bek from further down the room. 'Why don't you put them down the well?'

'We could, but we'd probably stand as much chance of being caught dropping stones down the well as we would throwing them over the wall. The sound is pretty distinctive,' replied Matim.

'Ah, yes, but I wasn't suggesting that you just drop them down the well. The bucket has a tilt rope attached to its base. If you simply place the stones quietly into the bucket and lower it gently until it reaches the water, you can then tilt the bucket and release the stones without creating any more noise than would be normal.'

'Excellent idea!' exclaimed Calvyn. 'Bek, you're a genius.'

Bek flushed slightly at the praise and returned to polishing the floor beside his bed. Calvyn quickly gathered the half a dozen or so stones and looked around at the nearer Recruits.

'Any volunteers to go get some drinking water for the barrack room?'

'I'll go,' offered Tyrrak, keen for a chance to redeem himself for his earlier outburst.

'Very well,' replied Calvyn. 'Good luck, and don't try anything fancy. Just keep to the plan, OK?'

'No problem,' replied Tyrrak and secreted the stones in various places about his person.

'Don't forget to march,' reminded Calvyn.

'Don't worry. Consider it done,' replied Tyrrak, his self confidence back in full flow.

Calvyn groaned inwardly, and began to wish that he had just gone back out to the well himself. It would have certainly saved some heartache. However, Tyrrak returned in short order with a container full of water, having disposed of the stones.

'Nobody suspected a thing,' Tyrrak assured everyone once the door had been secured behind him. 'I just can't wait to see Derra's face when she doesn't find us all crippled from today's beasting. It should be a real picture.'

'Let's hope so,' tempered Calvyn, not yet one hundred percent sure how long the anaesthetic properties of the cream would last, let alone how quickly it would effect a complete healing.

'One thing that is certain is that tomorrow won't start well if we don't get this place gleaming in time for Derra's inspection in the morning,' interjected Matim. 'She has a fearsome reputation for tearing barrack rooms apart.'

'You're right,' agreed Calvyn. 'Let's do our best to get this place spotless and grab some sleep. I've got a feeling that we're going to need it.'

CHAPTER 9

'Squad Two... atten... SHUN!'

The Recruits all snapped sharply to attention. Each of them was standing at the end of their bed, and all were straining to look smart as Corporal Derra entered the barrack room. The hard faced Corporal showed no glimmer of emotion as she walked in through the door, her face as flat and unfeeling as ever. As Derra halted just inside the door, she raked both the room and the Recruits with her piercing gaze. The Recruits, chests out and stomachs in, staring straight ahead, could almost feel the intensity of that look.

'Stand them at ease,' Derra ordered the Recruit next to the door, who had called the room to attention.

'Squad Two... stand at... EASE!'

Starting with the Recruit calling the orders, Derra began her inspection. Firstly, she looked closely at the individual whose bed-space she was assessing.

'Have you shaved this morning, Recruit?' queried the Corporal of her first victim.

'Yes, Corporal,' the Recruit replied, maintaining his focus on a point on the far wall.

'What did you use? A breakfast spoon? Make sure that you shave properly before you appear on parade this morning.'

'Yes, Corporal.'

'Your boots need polishing, your shirt is wrinkled... you are a mess, Recruit!'

'Yes, Corporal.'

'This is your bed?'

'Yes, Corporal.'

'And I suppose that you are going to tell me that this is a bed pack?'

'Yes, Corporal.'

'This is not a bed pack. I've seen neater piles of horse dung than this effort!' shouted Derra, and hurled the offending pile of bedding to the top end of the bed. 'Sort it out, Recruit, or you'll find yourself on cleaning chores for the next month in addition to your training program.'

The Recruit turned to go and start rebuilding the bed pack.

'NOT NOW, YOU IDIOT! As you were.'

Derra moved on down the barrack room and proceeded to tear apart everyone's efforts, one by one. No one escaped unscathed from her tongue, and the wrecked remains of the carefully folded bed packs lay strewn in her wake as if a raging tornado had smashed through the room, leaving a trail of devastation as it went.

Calvyn, being at the far end of the barrack room, was last in line. Having heard Derra virtually disassemble the dormitory as she went, it was with a certain amount of trepidation that he awaited his turn. Standing as still as he could, he watched as the Corporal annihilated Jenna's bed pack and ordered her to get a hair cut that was more in keeping with her new status as a trainee soldier. Then the formidable woman was standing in front of him, her dark brows furrowed in annoyance and her eyes burning with an inner fire.

Calvyn stood with his eyes locked on a point on the far wall, and worked very hard at not being drawn to looking to the Corporal's eyes. Despite looking through her, Calvyn could 'see' the muscles in her angular cheeks expand and contract as she clenched and unclenched her jaw. There was a slight pause as Derra stared into his distant eyes, almost willing him to look at her. Then, looking him up and down carefully without saying a word, Derra stepped aside and inspected his bed space.

'This bed pack is... not bad, Recruit. However, it is not

good enough,' Derra stated, and tipped it onto the floor. 'Keep working at it.'

Striding down the dormitory, judiciously avoiding the scattered bedding, the Corporal made her way back to the exit. On reaching the door, she turned and surveyed the wreckage.

'Frankly, Recruits, you are pathetic. You are undisciplined, untidy and scruffy. You lack pride, both in your appearance and in the state of your accommodation. When we do this tomorrow morning I expect to see a marked improvement or there will be hell to pay. This floor should be shining so brightly that I could use it as a mirror. Your boots, likewise. Your uniforms should be clean and properly pressed, your bed packs folded precisely and uniformly. I will not accept a repeat of today's effort, Squad Two. Do you hear me?'

'Yes, Corporal.'

'Very well. Get yourselves some breakfast. I will see you at the first call after breakfast on the drill square. Make sure that you all look presentable by then.'

The Corporal exited and closed the door firmly behind her. A collective sigh of relief sounded through the dormitory like a gust of wind. Recruits sat down on their beds, or just looked around at the mess in shocked silence. The room that had been immaculate to their eyes only minutes before, was now a mess of linen, blankets and pillows.

'That went well!' laughed Calvyn with a chuckle that cut through the silence. 'The Corporal obviously likes us or she wouldn't want to see us again so soon! Come on, let's just pile up the linen on the beds for now and go get some food. We'll work at the room later. Let's just make sure that we're sharp on the drill square this morning, shall we? Remember that Derra is expecting us all to be in agony out there today. Maybe she'll lighten up a little when we turn out to be a bit tougher than she's expecting. Why don't we form up outside in two minutes and show the rest of this place that Squad Two won't be broken that easily, and that we're going to stick together whatever Derra throws at us.'

A few smiles broke out around the dormitory and everyone started to murmur amongst themselves and make moves to gather their scattered linen onto the beds.

'So when did you turn into a leader?' whispered Jenna to Calvyn as she recovered a blanket from next to his bed.

'Somebody needed to say something,' he shrugged. 'When I first arrived here they all seemed so confident and knowledgeable, but now that we're all in the same boat and being treated like dirt, they've all suddenly become as vulnerable as you and I. I just want us to minimise the amount of time that we're given no respect.'

'Well, you get my vote. Let's hope it works.'

Jenna and Calvyn tossed the last of their scattered linen onto their respective bunks and walked down the barrack room together.

'Come on, Squad Two,' called out Calvyn in a loud voice. 'Let's get our act together. Fall in outside and we'll go get ourselves some good old greasy army breakfast inside us. The beds can wait.'

Squad Two formed up rapidly outside and, calling out the orders, Calvyn brought the twenty Recruits to attention and marched them smartly across to the mess hall. On the call of "Dismiss", the Recruits filed in an orderly fashion through the double doors into the dining hall.

Calvyn was in his normal position towards the back of the squad and so was one of the last to join the queue for breakfast. Consequently, he saw one of his fellow squad members step politely aside to allow two Privates to join the line ahead of them. By chance he was also just within earshot of the brief exchange that followed.

'Thank you, Recruit,' the taller soldier said gratefully. 'I see that your squad is getting the hang of this place already.'

'What do you mean? Letting you qualified Privates into the breakfast line ahead of us?'

The second Private smiled in amusement.

'No, though I appreciate it,' the first replied. 'I meant

arriving at meals as a squad. The Corporals love it. It shows team spirit and all that. Did someone tip you off?'

'Not that I know of. One of our squad members suggested that we stick together and come to breakfast as a squad after our barrack room had just been torn apart by Corporal Derra. It sounded like a good idea, and we just did it.'

'Well good for you. Take it from me, the more you stick together, the better Derra will like it.'

'Really?'

'You can bet your last copper penny on it! You must have had the speech about doing everything together by now. Eat together, sleep together and all that?'

The Recruit nodded, and other members of Squad Two standing nearby had begun to take an interest in what the unusually forthcoming soldier was saying.

'It took us several weeks to take the team spirit speech to heart, and we were amazed at the difference that it made when we finally did,' the soldier continued. Then, looking around quickly to see who was watching, the Private lowered his voice even more and Calvyn really had to listen hard to hear the advice that he was offering. 'Take the speech as literally as you can without being stupid about it,' advised he taller soldier. 'If one of you goes to eat, everyone goes. If one visits the lav, everyone visits... and if one of you is punished for any reason – everyone turns up for the punishment. Trust me. It may seem a pain in the rear end for the first week or so, but once you get used to it, the tasks that they set you seem a lot easier somehow. Also, you'll gain the respect of the hierarchy in short order, which is a definite bonus.'

'Thanks for the tip.'

'Don't mention it... and I mean don't mention it - to anyone outside of your squad, OK?'

'No problem. Thanks again.'

There were several very thoughtful faces at the breakfast table as Calvyn surveyed the expressions of his peers. As he scanned the room and worked mechanically through his plate of food, he found his own mind digesting the words of the Private. The principle of sticking together seemed plain common sense, though not perhaps to the extreme that the Private had advocated. However, the idea that doing absolutely everything together would be highly thought of by the senior ranks did not deviate from his early impressions of army life. It just grated a bit that the mentality left very little room for initiative and independent thought, and virtually none at all for any privacy.

Calvyn wondered again how on earth he would be able to progress in his study of magic if he was going to spend every waking moment with his fellow Recruits. It would not be an easy problem to solve. He could meditate easily enough whilst he was running or cleaning the barrack room, or doing any one of the several repetitive chores that the Recruits undertook. However, it was the physical practice of casting spells that would be risky, and he dreaded to think of the penalty for getting caught doing so within the castle walls.

The success of Calvyn's inspired 'bringing' spell had filled him with encouragement, and had also filled him with a keen desire to experiment further at devising his own spells. He remembered again his exultation when he had opened his eyes and seen the pot of ointment in his outstretched hand. An intense longing to repeat the experience consumed his thoughts, and the realisation of what it would be like to begin his own grimoire left him frustrated. The realisation that it may be months before he would be in a position to achieve any further success left a sour taste in the back of his mouth.

'One thing at a time, Calvyn ' he muttered to himself softly, and then realised that Jenna was watching him with a slightly amused expression on her face. He forced a smile. 'The first sign of madness, and it's only day two!' he laughed.

'Sorry?' asked Jenna, raising her eyebrows quizzically.

'Talking to myself... the first sign of madness. I was just wondering what I'd be like in a few months time.'

'Fatter if you keep eating that stuff,' laughed back

Jenna, and pointed at his almost empty plate.

'Nonsense! I'm a growing lad who needs his food.'

'Yes, growing... outwards!'

'We'll see, but what about you? You really should eat a bit more than that, you know,' Calvyn said, his voice tinged with concern.

'I'm fine. I just haven't got into the swing of three large meals a day yet. Give me time,' replied Jenna. 'No doubt given a few days of Derra's regime I'll be keen enough to monster everything in sight too,' she added with a wink.

Calvyn laughed along with Jenna and finished off the last few mouthfuls, casting the knife and fork onto the plate with a flourish. Giving a mock bow to Jenna, Calvyn sat back in his chair with his hands resting lightly on his stomach and sighed, replete.

'Well, if you've finished then we may as well gather the squad and head back to the barrack room together. We can at least make a start on clearing it before drill.'

*   *   *   *   *

Wiping the dripping rainwater from his eyes, Perdimonn looked back down the steep rise. Nothing but the rocky mountainside was visible in the driving sleet, but he could 'feel' that Selkor was not far away. It was galling that he could not shake the Shandese Magician from his tracks, and he ground his teeth in frustration as his mind raced again and again through the spells that he had at his command.

'If only I had taken the time to study shape-shifting properly,' he thought to himself, and then mentally chastised himself for such futile wishes. Shape-shifting was a discipline that took an extremely focused mind with a vivid memory for detail, and Perdimonn was nothing if not a realist when it came to his abilities. The old man's mind flashed back to his younger days when he had been foolhardy enough to attempt changing forms,

146

and he grimaced slightly as he remembered his almost disastrous venture when he had altered his shape to that of a falcon.

The young Perdimonn had been fascinated by flight, and in particular the possibility of trying it out for himself. What better and more prestigious form to try it in than a falcon, one of the swiftest and most elegant of birds? For days he had studied the shape at a falconry in Mantor before attempting the shift, but he had forgotten one vital element of the process – that of studying his own form in order to effect the shift back afterwards. Perdimonn allowed himself a wry little smile as he remembered the startled expression of the falconer who had come face-to-face with a subtly different young man from the one that he had left only minutes before. Perdimonn had been forced to leave the city in a big hurry after that little episode as, not surprisingly, rumours had spread rapidly in the wake of his experiment.

Turning back into the driving wind, Perdimonn pressed onward, ever deeper into the mountains. He shivered slightly in the cold, wet wind, and wrapped his cloak even tighter around his body. With a single word he drew energy from the earth around him and continued forward with renewed strength.

'Even the form of an old mountain goat would have been useful right now,' mused the old man as he stumbled slightly on a loose rock. 'Still, at least Selkor would be equally as uncomfortable,' he thought to himself with a grin. He could almost imagine the Shandcse Magician's annoyance when realising that Perdimonn had turned his horse loose and opted to leave the dubious safety of the Knife Edge Pass in order to enter the mountains on foot. Selkor hated heights, and the knowledge that Perdimonn was in the very place where his power was strongest, might at least give him some cause to hesitate in any use of direct force.

It had been a long chase. Ten days had passed since he had parted from Calvyn, and Perdimonn had pushed himself to his very limits ever since. He had also tried every concealing and camouflaging spell that he knew to hide his tracks, with no success. Selkor was still behind him, and still gaining slowly.

'Not long now,' whispered Perdimonn to himself through gritted teeth.

Grunting slightly with the effort, the old Magician hauled himself up to the minor summit where the ground flattened in an almost circular plateau, raised high above the valley floor. A huge single granite rock stood upright in the centre of the flattened area, towering a full ten feet tall and pointed like the lost tooth of some mighty stone giant of old.

Perdimonn walked over to the rock and placed his hands almost lovingly against its rough, textured surface. 'Yes,' he murmured. 'Perfect! This is the perfect place.'

Shielding his eyes against the driving sleet with his hands, the old Magician walked slowly around the monolith and looked out into the wild weather. On three of the four cardinal headings he could just make out the shoulders of huge mountains thrusting up into the clouds. Only southward could he see nothing, but he could sense the presence of lofty peaks in that direction also, just beyond the range of his normal vision.

Smiling to himself, Perdimonn sat down and leant against the rock, facing back towards the southern slope where, even now, Selkor would be struggling upwards into the howling wind. His position had the added bonus of sheltering him from the worst of the elements, and the old Magician relaxed and pulled his thick cloak over his raised knees to form a small tent of warmth. As Perdimonn sat waiting with nervous anticipation of the arrival of his challenger, his eyes suddenly began to sparkle as it dawned on him that he still had one avenue of escape that Selkor would neither expect nor even comprehend. However, it was nowhere near certain yet that he would need to escape. Perdimonn felt strong. Power flowed into him from all around.

At peace with his surroundings, Perdimonn reached

out with his thoughts to touch Calvyn' s mind. As clearly as if he were there, Perdimonn found himself 'with' Calvyn and a group of other youngsters marching across an enclosed and paved area. He perceived the depth of Calvyn's commitment to excel in this new environment and flashes of both frustration and triumph with his attempts at magic. Friendships too sat at the surface of Calvyn's thoughts, bringing a warm glow of good feeling to the old man as he withdrew and returned to his own situation on the bleak mountain peak.

'An army, Calvyn? Why an army?' Perdimonn asked himself quietly. Still, it may not be a bad idea in the long run for the boy to learn some controlled aggression, he reflected. Calvyn had a tough road ahead, that much was clear to the old man. Indeed, for some reason, whenever Perdimonn had thought of Calvyn over the past few days he had envisioned him holding a beautifully forged, brightly shining sword aloft in his right hand. This had seemed most strange to the old Magician, as he knew for a fact that the boy had never handled such a distinctive weapon, let alone possessed one. Yet the impression was that the sword and the boy were somehow linked, that they were destined to be together. There was obviously something deeper at work here than just an old man's imagination, and from his brief touch on the boy's mind Perdimonn instinctively knew that the path that Calvyn had chosen was 'right', just as this place was 'right' for his imminent confrontation with Selkor. For the first time, Perdimonn began to dimly sense what the seers and fortune-tellers had made their living from for centuries. The feeling of prescience was amazingly strong, and the old man knew with unquestioning conviction that events were taking a predestined course. Somehow the sleet and wind, his cold damp clothing, all of the things that had seemed negative or depressing, suddenly became a blessing as his heart and mind soared with joy at the revelation.

'This is *meant* to happen. It has purpose, and that purpose feels good. I just wish that I knew *what* it was,' muttered Perdimonn with a wry smile to himself. 'Still, you can't have everything all of the time.'

Once again Perdimonn reached out with his mind, searching this time for Selkor. He did not have to reach far, for Selkor was at that very moment approaching the summit.

Perdimonn stood up and leaned back casually against the rock. The old man's long dark cloak remained wrapped around his body, and rivulets of water ran from his bald pate into the iron grey hair that still grew at the back and sides of his head. His eyes sparkled, the old inner mirth bubbling back to the surface that had, for the last fortnight or so, withdrawn deep into his heart. It felt so good to be in the mountains again, where the earth was strong and unpolluted by the influence of mankind. Perdimonn breathed deep breaths of pure untainted air in through his nostrils, and watched with complete unconcern as Selkor climbed the last few feet to the edge of the plateau.

'It's over, Perdimonn. There will be no escape for you this time. I will not be taken in by your tricks and illusions any more,' Selkor stated coldly, his feet planted firmly shoulder width apart, and his eyes blazing with anticipation.

'You've got to admit that the last one was rather good though,' replied Perdimonn with a grin that was pure mischief. 'I really had you going for a while back there.'

'Pah! Tricks and deceptions are the domain of fools,' spat Selkor. 'Power is what commands respect, old man, and only the fact that you possess access to such power has kept me from this moment for so long. You are nothing but an old fool who refuses to wield his power for fear that you might inadvertently cause someone harm. Well, the time is long overdue for you to pass on that power to someone who is willing to use it for the common good – someone who will not balk at using force to crush evil and oppression, and will not hesitate to fight for what is right. It is time that you passed it to me.'

'I would gladly do so Selkor... if you were the one

destined to be my successor. However, you are not. The Council has already dismissed you as being unsuitable to be a Warder.'

'The Council,' laughed Selkor, placing his hands on his hips and shaking his head in derision. 'Those tired old idiots are worse than you are. At least you have a bit of spirit about you – they wouldn't know "suitable" if it jumped out and bit them!'

'But they do have the authority to make that decision, whether you like it or not.'

'Their authority is meaningless out here, old man, and you know it. Once the power is mine they will have no choice but to accept me.'

'And you want to *fight* oppression!' Perdimonn chuckled. 'Might I suggest that you get out a mirror and start throwing a few punches.'

Selkor's eyes narrowed at the scornful laughter.

'You are in no position to mock me, Perdimonn. There is nowhere that you can run that I cannot find you, and you know that without breaking those pacifistic morals of yours, there is no way that you can prevent me from taking what I want from you. It is my destiny to become the most powerful Magician ever to walk these lands. You and that rabble of a council may try to deny me, but in the end I will achieve my destiny.'

'That remains to be seen,' Perdimonn replied, his face still smiling but his eyes no longer displaying merriment. 'I will never willingly allow you to wield the power that has been placed in my trust, Selkor, and I honestly believe that no matter how strong you believe yourself to be, you will not gain access to that power by force. The earth possesses a power that can never be broken, Selkor. It can be shaped and changed, but never completely destroyed. I ward that power from abuse, and despite all your protestations of good intention I see no good in your methods of obtaining power. Power in the wrong hands can lead only to corruption and disaster, and this power in your hands could cause a major catastrophe. You may as well leave, Selkor. You are not going to get what you came for today.'

'Oh, but you are wrong, Perdimonn, for I will gain knowledge of your Key, as I will gain Arred's, Morrel's and Rikath's. Yes, I know you all, and I will gather knowledge of all the Keys. I have foreseen it. It will happen. I will ward *all* of the Keys, and I will use them as they were *meant* to be used.'

Drawing himself up to his full height, Selkor twirled his hands dramatically and released his first spell. An expanding wave of darkness like a blanket of pitch black emptiness flew from his hands to settle around Perdimonn, cocooning him in an amorphous blob of shifting darkness. However, it hardly had a chance to settle before it shattered outwards into a thousand shards, leaving Perdimonn standing resolutely unmoving and apparently unconcerned at Selkor's assault. The aggressor was given no time to launch a second attack. Perdimonn raised his hands and Selkor gasped as the rock beneath his feet shot upward at a frightening rate. His knees buckled slightly at the acceleration, and his mind and stomach reeled as the upward motion stopped abruptly, leaving him standing atop a sheer pinnacle of rock that dropped away vertically on all sides. Cloud and rain swirled all around Selkor, severely limiting his visibility from the suddenly imposed imprisonment of the rock spire. However, the lack of visible features did nothing to abate the rapidly rising panic of vertigo that the Magician found himself fighting to control.

Selkor dropped to his knees and closed his eyes. Hands palm down on the rock, he marshalled his thoughts and calmed his racing heartbeat.

'Think, damn you! Think!' he muttered to himself as he struggled with the unexpected tactic. 'The crafty old...! He knew that you hated heights and prepared this... who knows how long ago? Calm. Discipline. Think. He used no major power or you would have felt it, so this must be...' Selkor, maintaining his eyes tightly shut, carefully felt the ground in front of him for the edge of the drop. His hands felt further and further forward until he found himself crawling forward. '... An illusion!'

Still with his eyes firmly closed, Selkor stood up once more and boldly stepped forward. One, two, three paces. If his prison had been a real one, he would now be falling into nothingness. Gritting his teeth, Selkor opened his eyes and found himself once more on the flat hilltop facing the old Magician. However, Perdimonn had not been idle, and was now surrounded by a glowing wall of magical power that was growing more impenetrable by the second.

With barely a pause, Selkor began hurling balls of incandescent fire at the softly glowing barrier, but the lethal fireballs merely sputtered and fizzled out on impact with the blue-green wall of magical energy. Quickly, he realised that an assault of this sort would not only take inordinate amounts of magical energy, but also that even if it was successful, the attack would defeat his own ultimate objective. He could not afford to kill Perdimonn yet. He needed to keep him alive long enough to obtain the Key that would open his way to greatness. Selkor forced himself to calm his anger at having been fooled. He paused and considered the old Magician's tactic. It was a good one. Perdimonn had lots of readily available power here, and Selkor would be hard pressed to force the old man to give in without killing him.

'If only I can force the old fool into bringing the Key to the surface of his mind, it will be mine,' thought Selkor as he considered his options. Whatever he did would have to be fast as the old Magician's shield was rapidly becoming very strong indeed. The only way to get Perdimonn to use the Key would be to apply so much pressure that he would have no choice but to use it to defend himself. Then, whilst the old man was concentrating on the spell, he could insinuate his mind into the old man's and pluck the runes from his thoughts.

With the plan firmly settled in his mind, Selkor began to work on something that would begin to force Perdimonn along the path of no return. Out of the very air in front of him, Selkor began to create bolts of energy-sapping nothingness. They were not exactly black, but more like holes in the air that, once cast, impacted Perdimonn's barrier with an audible snap. With each bolt Selkor drained the magical force-field further until it started to shimmer and flicker as its cohesion began to fail.

Perdimonn grimaced with the effort of maintaining his shield and reached out further and further afield to draw in more and more energy. It was obviously a losing battle. Selkor's spells appeared to actually negate or destroy magical energy somehow, and the more energy Perdimonn pulled into the barrier, the more the anti-magic bolts destroyed. The old man needed to change tack again, but it was becoming progressively more difficult for him to think clearly, as the concentration required just to maintain his current defence was taking all of his spare mental capacity.

The temptation for Perdimonn to use the Key and employ the power that he had guarded for so long in order to aid his defence, was almost overwhelming. However, he resisted the urge, pushing all thoughts of that course of action firmly aside. He sensed that Selkor was willing him to use the Key, and decided that death would be a preferable option to complying with the Shandese Magician. Perdimonn needed breathing space, a respite in order to restructure his defence. Despite the cold, the old Magician was sweating profusely. He knew that he could not stave off Selkor's attack long in this manner. He needed to create a diversion that would cause sufficient confusion in his adversary's mind to give him the edge back. It would have to be simple, quick and not require too much energy.

The wind swirled a fresh wave of sleet across the hilltop, giving Perdimonn the inspiration that he required. Even as he allowed his defensive shield to drop, the old Magician completed his next spell and plunged the hilltop into thick, swirling fog as the cloud base abruptly lowered at his command.

Momentarily surprised, Selkor took a few seconds to marshal a counter spell to lift the fog. The visibility was extremely poor, a few yards at best as Selkor worked to raise the cloud base. Even as he worked, he could sense something strange happening around him, and so raised a shield of his own against the remote chance that Perdimonn might actually counter-attack rather than just defend or run away. The old Magician could not hold out for much longer, Selkor was certain of that. Furthermore, the old man would not be able to run far before Selkor lifted the fog.. There seemed to be no point to the fog other than to delay the inevitable for a mere handful of seconds.

The counter spell was cast and the fog lifted. For a second or two, all Selkor could do was stand and stare around in semi-disbelief. Then he put his hands on his hips and laughed long and loud as his gaze swept around the dozens of Perdimonns, all busily working away at their blue-green magical shields, spread right across the hilltop.

'This is all very entertaining, old man, but it will do you no good and will no doubt become tiresome all too quickly. Why don't you just concede that I will take what I want from you eventually, and cut short the agony? Give me the Key and be done with it.'

All of the identical-looking Perdimonns stopped what they were doing and turned to face Selkor. As one they emphatically cried out 'NEVER!' and then returned to strengthening their magical shields.

'Oh, very well. Have it your way,' said Selkor in a resigned voice and began once again to fashion his 'nothing' bolts and fire them at the figures at random. Each illusion that was struck by one of Selkor's shots of anti-magic was destroyed instantaneously, and disappeared with a soft popping noise. Before long, Perdimonn's army of phantoms began to reduce in number at a rapid rate, and Selkor became progressively more annoyed as each bolt that he fired failed to identify his real opponent.

Meanwhile Perdimonn, who had slipped around to the far side of the large central rock whilst the fog had hidden him from Selkor's view, was preparing his final defence. It was a drastic measure, but he knew that it would prevent Selkor from achieving his goal in the short term. The old man was no fool. He could see that Selkor was strong in his magical abilities, and that the younger Magician was more than a match for him even here in the mountains. However, Perdimonn had one last refuge that Selkor would be unable to breach without destroying that which he so much wanted to gain.

The concentration required was immense, but he managed to complete the unique spell flawlessly, and as he pressed his hands against the face of the granite monolith, his hands appeared to melt into the stone itself. Still maintaining his new magical field, Perdimonn pulled his hands back out of the rock and turned to face outwards. Then, with slow deliberate movements, he pushed his entire body back against the stone and felt himself sliding into it. Just before his face melted into the rock face, he could not resist calling out to his adversary with a final parting shot.

'Goodbye, Selkor,' he shouted with a mischievous chuckle, and then he was gone.

By chance, Selkor, who was by now striding around the hilltop in a towering rage and firing bolts of anti-magic in rapid succession, heard the shout, and turned just in time to witness Perdimonn's face disappearing into the stone.

'NO!' he cried, and ran over to where Perdimonn had disappeared. 'Damn you, old man! You can't stay in there forever. Come out and get it over with.'

Selkor concentrated and reached out with his mind to try to touch Perdimonn's consciousness, but all that he could sense was the rock and a vague whisper of the old man's lingering laughter. Intensely frustrated, he slapped his hand hard against the rock face, and then, cradling his stinging palm to his chest and wrapping his dark cloak around his body, he sat down cross-legged on the ground. A brooding frown settled on his face as he prepared himself to wait and think.

CHAPTER 10

Standing shoulder to shoulder, Calvyn and Jenna, together with eight others from their squad, faced Bek and the rest of Squad Two. All were perspiring heavily in the warm afternoon sun as they swung their heavy torps through the clattering paces of their latest exercises.

Until recently, Derra had concentrated their lessons on individual skills, emphasising the development of speed and strength. However, over the last few weeks the Corporal had introduced the concept of fighting as a team, and the skills and responsibilities of fighting alongside one another in a pitched battle. Everyone, without exception, had suddenly picked up a new collection of bruises and minor injuries as this latest phase of their training had begun, and Calvyn could feel the ache of his most recently acquired contusion as he swung his torp again and again through the pattern of the drill.

The progression from fighting solo to fighting as part of a line had been rapid but logical in its development, Calvyn mused as he blocked and swung at his opponents. Derra had introduced it by demonstrating how she would fight against two opponents who were attacking her simultaneously. With her speed and skill, she exploited the weaknesses of both with relative ease. However, having done this, the fierce looking Corporal had gone to great lengths to show how by working together as a unit, her opponents could learn to cover for each other and become a much more effective fighting force.

Practising with two against one had been entertaining and challenging, with some of the best swordsmen picking up bruises from some of the worst. Calvyn still revelled in the pride that he had felt when Derra had selected him along with Bek, Tyrrak and other more experienced swordsmen to fight solo against two opponents. He had been even more pleased when he had held his own for several sessions. Later, as his adversaries became more competent at working together and covering for each other, Calvyn had been forced to be ever more on the defensive.

Once the initial pairings had practised together for a couple of days, everyone had been shuffled around. Calvyn was partnered with Matim, who was at best an indifferent swordsman. His strokes were all correct, but far too slow to be effective. As a result, both he and Calvyn had received more than their fair share of bruises.

The practices had progressed to two against two and three against three, until this morning they had involved the entire squad in the exercise. The lunch break had passed and the afternoon had come all too quickly for Calvyn and the others, and all of the Recruits were feeling the weight of the torps on their straining arm muscles. Mistakes were coming thick and fast, but there were few with enough strength left to exploit them.

'Hold! Squad Two, for Tarmin's sake sharpen up! What are you? Slug spawn? No, that's unfair on slugs! I've seen slugs move much faster than that. Sit down, the lot of you, and listen in...'

Derra paused whilst Squad Two collapsed into a semblance of an orderly seated line, and prepared herself to give one of her famously encouraging shouting sessions. These "pep talks" were invariably laced with numerous vivid comparisons and illustrations that were often mind-boggling in their frankness. The Corporal pulled no punches in her debriefs on how each exercise had gone, and no Recruit was ever left in any doubt as to the areas that were in need of improvement.

Before Derra could begin the onslaught, however, two

other Corporals, both unknown to the Recruits, appeared around the side of the armoury and marched purposefully towards the resting squad. As it was obvious that the two NCOs wanted something from Derra or her squad, the female Corporal stood and waited patiently for them to approach.

'Yes?' she asked, her voice conveying a cold annoyance at the interruption to her class. Derra scanned her fellow Corporals' gleaming blue and black uniforms as if inspecting a parade. 'What is important enough that it cannot wait until the end of the training period?'

'We are here to place two of your Recruits under arrest on the orders of Captain Tegrani,' replied the older of the two Corporals in a solemn voice. 'You do have Recruits Calvyn and Bek in your squad, do you not?'

One of the Recruits gasped audibly, otherwise a shocked silence settled over the group as all heads turned toward Calvyn and Bek in surprise. There was a pause whilst the information sank in, during which Derra afforded the two Corporals one of her most withering stares. Neither flinched under the unwavering gaze of Squad Two's instructor; they just stood, patiently awaiting a response. Eventually, after what seemed like an eternity to Calvyn, Derra gave a slight nod, and beckoned for Calvyn and Bek to come forward.

Calvyn's heart was pounding as he stood up and stepped smartly out in front of the rest of the squad. Out of the corner of his eye he could see that Bek was almost as pale as the whitewashed walls of the stables beyond him. The two Recruits stood side by side at attention, facing their fiercely frowning Corporal.

'Do you know what this is all about?' Derra asked them in a gravelly growl.

'No, Corporal,' they answered in turn.

'Would you care to tell me what my Recruits are being charged with? They appear to be as much in the dark about all this as I am,' Derra queried of the two waiting Corporals.

'They are to be tried by Courts Martial for the theft of

certain personal effects belonging to Captain Tegrani.'

There were several sharp intakes of breath from the Recruits, but Derra, still frowning, regarded first the accusing Corporals and then the two shocked Recruits who stood with faces that mirrored their disbelief at the charges made against them. Derra's expression softened slightly as she motioned Calvyn and Bek to go with the two Corporals.

'I will talk with you both shortly,' the training Corporal said to them in the friendliest tone that Calvyn had yet heard her use. Looking into the eyes of her Recruits, Derra could see that they were not responsible for the crime and she decided there and then to do all that she could to help. 'Go with them for now. Be sure that you answer no questions until I get there. Understood?'

'Yes, Corporal,' Calvyn said crisply, and together with Bek he marched the few intervening paces to halt next to the unknown emissaries of Captain Tegrani.

'As for you, gentlemen,' Derra directed, turning to her fellow Corporals, 'Please ensure that no formal proceedings or questioning begins until I am able to be in attendance, or there will be hell to pay. Is that clear?'

'As a Vortaff mountain stream, Derra,' the older of the two Corporals replied with a nod of acknowledgement. 'We will hold them in Dren's office for now, and will await your arrival.'

With the two grim-faced NCOs flanking them as they marched across the training ground towards Dren's office, Calvyn and Bek both did their best to stay calm about their situation. Calvyn spent the short duration of the walk trying to think of any times that he had even been near the officers' accommodation. The only periods that he could remember were whilst he had been on guard patrol duty around the wall, but he had never been on shift with Bek, so that did not explain why they were under suspicion.

Nothing fitted. The only time that Bek and he had spent together over the past few weeks had always been in the company of someone else. When were they supposed to have committed this act of theft, and why? Calvyn certainly did not need money as he had what was almost an embarrassing amount of money held in the Quartermaster's store, and to his knowledge Bek was not hard up either. The Corporal had said 'personal effects' though... not money. What on earth would the Captain possess that would supposedly entice Bek and himself to risk everything to steal? Calvyn had absolutely no idea.

As the two Recruits entered Sergeant Dren's office they did so in different states of mind. Calvyn, although apprehensive, was by now also curious to try to find out what it was that he was supposed to have stolen. Bek, however, was verging on panic, his overactive imagination running wild with possible consequences of having been arrested. His mind already had him flogged in public, chained in darkness and left for years to rot in some forsaken hell-hole. His breathing and pulse rates were up, and his eyes were flicking nervously from object to object without actually taking anything in.

'Relax, Bek,' Calvyn whispered to his friend as they entered the office. 'You haven't stolen anything, have you?'

'No! Of course not!' replied Bek in an outraged and considerably louder whisper.

'Oi! No talking, you two,' ordered the Corporal entering the room behind them. 'You,' he continued, pointing at Calvyn, 'sit on the floor in the corner over there. You,' he said, gesturing to Bek, 'sit over there.'

Calvyn and Bek moved to their designated spots, and each sat in silent contemplation. Almost immediately after the Recruits were seated, the two Corporals held a brief muttered conference and the younger of the two left the office. The door closed with an echoing thud, and the three remaining occupants regarded one another thoughtfully as quiet seconds ticked by into minutes.

It was some time later that the door reopened, the clank of the latch startling all three from their introspective thoughts. The two Recruits, together with the Corporal, all leapt to their feet and stood stiffly to attention as Captain Tegrani and the younger Corporal strode into the room. The two Recruits were ushered forward to stand side by side in front of the Captain.

Tegrani was certainly a striking figure in his blue and black uniform. He stood tall and slim, his boyishly youthful face set in a frown as he fingered the silver belt buckle at his waist. The silver rank knots of a Captain stood proud on Tegrani's shoulder, and the silver spurs mounted on the highly polished black leather boots left no doubt as to the man's position of authority.

'You are Calvyn and Bek, I take it?' the Captain stated more than asked.

'Yes, Sir,' the two Recruits replied in unison.

'So would you like to explain to me how items of my personal property came to be found under the mattresses of your beds?'

'Sir,' Calvyn replied hesitantly, 'Corporal Derra ordered us specifically not to answer any questions until she arrived. So whilst I don't wish to appear insubordinate...'

'You are going to wait for Derra,' finished Tegrani with a quirky sort of half smile. 'Well, I suppose that I can't fault you for that. You will not have to wait long. The good Corporal undoubtedly observed me making my way here, and will almost certainly dismiss the class early to join us as soon as she can.'

The Captain strolled forward to Sergeant Dren's desk, spun the topmost parchment around casually and scanned the document quickly. With a slight 'Humpf,' he placed the scroll back on the pile and wandered back across the room to the window. As he walked, the Captain gestured to the two Corporals to stand at ease and then stood silently staring out over the weapons training area from the office window.

Calvyn and Bek remained at 'attention', standing as smartly and as still as they possibly could. The office was quite warm, with the afternoon sun still spilling in through the south-facing windows, and it became progressively harder for the two Recruits to maintain their posture. The weapons training that afternoon had been a particularly demanding and sweaty session. Despite having cooled off whilst sitting in their respective corners of Sergeant Dren's office, both Recruits now began to feel the afternoon heat once more, and had to draw on several of the tricks that Derra had taught them during their drill sessions to prevent themselves from passing out.

Calvyn concentrated on wiggling his toes inside his boots. Although invisible to anyone looking on, this was enough movement to prevent his blood from pooling in his feet and lower legs, and to promote sufficient circulation to maintain his level of consciousness. Bek was achieving the same ends by twitching his kneecaps. Both, however, were more than a little relieved when a knock at the door proved to be Corporal Derra, who saluted the Captain smartly and briskly entered the room, closing the door firmly behind her.

'Welcome Derra. Now let's see if we can sort this out with as little fuss as possible, shall we?' Captain Tegrani said, his tone business-like.

'Sir…'

'You will have your chance, Derra. Let's see what your boys have to say for themselves first, shall we?' interrupted the Captain, holding his hand out in a silencing signal to the defensive Corporal.

Derra nodded her head in quiescent acceptance of the Captain's right to question the Recruits.

'Thank you Corporals. You may leave us now,' Tegrani continued, dismissing the two silent figures by the door.

As one they saluted, turned and left the room, closing the door quietly behind them.

'Now then, Corporal Derra is here and poised to leap to your defence should I try to trick you into saying anything that you might regret,' Tegrani said, his youthful features set in determined lines. 'I ask you again, would you like to explain how items of my personal property came to be found underneath the mattresses of your beds?'

'Sir, I have no idea even what the items are that you

refer to, and even less how they might have found their way under the mattress of my bed,' replied Calvyn as calmly as he could.

'Me neither, Sir,' Bek stated, his voice cracking slightly as he spoke.

'Ah yes. Of course. No innocent man would know what had been stolen, how foolish of me. However, if I were to tell you, Recruit Calvyn, that my silver flute was found in your bed, and that a highly valuable dagger was the item recovered from underneath Recruit Bek's mattress, would that change your statement at all?'

'Sir, I make no secret of the fact that I play the flute, or that my flute is old and has seen better days, but I have no need to steal one. My own instrument has many years of playing left in it yet and holds great sentimental value to me. I have no reason to resort to thievery to obtain something that I could possibly afford to buy if I wanted it that badly.'

Captain Tegrani nodded thoughtfully for a second or two, and then turned to Bek who was still looking woefully pale.

'Well, Recruit Bek? What have you got to say for yourself?' the Captain asked.

'Sir, I would never steal anything from you, Sir. All I ever wanted to do was to join the army, and I would never do anything to jeopardise my chance here, Sir. Honest, Sir,' Bek blurted in a rush, and then abruptly shut up, his cheeks flushing red against the rest of his face which remained a determined pale shade of grey.

'Hmm... well I have to say that it's no great surprise that you deny everything. The whole feel of this situation is wrong somehow but the evidence clearly points a guilty finger at you two. Unless you can prove to me that you are innocent of this theft then you will be punished for it... and believe me, the punishment will be severe.'

The Captain eyed Calvyn and Bek in turn, his eyes probing for some sort of reaction. The two Recruits remained standing rigidly to attention, their thoughts racing in circles but getting nowhere. With a slight snort,

Captain Tegrani turned and strolled around behind the desk before sitting in Dren's chair and leaning back, began to stroke his chin thoughtfully.

'Captain, you must suspect, as I am already certain, that my Recruits are innocent, so why subject them to this, Sir?' Derra asked, her voice straining to control the anger behind the question.

'On what basis should I believe their innocence, Corporal? My possessions were found in their bunks and I have no evidence to implicate anyone else. You know as well as I how the Baron feels about discipline. The rules here are hard and the punishments severe to prevent circumstances just such as these. We cannot afford to have thieves operating in and around the castle. Army life depends upon the total trust of your fellow men. If suspicion and distrust abounds then soldiers no longer act as a unit and any hope of a cohesive force is gone.'

Derra fought her growing anger down, grinding her teeth silently for a moment before replying.

'I appreciate the need for discipline more than most, Sir,' Derra replied, the rasp in her voice dropping almost to a growl, 'but the fact remains that if that discipline is meted out unjustly on the innocent then it will achieve nothing. There are a few facts that you should know about these two particular Recruits that make this whole situation particularly ludicrous.'

'Oh?'

Tegrani's eyebrows raised slightly at this, his eyes questioning. Leaning back even further in the chair, he crooked his right leg over his left such that his ankle rested on his knee and he grasped his right ankle loosely with both hands.

'Very well,' he said, 'continue.'

'Well, Sir, for a start you say that the items were found under the mattresses of their bunks. That is such a ridiculously obvious hiding place that it was bound to be one of the first places searched. Neither of these Recruits is that stupid. If either of them had been involved in this theft then I suspect that your search would in all probability still be going on now. Also, what is not generally known amongst the other Recruits is that both of these two have more money than most veteran Privates, and probably most Corporals too.'

'And this makes them less suspicious, Corporal? Surely it should make them more so?' interrupted the Captain, slightly surprised.

'It's not the amount of wealth that they hold, so much as its source, Sir. I make no secret of the fact that I like to know all I can about my Recruits. It is my belief that if I can identify their strengths and weaknesses then I can better know how to push them to their limits and to mould them into the sort of soldiers that the Baron wants and needs.'

The Captain nodded.

'Well, Sir, you should know that Calvyn arrived at the castle with two horses and enough money and equipment that he would not need any other source of income for some time. Furthermore, according to Sergeant Dren he sold one of the horses to Captain Strexis – that beautiful thoroughbred mare that he has been riding recently – for a considerable sum of money. The Quartermaster informs me that Calvyn has neither added nor taken anything from his holdings at the stores except to sign out his flute and an old storybook on rest days. Bek, on the other hand, is the son of one of Lord Valdeer's senior captains. He has independent means and no need to steal for financial gain.'

'People don't always steal for the monetary gain, Corporal,' the Captain stated, his lips set in a thin line. 'And who is to say that Calvyn here did not steal the horse and equipment before he arrived?'

'Sir, I would never...' burst out Calvyn indignantly.

'Silence, Recruit!' Derra growled. 'I will handle this.'

'Yes, Corporal,' Calvyn replied meekly, clamping his lips together so tightly that they were virtually white with the pressure.

'You are right of course, Captain. However, if you add to these circumstances the fact that Bek here has won

Mark Robson

every inter-squad sword competition to date and that
Calvyn is top of the list to assume the Squad Leader
position for the forthcoming Squad Training phase, both
become obvious targets for someone to aim their jealousy
at. This to me looks like a poorly disguised set-up job.'

Calvyn shot Corporal Derra a quizzical look at the
mention of Squad Leader, which she returned with a tight
grin.

The Captain once more surveyed the two Recruits, a
deep frown creasing his face as he assimilated the
Corporal's information. His two forefingers started
tapping idly against his ankle as he thought.

'What you say has a ring of truth about it, Derra. I
believe that you may be right in this but even if you are,
it is not going to be easy to convince the Courts Martial.
All your arguments are circumstantial and no matter
what sort of character depositions you give, the Court will
always tend to convict on the weight of hard evidence.
Even assuming that you are right and that these two
have been set up, the unfortunate fact is that the stolen
items were recovered from their bunks. My lack of
seniority as a Captain, and my involvement as the injured
party in this case, will dictate that my only involvement
in any trial will be to identify the items found as the items
stolen from my quarters. The only way that I could
become involved further would be to find evidence
implicating someone else. The big question is – who
else?'

The Captain let the question sink in for a few
seconds.

'Can either of you think of anyone in your squad who
might hold a specific grudge against you? Or maybe
someone who would be jealous enough of your success to
wish to harm you in this way?'

Unbidden, Tyrrak's face flashed into Calvyn's mind,
but he firmly dismissed the idea. Tyrrak was self-centred
but not malicious, he told himself resolutely. Carefully
he considered the rest of Squad Two, but decided that
none would do such a spiteful deed to one of their own.

'No, Sir, there is no one in Squad Two that I could believe evil-minded enough to do such a thing,' Calvyn replied with certainty.

Bek shook his head silently as the Captain's gaze fell on him.

'What about you, Corporal?' enquired Tegrani of Derra, whose brows were deeply furrowed in thought.

'I think that the two of them are more forgiving than I am, for I would have named Recruit Tyrrak as a possible candidate,' she said with a sharp look at Calvyn. 'However, on reflection I am forced to agree with their judgement. He is a loud mouthed braggart, but he is not calculating enough to commit a crime of this nature.'

'As you are not known for your soft-hearted nature,' Tegrani said, smiling at the fierce-looking Corporal with a lopsided grin that dripped sarcasm, 'I will accept your professional judgement of your Recruits. Nevertheless, if someone out there is attempting to frame these two young men, then you had better nail them somehow, and quickly.'

'Can either of you think of anyone who might wish you ill? Anyone at all?'

'No one here at the castle, Sir,' Calvyn answered, then he shuddered. His mind had suddenly filled with a vision of Selkor, hand outstretched towards him with his long index finger pointing malevolently.

'Me neither, Sir,' Bek added at just the right moment to draw attention away from Calvyn's uncontrollable reaction to the mental image of the dark Magician.

'All right, Corporal, I will buy you some time to carry out an investigation. You can have a week but not a day more. In the meantime these two will be kept under arrest and detained in the castle dungeons.'

Uncrossing his legs, the Captain got to his feet and began to pace around the room. With the thumb of his left hand hooked behind his silver belt buckle and the fingers of his right hand tapping once more at his chin, the Captain looked the very picture of contemplation. The Corporal and the two young Recruits remained still and silent, the click of his heels and the slight jingle of his spurs sounding unnaturally loud in the stone walled office.

'I think that based on what you have told me, it stands to reason that the culprit is most likely to be a Recruit, so I suggest that you concentrate your efforts there. Just be sure of this though, Corporal... I will not stand in front of the Courts Martial and protest the innocence of these two on your word alone. You will have to come up with some real, substantiated evidence. You may have two minutes now to talk with Calvyn and Bek but then I expect to see them being marched across to the cells. Is that clear?'

'Perfectly, Captain,' Derra replied shortly.

'Good luck, Corporal.'

'Thank you, Sir.'

With one last glance at the two accused Recruits, the Captain strode over to the door and left. The door squeaked slightly as it shut and despite being solid oak, in Calvyn's mind it closed with a distinctly metallic clang.

Corporal Derra, her hard angular face set in angry lines, faced the two young men and took a deep breath.

'Having you locked away is going to hinder the investigation in some ways... but maybe it will help us in others. The advantage that I see of having you two in prison is that the real perpetrators will almost certainly believe that they have succeeded. We can only hope that they've lowered their guard a little on that premise. We will need to keep them thinking that they've succeeded and we'll need a few spies in the camp. Is there anyone that you would trust your lives with amongst Squad Two?' Derra asked, her piercing eyes virtually drilling into them for answers.

'Recruit Jenna,' replied Calvyn without hesitation.

'And Matim,' added Bek.

Calvyn nodded in agreement.

'Good choices both, I think,' Derra confirmed. 'Very well, boys, what I'm going to do is to brief Squad Two that you will be tried by Courts Martial in approximately a week's time. I will direct Corporals Gan and Beren to do likewise to Squads One and Three. At the earliest opportunity I will brief Recruits Jenna and Matim to keep their ears and eyes open for any signs of smugness amongst the other Recruits and I will ask Gan and Beren to maintain a close watch on their Recruits as well. We have seven days to sort this out. Let's hope that it's enough.'

Calvyn swallowed hard at that and Bek, who was already as white as a sheet, looked to be on the edge of tears.

'And if it's not enough, Corporal?' Calvyn asked tentatively.

'Listen, both of you. For the time being I'm afraid that you two lads are just going to have to trust me to try to sort this mess out. I can offer no promises other than that I will do my very best to prove your innocence. Life will not be pleasant. The cells are not exactly luxurious and I have no influence to speak of with the guards. Besides, if word got out that you were being treated in any way different from past prisoners, our hopes of catching the real culprits would disappear very quickly. This whole plan hinges on lulling our adversary, or adversaries, into a false sense of security.

'We understand, Corporal,' Calvyn stated with a calmness that he did not feel. 'Before we go though, Corporal, there is one other person that I would like to trust with this plan – Private Jez... tall, with ginger hair,' Calvyn continued, measuring Jez's height with his right hand. 'I believe that the Private is totally trustworthy, and with his easy going manner may get people talking where others would fail.'

Derra gave a tight grin.

'Yes, I know who you mean Calvyn. He's a good and interesting choice of confidant. I shall ensure that Private Jez is fully briefed. Have either of you anything to add? No? Very well then, let's go.'

The two young Recruits moved smartly into position, and Derra marched them out of the office and across the weapons training area. At the far end of the area, Squad

One were still involved in their archery lesson, being taught basic longbow techniques by Corporal Gan on the short range archery training area. However, as the Corporal and her prisoners marched around the side of the area there was no doubt in Calvyn's mind as to where the centre of attention was... and it was not on Corporal Gan's demonstration.

As he reached the top of the flight of steps that descended into blackness, Calvyn took one last look around at the sun drenched castle grounds. The clear blue sky, dotted with the occasional puff of pure white fair weather cloud would be a good memory to make the focus of his nightly meditation. In an instant, he captured as many details as he could. The scuffed sandy floor of the weapons training area, the three large straw archery targets bristling with arrows, the proud looking sentries patrolling the crenellated castle walls, and the fluttering blue and black pennant atop the roof of the central keep, all etched themselves into his memory. Then he was descending those steep steps into the very foundations of the castle.

Flaming torches mounted in brackets on the walls at regular intervals provided a flickering orange light as the last glimmer of the bright summer daylight was left behind. The footsteps of Calvyn and Bek echoed hollowly as they reached the bottom of the gently curving flight of stairs, and the small party halted as they approached a very solid looking oak door that blocked the passageway ahead.

A private appeared out of a side door and greeted Derra formally.

'Put these two in cell one. No visitors will be allowed without the express permission of Captain Tegrani,' the Corporal ordered.

'Yes, Corporal,' the duty jailer replied, and drew a big steel ring of keys from his tunic pocket.

The two locks were opened with large metal keys, and once unlocked, the Private drew back the thick steel bolts at the top and bottom of the door, each making a resounding metallic clank as they hit their stops. Then, taking a torch from the wall and pushing the heavy door open, the jailer led the two Recruits forward into the darkness that led to their cell. A similar series of bolts and locks barred the door to the chamber in which they were to be detained.

'In you go,' ordered the jailer, in a no-messing sort of voice.

Calvyn and Bek complied without delay. As they entered the cell there was enough light from the torch in the jailer's hand to make out two low canvas bunks, and what was little more than a grotty hole in one corner of the floor that was probably supposed to pass as a toilet. It was every bit as bad as Calvyn had imagined. The door swung closed behind them with a heavy thud, instantaneously shutting off all but the tiniest chink of flickering light at the base of the door. The jangle of keys sounded, followed by the clicking of the locks being secured. Then the snap of the bolts being driven back into place reverberated loudly in the enclosing blackness and the last remnants of light died with the echoing sound of receding footfalls.

Blackness and silence reigned.

Calvyn sighed heavily. He felt his way to the right hand bunk and sat down. The canvas sagged under his weight. This would not be a comfortable stay, he decided with resignation.

'I don't know if I'm going to hack this,' stammered Bek in a voice that sounded barely under control.

'Nonsense!' Calvyn replied firmly. 'You'll be fine. Just lie down on your bunk and catch up on some of that sleep that Derra's been working so hard to deprive us of. Get the rest while you can, because when Jenna, Matim and the others catch the swine that set us up, you can bet your life that Derra will show us no favouritism out on the training ground when we get out of this mess.'

'That's the truth,' Bek chuckled, the nervousness still present in his voice, but a hint of relief also spilling through.

A slight scraping in the darkness advised Calvyn that Bek had found his bunk, and by listening carefully to Bek's movements, Calvyn started to be able to hear his friend's breathing pattern across the black divide. As he concentrated, Calvyn sensed Bek's breathing settle into a deeper and more regular pattern. However, just as Calvyn began to think that Bek had regained control, his friend's breaths started to become shallower, faster and more irregular again.

'What's the matter, Bek?' Calvyn enquired, his voice sounding loud in the still blackness.

'It's the dark. I feel as if the walls are closing in on me. I've never known anything so... so completely black. I can't even see my hand if I wave it right in front of my eyes.'

'Hey! Come on now. Afraid of the dark? There's nothing to be afraid of in here,' encouraged Calvyn in a quiet and calm voice. 'We both saw the room as we came in. The air is fresh, and the walls and door are immensely solid. Just remind yourself that this place is designed to keep people safe. Safe and uncomfortable I'll admit, but safe nonetheless.'

Even as he was speaking, however, Calvyn began to experience the oppression of the complete lack of light. He suddenly found that his own heart was pounding in his chest, and his own breathing rate was increasing involuntarily. 'This is ridiculous,' he decided to himself, and consciously forced his respiration rate back to a slower rhythm.

'I know that,' Bek replied, his voice cracking slightly, 'but somehow it doesn't seem to make any difference.'

'OK... OK... just relax for a minute or two and I'll see if I can do something to help a little.'

'Like what?' Bek asked dubiously.

'Just trust me, Bek. I know what I'm doing, and I have a trick or two up my sleeve. Before I do anything though, at all, though, I'm going to have to get you to swear an oath of secrecy.'

'An oath of secrecy? Great Tarmin, Calvyn! What on

earth are you going to do?'

'Look, you trusted me once before, and I managed to help you successfully then. All I want is for you to promise that you'll speak to no one about what happens down here. I know that you are an honourable person, and I'd trust you with anything. Just give me your promise that if I help you now to get over your fear, you'll tell no one about how I did it, and I, in turn, will promise you that what I am going to do will in no way harm you. Will you swear?'

'Very well, Calvyn, if you really insist, then I promise,' answered Bek, who was more than a little intrigued by Calvyn's request.

'All right, now see if you can find a loose stone somewhere. Any size or shape will do.'

'A stone?' queried Bek.

'Just help me find a stone, Bek. You'll understand soon enough.'

'OK.'

The two young men fumbled around for a minute or two before Calvyn found what he needed. As he crawled along the floor towards the door his left hand came to rest on a loose pebble that was not much bigger than a marble.

'It's all right, Bek, you can stop your search. I've found just what I needed,' Calvyn said in a voice so quiet that it was barely more than a whisper.

'Great,' Bek replied. 'What do you want me to do now?'

'Just sit back on your bunk, close your eyes, and whatever you do, don't interrupt me for the next few minutes as I'm going to need all the concentration that I can muster,' ordered Calvyn as he felt his way back to his own bunk.

Turning the stone over and over in his hands, Calvyn built a mental image of the stone that he had never seen. Then, closing his own eyes to help his focus, the Novice Magician softly began his light spell. As he pronounced each rune Calvyn pictured a gentle white light emanating from his pebble, and without pausing he completed the spell which would lock the light in place before opening his eyes.

It took a moment for Calvyn to be able to see much beyond his hand where the small stone was emitting a muted glow. As his eyes adjusted, though, he found that he could just about make out the seated figure of Bek sitting a few feet away.

'All right, Bek, you can open your eyes again now,' advised Calvyn softly.

'What the...?'

'Shhh! Just give your eyes a while to adjust, and you should be able to see enough to allay any fears.'

'What did you do to it?' whispered Bek.

'I just used a trick that an old friend taught me, that's all,' answered Calvyn evasively.

'Magic, you mean.'

'If you want to label it as magic then fine, but just don't tell anyone about this, OK? If it were to get out then I could be in a lot worse situation than the one that we're in here,' Calvyn whispered, gesturing around at their small cell.

'No one will hear anything from me, Calvyn. Great Tarmin though! A Magician! I knew that there was something different about you, but I just couldn't place my finger on it. You've always been so focused on everything that we've done, and your evening meditations... it all makes sense now.'

'I can assure you, Bek, that I am no Magician. I have had a few lessons along those lines, and that is all. I swear it.'

Calvyn went on to give a whispered explanation of his chance meeting and subsequent travels with Perdimonn. He finished the tale with the encounter and flight from Selkor, and a summary of his reasoning behind joining Baron Keevan's army. Bek sat wide-eyed throughout.

'So you see, I'm not really a magician, Bek, but nobody must discover my abilities or I could get into a lot of trouble. I still have no idea what happened to

Perdimonn, but I've got a strong... well... almost premonition that he's still alive somewhere. I can't really explain the feeling, but I *know* that Selkor didn't kill him.'

'What about Selkor though? If Perdimonn is still alive...'

'I have absolutely no idea, my friend. He could be dead. He might be alive. I strongly suspect the latter, and if by some chance he were dead, I would find it very hard to believe that Perdimonn could have killed him. Violence just isn't in his nature.'

They sat quietly for a while, each immersed in their own thoughts. It felt good to have been able to confide his secret with his friend, Calvyn decided. Despite being risky, he felt sure that Bek would never knowingly let him down, and the shared secret would bind them closer in times of trouble. Calvyn almost burst out laughing at that thought. 'Times of trouble!' If these were not times of trouble then what were?

'Er... Calvyn? What are we going to do with the stone when the jailer returns? It is a little conspicuous.'

'Don't worry, it won't be a problem. If we keep the stone over by the door, then when the jailer comes back, the orange light from his torch will make the light from the stone undetectable. That's why I only made the light very dim,' assured Calvyn.

'You think of everything, don't you?'

'I try my best,' he grinned. Then, rising from his bunk, Calvyn walked over to the door and wedged the glowing stone into a crack in the wall. 'That should do the trick,' he said in a satisfied voice, and returned to his bunk. With a cat-like stretch he carefully laid himself down on the uncomfortable bed. 'Try to get some sleep, Bek. Let's make the most of the situation.'

'OK. I'll try,' his friend replied, and despite everything, physical tiredness won them over. Within minutes both young men were deep in slumber.

CHAPTER 11

Approaching footsteps in the darkness alerted the two prisoners that something was about to happen. It was not the single set of footsteps that heralded the jailer bringing food, but the multiple footsteps of a group of people moving purposefully along the corridor towards the cell where the two young Recruits sat waiting.

'There's more than just the guard coming, Bek. Something's happening,' Calvyn whispered loudly.

The glimmer of orange torchlight appeared at the base of the door and the loud snap of the steel bolts being undone echoed in the darkness of the small cell. Both Calvyn and Bek shielded their eyes and turned their heads away from the door as the rattling of keys sounded in the double locks. The two detainees had learnt quickly that looking directly at the bright light of the jailer's torch had destroyed their night vision and left them seeing orange blobs before their eyes for up to an hour afterwards. Obviously this was not desirable in an environment which was perpetually dark, so they had learned to avoid direct eye contact with the burning flames.

The cell door swung open, and someone stepped into the room.

'It's over. We've got the real thief. You can leave now,' advised the soft gravelly voice of Corporal Derra. 'Come on, lads. Let's get you out of here and cleaned up.'

Relief flooded Calvyn's body as water permeates a sponge, flooding every last pore of him with a feeling of release. His knees felt weak as he struggled to his feet and he found that even when he did manage to stand he could hardly move.

'How long?' croaked Bek, his throat parched dry from lack of water.

'Five days you've been down here, but that's not important right now. Come along. The good Private here has got a large mug of water for each of you. Once you have drunk that we'll take you up to get cleaned up, changed and fed. No doubt you'll be ready for a decent meal.'

Nodding in agreement, Calvyn looked up at the Corporal through heavily squinted eyes, with his right hand held out as a shield to prevent direct line of sight with the torch burning in the doorway. The background light was too bright for him to make out her facial expression, but the familiar lithe outline of Derra's athletic frame was a welcome sight.

The Corporal offered a hand to Bek who still sat unmoving on his bunk and hauled him to his feet. A large beaker was placed in Calvyn's hand as soon as he had stumbled out into the corridor. Gratefully he drank. The water gushed past his lips and down his throat like a glacial stream in springtime, making his stomach cramp as the icy fluid burned its way down his parched gullet.

The gurgling gulp of Bek, downing his water in similar fashion, sounded loudly behind him, but he did not contemplate turning around until the last drop of his own cup was tilted into his mouth and swallowed. Calvyn let out a loud sigh of satisfaction.

'Better?' enquired Derra.

'Much. Thank you,' Calvyn replied.

He looked around, his eyes barely open but beginning to respond again to the enhanced stimuli. Bek was just finishing off his drink and the duty jailer was re-locking the cell door. Derra was watching them, her face characteristically unreadable.

'So, can you tell us who did it?' asked Calvyn, trying to determine his Corporal's mood.

179

'Garth,' she stated. 'Squad Three.'

Calvyn thought for a second, and then shook his head. 'Don't know him.'

'Yes you do,' corrected Bek immediately. 'He was the guy that you beat to reach the last eight of the inter-squad sword tournament last week. He obviously wasn't happy about it at the time, but I would never have thought that losing a sword-bout would have resulted in such a vindictive response.'

'If that's the case, then why you, Bek? I remember him now and I've watched virtually every one of your bouts but I don't remember you ever facing him.'

'You're both correct,' interrupted Derra. 'However, I believe that Bek's inclusion in Garth's scheme was due to a mixture of jealousy and opportunity. He was obviously jealous of your unbeaten record, Bek, and I'm told that he had held high hopes of being the best swordsman on his course when he arrived. His hopes were dashed when Kaan from Squad One beat him in the semi-finals of the first inter-squad tournament. Then, when you annihilated Kaan in the final, he realised that First Sword was not going to be a position that he would hold for some time, if ever.'

Taking the empty beakers, Derra beckoned them to follow her along the passageway towards the steps that would lead them up and out of their imprisonment.

'It seems that during his shift of guard duty the evening after last week's tournament, Garth heard Captain Tegrani playing his flute in his quarters,' Derra continued as she led the way out. 'He must have seen you playing yours on one of the rest days, Calvyn, because he put two and two together and hatched this vengeful little plot of his. You can consider yourself lucky that he couldn't keep his mouth shut, or it may well have succeeded. However, the fool couldn't resist telling one of his friends in Squad Three and that proved to be his undoing. His friend was as disgusted at his actions as the rest of us were and immediately turned the little sneak over to Corporal Beren. He's still being questioned but there's no doubt that he is guilty.'

'So are we going to have to be questioned at the Courts Martial?' Calvyn asked tentatively, almost dreading the answer.

'No, I would think that unlikely,' Derra answered slowly, as she pondered the question. 'Captain Tegrani may wish to speak with you again. If he's in a good mood then you may even get an apology. I'll be disappointed in him if you don't receive one.'

Calvyn almost laughed out loud at the thought of Derra being "disappointed" with Captain Tegrani, and decided that it would have made an interesting conversation to be a fly on the wall for.

'I wouldn't hold your breath for the apology though, lads,' she continued. 'The man is infernally busy and although he is unlikely to forget, I expect that the occasion may not arise for some time.'

Corporal Derra led them slowly up the steps until they emerged into the sweet smelling fresh air and the half-light of dusk. Both Calvyn and Bek drank in great lungfuls as they looked around appreciatively at the shadowy interior of the castle.

'The next call is for dinner, lads. I suggest that you go get cleaned up and changed. I'll see you in the morning for our pre-breakfast run. You've got some catching up to do on the weapons training, but don't concern yourselves too much with that for now. I'll schedule extra classes if I feel that you require them.'

'Thank you, Corporal Derra... for everything,' Calvyn said gratefully.

'We look after our own in this army, Recruits. Never forget that. However, if soldiers act without integrity and honour then they are punished severely as you will no doubt see when Recruit Garth gets a taste of the justice he deserves,' Derra replied, her eyes setting once more into the hard lines of an instructor. 'I need to have another word with the Private on prison duty. Go. Enjoy dinner.'

The two friends needed no further encouragement.

Derra turned and disappeared into the dark descending stairwell as Calvyn and Bek squared up alongside each other. With a concerted effort they attempted to force their stiff limbs to march as smartly as they could across the weapons training area, around the Baron's keep and across the echoing stone slabs of the drill square to their dormitory. Lights were already on inside their sleeping quarters and the sound of familiar voices became identifiable as they approached the door. Waiting outside for them a tall, lanky figure was standing half concealed in the shadows.

'Calvyn? Is that you?'

'Jez! I mean, Private Jez. Yes, it's me. It's good to see you again.'

Jez grinned, his friendly features lighting up his face and his recently cropped shock of ginger hair giving his appearance an added glow.

'Not half as good as it is to see you, my friend,' he replied. 'Corporal Derra explained everything to me and I did all I could to discover the rotten sleethe spawn who set you up. I really did. Unfortunately I found nothing. Believe me, I was so glad to get the Corporal's message just now saying that he'd been caught and that you were being released. I just had to drop by straight away to say thanks for trusting me. I won't forget that. I'm just sorry that I couldn't do more to help.'

Calvyn smiled wearily.

'Don't be sorry, Jez. I really appreciate that you were willing to try. Believe me it was good to know that there was someone out here who was on our side. Incidentally, have you met my friend Bek?'

'No. I don't believe I have,' Jez replied, turning to Bek and extending his hand in greeting. 'So you're the new swordsman that everyone's been talking about. It's nice to meet you, Bek.'

'Likewise, Private Jez.'

'So where did you get to be so good with a sword anyway? There's a lot of speculation but no one actually knows anything, I'm sure.'

'Well I'm not really *that* good,' Bek said modestly, 'but my father's a Captain in Lord Valdeer's army. He taught me swordplay from an early age, but I felt that if I joined the same army as he had, I would be either constantly in his shadow, or people would treat me differently because of my father. I didn't want that so I came here where I could be a little more anonymous, and succeed or fail on my own merits.'

'Understandable,' nodded Jez in tacit approval. 'Maybe we could try a practice bout or two together sometime. I'm not much good of course...'

He let the sentence peter out, a twinkle sparkling in his eye that told Bek that he was probably very good indeed. Bek laughed.

'I'd love to take you on, Private Jez. Assuming of course that Derra gives either of us any free time now that we've missed five days of her sadism!'

'Excellent. Well, I'd better get going. Duty calls and all that, but I won't forget that you placed your trust in me Calvyn. That means a lot to me. If ever you need anything, I'll gladly do my best to help.'

Unable to do anything but thank him again, Calvyn watched his friend walk off into the rapidly deepening shadows before opening the door to the dormitory and a veritable roar of greetings.

*   *   *   *   *

Twelve complete squads stood to attention on the drill square, two hundred and forty witnesses to the harsh justice system of army life. As Recruit Garth was led out and tied to the sturdy wooden post that had been erected in the centre of the parade ground, Calvyn reflected that it was only by good fortune that it was not he who was standing, all but naked, with the eyes of the castle looking on.

Baron Keevan himself, flanked by Captains Tegrani and Strexis, emerged from the main door to the keep and walked out onto the square. The Baron's eyes were like flint as he took the proffered scroll that Sergeant Brett held out for him. Keevan scanned the document quickly and silently, his face betraying no emotion. Without so much as a glance at the accused, the Baron began to read from the scroll in a loud, clear voice that projected around the castle grounds with a volume that even a drill instructor would have been proud of.

'My Court has found you, Recruit Garth of the Province of Kelldorn, guilty: firstly, stealing personal effects from an officer; and secondly, attempting to use the said effects to incriminate your fellow Recruits of theft. This kind of devious behaviour is not tolerable in any society, and especially not in a military one. Trust in one's fellow soldiers is essential, and your actions have clearly shown that you are unworthy of any trust whatsoever. I therefore sentence you to fifty strokes of the rod and expulsion from training. Moreover, a letter will be sent to every Baron and Lord in the north of Thrandor detailing your shameful actions, and you will be branded on the right cheek with the sign of a thief.'

The Baron rolled up the scroll and handed it back to Sergeant Brett.

'Carry on, Sergeant,' he ordered.

Brett saluted, and spun around in an immaculately smart about-turn. He marched briskly into position alongside the flogging post, halted and addressed Corporal Beren who stood behind his convicted Recruit, rod in hand.

'The sentence is a count of fifty strokes,' he boomed. 'Begin on my count... ONE.'

Calvyn, together with many others, flinched at the whistling crack of the five-foot birch rod as it connected with Garth's back. The next few minutes were not pleasant. Garth's screams etched themselves into Calvyn's memory as he closed his eyes and wished with all his heart that he could close his ears as easily.

'FORTY NINE... FIFTY.'

The final smack of the rod sounded, and Calvyn shuddered a quiet sigh of relief, his eyes still tightly closed.

'PARADE... DIS... MISS!'

Making the half turn to the right, Calvyn opened his eyes and was gratified to see that many of his fellow squad members had faces the colour of parchment. Unable to so much as glance at the sorry figure being hauled away from the flogging post towards the smithy, Calvyn turned and walked straight to the door of the dormitory. Without pausing to close the door behind him, he walked to his bed and sat down. He felt sick.

The sound of footsteps alerted him to the fact that he was not the only one to come straight back. Jenna sat down on the bed beside him, and without saying a word she placed an empathic hand on his shoulder.

'Pretty grim, wasn't it?' she said in a subdued voice.

'You could say that,' Calvyn replied, his elbows firmly planted on his knees and his face in his hands. 'The worst thing was that with every stroke of the rod I kept thinking that it was so nearly me on that post. I all but felt each strike... and do you know what saved me from it? Do you?'

Calvyn paused and looked up at Jenna, tears streaking his cheeks. Her gentle brown eyes looked solemnly into his as she gave an almost imperceptible shake of her head.

'Bek and his family,' he said, his voice faltering slightly in a half sob. 'If Garth had just picked on me, he would have almost certainly succeeded. No one would have believed me. But Bek... it couldn't have been Bek! His father is a Captain. Did you know that? Dammit all, Jenna! What am I doing here? What have I done that merits being set up like that? Am I going to spend my entire time here dodging vindictive little snipes like Garth?'

'Hey! Calm down, Calvyn,' soothed Jenna. 'Let's get back to reality here, shall we? Even if nobody had believed you, Garth would still have been caught. Don't lose sight of the fact that it was one of his own that turned him in. The man is a fool. What's more, none of us ever believed for one second that you were guilty. Even Derra went straight on the defensive for you if you remember, and did she know about Bek's father? No, I thought not. As for what you're doing here... you're turning into a damn fine soldier, so snap out of it... Squad Leader! Yes, I know about it. Bek told me. You're a good man, Calvyn, and you will make one hell of a good Squad Leader. In many ways you've been our leader from day one anyway, but it's good to see that it's being made official.'

Calvyn placed his hand over the one that Jenna still had on his shoulder. He managed a weak smile of gratitude.

'Thanks, Jenna.'

'Any time, friend. And if any other idiot ever tries to set you up, you can bet your last copper penny that Squad Two will not rest until you are vindicated.'

'Nice touch,' he said, lifting one eyebrow in a sarcastic gesture, but his mouth betrayed a slight smile that gave the clue that he was teasing her.

'I mean it, you dim wit,' Jenna replied, and punched him gently with her other hand.

'And I appreciate it. Really. Thanks again. I feel a lot better, but I don't know whether I'm going to be able to face lunch after that.'

'Call the medics,' Jenna half shouted jokingly. 'Calvyn's refusing food. It must be serious!'

They both laughed at that.

* * * * *

It had not stopped raining for the best part of a week, and the leaden grey sky showed little sign of relenting. All of the Recruits were gathered in front of the castle preparing for the team obstacle challenge. Water sheeted out of the sky in torrents as each squad held a final tactical conference before the race.

'OK, boys and girls, we've all been through this a hundred times or more. You know what to do. Let's show the other squads what teamwork is all about. Any questions? No? Good. And one last thing... be careful! The course is a quagmire, so take it easy over the obstacles. Any heroics will probably result in injuries that will only slow us down. Remember: smooth, slick and methodical. Understand? To your places then. Let's go,' ordered Calvyn.

Squad Two split from their conference huddle and gathered their equipment to the start line. Each squad had to carry two long ladders, five long pieces of rope, two small tree trunks (each about fifteen feet long and about eight inches in diameter) and a stretcher with a weighted dummy strapped to it. At first sight it did not seem too daunting a load to share between twenty fit young men and women. However, the reality was a different story. Over a distance of four miles, with several major obstacles to negotiate, the equipment would quickly begin to feel as if it was made of lead. The added difficulty of the soft muddy ground and the gusty wind, laden with streaming rain, would make it a doubly tough challenge.

'SQUADS READY... GO!' hollered Sergeant Brett at the top of his voice.

At the executive word of command the three squads leapt forward and set forth across the muddy field towards the first of the obstacles. The pace was fast, but not blisteringly so. All of the teams were fairly evenly matched when it came down to straight fitness, so there was virtually nothing between the three squads across the first three quarters of a mile of fields. The real differences started to show in the different interpretations that the three squad leaders had about teamwork.

Squads one and three stuck together rigidly, and approached each obstacle as a group. Calvyn had different ideas for Squad Two.

As a team, Calvyn and his squad had discussed the relative strengths and weaknesses of each of their members. Having graded everyone's strengths, they had brainstormed each obstacle in turn and formulated a plan to safely negotiate it in the most expeditious manner possible. Once everyone had agreed on the plan it had been practise, refine, practise, refine, until the squad barely had to pause at the obstacles at all.

The first hurdle was the ten foot high section of wall that had been purpose built for this competition. All of the teams used similar techniques to get their people and equipment over, but the difference showed in their execution.

At a predetermined point about four hundred yards before the wall, the four best runners in Squad Two sprinted ahead with the two ladders which were then placed against the wall about six feet apart. They did so under the watchful eye of Corporal Gan who was the designated Obstacle Marshall. Two of the four then went straight up the ladders and over the wall whilst the other two braced the foot of the steps. With about one hundred yards to go to the wall, the two strongest remaining members of the team also sprinted ahead and climbed two thirds of the way up the ladder before stopping to await the rest of the group. On arrival at the wall, the two stretcher bearers, aided by a third man, heaved the stretcher up between the ladders for the two strong men to grab and manhandle over the top to the two sets of waiting hands on the other side. Rather than then going over themselves, the two strong men remained astride the wall between the two ladders and facing inwards towards one another. The two tree trunks were propped against the wall between them. They waited whilst the bulk of the group scaled the ladders and dropped with consecutive splats into the thick mud on the other side. Simultaneously, the ropes were systematically thrown over the wall to one side of the ladders, and gathered and distributed by those on the other side.

Once everyone was over except for the two men on the wall and the two bracing the ladders, the ladder men lifted the ladders out of the sucking mud and tilted them over the top of the wall. Whilst the team members on the other side dragged the ladders away, the two remaining men yet to scale the wall prepared to lift the first of the tree trunks.

'Clear!' called one of the men on the wall.

'Now,' grunted one of the lifters as they heaved the thick wooden pole upwards. At the same instant that the pole reached the top of its upward motion, the two men on the wall grabbed it and flipped it over the top.

'Clear,' came the call again, and the process was repeated. All equipment now over, first one and then the other of the two remaining squad members reached up to the waiting hands of the two astride the wall, who hauled the ladder men unceremoniously over the top before dropping down themselves.

All three teams made easy work of the wall, but Calvyn's initiative of sending the ladders ahead had saved them a few valuable seconds which allowed Squad Two to get away marginally in the lead. By the time that they reached the penultimate obstacle, it was a two horse race between Squads Two and Three, with Squad Two holding a marginal advantage. Squad One had incurred time penalties at the previous two obstacles and was now, barring a complete disaster striking the other two teams, out of the running.

Wet, sticky mud clung heavily to everyone's boots, making every step a struggle. The wind and rain made every mile feel like five as the Recruits battled against the course, the other teams and the elements.

The final two obstacles were both within sight of the finish line, which awaited them at the road outside the main gates. The first was a stream crossing while the second was a large ground net. The rules were simple: all people and equipment had to cross the stream without touching the water and then scramble underneath the ground net before the final dash to the finish line.

Squads Two and Three approached the ten foot wide stream almost simultaneously, but once again Calvyn had sent his best runners ahead to prepare the way. Even as the main body of the squad approached, a ladder had been laid as a bridge from bank to bank. Also, two ropes were being held at waist height, stretched taught by

Recruits pulling on opposite ends. The ropes were not intended to prevent people from falling as much as to offer the confidence booster of having something to grab at in the event of someone losing their balance slightly whilst crossing the ladder bridge.

The preparation gave Squad Two the edge that they needed to hold on to their slight lead, and the team were all crossing smoothly when the mistake came. Halfway across the ladder, Tondi's muddy boot slipped off the rung that she had just put her weight forward onto, and she pitched headlong into the cold water of the stream.

'Time penalty. Squad Two will hold for a count of ten before leaving this obstacle,' shouted out Derra, who was the Obstacle Marshall.

'Are you all right?' called Calvyn anxiously to Tondi from the far bank.

'Fine,' assured Tondi, picking herself up and shaking her head slightly as if to shed some of the water from her hair.

'Quick! Get back and cross again,' encouraged Calvyn urgently.

Tondi did not need asking twice, and waded as fast as she could back out of the thigh deep water and scrambled back up the bank to the ladder. This time she crossed without incident, and with the last of the team hot on her heels, the last of the equipment was hauled across and the time penalty began.

'ONE... TWO...'

'I'm sorry, guys,' apologised Tondi, who watched with dismay as Squad Three completed their flawless stream crossing and set off towards the final obstacle.

'FIVE... SIX...'

'Don't beat yourself up over it, we can still take them,' panted Bek with a grin. 'Besides, I needed a break anyway.'

'NINE... TEN.'

Squad Two raced forwards and up the hill towards the final obstacle. Jenna and Calvyn led the way, sprinting ahead of the rest of the squad and diving under the front edge of the ground net. However, instead of crawling forward towards the far side, both halted and arched their backs as high as they could to lift the net and form a bridge between them. The next pair dived in under the raised front of the net between Calvyn and Jenna, crawled about halfway to the other side, and then they too moved aside and arched their backs to help form a tunnel under the net for the next pair. The third pair of Squad Two went almost to the far side and repeated the procedure to form a completely raised tunnel under the net.

Calvyn looked across to where Squad Three had used exactly the same tactic, and his face broke into a grin as he saw two of the opposition struggling through the net with the team stretcher.

'We've got 'em,' he said in a quiet voice to Jenna.

'Haven't we just,' she replied, her eyes sparkling with amusement.

Squad Two poured under the net in a rapid stream, two abreast, and rapidly assembled on the other side of the net. However, the only piece of equipment that they took with them was one of the five ropes. Matim, Tyrrak and two of the others had remained behind, busily tying the remaining four ropes to the two arms of the stretcher and to the two tree trunks, whilst the rest of the team scrambled to the other side. Having secured one end of each rope to the equipment, the opposite end of each was then secured around the waists of the four Recruits who then also went under the net in pairs.

The first of the final two pairs was attached to the two arms of the stretcher. The coils of slack rope gradually unravelled as the Recruits crawled through the mud to the other side of the net. On reaching the far side, the two stood up, took up the last of the slack and ran forward, dragging the stretcher like a sled behind them. The stretcher skidded easily under the net and was followed rapidly by the final pair of Recruits tied to the tree trunks. Half a dozen other team members helped to drag the heavy poles under the net, and in no time flat,

Squad Two had reassembled, untied the equipment and left Squad Three floundering in the mud.

On reaching the finish line, Calvyn had his team stack the equipment neatly, form up smartly as if on parade, and brought them all to attention. Then he whirled about, marched up to Sergeant Brett, saluted, and using every decibel that he could muster, announced that Squad Two was "Task Complete".

'Well done, Squad Leader. Stand them at ease,' Sergeant Brett responded formally.

'Sergeant,' Calvyn acknowledged, and turned once more to face his Squad. 'Squad Two, stand at... ease!'

Chests still heaving for breath, Squad Two complied, and then watched with pleasure as Squad Three laboured up to the finish line whilst Squad One was still only just beginning to tackle the ground net.

Corporal Derra walked up the slope from the stream where her job as Marshall was now complete. The catlike grace of the Corporal's fast gait brought her striding rapidly up to where Calvyn and the others waited.

'Dammit! Does that bitch never smile?' muttered someone from behind Calvyn.

Almost as if in answer to the question, Derra's face softened from her customary frown into a wickedly mischievous grin just as she came to a halt in front of her squad.

'Good job, Squad Two. Good job,' she said, her mirth evident in her voice. 'I thought you'd blown it down there at the stream, but that was an excellent tactic at the net. I've never seen the ropes used like that before, but I've got a funny feeling that I might be seeing it again in the future. You can be sure that Squad Three are going to wish that they had thought of it in about a minute's time,' she added, nodding back down the slope to where Corporal Beren was striding up purposefully toward his squad.

'Go get washed up and take the rest of the afternoon off. Squad One will get to put all this equipment away. Practice swords and bows will be available from the armoury for any that wish to put in any last minute work before tomorrow's final inter-squad tournaments. March them back to the barracks, Squad Leader.'

'Yes, Corporal. Squad Two atten... shun. To the left, left... turn. By the left, quick... march.'

Calvyn marched Squad Two in through the main gate and around to the barrack room door where he dismissed them. Everyone pulled off their muddy boots and put them down just outside the door. Once inside, all formality dissolved, and the air was filled with laughter and whoops of victory as the excited babble of competing voices discussed the finer points of the race.

'Any chance of some last ditch practice later, Bek?' Calvyn asked his friend, slapping him jovially on the back.

'No problem. Give me an hour or so to get myself cleaned up, and the worst of this filth off my clothes, and I'll do battle 'til the sun goes down if you wish,' replied Bek with an extravagant bow.

Calvyn laughed.

'I'll be lucky to have enough energy to last ten minutes after that run! Besides, I want to hold enough back to be able to beat your sorry butt in the tournament tomorrow.'

'Ah ha!' exclaimed Bek in a loud voice, drawing the attention of several of the other Recruits around the dormitory. 'The Squad Leader seeks to challenge the supreme arm of the First Sword!'

Many of the other squad members made loud 'Ooooo' of light-hearted encouragement at the banter between the two friends, and Calvyn smiled in amusement at the reaction.

'It's time somebody took your supreme arm down a peg or two, Mister First Sword, and if nobody else can be bothered to do it, then I will,' said Calvyn, and then stuck his tongue hard against his left cheek.

Those looking on laughed at the gesture.

'One hour then.'

'With pleasure!'

'You don't seriously think that you can beat him, do

you?' asked Jenna as Calvyn walked down to his bunk.

'Are you kidding? Not in a million years! Bek and I have practised together a lot over the last few weeks and I've never even come close to touching him. However, our sessions on the practice grounds have certainly sharpened me up no end and another quick practice before tomorrow won't do me any harm.'

'Oh, I just thought that I caught a hint of serious challenge in that bit of banter, that's all.'

'Hey! Never write me off completely. Bek isn't unbeatable, and if I get far enough in the tournament tomorrow to meet him, he won't be getting any favours from me. I intend to win out there. Let's get realistic for a second, though. Bek has remained undefeated throughout the last five months. No one has even got close to him. My chances can't be rated as great! They're certainly not as good as yours in the archery.'

'I shouldn't wager too heavily on me winning if I were you. Tamar has as much of a stranglehold on First Bow as Bek has on First Sword.'

'You could beat Tamar if you just forgot about him and concentrated on putting those arrows in the middle of the targets. There isn't a shot in the competition that you couldn't make.'

'Maybe, but as many as I hit, Tamar hits more. The man has a heart of ice and a bow arm made of granite. I've never seen anything so steady in my life.'

Calvyn sat down on his bed and started to unbutton his mud-coated tunic. He paused, and looked up into Jenna's serious brown eyes with a friendly smile.

'That's why you can't beat him, Jenna. You look at him and watch him shoot. Don't. For tomorrow's competition, blank out all thoughts of Tamar and his scores. You can be sure that I won't be thinking about him or you as I let my arrows fly.'

'What? Not even a little bit?' asked Jenna, and her hands went to the top buttons of her tunic suggestively, her face twisting into a coy smile.

Calvyn choked slightly, and his cheeks flushed bright

red.

'I thought you might,' Jenna laughed.

'That's not fair! And it's not what I meant!'

'I know. That's why you're such a good friend, Calvyn. Your honesty and genuine care for others have made you both an excellent Squad Leader and the best friend that any of us could ever want. Good luck for tomorrow, and I'll do my best to take your advice and ignore Tamar. You never know, we might pull off a famous double upset.'

Calvyn grinned.

'Now wouldn't that be something?' he chuckled.

CHAPTER 12

Calvyn was tired. It had been a good morning, with plenty of success for Squad Two in the final inter-squad competitions. The weather had been particularly kind. The rain that had plagued the Recruits for the previous six days had given way to clear skies, and the sun had lifted everyone's spirits without making the air so hot as to make this culmination of the months of training unbearable.

It was just perfect, Calvyn thought to himself as he joined the queue for lunch. The line for food was quite long as he began the orderly wait, and he was tempted to just sit down and wait for the rush to subside. However, the Recruits were all buzzing with the events of the day, and before he had a chance to move, Calvyn found himself included in the excitement, making his tiredness fall away like a dropped cloak.

'Great fight, Calvyn! Brilliant! That's some of the best swordplay that you've ever produced in the comps,' Bek enthused, giving Calvyn a hearty slap on the back as he strolled jauntily up to the back of the line.

Jenna was hard on his heels, wearing a grin that threatened to split her face in two.

'Make way. Make way. The mighty First Bow wishes to dine,' teased Calvyn in a loud voice, genuflecting in mock worship towards her at the same time.

Everyone around him laughed and joined in with the fun. All around bowed in pretend homage to the highly embarrassed Jenna.

'Enough! Enough! You can all pay as much tribute as you like after I've had some food to fortify my grumbling stomach. I'm starving,' protested Jenna, waving her hands in a shooing gesture and doing her best to assume a haughty voice and an imperious stance.

'Now that is definitely *not* the same Jenna that I met five months ago!' stated Calvyn in an overacted aside to Bek.

'No! You're right. She must be an impostor,' Bek joked back. 'Quick, grab her!'

A rapidly raised warning finger halted Bek and Calvyn in their tracks, as Jenna's face took on a frown, but she only managed to hold the pose for a couple of seconds before bursting out laughing. First Calvyn and then Bek gave her a congratulatory hug.

'You were awesome out there this morning,' Calvyn stated with feeling. 'Poor old Tamar couldn't believe his eyes when you hit that third long range moving target in a row! His face looked as if your arrow had smacked straight through that icy heart of his.'

'Tamar? Who's he?' asked Jenna innocently.

They all laughed again.

'Hey, you didn't do so badly yourself, Calvyn. I did just happen to notice a few of your arrows hitting their marks as well. Where did you come in the end?'

'Oh, about fifth, I think,' replied Calvyn modestly.

'Fifth out of sixty-one is certainly no disgrace,' stated Jenna.

'You came fifth in the archery!' exclaimed Bek in surprise. 'And you're into the last eight of the sword tournament! You are having a good day.'

'Yes, I can't complain. What's more, I've got Tyrrak in the quarter finals straight after lunch, and I fancy my chances against him this time.'

'Now that's a match to look forward to!' chortled Jenna. 'I'd love to see you kick his butt after he gloated so much last time he beat you.'

'And if you beat him, you'll not only have got further than you've ever been in the tournaments before, but

197

you'll get another crack at me,' grinned Bek, waggling his eyebrows with the anticipation of another challenge.

'Don't get too cocky, my friend. You've still got to beat Garret yet, and he's no mean opponent,' advised Calvyn seriously.

Bek sniffed derisively, and then thought about it for a few seconds before replying.

'You're right of course, but I have no intention of losing to anyone today, and definitely not to Garret.'

'How did you do with the sword, Jenna?' Calvyn enquired. 'I'm afraid that I didn't see you fight.'

'Oh, I met Kaan in the second round. I only lasted a few seconds. He was like lightning,' she answered with a shrug. 'But Tondi has held up the flag for the Squad Two girls in the hunt for First Sword.'

'Is she still in?' asked Calvyn in surprise.

'Yes. She beat that tall guy from Squad One in the third round. He looked as surprised as hell when she disarmed him,' Jenna chuckled.

'I'll bet he did!' Calvyn said with a grin. 'So, four out of the last eight left in the sword competition are from Squad Two. A good morning's work I'd say.'

'Is that old mother hen Calvyn I hear clucking around his fledglings?' taunted Bek, putting a hand to his ear and looking up at the ceiling as if listening hard.

There were a few sniggers at that, but Calvyn refused to rise to the bait and casually ignored them.

'So Tondi must have got Kaan in the quarter finals then,' Calvyn said thoughtfully.

Jenna nodded.

'Well, I have to say that the odds favour Kaan, but that won't stop me from cheering Tondi on. That would be one upset that would really change the tournament if she could beat him.

'You can say that again,' agreed Jenna. 'It would be a minor miracle, but stranger things have happened.'

The three friends reached the front of the queue at that point. They collected their food in short order, and made their way to three adjacent empty seats at one of the long mess hall tables. The chatter continued right through lunch about who beat whom in the sword tournament, and who had hit which targets in the archery. There was also a lot of speculation on the unarmed combat competition that would finish off the day's events. Somewhat surprisingly considering her slim build, Jenna had always out performed both Calvyn and Bek in the field of unarmed combat, and she was the only one of the three who was really looking forward to it. Calvyn had developed a fair amount of muscle over the previous five months of training, and all vestiges of any fat had long since disappeared. However, he had never managed to develop Jenna's speed and balance when it came to hand to hand combat, and whenever he had practised with her or met her in competition, he had invariably come off worst.

Today it was Calvyn who could not finish his lunch. His stomach was bunched with anticipation at his impending duel with Tyrrak for a place in the semi-finals, and Jenna took great delight in pulling his leg over it.

'You'll never grow up to be a big strong lad if you don't eat your greens,' she teased, as Calvyn pushed the plate away. 'And I'll be forced to dump that sorry undernourished excuse for a body of yours in the dust again this afternoon.'

'You may well do just that,' acceded Calvyn with a grin, 'but you're going to have to find a few new tricks to do it.'

'Oho! All this success must have gone to his head,' Jenna chuckled. 'Give him a shake, would you, Bek? He seems to be daydreaming, and he's going to need to wake up for his match with Tyrrak in a few minutes.'

The friendly repartee continued until the eight remaining contenders for the title of First Sword were handed their weapons about a quarter of an hour later. During the previous rounds there had been at least four contests being fought at any one time, but for the final stages a single fighting area had been marked out in the centre of the sandy weapons training area. The Recruits who were no longer in the competition, together with many of the off-duty Privates, all lined the area to cheer on their squad mates, and a buzz of anticipation swept through the crowd as the quarter finalists began to run through a quick series of warm up exercises.

To many of the Recruits' surprise, a length of one side of the perimeter was cleared and five wooden chairs were placed in a line at the edge of the duelling area. The buzz increased in volume as speculation ran riot over which captains and Segeants would be spectating. Virtually all the Recruits were surprised when the Baron himself, together with all four of his resident Captains, appeared from the keep.

The butterflies that had been causing havoc with Calvyn's appetite suddenly redoubled their efforts as he noticed the latest additions to his audience. It took all of his months of mental control exercises to calm his nervousness. However, once the first two contestants were called forward, Calvyn found that his tension dissolved and was replaced with a deep sense of calm and self-confidence.

Bek and Garret were up first. The ritual salute of blades was made, and the match began. The clashing ring of steel brought a loud cheer of encouragement from the rest of the Recruits, each shouting for their favourite. Calvyn, though, found himself watching the Baron and his Captains, who sat quietly intent. No flicking blow escaped their notice. Every change in poise or balance was keenly followed by those five sets of impassive eyes. The only one who appeared to have any emotional involvement was Captain Tegrani, who gave a tight smile of satisfaction when Bek turned aside Garret's attack and nicked him with a winning touch on the chest. Squad Two let out a huge cheer as Bek raised his sword in salute, first to his beaten opponent and then to the Baron, before walking smartly out of the fighting area.

'Recruits Tyrrak and Calvyn,' called Sergeant Brett, who was acting as referee.

Calvyn forced himself to relax, and made his way

forward to the centre of the duelling area. Smartly raising his sword in salute to the Baron, he turned and repeated the gesture to Tyrrak, who was mirroring his actions.

'Begin,' instructed the Sergeant in a loud voice.

Tyrrak leapt forward to take the initiative by making a strong and fast attack, evidently attempting to finish the fight quickly and with the minimum of effort. His attack succeeded in bringing the fight to a swift conclusion, but not with the result that he was expecting.

Calvyn had spent weeks practising with Bek, and as a result, his reactions were razor sharp. Almost without thinking, he twisted one of Tyrrak's attacking strokes away, and in the blink of an eye he struck not one, but two winning strokes, before catching his opponent's blade on its return stroke.

The encounter had lasted but a few seconds, and Tyrrak was obviously having a few problems coming to terms with how easily he had been defeated. Having dealt the winning strokes, Calvyn jumped back and began to salute, only to find Tyrrak still attacking. Neatly catching his squad mate's blade on his own once more, Calvyn slid the blade down his adversary's until they were hilt to hilt, locked together in a straining fight for supremacy of sheer strength.

'Stop, you fool! It's over,' muttered Calvyn through clenched teeth.

'HOLD!' called the Sergeant a second later. 'Match to Recruit Calvyn.'

Most of Squad Two, together with many from the other two squads, let out a huge cheer. Tyrrak, it appeared, had not won many supporters amongst his peers.

Grudgingly Tyrrak pushed away from Calvyn and, with the most cursory of salutes, he stomped away. Calvyn found himself saluting his erstwhile opponent's back, but refused to have his moment of glory rushed. He therefore smartly turned towards the Baron and offered him a salute whilst the rest of the Recruits continued their loud and enthusiastic clapping, cheering and whistling approval of the rapid victory.

'That was amazing!' Jenna exclaimed, running up to Calvyn as he walked out of the square. 'I don't think that even Bek could have finished Tyrrak that quickly!'

'Sure he could. Tyrrak just made exactly the same arrogant assumptions that he always makes,' Calvyn stated in a "matter-of-fact" tone. 'That guy just never learns... but I do, and I wasn't going to let him get away with exactly the same tactics that he beat me with last time.'

'Well, he is certainly not going to forget that drubbing in a hurry! That loss is going to smart for some time – especially as he was dealt it in such august company,' Jenna replied, with a nod in the direction of the Baron.

Calvyn followed her nod with his eyes to find that the Baron was still looking directly at him with an unreadable expression on his face. Almost guiltily, Calvyn turned his eyes back to look at Jenna, whose face was still beaming with enthusiasm. Her large brown eyes were really most attractive with that sparkle of enjoyment in them, he decided, and then shook himself slightly, mildly annoyed that he had managed to be distracted so easily.

'Did you notice Bek's face after you won?' Jenna half whispered.

Calvyn shook his head almost imperceptibly, and forced himself not to look around immediately for Bek.

'He's sobered up a bit after his little bragging session at lunch time,' she continued. 'He was obviously happy that you'd won, but there was definitely surprise there as well. I think that you've got him worried... speak of the devil...'

'Great win again, Calvyn. That was some turn of speed you pulled off there.'

'I had a good teacher.'

'Yeah, well, this teacher was more than a little humbled. I'm looking forward even more to our match later on,' Bek replied, but his voice lacked a little conviction as he shook Calvyn's hand in a congratulatory gesture, and Calvyn just caught a hint of self doubt in his friend's eyes.

The next match started, and cheers of support broke out for the two new contenders. However, Calvyn now had a lot to think about, and his attention wandered as the closely fought match waxed and waned. The victor, one Geldarian from Squad One, also proved a popular winner with the crowd, and was given a massive cheer as he made his final salute.

'Recruits Tondi and Kaan,' called Sergeant Brett, bringing Calvyn out of his reverie.

'Sort him out, Tondi!' yelled someone, inducing a smattering of giggles and sniggers from the crowd.

The customary niceties were conducted, and the contest began. Calvyn, Jenna and the rest of Squad Two all gave maximum volume to their support of their team mate, but despite acquitting herself well, Tondi was clearly outclassed from the outset. The inevitable ending took a bit longer to come than Calvyn felt was absolutely necessary. Kaan, it seemed, liked to play to the crowd and toy with his victims a little before finishing them off. That was a dangerous habit to get into, mused Calvyn to himself. Kaan might not live to regret a habit like that if it ever came to a matter of life or death.

As Tondi made her way out of the duelling area, Calvyn gave her a pat on the shoulder.

'Good effort, Tondi. He's a tough opponent,' Calvyn said in a conciliatory voice.

'Thanks, and good luck yourself,' she replied with a disappointed little smile that spoke volumes. 'You're gonna need it,' she muttered under her breath as she turned away.

Although he realised that he had not been meant to hear the tagged-on comment, Calvyn also appreciated that it was not meant in a derogatory fashion. Tondi was merely stating a fact. He would need all the luck that he could find against Bek.

'First semi-final. Recruits Bek and Calvyn,' Sergeant Brett boomed over the noise of the spectators.

Calvyn and Bek walked forward into the centre of the square and carried out the ritual salutes. Strangely, Calvyn felt no nerves this time. Whether it was because he had already fought and prevailed against Tyrrak, he was not sure. However, it was with a clear calm mind and heart that he faced his friend, sword at the ready.

'Begin,' boomed out the loud command.

Blades flashing their deadly dance, the song of metal on metal sang out once more as the two friends applied every ounce of their skill towards the goal of a place in the final. The shouts of the crowd went unnoticed as the two circled each other, blades in constant motion as the fiercely quick tempo of the fight was unrelenting for several minutes. Bek pressed home attack after attack only to find each stroke countered swiftly and surely by Calvyn's blade. In turn Calvyn's attacks were met by an equally solid defence.

The match hung in the balance, neither having a clear advantage. The crowd was going wild, with screams of encouragement reaching fever pitch. They had not seen Bek so hard pushed since Derra had beaten him during the first weapons training session, and as is often the case, were doing their utmost to lift the underdog. Calvyn, however, was oblivious to everything but Bek. He remained completely focused, not wavering in his concentration for so much as a second as he coolly turned aside everything that Bek tried.

Driving home a blindingly fast attack of his own, Calvyn reacted automatically as he saw Bek stumble back slightly. Leaning his weight forward into a lunge, Calvyn realised that he had been suckered into a trap as Bek's blade swung under his stabbing thrust and whistled towards his midriff. In a contortion that surprised even himself, Calvyn sucked in his stomach and arched his back away from the sword tip whilst twisting his own blade into a slice at Bek's upper arm. Both men felt material rip as Calvyn's blade tore Bek's sleeve and Bek's blade sliced through the front of Calvyn's tunic.

'Hold,' called Sergeant Brett somewhat unnecessarily, as the two opponents backed off to assess the damage.

Calvyn's eyes locked with Bek's as the Sergeant came in to inspect both combatants for the cut that would end the contest. With a grin, Calvyn gave Bek an almost imperceptible shake of his head as he unbuttoned the front of his tunic for the Sergeant to see his unbroken skin. The grin was returned as Bek rolled up his torn sleeve to reveal that he too was unmarked.

'No score,' called the Sergeant. 'Continue.'

The rest of the Recruits had quietened to a breathless whisper of anticipation as Sergeant Brett had made his inspection, expectant murmurs running right around the square. With the call of 'continue', a resounding wave of cheers reverberated around the castle, and the clashing, spinning contest recommenced.

The next stumble came a short while later, and this time it was no ruse. Calvyn felt his ankle turn as he side-stepped, and instantly knew that he would not recover in time. Sure enough, Bek's blade snaked in and nicked Calvyn's arm as he staggered off balance. As soon as he felt the touch of the blade, Calvyn raised his own in acknowledgement of the winning point.

Both Recruits were breathing hard as they turned to pay their respects to the Baron. To Calvyn's amazement all four of the Captains, and the Baron himself, were all wearing smiles of obvious enjoyment at the bout that they had just witnessed, and all were clapping their applause enthusiastically. The wash of noise suddenly swept over him as the cheers of approval from his peers broke through to his conscious mind

'I almost wished that we hadn't practised together for a while there,' Bek laughed as they walked out of the square. 'You were very unlucky to lose the way that you did.'

'You still had to get the winning cut in... which you did. It was a good match. Just make sure that you don't make any mistakes in the final. OK?'

'You've got it, Squad Leader!'

Shortly afterwards, Calvyn found himself the centre of attention as many of the other Recruits offered their commiserations at his loss. Without exception the comments were all focused on how close he had come to victory. The tear in Bek's sleeve was the nearest that any of his fellow Recruits had ever come to beating him in a one-on-one sword fight since they had started training five months previously. Calvyn was a bit overwhelmed, and was more than a little relieved when the second semi-final drew the attention of his fellow Recruits away from him.

The rest of the competition was fairly predictable. Kaan completely outclassed Geldarian, and whilst the final between Bek and Kaan was hard fought, the outcome was almost inevitable. It was almost as if Kaan had got used to being beaten by Bek in the final, and for all his speed and style he never really looked like winning. Bek had once again retained his title as First Sword.

Once the final had finished, the Baron and his Captains made their way back to the keep, smiling and chatting animatedly to one another as they went. The draw was then announced for the unarmed combat competition and four circles were drawn out, one in each corner of the weapons training area. The bouts began shortly thereafter and continued right through until the early evening when the final was fought between two members of Squad Three who had dominated throughout. Bek and Calvyn had both lost to one of the two finalists, Bek in the second round, and Calvyn in the third. Jenna had also lost in the third round, but to the other finalist who had dealt her a stunning blow to the right cheek that had sent her spinning right out of the circle. However, on recounting the bout to Calvyn later in the evening, she did point out that the black eye that her victorious opponent wore into the final had been dealt with compliments of her left boot.

'Your boot!' exclaimed Calvyn in surprise.

'Yes, I landed a cracking drop kick that would have

felled a bear. Unfortunately he must have a harder head than a bear, and what I thought was a winning blow proved to be nothing more than an irritation to him. That guy is made of rock, and he was not best pleased with my attempts to sledgehammer him to rubble!' laughed Jenna with a wince as her laugh attempted to pull the swollen cheek into a smile.

'You never cease to amaze me!'

'You're obviously easier to amaze than he was, which was a little unfortunate as it turned out,' she said, prodding tentatively at the swelling.

'I've got some salve that will take that swelling down. It's in the Quartermaster's store. Shall we go and see if he's still there?'

'Another of your miracle cures? What are we waiting for? Let's go.'

*   *   *   *   *

'Great Tarmin! Will you look at that? Just when I thought that we were in for a few days of decent weather, we've got another dust storm on the way. Sound the alarm bell, would you Cieran?'

Cieran muttered something unintelligible and walked over to the large bell which hung in the corner of the gate tower, yawning as he went. The bleary eyed guard picked up a stout metal bar that was propped up against the wall, and clamping his left hand over his left ear, he hit the bell hard with the bar a good dozen times. The old bell still rang out a loud and clear tone despite being cracked and corroded after years of neglect. The internal hammer of the bell had long since broken off, and the handle that used to operate the swing mechanism was so corroded that it was now completely unmoveable. However, the faithful old alarm signal still performed its duty, and people all over the town began closing shutters and taking in anything that was not securely fastened down.

'Why me?' yawned Cieran to his fellow guard. 'What

did I do to deserve this, Petro?'

'Nothing. It was just your shift, that's all.'

'No, I don't mean the guard duty. I mean Kortag. Why did I have to get posted here to Kortag? There were no end of duties available in Mantor, but no... I had to get posted here to the furthest, most desolate, windswept, dust-ridden hellhole in the whole of Thrandor. And for what? To check caravans! I must have seriously hacked someone off during my training.'

'You're starting to hack me off too! Quit your moaning, and get us a cup of dahl from the pot, will you?' said Petro, still looking south at the distant cloud of dust which was boiling across the wastelands towards them.

The sun had just risen and the sky was completely cloudless, displaying that endlessly deep blue colour that promised so much. Weather in the wastelands did not often depend on moisture in the air. More often than not it was the surface wind whipping up the loose desert dust that determined what sort of a day the fortified town of Kortag would enjoy.

Today's storm appeared different, somehow, Petro mused to himself as he watched the wide line of low flying dust moving steadily across the desert towards him. Something was not quite right about it – something that nagged at the back of the mind with an insistent, but not quite audible, voice.

'Here you go,' said Cieran as he handed the mug of steaming liquid to his fellow watchman. 'Hey! That's an impressive looking blow,' he exclaimed, looking out at the storm that he had rung the warning bell for only a minute or so previously.

'Yes, but it's strange. I've never seen one quite like it before.'

'You've seen one storm, you've seen them all as far as I'm concerned,' snorted Cieran with a shrug. 'Dust is dust, my friend. You've been here too long if you start distinguishing between one type of dust storm and another. You seriously need to get back to civilisation before you start to develop any weird attachments to this godforsaken place.'

'Yes, you're probably right,' replied Petro thoughtfully, and took a sip from his steaming mug of dahl. 'I suppose that we might as well get inside and make sure that all the shutters are closed before it hits.'

'Now that gets my vote. In fact... there's no one out there. I'll nip down and get the gatekeepers to shut the main gates up,' said Cieran, having scanned the area briefly for any signs of movement.

The two watchmen went about their tasks quickly and efficiently. Before long, they were both sitting inside the shuttered little guard tower with their feet up on the low table, looking forward to spending the last few hours of their shift with nothing to look at but the bare sandy colour of the unadorned walls.

'So what have you got planned for this afternoon then?' asked Cieran, slouching even further into his chair in an effort to get more comfortable.

Petro ran his fingers through his hair and pursed his lips as he considered the question.

'I'll probably drop in on Ellen for a chat and a few cups of dahl,' he said finally, running a finger first one way and then the other, across the breadth of his thick moustache.

'A chat? Is that what it's called these days?' said Cieran suggestively, and barked a short laugh at his fellow watchman's flush of embarrassment.

'It's nothing like that at all,' retorted Petro defensively. 'Ellen is a good friend, and we enjoy each other's company. That's it. Nothing more.'

'Of course, my friend that's what they all say!' teased Cieran. 'But that's not really why I was asking. I just wondered whether you fancied coming for a meal at that new tavern in the West Quarter. The barkeeper has employed a cook who is a regular marvel. He uses some really unique combinations of spices on his meats, and his vegetables are perfection in culinary form.'

'Well, I don't know...'

'Oh, come on! A meal and a few jars of ale with some

of the lads won't do you any harm. Ellen will still be there tomorrow, but we don't eat out together that often. It'll be fun. Come on, what do you say?'

Petro considered the offer, his fingers playing continually with his moustache as he ran over alternative excuses in his mind. He really did not want to go. The rowdy, smoke-filled atmospheres of the town taverns held no enjoyment for him, and the heavily spiced foods that were in vogue played havoc with his stomach.

'Thanks for the offer, Cieran, but that spicy meat just gives me... son of a...!'

Petro leapt to his feet and flung open the window shutters.

'What? What is it?' demanded Cieran, also springing to his feet in alarm.

'Wind... there's no wind!'

'So?'

'So how's that damned storm moving so fast? Unless... Great Tarmin! Quick, I've got to check this out, but if my guess is correct we're both going to be far too busy to worry about taverns today.'

'Busy? Doing what?'

'Fighting for our lives.'

Petro ran up to the top of the tower with Cieran hard on his heels. They both ran to the south wall and looked out towards the rapidly approaching dust cloud.

'Holy mother of... there's thousands of them!'

'Don't just stand there, Cieran. Go rouse the messenger and send him to Mantor on the fastest horse that he can find. News of this must reach the King without delay,' ordered Petro.

'But what are you going to do?'

'Rouse as many men as I can before they get here. We're soldiers, remember? We're supposed to fight when the time comes. The time is here. Go! For goodness sake hurry. There's no time to waste.'

Cieran sprinted off down the steps. Before Petro started his own mad dash, however, he could not resist looking out just once more at the approaching army of nomads. They swarmed across the desert like a flood. Countless in number, many mounted on horseback, they surged onward towards the unprepared town.

'A time to fight... and a time to die,' he muttered to himself morosely. Then Petro too turned and ran, determined to raise at least something of a defence, if only to protect his beloved Ellen.

CHAPTER 13

Calvyn looked around at the bustling market place and was momentarily overwhelmed with a veritable flood of memories from his travelling days with Perdimonn. The cries of the more enthusiastic stallholders hawking their wares punctuated the buzzing hubbub of the crowded square. The smell of freshly baked bread mingled with that of the fresh herbs and spices sold on the nearest of the stalls. The occasional whiff of sizzling meat roasted on large spits filtered through the myriad other scents which characterised the typical Thrandor market place.

It was almost like coming home after an all day fishing trip, Calvyn thought to himself. Everything was so familiar and held so many good memories that it was almost as if he had never been away.

'Hey, Calvyn, come and take a look at this,' called Jenna, waving at him from one of the nearby stalls.

Calvyn smiled and nodded to her. Unconsciously he smoothed the front of his new blue and black chequered tunic before placing his left hand down to hold the sword on his left hip steady as he made his way through the crowd to where Jenna was lovingly caressing a beautifully crafted bow.

'Isn't it a beauty?' she asked, her eyes alight with enthusiasm.

'Yes, and no doubt an absolute bargain,' Calvyn replied with a wink at the stallholder. 'May I?' he asked, holding his hands out to take the longbow.

Almost reluctantly, Jenna handed the weapon to

Calvyn, who in turn made a careful inspection for any flaws in the wood. It was immediately obvious that no apprentice had made this weapon. The wood had been beautifully crafted and finished so that it was silk-like to the touch. The grip had been coated with a strange substance that was almost, but not quite, rough. Calvyn peered at it with interest, as he had never seen or felt its like before.

'Before you ask, the answer is no, I don't know what it is. The craftsman wouldn't tell me,' said the stallholder with a slight smile. 'But it certainly makes for a good grip that would never slip in your hand, don't you think?'

'Yes, it's excellent. What sort of wood is this? It's certainly attractive,' Calvyn replied, stroking the amazingly smooth finish either side of the central grip.

'It's Akar wood from western Shandar.'

'Really? I've heard of it, but never seen any before. I'm beginning to think that I'm not going to like the price of this bow.'

The stallholder chuckled. 'You're right there,' he acceded with a nod. 'The price is twenty-five gold pieces, and not a copper penny less.'

Jenna gasped in amazement, but Calvyn just nodded thoughtfully.

'Made by a Master, I suppose?'

'None other than Vandar himself.'

'Vandar? I've not heard the name,' Calvyn said, shaking his head slightly as he thought to himself that this was not really surprising, as he didn't know any of the names of the Master Craftsmen around these parts.

'You've not heard of Vandar!?' exclaimed Jenna in surprise. 'He's only the most highly respected bow maker in northern Thrandor – maybe in the whole of Thrandor for that matter.'

'Ah,' said Calvyn gravely, 'that Vandar.'

'You...!'

Lost for words, Jenna gave Calvyn a playful punch and retrieved the bow from him. With one last loving and regretful caress of the fine wood, she handed the weapon back to the stallholder.

'A bit out of my price bracket I'm afraid,' she said with a rueful smile. 'One day maybe...'

The stallholder nodded.

'I've got many more bows that might be suitable...' he offered hopefully.

Jenna raised a hand to stop him from getting too far into his sales pitch. 'Another day maybe. For today I think that I'd just like to dream a little,' she said. 'I'm sure that I'll be back to see your stall again.'

Calvyn nodded to the stallholder as he walked away with Jenna, moving in towards the heart of the market place. As they strolled through the aisles, it suddenly struck Calvyn that the other people shopping at the various stalls all moved respectfully aside to allow them to pass unhindered. The feeling of pride that he felt in the uniform he wore grew with every step. No one had ever treated him with such respect before, and he decided that he liked the way it felt. Whether it was the uniform, or the fact that they were obviously armed, trained fighters, he did not really care. He felt important, and it felt good.

'So is there anything that you want to buy today, Calvyn?' asked Jenna.

'Well it depends on the price, but yes, I've got my eyes open for some silver.'

'Silver? Silver what?'

'Silver silver. You know... the metal.'

'What on earth do you want silver for? Don't tell me that you're a silversmith in your spare time?'

'No! Not me. No, I need the silver for someone else to make something for me. I've been thinking about it for ages and... well it's just a crazy idea that I can't get out of my head. I want to have my own sword made. Not that this one isn't perfectly adequate, but I want a sword that's distinctively my own, and I thought that I might commission Gerran to make it for me.'

'In that case, I hope that the silver is to be his commission, or you're going to have a sword that's about as much use as a fireguard made of tinder.'

Calvyn smiled and nodded.

'Yes, I know how soft silver is, but an old friend of mine let me in on a kind of secret before I joined the army, and I'd like to try it out. It's a sort of experiment really.'

'Sounds like an expensive waste of money if you ask me, but if you've got money to waste, then who am I to stop you in your quest for knowledge?' Jenna said with a tinge of sarcasm in her voice.

It was plain to Calvyn that Jenna did not want to see him throw his money away on something that would be totally impractical, but his idea just would not be dismissed that easily. He had thought long and hard about this during his meditations over the last few months, and could see no reasons for it to fail. The biggest problem that he could foresee was convincing Gerran that his sword could be forged in the manner that he had in mind. The Master Smith would undoubtedly have serious misgivings about the whole venture, and was not exactly renowned for having a malleable nature. Calvyn, on the other hand, felt certain that he would be able to bring the sceptical craftsman around enough to attempt Calvyn's somewhat unusual plan.

'Come on, Jenna. Just give me a hand to find a jeweller who's willing to part with a small ingot of silver and I'll treat us both to some of that roasted meat.'

'You're on,' Jenna agreed enthusiastically, for the smell emanating from the barbecue pit was truly heavenly. 'I'll check out this way. You go that way. I'll meet you over by the baker's stand in ten minutes. OK?'

Between them, Calvyn and Jenna explored all of the market stalls and discovered that there were in fact two jewellers selling wares at the market that day. After bartering sessions with both stallholders, Calvyn eliminated one who gave him a vaguely uneasy feeling. Haggling with the other man proved straightforward, and Calvyn came away with his small ingot of silver feeling satisfied that he had struck a fair deal.

As he had promised, Calvyn then took Jenna across to where several large carcasses were being slowly spit roasted over a wide open firepit. The two friends stood and chatted as they munched their way through the large portions of roast meat that Calvyn had purchased. Initially they reminisced about the more memorable moments of their training, but it was not long before the topic inevitably shifted onto their latest patrols of the trade routes along the northern border lands of Thrandor.

'What do you think that Derra would do if we were to run into a Shandese raiding party?' Jenna asked, biting another succulent chunk of meat from the bone and wiping a dribble of juice from her chin with her other hand.

'Judging by the state of that ransacked caravan on the East Mistian Trade Route yesterday, I doubt that she would have much option but to fight,' Calvyn replied.

'But it looked like the caravan was hit by a pretty large group of raiders. If the odds looked bad, do you think that she'd hold back?' Jenna asked, her voice troubled.

'If you're asking whether I think that Derra would deliberately lead us into a fight that we had no hope of surviving, then I would say no – unless of course there was no alternative. But you must remember that we didn't just join the army to learn to fight when it suited us. We joined to protect these people,' Calvyn said, pointing his half-eaten hunk of meat around at the market square. 'We have a responsibility to Baron Keevan's estates now, and also to all those people in these parts who are unable to defend themselves.'

Jenna looked at him with surprise.

'Have you been eating those sentimental pills again or something?' she said with a laugh. 'Don't tell me that you didn't join the army for selfish reasons, Calvyn. Let's face it. We all did. Some were more selfish than others, but I'll bet you all the money I have, that nobody on our training course joined up to protect the weak.'

'All right, perhaps I was being a bit pompous,' conceded Calvyn with a grin. 'But like it or not, we do

216

now have responsibilities that we cannot discard lightly. Derra is the one who has the unenviable task of assessing the situations that we run into, and making the tough decisions. Whatever she decides will undoubtedly have to be accounted for to the Sergeants and Captains afterwards. Could you imagine her telling Brett or Dren that we stood back and watched raiders kill innocent merchants and steal their goods because they looked mean enough to hurt us? In reality, it would take a lot of raiders to best our squad in a fight. Some of these veterans in our patrol are excellent fighters.'

'Yeah, I know. It was a shame to have our squad split up after the course, but I'm certainly learning a lot since we got mixed in with the vets. I'm also glad that we still have Derra as our Corporal. I know where I stand with her.'

'Definitely,' Calvyn agreed, with a knowing smile. 'Derra might be a hard person to please, but it's been good to have a few constants. I just wish that Bek had been assigned to our patrol squad. I'm going to miss having him around.'

'Talking of Derra... here she comes,' warned Jenna with an almost imperceptible nod of her head towards the approaching Corporal.

'So, how are you enjoying life after training then, *Privates*?' asked Derra with a friendly smile that looked totally out of place on the fierce face of the person who had given Squad Two such a hard time over the last five months.

'It's great thanks, Corporal,' replied Calvyn a little warily, not sure whether the Corporal's smile was genuine or a front for another of her famous reprimands.

'Good. You two can count yourselves lucky that you landed a patrol that brought you into town on market day so soon out of training. Many new Privates end up waiting months before getting a duty like this, especially as we have enough flex to allow a little shopping time as well. Have you found anything that you like?'

'Oh yes,' enthused Jenna, all barriers dropping in an

instant. 'There's an absolutely fantastic longbow for sale at the stall over there on the right hand end of that aisle. I've never seen such a weapon. The stallholder says that it's made of Akar wood, and that it was made by Vandar himself. Unfortunately, he wants *twenty-five* gold pieces for it.'

'Ah yes! I know the bow that you mean. He's had it for some time now. Unfortunately for him, he'll probably have it for some time to come unless he gets extremely lucky.'

'Why?' asked Jenna in surprise. 'Surely a weapon of such quality is a desirable enough item to be saleable.'

'True,' Derra replied. 'High quality weapons are in short supply, and the nobility and the more wealthy captains are always on the lookout for such things. However, how many captains or nobles do you know who are bowmen? Not many. Almost to a man, their preferred weapon is the longsword, so the people who could afford such a high quality longbow are unlikely to spend such a large sum of money on something that they'd probably never use.'

'That makes sense,' Jenna said thoughtfully, 'but it seems a great shame that such a fine weapon should spend its days lying unused on a merchant's table when there are people like me who would willingly give everything that they owned to get their hands on it.'

'Unfortunate, but unlikely to change,' agreed Derra. 'How about you Calvyn? Found anything interesting?'

'Many things, but mainly I've just been enjoying being away from the castle. The change of scene has been very refreshing.'

'And the change of food, I see,' Derra grinned.

'Sorry! I should have asked. Would you like some?'

Derra held up her hand in a gesture of denial, and shook her head.

'No, thank you. If anything it should be me treating you after what you've been through over the last five months.'

Calvyn and Jenna exchanged a rapid glance of

surprise, which Derra spotted and laughed at.

'I'm not quite as heartless as you might think,' she said, still chuckling at her two protégés' reaction, 'However, don't think that I'm not going to continue to be hard on you just because you've finished your training, because I will. Hopefully, though, we might just begin to have a bit of fun along the way too.'

Calvyn and Jenna could hardly believe their ears. The thought of having fun with Corporal Derra was a little difficult to take in. The fear of her ferocious temper was too deep-set to just discard in a moment of mild mannered joviality. However, the mischievous glint in Derra's eyes was unmistakable, and shattered Calvyn's image of her as the completely humourless, cold and autocratic leader that he had taken her for. The facade that she had put up for Squad Two had been solid enough to prevent any from seeing beyond that rock hard exterior.

'Tell me, have you two ever had your fortunes told?' Derra asked suddenly.

'Once. A long time ago,' Jenna replied. 'But it was a load of drivel. None of what the old crone said has come true.'

Calvyn shook his head as Derra looked to him, remembering how Perdimonn had always avoided the fortune tellers in the markets that they had visited together. He had approached the old Magician about it one day whilst they were packing their wares into the wagon in preparation to depart.

'Can fortune tellers really look into the future, Perdimonn?' the young Calvyn had asked innocently.

'Some can, in a limited sort of way,' the old man had replied after a short pause. 'Most are fakes, charlatans who are merely putting on an act to line their pockets with the money of the more gullible and superstitious townspeople. However, there are one or two who have a definite ability to sense fragments of the future. The big problem with the future is that even if the vision of a true prescient is strong and sure, the events seen may still alter, or not happen at all. There are many possible futures, Calvyn, and every choice that you ever make will eliminate possibilities from existence.'

'So why do they bother to look at all if nothing is certain?' Calvyn had asked.

'Oh, various reasons. Some look because they keep seeing their visions coming true, others because they are led into it by parents who are also mystics. Many, though, just see it as an easy way to earn money.'

Calvyn had always watched the market mystics with wary scepticism since that day, wondering whether the strange characters who were apparent in most of Thrandor's markets were genuine or fake. It had always fascinated him to see the wide range of customers that he had observed visiting the fortune tellers, but he certainly had not expected to find that Derra was the superstitious sort.

'Well, you might be surprised by this old crone, Jenna,' the Corporal continued. 'I've seen many of the things that she has predicted come true. I never used to think much of such things myself, but one of the other Corporals was having his fortune told a couple of years ago, and he convinced me to have mine done too. I was still a Private at the time. The old crone predicted my promotion to the day. Believe me, no one was more surprised than I was when I was promoted, as I never saw myself as any more than an average soldier. Who knows what she might see for you two.'

'Well, I don't know...' Calvyn hedged uncertainly.

'Oh come on, Calvyn. What harm can it do?' asked Jenna. 'Don't tell me that you're afraid of an old crone!'

'Never judge an enemy by their appearance,' quoted Calvyn, using Derra's words in his defence. However, he said it with a grin to let Jenna know that he was only kidding.

'Enemy! I think you'd better keep an eye on Calvyn, Corporal. It seems that he's looking to start picking fights with little old ladies. The uniform and sword must have gone to his head,' Jenna laughed.

Calvyn and Derra joined in with the laughter.

The Corporal's laugh was strange to hear for the two new Privates. Calvyn suddenly realised that today had been the first time that he had actually heard Derra expressing genuine mirth since they had met her, and his heart lifted. Much as he was enjoying the challenges of army life, it struck him that this was probably the sound that would herald a whole new level of appreciation for his profession.

'OK, OK, I give in!' chuckled Calvyn, raising his hands in a sign of surrender. 'Let's go see what the future has in store for us, shall we? Lead on, Corporal, though I think that I know where you're going because...' Calvyn closed his eyes, and placing his fingers either side of his temples, he started speaking in an impression of the low creepy voices that many of the mystics used. '...I see you leading us down the second aisle on the left.'

Jenna punched him.

'Thanks, Jenna. If you hadn't done that, I would have,' Derra said, her face back to her normal hard frown, and her voice harsh.

Calvyn gulped, thinking that he had overstepped some unseen line. Then Derra's face broke back into a grin.

'I do that hard act quite well really, don't I?' the Corporal chuckled, amused at Calvyn's discomfort.

'Believe me, you're the best,' replied Calvyn with a sigh of relief.

The three blue and black garbed soldiers made their way through the crowds to where an old woman sat at a simple table covered in black cloth. She was dressed in a plain robe that might once have been white but was now a dull and dusty grey. Her thin straggling grey hair was tied back in an untidy attempt at a bun, and her weathered, deeply wrinkled face betrayed no emotion as she sat staring forward into space awaiting her next customer.

As Corporal Derra sat down at the table opposite the old woman, Calvyn suddenly noticed that the seeress's eyes were covered with the filmy coating of cataracts.

The old woman must be virtually blind, he thought to himself as Derra placed a copper penny in each of the gnarled hands that were waiting, palms up on the table.

The old woman pocketed the money and then grasped Derra's hands in her own. The crone's face split into a grin, revealing a few stumpy pegs of teeth as she let out a harsh sounding cackle of delight at the feel of Derra's hands.

'So the Hard One returns to see more, I see. What would you know?'

'I wish to know what you see of my future, old mother,' Derra replied.

'Of course, of course. But *what* would you know? Would you know of your death? Or of your life?'

Calvyn's blood suddenly ran cold as the old woman mentioned death, and he began to wonder why he had agreed to go along with this.

'Please, old mother, just tell me what you see,' Derra asked firmly, but politely.

'I see war. War and death. Death and sorrow. But not death for you. You will live and be advanced. Oh yes, hard one. You may be reluctant, but you will be advanced again.'

'War? With the Shandese?' Derra asked in surprise.

'The Shandese!?' the old woman exclaimed, and then burst into cackles of laughter again. 'The Holy War is coming, hard one. Be ready, for it spells doom.'

'Doom? Doom for what?'

'No. No more will I tell you. I have already said too much. Your fortune is told, but who are your friends? Do they too wish to hear of their futures?'

Derra stood up and signalled to Jenna to take her place. Somewhat reluctantly, Jenna sat down and placed a copper penny into each of the old mystic's hands. Derra looked very thoughtful as she stepped aside and joined Calvyn in watching on as the old woman took hold of Jenna's hands.

'Ahhh,' the old woman breathed, 'The Huntress. Yes, that makes sense. The Huntress and The Hard One together. Interesting. Well, bow mistress, what would you know?'

Taking Derra's lead, Jenna just asked the old woman to tell her what she saw.

'Well, the war and sorrow will touch you too. From that, few will escape without some hurt, but... a long journey. Yes. A hunt. But what will you hunt with that bow of yours? Be sure of your target lest you find yourself as the hunted.'

'What do you mean, old mother?'

'What do I mean? I mean what I say,' the old woman cackled. 'Your quarry will be the most dangerous of all time. Just be sure in your own heart that you know what it is. Now I can say no more. Your fortune is told.'

'But it makes no sense to me,' Jenna said, somewhat disgruntled.

'Oh it will,' the old woman crooned. 'Mark my words, it will. Now, who is the other? I sense something...'

The old woman paused, cocking her head slightly to one side like a dog intently listening for some slight sound. A chill shot down Calvyn's back as he watched, and he almost turned and ran like a frightened rabbit. However, at that precise second Derra placed a hand on his shoulder. The touch made him jump slightly as it was unexpected, but it did lend him a bit of confidence. After all, he thought, what has the mystic done to either of the others? Apart from giving them a couple of riddles... nothing. So why was his heart racing?

'Stupidity,' he muttered to himself, and sat down in the chair that Jenna had now vacated.

He placed the requisite copper pennies in the old woman's hands, which she duly pocketed. Then she gripped his hands in her gnarled, bony fingers. The reaction was startling and immediate. The mystic jerked back as if shocked.

'You... The Sword!' she gasped, sitting bolt upright, her blind eyes open wide.

In the next split second several strange things happened. Calvyn heard Perdimonn's voice by his right ear clearly and loudly give the warning 'Calvyn, look out!' In surprise, Calvyn turned in his chair to look for the speaker just as, seemingly from nowhere, the old crone pulled a dagger and lunged across the table like a striking snake.

A screaming pain exploded in Calvyn's shoulder as the dagger bit deep into his flesh. The old woman wrenched the blade free and went to strike again, but Derra was faster and caught the crone's wrist in a vice-like grip. Twisting the dagger free, the Corporal held the mystic fast and shouted for the Market Master.

Jenna, who had found herself almost frozen in shock at the sudden attack, moved to Calvyn's side as he clasped his bleeding shoulder and squirmed in agony at the waves of pain that cascaded through his body.

'You'll need to get that seen by a medic, and fast,' Jenna said in a low voice.

'No kidding!' gasped Calvyn through gritted teeth. 'See if you can find one. If you can't then just get a needle and thread... and something to bind it with,' he added as an afterthought.

Blood was dribbling through Calvyn's fingers at a frightening rate, and so despite the pain he pinched the wound together even harder. A sudden rasping cackle of laughter from the old crone, who was no longer struggling against Corporal Derra, caused Calvyn to look up at her wrinkled face. The blind eyes looked back at him and the gap-toothed grin mocked his pain.

'You will burn by the power of the Chosen One,' she all but screamed. 'I see your hands consumed in his holy fire. The Sword will burn. Ha ha ha ha...'

The old woman was wracked by hysterical laughter, unable to speak any more, and shivers ran up and down Calvyn's spine that had nothing to do with his wound. Then the Market Master arrived demanding to know what was going on.

'This crazy old woman stabbed my soldier with that dagger on the table. There was no provocation or warning. She just pulled the knife and stabbed him. If he hadn't turned aside as she struck, the wound could have been fatal.'

'Did anyone else witness this?' asked the Market Master in a tone that betrayed his annoyance at the whole situation.

Several people stepped forward.

'And you corroborate this story?'

The witnesses all nodded.

The old crone, still being held firmly by Corporal Derra, remained consumed by her hysterical laughter. Every now and then she croaked 'burn' or 'sword' but nothing comprehensible. Obviously disgruntled by the disturbance of the entire affair, the Market Master signalled to two of his deputies to take the old crone away.

'Lock her up until we can quieten her down enough to question her properly,' he ordered.

As soon as the deputies relieved Derra of her captive, she went straight to Calvyn.

'How bad is it?' she asked, her face back into a dark frown.

'It's deep, but I'll live,' assured Calvyn, who was fervently wishing that he could get somewhere private so that he could fix the wound with a healing spell. Unfortunately, too many people had seen how bad the cut was, so he would not be able to just heal it without raising suspicions. This was one time when he would have to just let nature take its course, he decided. Well, superficially at least.

Jenna arrived back on the scene with a medic, who immediately got to work cleaning and stitching Calvyn's shoulder. The crowd that had built up around the stall started to disperse, as the main excitement was obviously all over. Just a few people remained, watching with interest as the medic's needle dipped in and out of Calvyn's skin, the thread pulling the flaps of skin tightly together and staunching the flow of blood.

Calvyn just sat looking straight ahead, deep in thought, his teeth firmly clenched together against the pain. He was absolutely certain that it had been Perdimonn's voice that he had heard behind him, but there had been no sign of the old Magician anywhere. Nothing about the entire incident made any sense. However, the mystic had mentioned "The Sword", and she certainly would not have been referring to the one that he wore now. At least that reference gave him some hope that the sword that he planned to have made might prove to be special somehow.

Once the medic had completed stitching up the wound, he placed a dressing over it and wound a bandage over the top.

'Nice job,' complimented Calvyn, rolling his shoulder slightly to test the tightness of the bandage. 'Many thanks.'

'No problem. You've livened up my day no end,' replied the medic with a grin. 'I haven't had a chance to play with anything quite that serious for a while now. It's good to keep your hand in, you know.'

'Well, I'm glad that you enjoyed it,' Calvyn said, with just a hint of sarcasm. 'But forgive me if I try not to keep you amused too often.'

The medic laughed, waved, and walked away into the now bustling market place.

'We should be getting back to the meeting place,' Derra informed them. 'We're due to be moving on shortly. Are you going to be all right to continue walking with the patrol, Calvyn? Or do you want me to order a wagon to take you back to the castle? You lost a fair amount of blood through that wound, and I don't want to end up having to carry you back.'

'I'll be fine, Corporal. Walking won't be a problem, but I might not be quite myself if it came to a fight. At least she didn't stick the knife in my sword arm, so I could probably hold my own, but I can't say that I really feel like proving that right now.'

'Very well. We'll finish today's sweep back to the castle anyway, then I'll have you put on light duties until you're fully recovered. I just wish that I'd never suggested this stupid idea at all.'

'Oh, I don't know,' Calvyn returned, 'you were certainly right about one thing... we were definitely surprised by the mystic.'

Derra's scowl deepened slightly.

'That's one sort of surprise that I could live without,' she said firmly. 'I am definitely through with mystics from now on. Holy wars indeed! There's nothing holy about any war. Still, what can you expect from desert nomads anyway?'

'Desert nomads?' Jenna said questioningly.

'Yes. Someone told me that she originated from the Terachim wastes. Who it was I forget, but no matter. My days of worrying about the future are done. Let's go. I can see the rest of the patrol gathering together, and I'd rather not be late.'

CHAPTER 14

'What is it, Veldan? What is so important that you see fit to interrupt my dinner when I specifically told you that we were not to be disturbed?'

'I am sorry, your Majesty,' the Chief Butler apologised, bowing deeply. 'There is a message rider from Kortag, Sire, who desperately seeks an audience with you. So desperately, in fact, that he is threatening to try and cut his way in to see you with his sword.'

'Kortag? But there *is* nothing at Kortag of any great importance,' the King replied indignantly.

Settling his knife and fork down on his plate, King Malo II, ruler of Thrandor, heaved a sigh of resignation and annoyance. The Monarch dabbed briefly at his mouth with a large napkin, and looked around the table at his wife and guests. The King had been looking forward to this meal all day long, and the anticipation had helped to make the mundane boredom of his day at court pass relatively painlessly.

It had been months since the last time the King had been able to sit down and eat with his old friend, Baron Anton. The Baron had been unable to attend court because he had been dashing around the countryside trying to catch the group who had named themselves 'Demarr's Rebels'. To date Anton had suffered repeated frustration as the group followed no discernible pattern, struck without warning and then disappeared without ghosts. It had taken a lot of persuasion to get him to abandon his search for a few days to come and visit the palace, so the King was keen to monopolise the Baron's time whilst he was here.

'This had better be good, Veldan, or this message rider is going to be *very* sorry.'

'Yes, your Majesty,' the Chief Butler replied, allowing no emotion to show on his face.

'Well, you'd better show him in I suppose.'

'Right away, your Majesty.'

The Chief Butler gave another bow and left the dining room, only to return a few seconds later with a wild eyed man dressed in dirty riding leathers. The messenger's hair was unkempt, he was unshaven, and from the rings under his eyes it was obvious that he was very tired.

'Your Majesty,' the message rider acknowledged, dropping to one knee and bowing his head.

'Rise and give your tidings that could not wait,' ordered the King in a stern, unforgiving voice.

'War, your Majesty. We are at war,' the rider replied boldly, undeterred by the King's displeasure.

There were several gasps of amazement from the ladies around the table, and Baron Anton choked slightly on his mouthful of food.

'War!?' the King exclaimed in disbelief. 'And with whom are we at war, young man?'

'The Terachites, your Majesty. They attacked from the wastelands, and before I was even out of sight of Kortag I could see that the town was already burning.'

'Surely not! Doesn't Kortag have a strong outer wall and a full company of men guarding it?'

'Yes, your Majesty, it does, but the initial estimate of the attacking force was something in excess of twenty-thousand men.'

'What!' exclaimed Baron Anton, jumping to his feet. 'You can't be serious! A force that size implies more than just an attack. That's big enough for an invasion. Who made the assessment? Are you sure that it wasn't just some over excited young Private blowing things out of all proportion?'

'Yes, Sire. There was no time for an accurate appraisal

of the Terachite force, but personally I would have said that twenty thousand was a pretty conservative estimate.'

'And when did the attack take place?' asked Anton, his brow furrowed.

'Four days ago, Sire. I've been riding flat out ever since.'

'Four days from Kortag! That's an outstanding effort. My deepest thanks, young man. You will be well rewarded for your dedication. Veldan, take this young fellow to the guest quarters and see that he gets food and rest.'

'But, your Majesty...' interrupted Anton urgently.

'No, Anton, your questions can wait until the poor man has rested. He has given us the bones of the news. You can ask your questions tomorrow. In the meantime, we have much to do. We need to mobilise the army and send out messages to all areas of Thrandor. For all we know there may be reinforcements following the force that attacked Kortag, but the details can wait. Let's get things moving, my friend. We have little time to waste.'

'Of course, your Majesty. You are quite right,' Anton acceded with a nod toward the message rider.

The Chief Butler led the tired young man out of the dining room. A buzz of low voiced conversation swept around the table as the King and the Baron made their excuses and left the room hard on the heels of the messenger.

'I had no idea that there *were* twenty thousand nomads in the Terachim wastes,' admitted Anton as he strode down the palace corridor next to King Malo.

'To be honest, neither did I. But then as far as I know, no outsider has ever travelled the depths of the Terachim and returned. Who knows how many there may be roaming that dust blasted expanse? It is inconceivable to my way of thinking that the desert could support such a large number of people. Perhaps that is why they are riding north – to find lands which will support their people. Who knows? Whatever their number, they have broken the Peace Treaty of Kortag. We must now do what we can to protect our land and our people as best we are able.'

The King stopped suddenly at a junction of two corridors and turned to his friend. Placing his hand on the Baron's shoulder, the King looked him straight in the eye.

'Anton, I'm going to need you to lead the main force from Mantor. You have always been loyal, and I trust you more than any other man alive. Take the Mantor regiments southwest to Fallowsford. Combined with the militia there, you should have at least four and a half thousand men. That should give you enough to make the town reasonably defensible. Just make sure that you get there before the Terachites do.'

'Yes, your Majesty.'

'And Anton...'

'Yes, your Majesty?'

'Take care, my friend. Send me any intelligence that you can and I will direct reinforcements towards you as fast as I can raise them. I'll get the Kortag messenger to come with you in the morning. You will then get the opportunity to get what information, if any, that he has on the enemy's force composition as you ride along.'

'Thank you, your Majesty. I will do the best that I can,' Anton replied.

'I know you will.'

Baron Anton turned and strode off down the corridor towards the quarters that his men were billeted in. The King watched him go.

'I know you will, old friend,' muttered the King quietly to himself again 'I just hope that your best is enough.'

*   *   *   *   *

'No! Absolutely not! The whole idea is completely preposterous.'

'But, Gerran, this is not ordinary silver,' pleaded Calvyn. 'It comes from deep in the heart of the Great Western Forest, where the earth is strange and the properties of metals are different,' he lied smoothly. 'Please, trust me, you've never seen silver like this before. My father gave this to me before he was killed. He had another piece that he had forged into an axe head. That axe chopped trees like no other I have ever seen, and the edge never blunted. It was amazing.'

Calvyn walked around the smithy, following the huge blacksmith who was doing his best to ignore Calvyn's concocted story.

'Axe head?' he scoffed, stopping and glancing momentarily at the ingot that Calvyn held in his outstretched hand before moving off again. 'Ridiculous!'

'Look, Gerran, I've waited years for this opportunity. You are without doubt the best blacksmith that I've ever met. You make outstanding swords of the highest quality. I don't want anyone else to make my sword for me. I want you. That's why I am willing to pay ten silver pennies for your effort. That's ten silver pennies plus the cost of the materials, of course.'

'Ten silver? You do want this badly, don't you?' The Smith paused and thought about it for a few seconds. 'No. It's still ridiculous. The metals will never bind. Silver and steel together! It's crazy,' the Smith stated flatly, shaking his head.

'OK, fifteen silver pennies,' countered Calvyn.

'You would pay fifteen silver pennies to watch me attempt this fiasco? You're mad,' Gerran said in an amazed voice. 'Oh, very well then. Bring your money tomorrow morning and I'll try the impossible.'

'Thank you, Gerran. Thank you very much. I'll be here right after breakfast,' bubbled Calvyn, unable to contain his excitement.

The Smith just shook his head and walked away muttering 'foolishness' to himself as he began to prepare the forge for his afternoon's work. Calvyn left the smithy quickly in case Gerran had a change of heart, and walked with a bounce in his step to his new quarters.

The barrack room into which he had moved was not that dissimilar to the one which he had spent the last five months sharing with his fellow Recruits from Squad Two. However, one difference was that he now had a small locker next to his bed in which he could store personal items other than his precious new blue and black uniform. Unsurprisingly, his flute and Perdimonn's grimoire were the first items into the locker. These were followed by some of Perdimonn's ointments and potions, together with one or two that he had made himself using spells from the grimoire.

Calvyn had actually managed to progress far more with his magical studies than he had thought would be possible during the last two months of his training. From the very start of the course he had always been very disciplined with his practice of the mental exercises and meditations which Perdimonn had taught him. As his military training had progressed towards the latter stages, both he and his fellow Recruits had been given more regular rest days. Calvyn had put this spare time to good use with his studies and, when he could get out of the castle, with practising as many spells as he could.

The idea of having a magical sword must have been a part of most childhood daydreams for young boys across the whole of Thrandor during one stage or another of their growing up. However, the dream had actually begun to develop into more of a goal for Calvyn during the past two months. There had always been stories of magical weapons and enchanted armour. Minstrels the length and breadth of Thrandor made their living telling such tales and singing ballads of numerous such artefacts. Calvyn reasoned that even if most of them were pure fabrications, some would have at least a grain of truth at their core. Therefore, the young student of warfare combined his limited training and experience of weapons, together with his even more limited knowledge of magic, and came up with an idea to try to make his boyhood dream a reality.

The essence of Calvyn's idea revolved around one of Perdimonn's parting words of warning. The old Magician had cautioned his young apprentice against trying to bind magic into objects made of steel, and encouraged him to use receptive materials, quoting silver as a good example. As silver was obviously far too soft a metal to make a sword of any use from, Calvyn was forced to be inventive. It took time, but eventually inspiration came. He decided that if he tried infusing some silver into a normal steel sword at the time of its forging, the blade might keep the majority of its normal strength characteristics and also inherit some of the silver's receptiveness to magic.

The biggest problem that Calvyn could see with the whole idea was that the properties of the two metals on a purely chemical basis were completely incompatible. Limited though his knowledge of metal working was, even Calvyn was aware that silver melted at a relatively low temperature and became a liquid, whereas, even in the hottest blacksmiths' forge, steel might become white hot but it would not liquefy. To make a true blend of silver and steel would therefore require a distinctly unnatural process, and what the end result would be, Calvyn could only speculate.

Undeterred by the difficulty and uncertainty behind the whole hypothesis, Calvyn had spent many evenings deep in thought, meditating and formulating possible ideas and spells to accomplish his goal. The end result was a surprisingly short and simple binding spell and the more he thought about it, the more Calvyn could see no reason why it should fail. The binding was similar to that of sealing a healing property into a potion or ointment. The even diffusion effect was required in both cases, so Calvyn just adapted the known spell to suit the rather different ingredients.

Solving the problem of blending the metals was a major step forward, but then Calvyn had been faced with the question of what sort of special properties he would desire in a weapon. The options were really only limited by his knowledge of magic. Unfortunately, that was quite a big limitation as most of the spells that he had inherited from Perdimonn were for healing and were not easily adaptable into useful properties for a sword.

However, Calvyn put his imagination to work and came up with several elements of spells that would be useful.

The first, and most immediately obvious useful spell, was the one that Perdimonn had used to lighten his wagon when Calvyn had first met him. A lighter sword would give him an edge of speed and prevent his arm from tiring so quickly in battle. Moreover, the spell needed no adaptation other than a locking sequence to ensure that the effect was permanent.

Adapting the spells for lighting fires to produce flames on the blade at the utterance of a single rune of power was more difficult, as indeed was designing a spell to make the blade glow in the presence of true evil. However, Calvyn did find a spell for a protective barrier of magic that proved useful, and also adapted the spell that Perdimonn had used to make the grimoire appear to be an old story book to alter the appearance and handling characteristics of the blade. In theory, unless keyed into flame or in the presence of true evil, the sword would appear ordinary to those around him.

The final touch was to adapt a spell of 'finding' such that the blade would try to 'find' him if he ever became separated from it, effectively binding the sword to him alone for all time. Whether the magic would work this way around, Calvyn had no idea. The whole idea of instilling an inanimate object with an animate objective was dubious at best, but as he had nothing really to lose, Calvyn saw no reason not to try.

The final result of his meditations and study was a complex and lengthy combination of spells, which would take some time to complete. This, Calvyn decided, could prove awkward, as he would have to begin the entire spell as the silver made contact with the steel or the precious metal would merely melt and run away. What he needed was something to explain his need to interrupt the Smith's work at the crucial moment, something that would give him a full five uninterrupted minutes in which he could be completely focused whilst he completed the conglomerate of spells. Gerran did not get to be such a well-respected Master Smith by allowing distractions to interrupt him during his work, so gaining the time to cast the spells was unlikely to prove easy.

As is often the case with problems that seem virtually unsolvable, the answer to Calvyn's predicament proved to be very simple. Furthermore, it presented itself at a completely unrelated moment and from a most unlikely source.

Calvyn had recently returned to the castle from the eventful patrol trip that had seen the incident with the fortune teller. Since his return he had been placed on light duties to allow his wound to heal. The majority of his duty time had been allocated to the mind numbingly boring task of watch duty up on the castle walls for the last three days. As a result, Calvyn had been on watch with members of several different squads, including several members of his training squad. It was at the end of a particularly tedious watch that Tondi and her watch partner had marched up to relieve Calvyn and his fellow watchman of their post. Tondi looked concerned.

'Calvyn, I heard that you were injured whilst out on patrol. Is it bad?'

Calvyn had smiled in reassurance.

'No. It could have been a lot worse. I got myself stabbed in the shoulder by a little old lady in the market place. Some hero's war story that would make!' he had joked, patting at his shoulder gently.

'Still, I bet it hurt,' Tondi had persisted.

'Oh yes. There's no getting away from the pain of being stabbed, no matter who does the stabbing.'

'Then I shall pray to Tarmin and Ishell for healing and relief from pain for you.'

Calvyn had never really known many people who had shown true faith in deities, and was a bit thrown by Tondi's announcement. However, he had thanked her in advance for her prayers, and had thought about her dedication to her gods all the way back to his new dormitory.

It was only later during his meditation time that it had

struck Calvyn that Tondi had just provided him with the perfect reason to complete his spell right in front of Gerran, with no need to cause a distraction. He would tell the Smith that he needed to carry out a ritual dedication of the blade to some deity that Gerran had never heard of. Moreover, he could pass the spell off as a prayer in an ancient woodcutter's language. The Smith would never know any better, and Calvyn would be able to complete his entire spell uninterrupted. Calvyn had been so elated at the solution that he had been sorely tempted to run, find Tondi, and give her a big hug. Instead, however, he had calmed his mind back into the discipline of his evening meditation, and had shot his own quick prayer of thanks to his friend's two gods.

Today had seen what Calvyn fervently hoped would be the last major obstacle between him and his dream of a magical sword brushed aside. Gerran's acceptance of the commission to forge the sword had not come easily, and Calvyn really felt pleased that he had not given up. True, the blade was going to cost him most of his money, and could still end up a disastrous failure, but somehow Calvyn knew that the end result was going to more than justify the expense and heartache.

Sleeping proved difficult that night, and Calvyn found himself laid long into the dark hours listening to the snores and sighs of his roommates. When tiredness finally overtook his active mind and excited anticipation, dreams of both failure and success troubled his sleep.

It was a gritty-eyed, but very alert young man who awoke with the dawn chorus the next morning. Quietly, so as not to wake his fellow soldiers, Calvyn got up and silently dressed. He collected the silver ingot from his locker and crept noiselessly from the dormitory out into the chill of the early morning air.

It was still not fully light as Calvyn strolled around the drill square and climbed the steps up to the top of the south wall. Looking out over the green countryside that surrounded the castle, Calvyn inhaled a deep breath of the clear country air. Only a faint smell of wood smoke from the fireplaces that heated certain parts of the castle accommodation tainted the otherwise pure, sweet smelling air. Maybe it was the proximity of the mountains, mused Calvyn to himself, and looked around at the purple-headed heights off to the north.

'Well, Perdimonn,' Calvyn muttered to himself, 'if you were here now, you would probably think that I was half crazy. Maybe I am, but I've got to give this a try or I'll spend my whole life wondering about those "what ifs" that you spent so much time trying to get me away from.'

Calvyn chuckled out loud. 'I am going crazy,' he thought to himself, shaking his head. 'Talking to someone who is either dead or half a world away – It's almost as mad as what I'm going to attempt in the smithy later!'

The time dragged mercilessly through until breakfast, and Calvyn must have gone over the spell in his head a hundred times or more by the time that the bugle sounded announcing the morning meal. For once, the thought of food was almost repugnant as Calvyn, unable to wait another second, made his way around the castle to Gerran's domain.

'You're early,' growled the big smith as Calvyn entered. 'Do you have the money?'

'Yes, Gerran, it's all there,' Calvyn replied, a little annoyed by the Smith's gruff, confrontational attitude, and tossed a small pouch casually to him. Calvyn also removed the silver ingot from his tunic pocket. 'And here's the silver.'

'Humpf,' grunted Gerran, and having counted the silver pennies, he took the proffered silver ingot in his huge, rough skinned hands. 'Looks like normal silver to me.'

'Believe me, that is like no silver that you have ever seen before,' assured Calvyn as the Smith scrutinised the ingot, turning it over and over in his enormous hands.

'We shall see.'

'Oh, and there's one thing that I forgot to mention the other day. There is a traditional ritual that I need to carry out when you join the two metals. It's a very old prayer to the woodsman's gods that I was taught as a small boy. It's normally carried out when commending a new axe to the gods, but it would mean a lot to me if I could complete it for my sword. It's sort of in memory of my father.'

The Smith rolled his eyes heavenward as if looking for divine inspiration himself.

'And how long will this prayer take to complete?'

'Only about five minutes,' Calvyn replied, trying to sound casual about it.'

'Five minutes!' exploded the Smith, looking at Calvyn with an expression that said 'Are you a complete idiot?' 'Why me?' and 'You have got to be joking' all in one. Then, placing his hands on his hips he laughed a deep, long, loud laugh that boomed around the smithy.

'You really are determined to make a mess on my anvil, aren't you? Great Tarmin, boy! You are going to have molten silver running all over the place once you place it against the hot steel, and you want to pray whilst your money melts away! You must be an arrow or two short of a quiver! Come on. Let's get on and get this over with. I've got some real work to do today after this... this...'

At a loss for words, the Smith shook his head again and walked across to his metal store, tossing the ingot of silver in the air and catching it as some might flip a coin. Together, Gerran and Calvyn chose a suitable piece of steel with which to make the blade. Then whilst heating the metal in the forge, the Smith explained how he intended to heat the steel wider than normal, hammer the silver to a thin sliver, lay the silver on the steel and then fold the steel around it before beating the blade into its final shape.

'If I don't fold the steel quickly enough, the silver will probably melt and just run all over the place... and if I have to reheat the folded metal... well! Let's just say that the odds are not good that you will have any of your silver left in your blade.'

Calvyn smiled and nodded.

'I understand what you're saying, Gerran, really I do. And I appreciate that you've put so much thought into this. However, none of what you've suggested will be necessary. Just make the blade as you would any other. The only extra thing that you'll need to do is to beat the silver out into a strip and to lay it onto the hot steel blade. The silver will join to the steel, and you'll just need to finish off the edge and the hilt.'

'Listen, Private Calvyn, I haven't been a Master Smith for ten years without knowing how to work metal...' started Gerran in an angry voice.

Calvyn held up his hands to stop the irate smith and interrupted him mid-flow.

'This is *my* sword, Gerran, paid for with *my* money. Just make it the way that *I* want it. Please. Don't make me go elsewhere. I really want your expertise on this, but I want it on *my* terms.'

The Smith let out a growl of frustration, plucked the steel from the forge with his tongs and began beating it against his anvil with a large hammer. Despite his anger, Gerran did not vent his feelings on the steel. Metal was sacred to the Master Smith, and he could no more abuse it than he would harm a small child. To do anything less than craft metal in his smithy would defile his tools, so he bent his mind to producing another fine blade, the very best that he could. Anything less would dishonour his name and reputation.

Gradually, the blade took shape and the skill of the Smith held Calvyn rapt in wonder and fascination. The 'tip, tip, tapping' of the Smith's hammer created a spell of its own as the young man watched magic of a different kind, worked with consummate skill before his very eyes. Time held no meaning as Gerran laboured, wielding his hammer tirelessly in his quest for perfection.

When Gerran finally inspected the blade and found it to his satisfaction, he returned it to the fire one last time and switched his attention to the small bar of silver. In what seemed like no time at all, the silver had been hammered into a long, even strip, and Gerran reached for the heated steel blade with his tongs.

'Whatever you're going to pray about, you might as well start by praying for a miracle, 'cos this is going to be messy,' Gerran growled.

With one last quick inspection of the red-hot steel sword the Master Smith placed it on the anvil and, reluctantly but precisely, laid the strip of silver along the length of the blade.

The sizzle of the contact of silver and red-hot steel snapped Calvyn out of his trance-like fascination at the Master Smith's skill. He stepped forward, adopted a prayerful pose over the blade, closed his eyes and began to recite his carefully rehearsed spell. Picturing the runes sinking into the silver, Calvyn saw in his mind the precious metal strip sinking into the steel as if being soaked up like water into a sponge. Gerran let out a gasp of amazement. Calvyn ignored him. The endless flow of runes in Calvyn's mind melded into the sword, absorbed as the silver had been absorbed. With concentration every bit as absolute as the Smith's had been only minutes before, Calvyn worked flawlessly through his spell. The final rune pronounced and visualised sinking into the blade, Calvyn opened his eyes and turned to the Smith, signalling to him to finish off the sword.

Almost reverently, Gerran picked up the blade with the tongs and made a careful inspection of its shape and finish. Tapping a few spots with his hammer, the Master Smith was soon satisfied and quenched the newly forged blade in a trough of pure mountain spring water. Again, the inspection. Again the concentration and focus of energy as Gerran began to grind an even edge to the blade.

No word passed between the Private and the Smith until, finally, Gerran was satisfied that the blade was as perfect as he could make it.

'A fine blade, young soldier. May she be used in righteousness and justice,' Gerran stated, raising the sword high in a ritual salute.

'And may she bring honour to her maker's name,' replied Calvyn with the traditional response.

'Amazing! I have never seen silver dissolve like that before. It was fascinating. My apologies for doubting your word, Calvyn, but that was probably the most unusual thing that I've seen in all my years of working metal. Where did you say that the silver came from?'

'Deep within the Great Western Forest.'

'Do you think that you could get me some more? I'd like to get some, if only to watch it soak into steel again. That really was something else!'

'As far as I know, the forest people don't trade their special silver with outsiders. I don't even know how my father got hold of the small amount that he gave me,' lied Calvyn smoothly.

'A shame. The silver adds something to the finish of the sword. A sort of slight gleam. It's a bit of a shame about those concentrated lines of silver though. I just hope that they don't weaken the sword too much.'

Calvyn looked at where the Smith was pointing on the blade, and his eyes widened slightly in surprise. Fortunately, the Smith was too engrossed in his handiwork to notice, for the lines that Gerran's large finger was tracing had formed runes of power on the blade. Three in all. The key runes for light, fire and air.

'May I?' asked Calvyn, extending his hand to accept the sword.

'Of course.'

Gerran proffered the sword, hilt first. Calvyn grasped the bare metal hilt and gasped as he gripped the cold handle.

'Are you OK? Did you cut yourself?'

'No, no, I'm fine,' Calvyn assured the Smith with a beaming smile. 'Everything's fine.'

On first contact with the sword, Calvyn had experienced a strange melding, as if his hand had somehow joined itself to the hilt. The sword was undoubtedly his. He felt it in every fibre of his body.

As he lifted the tip, he was surprised at just how light

the sword felt, and was momentarily confused because the Smith hadn't said anything. Then he realised that to Gerran, the blade would have felt like any other. The magic was keyed to Calvyn, and Calvyn only.

Lifting the blade in salute to the Smith's skill, Calvyn was about to thank Gerran for his time, patience and expertise, when a very strange thing happened. As clearly as if the old man had been standing right behind him, Calvyn heard Perdimonn's voice pronouncing the runes of a spell in his mind. Without knowing why, Calvyn found himself echoing the spell out loud, and yet more runes, many of which he did not recognise, flowed once more into the blade held aloft in front of him. When the spell finished, Calvyn immediately noticed that a fourth rune had appeared on the blade. The Smith, however, was no longer looking at his handiwork but regarding Calvyn with a suspicious expression on his face.

'What was all that about?'

'It was just a prayer of blessing on you and your work,' Calvyn lied. 'My thanks, Gerran. Your skill is definitely without equal, and I shall recommend you for so long as you remain in the trade. If you don't mind, I'd like to go and get to work at binding and dressing the hilt to fit my hand now. So if you'll excuse my abrupt departure, I'll leave you in peace to get on with your work.'

'No problem,' grunted the Smith at the rapidly retreating Calvyn. Then as Calvyn left through the main doors, the Smith muttered 'Strange... very strange,' before turning to the first of his regular pieces of work for the morning. Outside, Calvyn looked again at the fourth rune that had appeared in silver on his new sword, only to find that it was no longer there. The rune had not been one that he had recognised, but it had been strangely familiar somehow, as if he should have known it. The strangest thing was that now, when he tried to remember the shape of the rune, he could no longer picture it in his mind at all. The only thing he could remember was tantalising snatches of that strange spell, none of which meant anything on its own. If it had not been for that spontaneous spell he might have doubted that the rune had ever been there at all. It was not one that he recognised. He had no idea why he had heard Perdimonn's voice, but was vaguely reassured, because he had wondered all week whether or not it had been his old friend's voice that he had heard in the market place when the old seeress had attacked him. The appearance of the fourth rune on the sword had been something of a confirmation that he had not imagined it. However, the rune had disappeared leaving no hard evidence and so what the final spell had been that he had cast, echo fashion onto the blade, he had no idea.

With his finger, Calvyn carefully traced the area of the blade on which the mysterious symbol had appeared and focused his mind on an image of his mentor.

'What was that all about old friend? What did it mean?' he asked out loud.

In his mind came only a familiar echoing chuckle, that spread its infectious nature to Calvyn's lips, which immediately turned upwards in an answering grin.

CHAPTER 15

'Where's Derra? She's never late,' muttered Jenna to Calvyn as they waited with the rest of their patrol at the gates of the castle.

Corporal Derra had always led by example and, if anything, had been habitually early. At the very least the Corporal would turn up as the bugler began the hour call, and woe betide anyone who was so much as a second late. Today, however, the time for her squad to begin their patrol had come and gone with no sign of Derra anywhere. The squad was becoming restless. Something had to be wrong for Derra to be late. Whispering amongst the squad members was steadily growing louder as the patrol got later. Suddenly one of the veterans spoke out in a loud voice.

'OK, quieten down everyone. If Corporal Derra doesn't arrive in the next two minutes, then we'll send someone out to find her. Until then, let's keep the noise to a minimum. We are supposed to be professionals.'

Silence fell. The seconds ticked by. Calvyn ran through some possibilities in his mind. Derra could be ill, but then a replacement Corporal would have been sent. She could have overslept, but that was highly unlikely. Then it struck Calvyn that he had not seen a single Corporal or Sergeant all morning. Normally there would be a smattering of them at breakfast, but he could not remember seeing any this morning. So it was not just Derra who was late. Something involving all of the

NCOs was going on. A shiver ran down Calvyn's spine. It was something bad. He could feel it.

Just as the two minutes were about up, Corporal Derra, in company with several other Corporals, appeared striding around the corner of the stables towards the gates.

'Squad, atten... shun!' called the veteran who had called for quiet earlier.

Derra nodded a farewell to her fellow Corporals who split and headed off in various directions. With a deep frown creasing her brow and making her look particularly fierce, Derra approached her squad and called for them to stand at ease.

'Well, people,' she began, and then paused to take a deep breath, 'we will not be going out on patrol today. However, there is much to be done. Tonight we march to war.'

There were several gasps from squad members at the word 'war'. Calvyn was not among them. It was not by chance that Derra had been looking straight at Jenna and himself as she had pronounced their objective, and Calvyn's mind immediately flashed back to the old seeress in the market place.

'The Holy War,' he breathed to himself.

'Who are we at war with?' asked one of the other veterans in a puzzled voice. 'I didn't think that the King had the stomach to fight the Shandese because of the raiding parties.'

'No, we are not at war with the Shandese. The Desert Nomads of the Terachim Wastes are our adversaries,' answered Derra, again glancing across towards Calvyn and Jenna. 'Apparently they have invaded through the Kortag Gap with an army of more than twenty thousand men. A messenger from the King arrived last night calling for support, and the Baron is mobilising a force to join the armies of the south. As such, there is much preparation to be done, and very little time in which to complete it. We are assigned to loading food wagons, the first of which will be with us imminently. All of you are to report to the food stores in ten minutes. Any questions?'

'Is everyone heading south?' asked someone.

'Virtually,' replied Derra. 'Two squads only and the new batch of Recruits will be left to guard the castle, but the Baron himself will be leading everyone else in the campaign to the south. Anything else?'

No one spoke.

'Very well, Squad, dis... miss,' she ordered. 'Food stores. Ten minutes,' she added in a loud voice.

Calvyn and Jenna looked at one another meaningfully, and an unspoken understanding passed between them. The fortune teller had been right. War was coming. Indeed, it had already arrived.

The rest of the day was a blur of activity. Wagons rumbled in through the gates of the castle empty, and groaned their way out again a short while later, packed full of food, weapons, tents, blankets, armour, and all the paraphernalia of war. By late afternoon the stores were all but empty, and the aching soldiers were all called into the mess hall for an early dinner.

Calvyn had never seen the dining hall so full. The Baron had apparently called in all of the squads that had been out on patrol, and those that had been on resident tours of duty in the local towns and villages. Keevan's entire army was assembling, and there were dozens of faces that Calvyn had never even seen before, all crowding into the heaving mass of excited, apprehensive, and determined soldiers who were sharing a last meal together before taking the road into battle.

It was sort of exciting, Calvyn decided, but frightening at the same time. More so perhaps because of the words of the old seeress in the market place which now haunted his thoughts. Over and over he heard the rasping voice screaming. 'You will burn by the power of the Chosen One. I see your hands consumed in his holy fire. The sword will burn,' and the old woman's maniacal laughter echoed around and around in his skull like the never-ending screeches of the skrii lark. This unfortunate bird's demented-sounding cries had caused it to become the most hunted species of bird in Thrandor, for no other reason than to rid the countryside of its intensely irritating call.

Calvyn would have given much to remove the equally aggravating laughter from his mind. It was disquieting to think that he was heading along a predetermined path that would cause him to meet with this mysterious 'Chosen One'. Quite what the old crone had meant by her riddles was unclear. If Derra was 'The Hard One' and Jenna was 'The Huntress', did that make him 'The Sword'? If so, then his premise for being so confident during the forging of his sword had been misguided. But then she had said that his hands would be 'consumed in his holy fire', and that 'The Sword would burn'. Well, he knew already that his sword burned, as he had tested the binding of his specifically designed spells shortly after the sword had been forged. On uttering the appropriate rune of power, the blade had burst into flames which flickered back and forth, licking up from the hilt to the tip, and yet his hands had felt no heat whatsoever from the magically induced tongues of fire.

'Hello. Is anyone at home?' asked Jenna, startling him out of his troubled thoughts by waving a hand in front of his eyes.

'Sorry. I was miles away.'

'Want to talk about it?'

'I'm not quite sure.'

Calvyn's eyes unfocused again for a second or two as he started to ask himself Jenna's question. Did he, or didn't he want to talk about it? The gentle touch of Jenna's hand on his arm snapped him straight back to the present.

'The old crone?' Jenna asked perceptively.

'Yes. She raised more questions than she gave answers.'

'I've struggled with those questions myself, and with her prediction of war coming true so quickly...' Jenna paused whilst she gathered her thoughts. 'There must be a thousand interpretations and explanations for the old crone's predictions, not least of which is that she could still be a fake.'

'But the war...' Calvyn objected, surprise colouring his tone.

'Derra said that the old woman was of Terachite origin,' interrupted Jenna immediately. 'I'm sure that many a "seeress" has used a bit of inside information to lend credibility to their visions. For all we know, that could be how she gained Derra's trust in the first place. Maybe the old woman had heard from some other source that Derra was to be promoted and when. Who knows? But even if that isn't the case, the prophecies that she made are so vague, and open to interpretation, that they could apply to virtually any soldier.'

'So how would you explain the old woman's designation of you as 'The Huntress', and her prediction of your quarry being the most dangerous of all time?' asked Calvyn, intrigued by Jenna's obvious scepticism in the face of reasonably convincing circumstances.

'Well, it is fairly common for a woman soldier to favour the use of a bow over the sword. The bow is also the favoured weapon for hunting. Hence, "The Huntress". As for the most dangerous quarry of all time, who is to say what that is? It could be anything from a lion to a person. The perception of what is dangerous is unique to the individual, so how could her statement fail to be true? Any dangerous prey could be perceived to be the most dangerous of all time to the individual concerned. It's just a matter of perspective together with the willingness to look for an explanation.'

Calvyn considered Jenna's ideas carefully, but whilst he could see the logic of Jenna's argument, he could not evade his feeling that there was more going on than met the eye. Using Jenna's logic, the 'Chosen One' could be anyone that Calvyn decided in the future to designate with that title when the circumstances even slightly resembled those that the old woman had described. However, the old crone had implied with her tone that this 'Chosen One' to whom she referred was a person of importance and power. Maybe even magical power. The questions in his mind seemed unending, and all of them remained without answers.

'Well I'm not quite sure that you've answered the old woman's riddles Jenna, but I'm glad that you shared your feelings on this with me. Somehow, I feel better about the entire business. A trouble shared is a trouble halved so they say.'

Calvyn smiled warmly at his friend and grasped her hand in his. He squeezed Jenna's fingers gently to convey his gratitude, and locked eyes with her. A wealth of feeling transmitted between their touching fingers, and in that shared gaze an even closer bonding formed.

'I'm glad that I've been of help, but what of you? You've said nothing of your thoughts on the prophecies,' said Jenna, her large brown eyes still watching Calvyn's face for further clues to his thoughts and feelings.

'My thoughts are very confused,' Calvyn replied carefully without looking away. 'I can give you no answers because I have none. Only more questions. But all of that will have to wait. We have to go. The rest of our squad is already leaving to gather their kit and make ready to march. We should join them or we'll incur the wrath of Derra, and I wouldn't want to lose the friendlier side of her character before it's had a chance to establish itself.'

'Agreed,' nodded Jenna with a tight grin. 'Let's go. We'll most likely get a chance to talk on the long march south.'

'Undoubtedly. And maybe by then I'll have some answers to give.'

A short while later, Corporal Derra and her squad of twenty soldiers stood at ease in two ranks, breathlessly awaiting the commands that would begin their long trek to war. Each soldier was dressed in their normal blue and black patrol uniform, but with certain additions. Everyone had been issued with a hardened leather skullcap, strengthened with a band of steel that encircled the head at forehead height. Furthermore, everyone wore a chain-mail vest under their tunic, and each carried spare clothes and a set of eating utensils in a lightweight backpack. Each squad member was also expected to carry a flint and tinder with which to start a fire should they be called to do so.

Calvyn was uncomfortable. The chain-mail was heavy. Having taken the strain of the loading duties all day, his aching back and legs now protested at the weight of both mail and backpack. Already, his tired body craved for a shower and a warm bed, and yet his mind had accepted that he was unlikely to see either for the foreseeable future. Maybe never.

Baron Keevan, together with his Captains, trotted sedately out of the gate on horseback, their full knightly armour clanking and spurs jangling with every hoof fall. Making their way forward to the front of the column, each squad in turn came to attention as the exalted company passed, and then were called to turn 'in column of route', ready to move out. Finally, the Baron reached the front of the column and the long march southward began.

The normal formalities of marching were dispensed with almost immediately. Talking was allowed amongst the troops, and the straight-armed swinging gait of drill marching was largely abandoned, with the exception of passing through villages and towns, when the mere fact of being on show made precise, smart drill mandatory. However, the Corporals did ensure that their squads stayed in step with one another at all times, as they were well aware that the crunching rhythm of booted feet would imbue the soldiers with a momentum which would carry them onward through their fatigue.

Any talking amongst the men and women of Baron Keevan's force quickly died out as the initial excitement of the march to war faded into the weariness of a long day of hard labour and exercise. The light packs soon felt as if they were weighted with lead, and many would willingly have cast aside the protection of their mail shirts just to shed the weight from their shoulders. Heads drooped, feet dragged, and shoulders slumped as the daylight faded into the twilight of dusk. It was full dark by the time that the Baron called a halt for the night. Calvyn estimated that they had marched for at least three hours, and his legs were painfully informing him that this was two and a half hours too many.

Corporal Derra called four of the squad members, including Calvyn, to fetch from the waiting wagon the two tents that would house their squad for the night. Unshouldering his pack next to Jenna, who had sat down by the roadside when the halt had been called, Calvyn trudged with his three fellow squad members to join the queue for the canvas shelters. Before they knew it, Calvyn and the others were groaning under the weight of the heavy bundles of canvas and wooden poles. Staggering under the load, they wended their way back to where the rest of the squad was preparing two areas of ground next to the road on which to erect the shelters.

Derra, still seemingly full of energy, directed the operation with her normal brusque manner, and despite the weary fumbling of her subordinates the two tents were quickly constructed and a fire was swiftly lit at the entrance to each. To the consternation of some of the squad members, Derra refused to allow her soldiers to go to sleep until they had each drunk a hot cup of dahl and stacked their backpacks neatly under a canvas cover. However, once Calvyn had got the steaming mug of liquid in his hands, he appreciated the Corporal's discipline. The hot dahl warmed his stomach and soothed his aching muscles. It was with huge relief that the squad received Derra's news that there would be no watch rota that night, and all were fast asleep within seconds of laying down on the cold groundsheet of the tent.

The next eight days settled into a routine that began at dawn and ended some time after sunset each evening. The weather proved cold, and often wet, but not unusually so for the time of year. Not surprisingly, the troops soon became very weary with the long daily marches, and the Corporals and Sergeants quickly found that they had their work cut out to maintain morale and discipline at a level acceptable to the Captains. Marching songs and chants were frequently employed to pass the time and help the long miles pass more swiftly.

Corporal Derra had insisted that from the first full day of the journey to Mantor, each and every member of her squad was given the task of either constructing the tents, drawing water, gathering firewood or digging the toilet trenches. However, without exception all were involved with the nightly sentry duties that maintained the security of the campsites. Occasionally, one of the two veterans who had been trained in the past as a mounted scout would be allocated a horse and sent ahead on patrol. Otherwise, very little broke the set routine.

After the first night's rest, Calvyn had woken early, shivering with cold and his limbs stiff, both from the temperature and the rigours of the previous day. However, having resurrected the fire at the tent entrance back into life, and warmed up his chilled body, Calvyn found the rest of the march to Levanbridge relatively painless. He had used his watch shifts to practise the few spells which he felt might be of use in battle. In particular he practised the magical shield spell, which he had adapted into a part of the incantation that he had cast during the forging of his sword. Unfortunately, the glowing green barrier of energy that had formed on his first late watch practice had aroused the interest of the watchman from the squad next to them. Calvyn had subsequently been forced to do some fast talking to convince the Private that what he had seen was probably the result of looking into the fire too much. Unconvinced, the sentry had gone back to his watch post grumbling, and Calvyn had subsequently limited his nightly exercises to merely learning and rehearsing the runes without picturing, and therefore producing, the end results.

At times, Calvyn and Jenna had managed to get together with Bek, Tondi, Matim and some of the other members of their old training squad. Everyone seemed in reasonably high spirits under the circumstances. Their reunions never lasted long, as they were almost invariably too tired for much more than a quick cup of dahl together by the watch fire before turning in for the night.

The only exception to this was about four nights into the march when Bek appeared at the fireside outside Calvyn's tent. Calvyn noted immediately that his friend looked thoughtful and slightly troubled by something, but did not have the opportunity to ask him what was wrong until the rest of Calvyn's squad had turned in for the night.

Once the last of Calvyn's compatriots had gone to their beds, Bek quietly ushered Calvyn away from the fire to a spot that was as far from anyone's hearing as they could get in the huge campsite of the Baron's army.

'What's the problem, Bek?' Calvyn whispered to his friend, straining his eyes to try to see him properly in the darkness.

'I don't wish to pry Calvyn, but have you been practising magic recently?' Bek returned, saying the word "magic" as softly as he could. 'It's just that I overheard one of the Privates from the squad next to us telling his mates about some green glow that he'd seen during a night watch, and I thought of you.'

Calvyn sighed.

'Yes, Bek, that was me. I was careless, but it won't happen again.'

'What won't happen again? The magic or the carelessness?' Bek asked. 'And what was the green glow about anyway?'

'The glow was a spell from Perdimonn's grimoire. It forms a sort of magical barrier, which in theory is impervious to weapons, but I wasn't really thinking too brightly when I decided to practise it. I won't make that mistake again.'

'Wow! A magical barrier!' hissed Bek in excitement. 'Are you planning to protect us all against enemy arrows in the battle or something?'

Calvyn paused, wondering whether he should tell his

friend that the spell was designed for personal protection, but after a moment's thought, he decided to temporise.

'Well, the spell wasn't really designed for mass protection, but I'm working on it,' he whispered gently. 'The biggest problems with using magic are firstly that it is highly illegal and its use is considered all but treasonous. Secondly, and in this case more pertinently, it requires great concentration and focus of mind. Somehow I doubt that I'll be able to maintain that sort of focus whilst twenty thousand Terachites are trying to carve out my gizzards!'

Bek clapped his hand over his mouth to stifle a laugh, which he managed to muffle sufficiently that it sounded much like someone clearing his throat.

'You have a way with words, Calvyn,' he muttered, quietly chuckling to himself.

Calvyn failed to see what he had said that was so funny.

'Let me put it this way, Bek,' he said carefully. 'I'm more likely to be using what magic you've taught me with this sword to keep me alive than any half-baked spells that I've learned or invented.'

Bek thought about that for a moment or two and then sighed. 'One thing is for sure: we will all be put to the test one way or another.'

On arrival at Levanbridge, Calvyn and several of the other more junior members of his squad were awe-struck at the size of the campsite sprawled around the outside of the town. It seemed that the tents almost matched the houses in number, and Calvyn had suddenly felt a lot more comfortable about the outcome of this sudden and distant conflict. The veterans amongst the squad did their best to look nonchalant about the massing of troops, but in truth none of them had ever seen an army of this scale gathered in one place.

In reality, there were only about four thousand troops camped at Levanbridge. However, this was undoubtedly the largest force that had been seen in central Thrandor in living memory, and as such it made the soldiers there feel invincible.

As Baron Keevan's troops pitched their camp it quickly became apparent that they would not be remaining at Levanbridge for long. With more troops arriving almost by the hour, the gathering army was rapidly draining the resources of the local area.

Having established where his troops were pitching their camp, the Baron, together with his Captains, had immediately disappeared off into the mass of tents in search of the other army leaders. They had been gone some time before Captain Tegrani returned with the news that everyone would be breaking camp and marching south early in the morning. The young Captain had briefed the Sergeants and Corporals on the latest intelligence from the scouts, and from the message riders who had been sent north by the southern force to bring up to date information on the progress of the Terachite army to the gathering reinforcements.

Later that evening, Derra gathered her squad and gave them a rundown on the current situation.

'It sounds as if it's all got pretty ugly down south,' Derra grated, her voice harsh but her hard face impassive as her eyes glittered in the firelight. 'The Terachite force has now been estimated at approximately thirty thousand by scouts from Baron Anton's force.'

At the mention of that number, someone let out a long low whistle of surprise. After a short pause to let the facts sink in, Derra continued. 'By reputation his men are trustworthy, so I think that we can be certain of being fairly significantly outnumbered when we arrive at Mantor. The latest word is that Anton took a force to strengthen the garrison town of Fallowsford and delay the Terachites from reaching Mantor with their full army. The Terachim sleethe spawn have been destroying everything in their path. They've left nothing and no one alive in their wake. There will be no quarter in this war, people. It is going to be kill, or be killed. It's said that their leader is a fanatic who will stop at nothing.'

'How long before the Terachites reach Fallowsford?'

asked one of the older veterans.

'They already have,' replied Derra. 'Four days ago in fact. The latest information we have is that Baron Anton's main reinforcement army arrived at Fallowsford only hours ahead of the Terachites. We know that the defenders held the initial enemy assault, but the garrison was taking heavy losses. It's unlikely that they will hold out for long.'

Quiet settled over the squad as they absorbed this gloomy forecast. Calvyn looked around the fire at the other squad members, but all were too caught up in their own thoughts to meet his gaze.

Suddenly Jenna's voice broke the silence.

'Just how strong is our force, Corporal? I don't mean Baron Keevan's. I just wondered how many fighting men the King is going to field at Mantor. It would be nice to know how many Terachites each we have to kill. After all, I wouldn't want to get greedy and steal someone else's share.'

Laughter rippled around the fireplace at Jenna's light-hearted phrasing of the very serious question.

Derra too smiled as she answered.

'The force at Fallowsford is about four and a half thousand strong. The latest figures from Mantor suggest that a further three and a half thousand have already gathered there, and we should leave here with about five thousand tomorrow morning. Other reinforcements may arrive in dribs and drabs, but if you ignore those, then I would say that the Terachites have provided us with two to three men each to kill.'

'How very generous of them,' replied Jenna, gaining a further laugh.

'Outnumbered by three to one is a narfing poor way to start a fight,' grumbled someone at the back of the group.

'Agreed. It's not ideal,' Derra answered in the general direction of the disgruntled comment. 'However, you are a disciplined and highly trained fighting force. Providing that you remember what you have been taught and do as you are told, there is no reason why we shouldn't send this nomad rabble running back to the desert as fast as their sand-flea bitten legs will carry them.'

'I have no problem with fighting alongside any of my fellow members of Baron Keevan's army,' one of the veterans stated firmly. 'Even the most junior members of our squad are more than adequate sword brothers, but what of all these others? Are they too going to be disciplined in battle and solid enough to guard our flanks? Otherwise we have serious problems, Corporal.'

'It is true that a mixed force is weaker than one made up of people who have all been trained the same way, and consequently think and react as a unit. However, if it makes you feel any better, the Terachites have far bigger problems than just a mixed force. Their army is made up of many clans and tribes. Several of these clans actually hate each other more than they hate us. Therefore it stands to reason that the longer that this campaign goes on, the more divided our enemy will become. That is almost certainly why their leader is pushing so hard towards Mantor. He knows that Mantor is the key. If he can offer the combined tribes a crushing victory in short order, he will stand a good chance of healing some of the old enmities between the various clans. On the other hand, if things don't go the way he planned, very shortly we will become the least of his problems.'

'Now wouldn't that be something?' Jenna laughed. 'Let's just hope it doesn't happen before we get to claim our quota of Terachites.'

'What a depressing thought,' Calvyn added, his voice dripping with sarcasm.

A ripple of laughter ran through the group.

'Unless there are any more questions, the show's over, boys and girls,' Derra stated, her penetrating voice demanding attention once more.

No one spoke.

'Very well,' the Corporal continued. 'I suggest that those of you not on the first watch get some sleep. We'll be marching alongside a lot of other outfits over the next few days, and I expect you all to be the smartest, most disciplined soldiers in Thrandor. Is that understood?'

'Yes, Corporal,' came the chorused reply, and with that the group began dispersing back to their two tents and appointed guard posts.

Morning arrived all too quickly for Calvyn after a restless night of broken, half-remembered dreams. His eyes felt hot and gritty as he splashed icy cold water onto his cheeks and around the back of his neck from the cold stream. Slapping his cheeks gently to increase the circulation of blood to his face after the bracing wash, Calvyn looked down at his reflection on the settling surface of the water. Gradually, his features became more regular as the ripples settled into stillness in the small pool. Somewhat surprised, Calvyn noted that the face that looked back at him from the pool was no longer the face of a boy. It was a man's face. Youthful, but definitely adult.

'Strange,' he muttered to himself. 'I wonder when that happened.'

Somehow, having realised that his childhood was a thing of the past for him made what he was facing easier to accept. War was something that children played at, but that adults faced when it became necessary. The day of necessity had arrived much sooner for him than he would have liked, but having seen his reflection looking strong and determined out of the water had settled his heart towards his duty as a soldier. As he returned to his tent, he looked at the faces of his compatriots around the campsite with fresh insight. It was amazing. He found that he could actually see which of his fellow soldiers had still not made the mental adjustment from being the child out to play war, and the adult, willing to die for king and country.

'Are you OK?' asked Jenna, who was busy packing her clothes back into her backpack as he entered their tent.

'Yes. Fine thanks,' assured Calvyn, allowing his thoughtful expression to relax into a smile for his friend. 'I'm just a little preoccupied with the information that Derra gave us last night, that's all. I suppose that I'd feel better if I just knew the area that we are to fight in. Somehow I think that I'd feel more comfortable if the battle was being held say... back at the castle where I know the lie of the land. Then they could outnumber us by ten to one and I'd probably still be happy... well... not happy, but at least content that I was fighting on home turf. Do you know what I mean?'

'Exactly,' replied Jenna, nodding her head in affirmation. 'Although... I have been to Mantor once. It was some years ago now, but it doesn't feel totally alien. I must admit though, that I much preferred travelling this road in a carriage to walking it.'

'A carriage? I didn't realise that your family was rich or I'd have proposed a bonding ages ago,' jested Calvyn, rubbing his hands together and twisting his face as if thinking of pots of gold.

Jenna laughed.

'Perhaps I should have said "pony and cart" rather than carriage, as that would be a much better description.'

'Rats!' Calvyn cursed, shaking his down-turned head in mock disappointment. 'My chances of wealth and fame cruelly dashed again! Never mind, I'm sure that the second I walk into Mantor in this outfit, the maidens, both rich and poor alike, will swoon in my presence. I'll undoubtedly be able to take my pick of the dozens of beautiful, eligible, wealthy young ladies who'll be falling over themselves to bond with such a dashing hero of a soldier.'

'Undoubtedly,' agreed Jenna, keeping a deadpan face. 'In fact you'll probably need more skill and determination to fight off the women than to beat that excuse for a Terachite army. Thirty thousand raging Terachites will be a mere trifle compared with the ladies of Mantor.'

Calvyn laughed, but Jenna's face remained serious and a twinge of doubt gripped his stomach as his mind raced.

'You are joking?' he asked, his voice halting and uncertain.

Jenna managed to hold her serious expression for a good few seconds before abruptly bursting into fits of laughter. Calvyn ruefully joined her as he realised that he had been well and truly taken in. Dashing tears of mirth from her eyes, Jenna pointed a finger at Calvyn's face and then curled up again in an uncontrollable belly laugh that drew the attention of Corporal Derra, who poked her head through the tent entrance.

'What's the joke? I could do with a laugh,' she growled.

'I am,' answered Calvyn with a smile as Jenna was still convulsed, tears streaming down her face, unable to speak. 'Jenna managed to convince me that I would be irresistible to the women of Mantor, and that I would do better to worry about how to fight off the ladies than to get concerned about the Terachites. She keeps a very straight face,' he added.

Derra looked at Calvyn, and across to Jenna who had redoubled her laughter at this candid summary, and was now holding her sides as if in pain. A wry smile twisted onto the Corporal's face and she shook her head slightly in semi-disbelief.

'When you've had your little joke, perhaps we could begin breaking camp?' Derra suggested, not too unkindly. 'We won't be moving out for an hour or so, but I want to have everything packed and loaded well before then. There's a lot to do, Privates, so don't dwell too long on your merriment, though it's good to see that someone's still in good humour.'

A short while later, having made short work of the now routine packing of equipment and reloading of wagons, Calvyn and Jenna were standing in the column with their fellow soldiers, all awaiting the order which would recommence their march to Mantor. Jenna had shared the gist of their previous conversation with a small group of their friends who had all proceeded to rib Calvyn so mercilessly that Jenna began to feel twinges of guilt. Eventually, when she realised that Calvyn was just going to let them all laugh at his expense without replying in kind, Jenna butted in with a few choice put-downs which deflected conversations along a different line.

'Sorry about that, Calvyn. I should have known better,' she murmured to him afterward.

'No problem,' he replied amiably. 'As the NCOs keep pointedly mentioning, "If you can't take a joke, you shouldn't have joined." Besides, it was quite funny, and it gave them all something amusing to concentrate on for a while.'

'Yes, take a joke by all means, but don't just let them run riot over you! You are fine at one to one banter, Calvyn, but when a group starts poking fun you just clam up and take it. Don't. Take my advice on this. Don't bottle up so much. Hit back hard and fast. Be outrageous. Suggest the preposterous in order to deflect their attention. You make yourself an easy target otherwise, and if you allow yourself to become the brunt of too many jokes without fighting back, you'll eventually lose the respect of those around you. You're better than that, so don't give them the opportunity.'

'OK, Mum,' he said meekly, but with a glint in his eye that set Jenna chuckling.

'I mean it, you idiot!' she laughed.

'I know you do, and you're absolutely right. From now on I'll be vicious,' Calvyn answered, dropping his voice to a bass growl for the last three words.

'Impossible! Absolutely impossible!' Jenna laughed, shaking her head in disbelief. 'Why do my friends all turn out to be so difficult?'

Before Calvyn could think of a suitably quick response, however, Sergeant Brett called them all to attention, and within seconds the march was underway once more.

CHAPTER 16

Once the troops had left Levanbridge a nervous tension began to build steadily over the following few days. A large troop of Lord Valdeer's cavalry caught up with them the day after they had left the riverside town, bringing news of a further five hundred foot soldiers only a half day's march behind. After a brief halt for the leaders to discuss the merits of awaiting the additional force, the march was continued.

That evening, Corporal Derra explained what little she knew to her squad.

'The Baron and the other leaders are of the opinion that unless we get to Mantor as soon as we can, we may arrive too late to be of any help. There will be no let up in the pace from now on. We will be marching from dawn until dusk with no more than the standard halts to rest the mules and prevent you all from keeling over. Make sure that you drink water 'til you slosh, and top up your water flasks at every opportunity. Dehydration is going to be a serious problem with this sort of push, so be aware and don't allow yourselves to dry out. As we get closer to Mantor we will almost certainly push well ahead of the supply train, so eat what you can, when you can. Don't turn down food from now on, people. You will not be able to guarantee when the next meal will be available.'

'Is there any more news from Fallowsford, Corporal?' asked one of the older veterans, voicing a question that was on most of the soldiers' minds.

'No,' Derra replied in a tone that suggested that this was the limit of her answer, and that no further discussion on this subject was to be broached. 'Let's get our priorities straight. We must get to Mantor as fast as we can, but we'll also need to be in a fit state to fight when we arrive. Fighting whilst tired is hard. Fighting whilst tired, dehydrated and hungry is impossible. Therefore, starting tomorrow evening we will be having a half-hour of sword drill before making camp at the end of each day's march. The format will be ten on ten, and I will be designating the groups. The drill will serve dual purposes. Firstly it will show you firstly just how hard it is to fight whilst tired, and secondly to keep your sword arms both strong and in practice. Has anyone got any further questions?'

No one responded.

'Very well. Let's get some sleep. We're going to need all the rest we can get.'

So it went on: marching through the daylight hours and sword drill in the fading light of dusk; make camp, break camp, and through the cycle again. The miles and days rolled past, but at a seemingly slower and slower pace, as the tension heightened amongst the troops and the city of Mantor, together with the imminent battle, drew ever nearer.

Minutes dragged, but in reality the speed of the army's progress actually increased. Calvyn had noted a marked improvement in the quality of the roads as they had progressed southward. The major trade routes of the north were often little more than poorly cobbled tracks, which at times had deteriorated into muddy quagmires with the combination of the large troop movements and the bouts of heavy rain which had made sections of the long march particularly miserable. Trying to march in ankle deep mud had been virtually impossible at times, but now the roads were well constructed and wide enough to allow two wagons to pass with ease. Only the nervous anticipation and constantly rolling terrain made it seem as if they were not getting anywhere.

Calvyn gained some information about Mantor from Jenna, and more from some of the other soldiers. However, when he finally saw the city, his mental picture of a vast hill fortress containing the entire city within mighty walls proved somewhat inaccurate. In truth, the city walls, whilst strong, were not unassailable. Furthermore, whilst the vast majority of the city buildings ranging across the top of the hill on which Mantor had been founded were within the confines of that protection, there were also many buildings which had been constructed outside of that defensive circle.

The original concept of a hilltop city had been tactically very sound, especially as the great sweeping curve of the River Fallow gave the city a natural barrier to the west and south. A single stone bridge had been constructed across the swiftly flowing river to the northwest of the city with fortified gates on the city side of the span. All of the southern and western trade routes relied on this bridge, as it was the only way, aside from the ferry boats, to cross the Fallow without following the river upstream many miles into the heart of Thrandor. Backtracking in this fashion would lead northwest to the very base of the Celadorn hills, before gradually swinging back southward towards its source in the Terachim Mountains, which formed the southern border of the kingdom. However, the tactical advantage of the hilltop city had given way to the pressures of trade, commerce, and forty years of peaceful prosperity. As a result, the population of Mantor had outgrown its confining walls and many individuals and minor trading houses had ignored the possibility of any future military threat. In time, what amounted to suburbs had grown at the base of the northern side of Mantor Hill, though Calvyn's first sight of this extension of the city was of the last throes of its destruction.

*   *   *   *   *

King Malo was standing atop the city wall in the

northwest quarter of Mantor looking down towards the valley where the Fallow Bridge defined the last line of defence before the wall on which he stood. Dusk was setting in, and as the arch of night slowly crept up the sky behind him a grumble of distant thunder rolled up the valley from the east. The King glanced over his right shoulder towards the source of the threatening sound. A distant flash of lightning momentarily lit the eastern sky, and silhouetted a lone figure walking wearily along the wall towards him.

'Your Majesty,' the man said, bowing deeply.

'Anton, my friend, it is good to see you still alive. I have been hearing dire reports of the losses at Fallowsford and had feared that I might not see you again.'

The King gripped Anton firmly by the hand and looked into his friend's tired eyes. If anything the fading light accentuated the fatigue which was etched into every line of the Baron's face. Another rumble of thunder growled its menacing message of impending doom.

'It was bad, Sire. I... failed...'

The Baron's voice was faltering and soft, but the King interrupted him before he could continue.

'Nonsense, Anton. You did not fail. You held back an army of thirty thousand or more with a mere four and a half thousand men for a full six days. The minstrels will sing of your achievement for centuries to come.'

'But I lost more than half of those men, Sire. Unless you have a lot more men held in reserve somewhere that I am unaware of, then I fear that the city will fall within a day. This wall is far too long to hold with the few thousand men that we have here.'

The King sighed heavily and turned back to his previous north-westerly vigil.

'I know, Anton,' he admitted eventually. 'It seems that it is I who have failed – failed to anticipate this sort of attack. I suppose the comfortable complacency bred by forty years of peace could be my excuse, but I have had fair warning. Demarr and those others from the north warned us all of just such an assault three years ago. True, it was from the opposite border, and it never came. However, it may be that I should have listened to them after all. Instead, I did nothing. And I would undoubtedly have done nothing with similar warnings from the south. I have lost touch with my kingdom, Anton. I only have myself to blame.'

'You are too harsh on yourself, Sire...'

'On the contrary, Anton,' interrupted the King, 'I am not harsh enough. I should be down there with my men, fighting for my kingdom instead of cowering here and allowing my minions to die for my comfort.'

Anton remained silent, not knowing how, or indeed whether to respond to the King in his dark and gloomy mood. The two continued standing quietly for some time, staring out into the now rapidly darkening valley.

'Listen,' whispered the King quietly to Anton. 'It begins.'

The faint sounds of battle drifted up from the valley, a distant yelling and clashing of swords that seemed somehow surreal to the morose Monarch. King Malo turned to his friend and placed a hand on his shoulder.

'Come, Anton,' he said sadly. 'Let us go and find me some suitable armour.'

The King's troops held the Fallow Bridge for some hours despite being massively outnumbered. If the bridge had been narrower they might have held out indefinitely. However, it had been constructed for the large merchant wagons which had for so long been the primary user of the kingdom's roads, and despite the fortified gates on the city side of the bridge, eventually the sheer weight of numbers of the enemy fighters told. The defenders, having been forced to retreat did so quickly, and in an orderly fashion. The North gates of the city clanged shut behind them as their Captain marshalled his troops into the relative safety of the city walls. With a reverberating thud the heavy portcullis dropped into place behind the gates. A crash of thunder followed an instant later as lightning split the sky overhead and the

267

first of the threatening line of thunder-storms chose that moment to unleash its fury on the beleaguered city and attackers alike.

Great droplets of rain spattered on the stone streets and tiled roof tops, a scattered patter at first, building rapidly into a rushing crescendo as a second flash of lightning lit the city with its harsh light. The clap of thunder that followed was heart-stopping in intensity, and the defenders crouched behind their battlements and watched with dismay as the inky black mass of the invading army swarmed across the Fallow Bridge. The seething mass of humanity spread like a filling lake around the base of the northern side of Mantor Hill.

It was about midnight when the first of the fires started in lower Mantor, the ransacking of the more recently built suburbs being both rapid and thorough. The defenders on the walls watched in dismay as first one, then another, and then more fires in quick succession lit the midnight sky with their crackling orange glow. Thunderstorms came and went right through the night, but even their intense efforts at extinguishing the flames were to no avail. By the early hours of the morning the entire lower city was alight, and morale amongst Mantor's defenders had sunk to its lowest ebb.

King Malo and Baron Anton walked the walls of the north and west sectors of the upper city talking through what little strategy that they had, and taking time to encourage the troops awaiting the imminent assault.

A young soldier who was huddled, dozing with his back to the battlements was startled by their approach. Guiltily he leapt to his feet and bowed to the two dignitaries. The King smiled and waved him back to his resting spot.

'Get what rest you can, Soldier,' the King advised kindly. 'They won't attack until dawn.'

'Really, your Majesty?' blurted the young man, relief colouring his voice. 'How do you know?'

'Well, I suppose that nothing in life is totally sure, but

if I were leading that army down there I would want at least the bulk of it on this side of the river before commencing any assault. Add to that the fact that they have not yet even seen this side of the city in full daylight, and I think that even the most reckless of commanders would think twice before ordering his initial attack in the dark. Get your rest whilst you can, young man. It is refreshing to see someone who can.'

'Thank you, your Majesty.'

The King and Baron Anton continued their walk. The mere sight of the white haired Monarch in his burnished armour and brightly polished helm looking remarkably hale for his years, strolling along the wall with the solid and competent looking Baron by his side, lifted many men's hearts. Both took time to speak to the soldiers, listening to their ideas and making perceptive last minute suggestions on how best to defend each point on the wall. By the time dawn broke they had walked the north and west sections of the wall twice, and had stopped by the North gate to await the sunrise.

The sky brightened slowly as if night was reluctant to lose its grip over the heavens. The last storm had passed the city a couple of hours beforehand, and as the sun finally peeked its fiery face over the eastern horizon, the ground steamed as the wet earth released some of its recently gained moisture back to the air. Great towering clouds still rode the early morning breeze, but in isolation only, and a fresh deep blue clearness dominated the sky.

With the advent of dawn the Terachite army let out a huge cry, and the inevitable charge up the hill towards the main city wall commenced.

'Tarmin protect us,' muttered the King in horror as the true scale of the enemy force started to sink in.

'Amen to that,' grunted Anton, and waved at the nearest soldiers to move the vats of boiling pitch into position on the battlements.

*   *   *   *   *

Calvyn fingered the string of his longbow nervously as he looked through the few remaining trees at the orange glow, which he now knew was the burning remnants of Lower Mantor.

'I wonder if they know that we're here,' he whispered quietly to Jenna.

'Who? The enemy, or our allies in the city?' Jenna asked.

'The enemy, surely they'll miss their sweep riders soon and suspect something.'

'It's difficult to say, but I personally don't think that they're expecting to face anyone except those already in the city. Mantor seems to have been their goal from the start, and now that they're here on the doorstep I suspect that the city will dominate their thoughts.'

Calvyn thought about that. It certainly made sense. The small party of sweep riders, who had entered the edge of the woods on the hillside which formed the opposite wall of the valley to the north of Mantor, had been slain within seconds of entering the trees. The orange glow at their backs had made them easy targets for the waiting bowmen despite it being the middle of the night. The riderless horses had been quickly rounded up and led back to where Lord Valdeer's cavalry were waiting on the other side of the ridgeline.

The final stage of the march had been both hard work and, for the last mile or so through the trees, treacherous in the extreme. Walking through woodland at night was not something that Calvyn ever planned on doing again by choice.

Corporal Derra had informed them all during their afternoon rest stop that the scouts had just returned from the ridge-line north of Mantor and that they had reported sighting the enemy forces approaching Mantor from the south.

'They still have to take the Fallow Bridge before they can assault the city,' Derra had stated coldly, 'but from what I remember of the defences there, it is unlikely that we can reach the city before the bridge is stormed.'

The Corporal's estimates had proved accurate, and at about an hour to midnight the troops were halted whilst the leaders discussed the news that the enemy now held the north bank of the Fallow. At this point the Northern Lords' army was no more than a half-hour's march from the ridgeline to the north of Mantor. After some debate amongst the Captains and Nobles it was decided that trying to win through to Mantor at night would be too dangerous. Instead, a battle plan for daybreak had been drawn up and agreed.

The basic plan was to spread the army along the ridgeline short of the city, it being no more than half a mile from the tree line to the base of Mantor Hill. The battle ranks would be threefold. In the front rank would be all the troops who had been given training in the use of pikes. Calvyn had given a quiet sigh of relief at this news, as Baron Keevan had never ordered any of his men to undergo training with this cumbersome weapon, and Calvyn had no desire to be in the front row of fighters. Behind the pikemen were to be the swordsmen and the small company from Celadorn Fell who had trained exclusively with battle-axes. These fearsome warriors were some distance to the east of where Calvyn was stationed, which suited him fine. He found it very difficult to imagine how one would fight with a sword alongside someone swinging such a bludgeoning weapon.

Finally, some ten paces behind the ranks of swordsmen were to be a rank of archers. To his surprise, Calvyn was chosen to join the rank of archers. However, when he mentioned to Corporal Derra that he would have preferred to have been with the swordsmen she just smiled, and told him that he would run out of arrows soon enough to try out his new sword.

'Make every arrow count,' she advised him. 'There will be plenty of nomads left to play with when you're done shooting.'

Lord Valdeer's cavalry, together with all of the other minor groups of mounted troops, were planning to wait back behind the ridgeline. As Lord Valdeer himself had pointed out, the horsemen would only be in the way of the archers initially, but if they circled around the wood and attacked the eastern flank of the enemy force after the archers had done their work, the horsemen would be at their most effective.

With the plans laid and the troops in position, that left only a nervous wait for the rising sun. Corporal Derra moved amongst her squad and made them all eat some food and drink lots of water.

'If you get cramps through a lack of salt, or try to fight dehydrated, you will not survive this battle. Dying is not what you're paid for,' she said forcefully. 'Killing the enemy is. So give yourselves the best chance of doing your job.'

Several of the soldiers had vomited their food back up, their stomachs so knotted with anticipation that they could not keep the food down. These few were encouraged to drink lots of water, and by the time that the sun finally pushed itself up over the horizon, all had managed to get some sustenance into their systems.

Dawn finally arrived.

'All right, everyone. Wait for the word now. Don't anyone move forward until the signal is given,' Derra growled as the sound of the charge of the Terachite army up to the Mantor city wall drifted up the valley. 'Wait for it... wait for it,' she purred.

Then, from somewhere a good distance eastward of where Calvyn, Jenna and the rest of their squad waited, a horn trumpeted its brassy challenge. Within seconds a dozen or so more echoed the call right along the ridge, and the order to advance was given.

Marching forward into the bright morning sunlight, Calvyn and the others got their first clear view of the beleaguered city and the massive Terachite army sandwiched between where they stood and the city walls.

'OK, everyone, here they come,' boomed Sergeant Brett. 'Remember, men, whatever they throw at us we must hold our lines or we'll be finished. Archers – hold your fire until you can see the whites of their eyes.

Discipline, men. Discipline will keep you alive...'

Brett continued his exhortations at the top of his stentorian voice as a mass of enemy horsemen swarmed up the slope towards them and along the line other Sergeants and Corporals were being equally vocal.

The ground thundered at the approaching charge, and Calvyn held his breath as the clamour of Terachite voices raised in ululating war cries filled the air. Focusing everything on remaining calm, he looked briefly down at his feet before raising his head and drawing his bow in one fluid motion. Picking a target other than the two or three front runners, Calvyn held the bow rock steady, awaiting the order to fire.

*   *   *   *   *

Just as the first of the scaling ladders was placed against the city wall a faint fanfare of brassy horns cut through the battle cries of the attacking nomad tribesmen. The Thrandorian defenders on the city wall let out an almighty cheer as the ranks of their allies from the north marched out from the trees on the other side of the valley.

'Look, your Majesty,' a nearby soldier called, somewhat unnecessarily to the King, and pointed enthusiastically to the impressive formation of troops which were lined right the way along the opposing ridgeline.

Tears of relief sprang to the King's eyes, and his legs felt momentarily weak as the enemy assault faltered slightly in confusion and alarm. Baron Anton, however, had taken one look at the friendly forces and sprinted away along the wall towards the North Gate.

'Anton! Where are you going?' shouted the King at his rapidly departing General.

'To prepare the horses, Sire. A cavalry charge at the right moment might just tip the balance,' he shouted back over his shoulder, pausing briefly to answer before disappearing along the wall at a flat out run.

*   *   *   *   *

'Dammit, Ramiff! Why did I not know of this?' stormed Demarr, pointing northward up the valley side at the long lines of enemy soldiers emerging from the trees. 'Did I not give the order for scouts to be sent out? Do I have to see to everything myself?'

'The scouts were sent, Chosen One. However, they are only just overdue and with the bickering between the tribes as to who was entitled to what from the looting of Lower Mantor to settle, it was dawn before anyone even began to think about where they were.'

'Blast their greediness! Can they not see that the greatest prize of all lies within their grasp? Great Tarmin! No! Not the cavalry! Signaller. Quickly. Signal them back. What are they thinking of? They'll be slaughtered up there.'

The Signaller blew on the strangely curved horn a rapid series of blasts that should have halted the charging horsemen. However, the call was ignored, and the galloping mass of cavalry continued unchecked up the slope towards the waiting enemy lines.

'Again,' screamed Demarr at the Signaller, incensed that his orders were being ignored. 'Ramiff, find the Maharls of the Dagali and the Embara and send them to me now. We need to co-ordinate a sensible attack against those troops,' Demarr snarled at his aide, whilst the Signaller blew for all he was worth.

Ramiff did not need telling twice and he departed at a run, only too glad to have a valid excuse to get away from his furious Master. If it was possible, Ramiff would have been even more glad to leave had he seen the Chosen One's reaction when, on turning back towards the city, he had found that the signal to stop the cavalry charge had confused those assaulting the walls. The results were disastrous as the lack of direction amongst the attackers allowed the defenders on the walls to massacre huge numbers of their opponents at very little cost.

Demarr could only grind his teeth in frustration as he

watched his men die in large numbers.

*   *   *   *   *

'Fire!' bellowed Sergeant Brett at the top of his immensely loud voice.

The whooshing buzz of arrows leaving bowstrings filled the air, and a bridge of arrows arched over the swordsmen and pikemen, thudding with deadly force into the leading rows of charging Terachite horsemen. Horses and men alike fell dead under the lethal rain of shafts.

Calvyn drew again and again, trying to keep his calm as he aimed and released. Out of the corner of his eye he sensed Jenna releasing virtually two shafts for each of his, and he did not doubt for one second that each one was fired with unrelenting accuracy.

The leading ranks of the enemy cavalry were cut down as if someone had taken a great scythe to their legs. However, the sheer mass of numbers was such that despite hundreds of riders melting away under the withering rain of arrows, a wall of horsemen ultimately crashed into the front row of Thrandorian troops, and the hand to hand fighting began.

It quickly became apparent that the Captains had chosen well by putting the pikemen in the front row, as the Terachites had obviously never fought against weapons with such a long reach before. Indeed, it was only the sheer weight of the horses which enabled some of the riders to crash their way through the pikemen and into the swordsmen, and the majority of those who did so sustained wounds to themselves or their mounts in the process.

The archers very quickly had their pick of targets as the impetus of the charge was halted by the line of braced pikemen, and before long a large proportion of the enemy cavalry lay dead. The straggling survivors retreated back down the hill to where line upon line of Terachite foot soldiers were gathering.

Despite failing to seriously breach the ranks of the

Thrandorian troops, the defenders had not been without casualties. Unfortunately, amongst them was Sergeant Brett who had been trampled by a huge black Terachite horse that had smashed, riderless through the line of pikemen and crushed him before being cut down by the other swordsmen standing around him.

Whilst the remaining Terachite horsemen retreated down the hillside and the enemy foot soldiers formed their ranks, the Thrandorian Captains toured the lines and organised the removal of the dead and severely wounded back into the trees. Enemy bodies, both human and equine, were dragged forward and placed in front of the pikemen where they would hinder the next Terachite attack.

Captain Tegrani looked sadly at the body of Sergeant Brett as it was carried back to the trees, and waved Corporal Derra over to join him.

'Derra, I want you to take over Sergeant Brett's responsibilities,' he told her solemnly.

'Corporal Gan is the senior Corporal, Sir.   Surely...' Derra began to say.

'You are the better disciplinarian, Derra,' the Captain interrupted, swiftly overruling her line of reasoning. 'The troops need that discipline now more than ever. Just do it, and we'll argue over who should be the new Sergeant once we've sent these sons of bitches home.'

'Yes, Sir.'

If the stone-faced Corporal felt any emotion, either good or bad, it did not show on her face as she returned to the lines as the 'acting' Sergeant. The enemy forces were rapidly regrouping, and a huge mass of Terachite foot soldiers had been organised into some semblance of order at the base of the slope. To those around her, Derra appeared to slip into her new role effortlessly, and within seconds of her return the units under her command were snapped back into immaculate defensive lines.

'Archers, ready,' called Derra, her gravelly voice carrying to her troops just as clearly as Sergeant Brett's mighty bellows ever had.

The enemy was advancing up the slope steadily towards them now. However, unlike the rash charge of the cavalry these soldiers were prepared for the rain of arrows that would soon be slicing the air towards them. Each man carried a round lightweight shield made of toughened hides strapped to one arm, and held a wicked-looking curved sabre in their other hand. Although the rounded shields did not lock together to form a solid protective wall in the way that the more square-shaped shields of the Thrandorian troops did, the number of arrows which found their marks when Derra gave the order to fire this time was significantly reduced from the earlier success against the cavalry.

Calvyn had virtually run out of arrows by the time that the first of the enemy clashed with the pikemen. Jenna, he noticed, had already placed her bow down behind her and had drawn her sword. Releasing his last shaft on a trajectory that carried it over the heads of his fellow soldiers and into the mass of enemies beyond, Calvyn too discarded the longbow and drew his sword.

The Thrandorian formation held steady as the enemy forces struck, and despite the almighty din of clashing weapons, war cries, and the screams of the wounded and dying, Calvyn could still hear Derra's rasping orders above the cacophony of the battle. Together with the other archers, Jenna and he moved forward to the rearmost rank of swordsmen to await their turn at crossing blades with the enemy.

*   *   *   *   *

'You should get that seen to, your Majesty. It's bleeding pretty badly,' Baron Anton suggested in a tone that bordered on being an order.

'I don't have time for that. It's only a scratch, Anton. Look, they're massing for another push and we need every sword that we have up here. They nearly managed to overrun us on that last assault. We are so thinly spread that they will only have to take one small section of the wall and we'll never be able to dislodge them,' the King replied grimly.

'My King... my friend,' Anton replied more gently, 'you will be of no use to us at all if you keep losing blood at that rate. You'll be weaker than a newborn babe inside half an hour. Please. Get it wrapped.'

The King locked eyes with his friend, anger flashing in his gaze. Anton held his ground and his calm, solid expression quickly cooled the King's wrath.

How the man had changed over the last few days, Anton reflected. The Baron had always liked Malo, and respected the goodness that radiated from the reigning Monarch, but had never really felt that he had possessed the mettle to be a truly great king. Today he saw a different man. If only Malo had discovered this sort of drive and commitment as a younger man, Anton mused. Thrandor could truly have become a great nation again. Instead, they were fighting a losing battle and his friend's transformation looked very much as if it was to be in vain.

'You are right, Anton. However, I will not leave the wall. Order the medics to be armed and stationed up here on the battlements with us. If they don't fight as they heal now they'll probably have to fight alone later.'

'Very well, your Majesty,' Anton agreed and swiftly relayed the King's orders to a nearby Captain, who in turn ran off to action them.

Screaming, chaotic war cries again heralded the fact that the seething mass of Terachites was once more swarming up the slope to assault the city wall. The ear-splitting din from the marauding horde was largely met with calm and determination from the soldiers of Thrandor. One or two hurled curses back, but for the most part the defenders conserved their energy to meet the invaders with hurled rocks, boiling fluids, sweat, heart and steel.

Within moments, ladder tops were appearing again all along the walls, only to be shunted away with forked poles as fast as they were raised. The defenders walked a fine line, as it was pointless to push away an empty ladder, but to wait until attackers began to climb was like an invitation to them to reach the heights.

Sure enough, within a few minutes scores of small fights had broken out as some few Terachites had managed to reach the tops of their ladders. For a moment, Anton's heart almost faltered as it looked as if the defenders were about to be swamped by enemy fighters. However, slowly but surely the enemy were cut down and forced back until the momentum of the attack had been lost and the defenders once more held the upper hand.

'I'm too old for this, Anton,' the King grunted as he heaved the dead body of the warrior that he had just killed over the side of the battlements.

'Nonsense, your Majesty,' he replied with a grin. 'But you *are* going to let the medic bandage that arm. Hey! You... Medic. Over here! Now!'

*   *   *   *   *

'That one. The young one with the dark hair,' the Dagali Clan Leader stated, pointing at Bek who was systematically killing one Terachite warrior after another in quick succession.

'Yea gods, Maharl! He is like the Saastrani, the swirling whirlwind of death that plagues the Terachim hot season.'

'What's the matter, Zettar? Do you think that he will prevail against "The Hammer of the Dagali"? Is not mine the most feared swordarm in the Terachim aside from that of the Chosen One?'

'Of course, my Maharl. You are unstoppable,' Zettar answered mechanically. Inside, though, he was not quite so sure.

'Assemble me a dozen of our best blades and I shall drive a wedge through the soft-skin lines. What's more I shall do it right there,' the Dagali leader stated, pointing once more at where Bek was standing in the Thrandorian line. 'That one is to be mine,' he added through gritted teeth.

'Of course, Maharl. Right away,' Zettar said, hurrying as best he could through the massed throng of fighters jostling to get closer to the enemy ranks.

Ten minutes or so later Zettar returned with eleven others. All were hand-picked fighters of the highest calibre, chosen to join the Dagali leader. The Maharl was standing, watching in fascination as Bek killed again and again.

'Ah! There you are, Zettar. That young soft-skin will be a worthy opponent. He has killed eight of our Embara brothers since you left and I don't think that one of them so much as scratched him. Come, let us show the Embara how the Dagali fight and I can face an opponent worthy of my skill.'

A chill ran down Zettar's spine as he looked forward at the enemy line. There was something about the young dark haired fighter – something he had not seen before. Yes, he was fast. Yes, he moved with a balance and smoothness that displayed great skill... but there was something more, something different.

The Maharl pushed his way forward and his elite guard formed a wedge-shaped group around him. Together, they barged their way forward in short order to where the two lines were locked in combat.

In all the pushing and shoving, the Dagali Maharl had missed the mark by a few yards and to his chagrin the young swordsman was no longer fighting. He had fallen back from the front line and was talking to a lithe-bodied female with a fighter's visage. 'Now that was a woman worthy for a Maharl to sport with,' he thought to himself.

Inexorably, the small wedge of Dagali fighters pushed forward and the soldiers of Thrandor fell back or died before the swift blades of the Dagali.

'To me!' the female fighter was yelling as she sprinted across to stop the Thrandorian line from being pierced. Others followed. The Maharl's heart leapt as he saw that the dark haired fighter was among them and heading straight for him. With a flashing cut and a lightning-like thrust the Dagali leader disposed of the soldier in front of him. Bek smoothly moved into his place.

'Now we will see just how good you really are,' the Maharl snarled in the Terachim tongue and his blade clashed with Bek's in a rapid exchange of blows.

It took several seconds for comprehension to dawn that something was wrong. The Dagali leader felt a burning sensation in his chest and was unable to draw breath. His hand went to his throat and he was shocked to feel a huge slice, pouring blood. How had he fallen to his knees? There was no memory of a wound. No one could be that fast. 'Impossible,' he mouthed as he fell forward and life drained from him.

From the corner of his eye Zettar saw his leader fall. He was not surprised at the outcome of the encounter so much as the speed at which it was resolved. The Maharl, for all his overconfidence in his ability, was a fine swordsman – indeed, probably the best that Zettar had seen before today. However, there was something about that dark haired fighter. He had seen it from the start. 'No time to dwell on it,' he thought to himself. 'This woman knows how to handle a blade as well.'

Zettar had barely finished the thought when agony bloomed in his chest. He too had not even seen the thrust that felled him.

Derra moved on.

*   *   *   *   *

'Ramiff, have the Signaller sound the retreat to those attacking the city.'

'But, Chosen One... it is only a matter of time before we prevail.'

'I know, Ramiff, but we are wasting too many men trying to fight on two fronts and holding the worst ground on both. Pull them back. We need to destroy those enemy lines up on the North Slope before they get reinforced. This whole situation is galling but we still hold a huge advantage of numbers. Let's not lose that by throwing away lives unnecessarily. Sound the retreat.'

'At once, Chosen One.'

Demarr watched his personal aide go running and his fists clenched in pure frustration when, moments later, the horns started calling those attacking the city to fall back.

'Damn you, Malo. You will not hang on to your petty throne this time,' he muttered.

*　　*　　*　　*　　*

For the second time that morning a loud cheer went up amongst the defenders on the wall of Mantor. The Terachites were in full retreat from the walls. King Malo, however, was not cheering. He was looking across the valley at where his allies from the north were being hard pressed to hold their ground. Baron Anton stepped up beside his frowning King.

'They are being hit hard, Anton,' the King stated, his voice melancholic. 'We've got to do something to help them.'

'I agree, your Majesty,' replied Anton in an upbeat tone. 'We have six hundred horses prepared to ride. The enemy have no archers that we have seen as yet, and with the scarcity of wood in the Terachim Wastes I would find it hard to believe that they have a significant number of men trained with bow and arrow. It is my recommendation that we send out the cavalry to harry the enemy. Their own cavalry have been hard hit in that foolish charge up the North Slope. I think that if we hit them hard and fast at random time intervals, the nomads will be forced to hold back troops to counter us. It will afford at least a modicum of relief to our forces up there.'

'Very well, Anton. In addition to that I want you to know that if I deem that it has become necessary, we will commit all of our forces here in an attack,' the King replied. 'Let's face a few home truths here,' he continued.

'If the Terachites manage to destroy our forces on the North Ridge they will be free to attack the city again unhindered, which is undoubtedly why they are now concentrating their efforts in that direction. But I will not allow it, Anton. No longer will one Thrandorian stand by whilst another fights for their life. From now on we fight together whether we live or die.'

Anton turned to face the King and bowed deeply.

'A worthy policy, your Majesty. Let us pray that such a bold move shall bring such a victory as has never been seen before.'

With that, Anton departed once more towards the North Gate whilst the King gazed anxiously northward at the tightly locked lines of antagonists on the other side of the valley.

CHAPTER 17

Sensing the weakness on his opponent's left side, Calvyn launched a blindingly fast stroke past his enemy's guard and dealt the man a crippling wound to his sword arm. As the Terachite warrior screamed in pain and dropped his sword, Calvyn lunged and ran the golden skinned warrior through. Another man leapt into his dead countryman's place, and the pattern of stroke and counterstroke recommenced.

The opposing forces had been locked together for over two and a half hours now, with neither side making any significant progress. The Terachites were numerous, but despite being heavily outnumbered, the superior training of the Thrandorian troops was showing through. Charges by the cavalry out of Mantor and by Lord Valdeer's horsemen proved devastating, and for a while the Terachim forces were on the defensive. However, as time passed the fatigue of the long march south by the Northern Lord's men, combined with the superior numbers of the enemy forces, began to take its toll.

Gradually, the Terachites had forced the Thrandorian troops back step by step until they were virtually backed up against the trees. Many Thrandorian soldiers of lesser ability had been killed, but those who remained in the ever-thinning lines fought with ferocious skill and determination. Eventually, breakthroughs by the Terachites started to become more frequent, and at one point a wedge of Terachite soldiers managed to break through not far from where Calvyn and Jenna were fighting desperately hard to contain the relentless push of the sabre-wielding invaders. For a moment, Captain Strexis and a handful of others were all that held the Terachite thrust from disintegrating the line. It was only a charge led by the ever vigilant Derra, who attacked with Bek and a dozen or so men from one side, along with another attack led by Corporal Gan on the other side, which together managed to plug the gap and drive the Terachites back.

Bek's skill was causing havoc amongst the ranks of the enemy and his lightning-fast strokes felled opponents wherever he went. Death seemed to hang over him like a cloud as he rapidly gained a reputation amongst the soldiers of both attackers and defenders alike. However, individual prowess amongst the slowly dwindling numbers of Thrandorian troops was gradually proving to be in vain as they were pressed harder and harder, and continued to lose ground to the greater numbers of the invading forces.

Then, just as the Terachites had sensed that victory was within their grasp and the Thrandorian line appeared on the point of folding under the intense pressure, five hundred fresh troops had stepped out from the trees and bolstered the rapidly tiring Thrandorian soldiers. Lord Valdeer's foot soldiers had marched hard to reach the battle, but were now eager to join in with the fighting.

Calvyn was only too glad to step back from the front line to catch his breath. He had killed several Terachites in the fighting and the experience had left him feeling sick to the core. It was one thing to fire arrows at horsemen fifty paces or more away, but it was quite another to run a sword through a man and watch the light fade from his eyes. The smell of gore and sweat was overpowering and the stinging of minor cuts on his arms and upper body clouded his mind as he strove to find mental release from the mayhem of battle.

As it happened, by pure chance the King chose that very same moment to launch an all out counterstrike from the city. King Malo had been carefully observing the changing tides of fortune from his vantage point on the tower of the North Gate, and had sensed that unless something changed quickly his allies on the North Slope would be overpowered. In a last-ditch effort to support them, the King himself had led the strike down the hill at the mass of enemy soldiers holding the valley.

'Well, would you look at that?' Jenna said with a laugh, as she too stepped back from the fighting to catch her breath, the fresh troops having joined the lines. 'Those city boys have got jealous and come down for their share,' she added with that mischievous grin which Calvyn felt was one of her most attractive attributes.

'Glad to see that you're still in one piece,' Calvyn said with heartfelt sincerity. 'When I saw that really big guy swinging away at you out of the corner of my eye, I must admit that I didn't rate your chances too highly.'

'Oh, him,' Jenna replied, dismissively. 'Well you know what they say... the bigger they are, the harder they fall... and boy did he fall! A kick where it hurts most and he didn't look anywhere near as imposing,' she chuckled.

Calvyn winced.

'You didn't?'

'Oh, you men!' exclaimed Jenna, slapping her thigh with her hand and laughing out loud. 'You'll happily shoot each other with arrows, or slice one another up with swords, but even mention hurting a man's privates and you go all squeamish.'

'It's just...'

'... not the done thing?' finished Jenna, still grinning.

Calvyn nodded with a lopsided and embarrassed grin of his own.

'Well I don't know about you, but I intend to be around for the victory celebrations. I hear that the food is good in Mantor and I'm feeling remarkably peckish right now. Might I be so bold as to suggest that you curb your inhibitions a bit so that we can see this rabble off with a bit more urgency? I'd hate to miss lunch.'

Calvyn's smile broadened, and then changed from mirth to greeting as Jez walked over to join them.

'Calvyn, Jenna, nice to see that you're still with us.'

'Yes, we're quite pleased about that too,' Jenna replied glibly. 'Have you finished your quota yet?'

'Quota?' Jez asked, a puzzled expression forming on his face.

'It's OK, Jez. Jenna has been doling out the enemy to make sure that nobody gets greedy and kills more than their fair share,' Calvyn explained. 'I think that she might be forced to have words with Bek later though,' he continued, pointing at where their friend was still fighting with a speed and fury that defied belief.

'Hmm! Well I'm afraid that not everyone has managed to pull their weight on that score,' Jez said sadly. 'You may need to do some more sums, Jenna, because we've lost a lot of good soldiers today.'

'Anyone we know?' Calvyn asked, his face sobering instantly.

Jez nodded, his expression flat with grief.

'Sergeant Brett early on, but you probably already knew that. Corporal Gan was killed not that long ago, and we've lost...' Jez reeled off a long list of names, many of which were familiar to Calvyn and Jenna. Some of the names evoked pictures instantly in their minds whilst others were just tantalisingly familiar.

At the end of his list, Jez paused and looked reluctantly at Calvyn and Jenna as if unsure as to whether he should continue.

'Unfortunately, that's not all,' he said slowly.

'Who?' asked Jenna quietly, no longer in a jocular mood.

'Matim,'

Calvyn and Jenna fell silent, their faces ashen as the news sank in. Matim had been one of their closest friends through training and it was hard to conceive, even here amidst the biggest battle that Thrandor had seen in centuries, that he could be dead.

Tears welled in Jenna's eyes and Calvyn drew his lips into a tight, hard line.

'I'm sorry,' Jez apologised. 'Maybe I should have left

you to find out later...' Jez drew breath to continue talking but then paused, momentarily distracted by a strange sight down behind the enemy battle line.

'It's alright, Jez. Thanks for...' Jenna said comfortingly, thinking that Jez had run out of words.

Urgently he interrupted her.

'Jenna, tell me I'm going mad if you will, but that man down there directing those Terachite troops is no Terachim-born nomad, or I'm the Emperor of Shandar.'

'Great Tarmin!' Jenna exclaimed as she spotted the figure that Jez was pointing at. 'It's Earl Demarr!'

'Demarr? Are you sure?' Calvyn asked, his voice cold and hard.

'Absolutely. I met him once, and saw him on several other occasions. It's Demarr all right, but what is he doing dressed as a Terachite?'

Calvyn ignored the question, a great rage boiling up inside his gut which burned with fierce intensity. In his mind, chaos abruptly ruled. Torturous images haunted him. Pictures of his home village that fateful day when Perdimonn and he had ridden up the lane to find family and friends dead flashed through his mind like a carousel. First those from his home village and now Matim, Brett, Gan and all the others. It was all too much. Everything that he had ever heard or associated with Demarr tumbled through his head like an avalanche. What he had heard, good and bad alike, made no difference now. Demarr was one of the enemy. That was enough to know.

'*Ardeva!*' Calvyn yelled, holding his sword high.

At the pronouncement of that magical rune his sword burst into flames, the blue tongues of fire licking their way hungrily up the blade. Before he knew what he was doing he had cast aside his shield, barged his way between two of his fellow troops and was hacking his way through the enemy soldiers in a direct line towards the focus of his anger.

'Calvyn! What are you doing?' shouted Jenna in alarm, as Calvyn smashed his way into the enemy like some bounding boulder, crashing down the hill with unstoppable momentum.

Calvyn, however, was deaf to her cries. His whole consciousness was intent on reaching Demarr.

More magical runes flooded from his lips in an unconscious flow and a protective force field of magical energy sprang up around his body, glowing with the same fresh green as the first shoots of spring. Terachite soldiers scrabbled to get out of his way as his flashing sword carved a path through their ranks. As if from nowhere, amongst them had appeared this frightening apparition, whose aura shattered weapons and whose burning sword brought death wherever it turned. Calvyn's incensed visage and flaming sword gave him the bearing of a god of war, full of wrath and set on exacting justice. Unsurprisingly, none could stand before him.

'Chosen One! Look out!' Ramiff screamed as he saw Calvyn cleaving his way towards the Terachite leader.

The words hit Calvyn like a falling tree.

'Chosen One... Chosen One... Chosen One...' echoed through his mind, as the maniacal laugh of the old crone in the market place mocked him from the past.

'You will burn... you will burn... you will burn...' screeched the crazed old woman's voice in his mind.

Calvyn hesitated briefly, confused emotions cascading through his mind. However, he had come too far to turn back, and the brief faltering merely served to cool the blind burning rage to an icy cold determination. Gritting his teeth and marching onward, Calvyn swept away the last of the opposition until only Ramiff stood between him and Demarr

'Move aside, Ramiff. This opponent is not for you,' ordered Demarr to his personal aide.

'Never, Master. I will not let you face "The Sword" alone.'

With a yell of defiance, the faithful servant charged at Calvyn, his curved sabre raised high above his head. In an instinctive reaction that was born out of hours of practice with Bek, Calvyn blocked the down-swinging blow from Ramiff and whipped a slashing cut of his own across the Terachite's body. Ramiff folded over the massive wound, his sword dropped and his hands clutched at the great rent in his flesh.

A strangled cry escaped Demarr's lips that ended in a groaning sob. Then the silver talisman that was hanging against his chest began to glow with a sickly white light. The light brightened rapidly to a blazing brilliance, and as the malevolent gleaming intensified, so Demarr's face contorted from genuine anguish into an evil, vicious snarl. It was a frightening and unnatural transformation to behold, and the sight of this strange metamorphosis sent shivers running up and down Calvyn's spine. Almost unnoticed at first, but then more obviously, the sword in Calvyn's hands began to glow a rich blue green warning of the evil power of the talisman, and the flames which ran up and down the blade danced higher in anticipation of the forthcoming conflict.

Demarr strode forward, his eyes blazing under the malignant influence of the medallion. Calvyn moved calmly to meet him, the green aura of energy still sparkling its unpolluted protection around him. The conflict in Calvyn's mind no longer troubled him and his way was clear. This was not about vengeance any more, but about conquering evil. What faced him was no longer the man whom he held responsible for the death of his parents, but a force of darkness which needed to be destroyed.

The two adversaries smoothly circled around one another. Demarr prowled, predator-like in his motions. Calvyn maintained a solid defensive stance, moving easily but cautiously as he watched every minute motion of his enemy for a sign of weakness.

Without warning, a bolt of lightning-like flame leapt from Demarr's talisman and punched through Calvyn's magical force field. In that frozen instant of time it seemed almost as if the bolt changed direction in the air slightly before striking Calvyn's brightly glowing sword. The green protective barrier around Calvyn dissolved instantaneously with an audible pop, and he nearly lost his grip on the sword as it leapt in his hand under the impact of the bolt of magical energy.

Calvyn staggered, and Demarr leapt in behind that magical blow. For several seconds Calvyn barely managed to stave off the pounding rain of strokes which his opponent dealt with deadly skill, and the hours of swordplay with Bek were all that kept him alive during the following few minutes. Calvyn, although inexperienced in battle, had put in months of practice with his highly skilled friend. Demarr on the other hand was a renowned swordsman, but he had not faced a serious opponent in anger for months, if not years. The resulting duel was finely balanced, with each combatant alternately gaining and losing the upper hand on several occasions. Meanwhile, a magical struggle raged with equal intensity.

After the initial explosive bolt of flame from Demarr's talisman, more of the white, lightning-like fire was blasted at Calvyn with ever-increasing frequency. Somehow, each bolt of energy was caught and dissolved by Calvyn's magical blade. However, after the jolt of the first impact, Calvyn felt nothing except heat when subsequent bolts struck. The white fire was simply absorbed into the sword. It was as if the sword had adapted to the talisman's attacks and was cushioning the shock of each new burst of flame.

Calvyn and Demarr whirled and weaved in a flashing exchange of blows which drew the awareness of many of the soldiers around them. The flaming magic of talisman and sword gradually demanded attention from all, and bit by bit the two lines of the opposing armies drew back from one another. Before long the eyes of aggressors and defenders alike were transfixed by the stunning spectacle of the duel.

Twice in quick succession Demarr almost got past Calvyn's guard, but each time Calvyn blocked the stroke a hair's breadth before his opponent's sword tasted blood. The crackling energy of the talisman was flowing in an almost constant flow at the blade of Calvyn's sword now and the brightly glowing blue green weapon was getting hotter in his grasp by the second.

Sweat flowed down Calvyn's body like rivers as again and again he parried and swung, blocked and lunged at his enemy. Every sinew in his body was taut and straining to the limit to produce that vital winning stroke. Demarr's eyes glittered with evil as he pressed home attack after attack, only to find each assault blocked and the counterstrokes testing his own defences to the limit.

Pain began lancing up Calvyn's arms as the sword hilt became so hot in his hands that the skin on his palms began to blister, but with teeth gritted in dogged determination he fought on with a degree of skill which only months before he would never have believed possible. Then, with a move so unexpected that it caught Calvyn completely by surprise, Demarr leapt forward whilst blocking Calvyn's sweeping stroke and crashed shoulder first into him.

Thrown completely off balance, Calvyn lost his footing altogether and fell backward to the ground. Demarr's sword whistled down towards him in a vicious arc that many of the thousands of spectators fully anticipated would be the killing blow. Somehow, in a reflex action that defied belief, Calvyn managed to block the descending sword with his own. At the same time, the motion of leaning forward to put weight behind his stroke caused Demarr's medallion to swing away from his chest, suspended on the silver chain that looped around his neck. In blocking Demarr's descending blade, Calvyn's own sword tip made brief contact with the silver chain of the magical talisman. A massive explosion rocked the earth in the instant of that contact and the resulting force hurled Demarr off his feet. The former Earl flew several yards through the air and landed heavily in a stunned and crumpled heap.

Calvyn too was stunned by the blast. His ears rang with the aftershock but, strangely, his body had remained untouched by the force of the explosion.

Slowly, he pushed himself to a sitting position and looked across to where the crumpled form of Demarr lay some distance away. From where Calvyn was sitting it was impossible to tell whether the former Earl was alive or dead, but whichever was the case his opponent no longer posed a threat.

A sort of low groaning sound ran through the ranks of the Terachite army, but around him no one moved. It was eerie. All sounds of battle had now ceased, but the quiet was somehow unnatural.

Calvyn staggered to his feet with his glowing sword still grasped tightly in his blistered right hand. As he looked around in suspicion at the motionless armies around him he spotted a slight movement on the hillside to the east of where he was standing. A path was forming amongst the mass of troops there. Without a sound, the soldiers were all moving aside to allow a single horseman passage through to where Calvyn was standing. The rider was dressed in black, with a long dark flowing cloak that fluttered behind him in the breeze. His horse, also black, moved at a dancing canter through the parting sea of warriors, and the horseman's long black flowing hair was tied back in a single pony tail that patted against his back as the huge horse pranced along the side of the slope.

Calvyn waited. Setting his feet shoulder width apart, he placed his hands on the pommel of his sword and used the point of the blade against the ground as a tripod-like brace to help him stand firmly.

The rider approached, halted, and dismounted, landing lightly on his leather booted feet.

'Hello, Selkor. I would say that it's nice to see you again, but it's not,' Calvyn said casually, his voice calm and his face set in what he hoped was an unconcerned and relaxed expression.

Inside, Calvyn's heart had sunk at the appearance of the Shandese Magician. He knew that he was in no fit state to fight again, and from what little he knew of the enigmatic Selkor from his conversations with Perdimonn,

293

Calvyn doubted that he would ever be able to challenge the Shandese Magician.

'Ah! The apprentice. My, haven't you grown a few teeth, boy,' Selkor returned, his face sneering and contemptuous. 'Read any good books recently?' he added with a mocking laugh.

'Actually, yes. But nothing that you would consider worthy of study.'

'Maybe. Maybe not,' Selkor temporised, walking forward until he was only a few paces in front of Calvyn, staring straight into the young soldier's eyes the whole while.

Calvyn blanched slightly under that gaze, his heart pounding heavily in his chest as he remembered what Perdimonn had said about a Magician being able to take his precious grimoire from him by force.

'Don't mess with me, boy. You are not in my league,' the Magician said quietly, his voice flat and his face no longer amused. 'Your mentor could not stand against me, so don't think for one second that your little toy there will avail you one iota,' Selkor continued, gesturing at Calvyn's still brightly glowing sword. Flames still ran their blue tongues along the length of the blade, but seemed to sputter somewhat under the Magician's steely gaze.

Calvyn's heart seemed to skip a beat at the mention of Perdimonn, but the voice of his old friend once more sounded quietly in his ear. 'Don't rise to the bait. He is right. You cannot challenge him.'

The familiar voice sounding so clearly in his ear relaxed him.

'So why are you here, Selkor? Surely you didn't come all this way south just to talk to me?'

'My deeds are my own concern, boy. As it happens the crossing of our paths is pure chance, so don't let it go to your head. I heard rumours of an invading army led by someone bearing a magical talisman. Such items are rare. Indeed, I have only confirmed the existence of a handful of them, and each of the others is in the possession of the Council of Magicians.'

Before he could stop himself, Calvyn's eyes looked across to where Demarr lay unmoving on the ground. Selkor followed the glance.

'Ah! So that was the said leader I take it?' Selkor stated more than asked. 'That would explain the fireworks earlier on, and would make this...' the Shandese Magician continued, stooping in the grass to pick up the silver talisman from where it had fallen in the grass nearby. '... the magical item in question.'

Calvyn took an involuntary half step forward in dismay, but Selkor's head turned and his icy stare froze Calvyn to the spot.

'Don't even think about it,' Selkor hissed.

The Shandese Magician looked once more at the silver medallion on its now broken chain and turned it over and over in his hands. As he studied the runes on the beautifully crafted talisman Selkor's eyes opened wide in amazement, comprehension of the origin of the masterpiece dawning in his mind.

'Darkweaver's amulet!' he gasped. 'It must be. There could not be two such works in existence. Darkweaver's amulet in *my* hands!'

Selkor threw back his head and laughed out loud. The sound of that laughter chilled the wind.

'Well, boy, you have undoubtedly saved me what could possibly have proved a tricky confrontation today. For that you have my thanks. Even in the hands of one who has no knowledge of this amulet's potential, or how to use it properly, the power would be difficult to overcome. What intrigues me is that you managed to do so. Indeed, you broke the chain, which I would have thought impossible for one of so little training. Perhaps I have underestimated the power of your sword after all. Come. Let me see.'

Calvyn's hands clenched tightly around the hilt of his precious sword, and the pain from his burned palms gave him a focus for his thoughts. Involuntary tears sprang to his eyes with the wave of pain that raced up his arms as he braced himself to fight in order to prevent Selkor from taking the magical weapon from him. A short-lived battle of wills ensued, but before he realised what had happened, Calvyn found that under Selkor's dark gaze he had handed the sword over even as he had been mentally preparing to strike. The dark eyes held him transfixed for a moment longer before turning their attention to the blade of the sword.

As soon as Selkor took hold of the sword, both the flames and the glow extinguished abruptly. The Magician looked carefully at the blade whilst Calvyn looked helplessly on. The visible runes glowed briefly as Selkor muttered a spell under his breath, but apart from that the sword did not react to him in any way. After the explosive contact with the silver talisman, Calvyn was somewhat surprised by the blade's quiescence.

'Ah yes. Just as I thought. The blade acted like a magical lightning rod,' Selkor said thoughtfully. 'An interesting idea. Not something for which I have any great use though. You may keep your toy, lad.'

Selkor tossed the sword back to Calvyn who caught it mid-flight and winced at the pain of that contact with his palm. The blade blazed back into light, and flames once more danced in the morning sun.

'It's a cleverly constructed toy, Apprentice. However, a toy is still a toy. Be warned... think again of swinging your pretty little weapon at me and you will not live long enough to finish that thought,' Selkor stated coldly.

With that, Selkor turned and walked back to his great black horse, which was casually munching at the grass where the Magician had left him. Carefully placing the silver talisman into his saddlebag, he placed his left foot into the stirrup and swung himself up onto the horse's back.

'It's been an interesting and profitable afternoon, but if you'll excuse me I must be going,' Selkor said, his face twisting in an unpleasant smile. 'I apologise for interfering in your morning's entertainment,' he added with a sweeping gesture that encompassed the two armies. 'I'll leave you to it.'

With that parting comment, Selkor wheeled his horse around and cantered sedately back along the waiting path through the mass of Terachite soldiers. The gap closed silently behind him as he made his way eastward along the ridge and away from Mantor, and with his departure the green blue glow of Calvyn's sword faded until the blade appeared steel grey once more. However, the magical flames continued to dance along its length, undampened by the withdrawal of the evil talisman.

The moment that Selkor cleared the eastern extreme of the battlefield, movement and noise broke out afresh. Terachite horns signalled a retreat and the Thrandorian troops marched forward in response.

'*Damok*,' Calvyn said quietly, and the flames that had been continuously licking along his blade died instantaneously at the pronouncement of that rune of power.

With complete unconcern at what was going on around him, Calvyn walked over to where Demarr still lay unmoving on the grassy hillside. Terachite soldiers poured past him, but all gave him a wide berth, terrified of getting within reach of the sword that had defeated the power of the Chosen One. It was with great satisfaction that Calvyn noted a slight rising and falling of the erstwhile Earl's chest. Demarr still lived. The so-called 'Chosen One' had a lot to answer for, and Calvyn wanted to be sure that he did just that.

Clearing his mind of the clamour around him, Calvyn closed his eyes and focused on his badly burnt hands, which were still causing rivers of pain to rush up and down his arms. Seeing the healing runes in his mind's eye, he pronounced the requisite spell and immediately felt the cooling balm of magic smooth away the heat from his palms. Without pausing, Calvyn continued to use his magic to heal each of the minor cuts and wounds that he had sustained during the fighting. When he had finished, he felt whole and invigorated by the process.

On opening his eyes he found that Derra and Jenna

were standing nearby and watching him with open curiosity.

'Who *are* you?' Jenna asked, the question ripping from her mouth like an explosion and her voice clearly portraying the sense of betrayal that she felt.

'I think that you have some explaining to do,' Derra added coldly.

'I'll second that sentiment,' interrupted Captain Tegrani, as he arrived and assessed the situation with his intuitive gaze. 'Private Calvyn, it seems that whenever there is something unusual going on, I find *you* in the middle of it. I want answers, Private. I don't know what's going on here but I cannot ignore what I, together with half of Thrandor, just witnessed. You will be held to account so you had better start formulating some damned good answers and fast.'

'The truth will not take any formulating, Sir,' Calvyn replied calmly, 'but it will take some time to tell, and is strange enough that even the most open-minded might have difficulty in believing it.'

'After the light show that you just put on, I think that I'll suspend judgement on that, young man.'

Tegrani nudged at the unconscious enemy leader with the toe of his boot and a look of surprise flashed across his face.

'Demarr! The Baron will want to be told of this development immediately. The outcast will undoubtedly have some questions of his own to answer.'

Tegrani turned to Derra.

'Sergeant, make sure that this prisoner is well guarded. Also, ensure that Private Calvyn is available for questioning as soon as the enemy are on the other side of the River Fallow.'

'Yes, Sir,' Derra replied, saluting smartly.

The Captain strode off, shouting orders at the troops as he went, whilst Derra turned her gaze back to Calvyn, her eyes sharp and penetrating.

'I too will want answers, Calvyn,' she stated coldly.

'And I will do my best to give them, Sergeant.'

'In the meantime I am somewhat busy. Jenna, you stay with Calvyn and guard Demarr. And for Tarmin's sake, keep him out of trouble for a couple of hours would you, Private? He's caused me more headaches than this lot,' she added, gesturing broadly at the retreating army of Terachite warriors.

'I'll try, Sergeant,' Jenna said somewhat uncertainly.

'Well, you captured him, Calvyn. I trust that you are not about to let him get away?'

'Not likely, Sergeant,' Calvyn replied with a grin.

'Very well, Privates. See that you don't.'

Calvyn and Jenna watched Derra stride off in the same direction that Captain Tegrani had gone only moments before. Demarr stirred slightly. An uneasy silence settled between the two friends as they began their guard duty together.

The distinct battle lines of earlier in the day had totally dissolved now. Calvyn noted with interest that the enemy army was in total disarray as they retreated. Even within the individual clans there seemed to be no effective leadership or cohesion. The Thrandorian troops on the other hand were now being marshalled into new lines and advancing in an orderly fashion to shepherd the enemy towards the Fallow Bridge.

Some minutes passed before Jenna finally broke the ice and started talking again, her question of 'Who are you, Calvyn?' a gentler repeat of her earlier demand, softly recommencing dialogue between them.

'I am the same Calvyn that you trained with Jenna. I haven't changed. I have kept certain abilities hidden from you for reasons that should be obvious, but that doesn't change who I am.'

'No, Calvyn, you are wrong. Of course it changes who you are. Magic could do nothing else. It sets you aside from everyone else no matter how you use it. Everything is starting to make sense now. You were always different from the other guys but I could never put my finger on what it was about you. Those lotions you used to heal the squad with – magic I suppose?'

Calvyn nodded.

'Made by my mentor, an old Magician named Perdimonn,' he confirmed.

'No wonder they acted so fast. Was that him on the black horse just now? I couldn't hear you talking but I gathered that you knew each other.'

'No, that wasn't Perdimonn. That was big trouble. The man on the black horse was a powerful Shandese Magician called Selkor. All I know of him is that he is at odds with Perdimonn over something that he called a "Key of Power". It was Selkor who caused Perdimonn and I to part company, but that's a story for another day... Demarr was the "Chosen One".'

'What?'

'You remember the crone in the market place?'

'How could I forget?' Jenna answered with a shudder.

'Well, Demarr was referred to by the Terachite nomads as "The Chosen One". The old seeress was right, my hands did burn by his power. The only thing was – it wasn't really his power. All the magical power belonged to the silver amulet that he was wearing. What's more, Derra has been promoted again... also as predicted. I don't want to worry you, Jenna, but the only one of us that has not yet seen the old woman's words come to fruition is you.'

Jenna's face was thoughtful as she contemplated Calvyn's words, and she was still thinking over all that had happened when five horsemen rode up the slope towards them and brought their horses to a halt nearby. Demarr stirred again and groaned as he lapsed back into unconsciousness.

The five riders all dismounted and, noting by the dress of the horsemen that they were of high rank, Calvyn and Jenna stood to attention and saluted. Acknowledging the salute, two of the riders handed the reins of their horses to the others and then walked across to where Calvyn and Jenna were standing smartly by their prisoner.

'Tell me, young soldiers, was it one of you who fought that duel up here on the hillside?' asked the silver haired old man.

Calvyn's eyes took in the burnished breastplate and shining helm. Comprehension flooded his mind as suddenly as if a tidal wave had struck, and he stammered out a jumbled affirmative with a 'your Majesty' mixed somewhere in the middle.

The King smiled kindly.

'Relax. I did not come to chastise but to convey my thanks to you. That you fought using the illegal powers of magic was obvious. However, considering the results of your intervention I am sure that I can overlook that use on this occasion. I am led to believe that you fought the leader of the invading army... the one they called "The Chosen One". Is this he?'

'It is, your Majesty.'

'He doesn't look like a Terachite to me.'

Demarr had rolled over and lapsed back into unconsciousness. He was now lying on his stomach with his face away from the King. Calvyn reached down and rolled the banished Earl over onto his back so that the King could see his face.

'Demarr!' the King exclaimed, his face suddenly angry. 'I should have killed that troublemaker the first time he tried to take the throne. Is he dead?'

'No, your Majesty,' Calvyn replied.

'Then kill him now, before he causes any more trouble.'

'Before I do so, your Majesty, I think that you should be aware that Demarr was not really responsible for all this,' Calvyn said quickly, nervous in the extreme at questioning the King's orders.

The King's eyes widened slightly, but he contained his emotions.

'Go ahead, Soldier, explain how this is so. But I warn you, this will have to be an exceptionally good defence, for I am in no mood to forgive the man who has caused thousands of my subjects to be killed and my kingdom to be invaded.'

'I understand, your Majesty, and until about half an

301

hour ago I would not have hesitated for one second to run him through,' Calvyn replied.

'Wake up the traitor first, Private. He should hear this,' the King directed, gesturing to Jenna to wake Demarr.

Jenna shook the unconscious Earl with no effect, so she took her water flask and emptied it over Demarr's face. With a slight splutter Demarr awoke and looked around bleary eyed, obviously confused by his whereabouts and the company that was standing around him. Slowly, a horrified realisation spread across his face.

Quickly outlining the circumstances of the murder of his parents by Demarr's Rebels, Calvyn told of his taking to the road with a kindly old stranger who had offered to take him under his wing and teach him a trade. The King appeared sympathetic, and Baron Anton confirmed that what Calvyn had said about the village was true. Calvyn did not elaborate on the arcane side of his tuition, but skipped on to his joining Baron Keevan's army and to the very different views of his fellow soldiers on the character of Earl Demarr, and the virtual hero status that the banished traitor had held amongst them. The King nodded thoughtfully at that, and Demarr hung his head in shame. Finally, Calvyn told of the silver talisman that Demarr had been wearing, and what little that he knew about it.

'Darkweaver? Come now, surely you don't expect me to believe that Derrigan Darkweaver, who if he ever even existed would have died at least two hundred years ago, could be responsible for the actions of this man?' the King said, incredulous at the suggestion. 'What proof can you offer?'

'Nothing that I can physically show you, your Majesty,' Calvyn replied, cautiously. 'However, you must have seen the strange rider dressed in black, who rode through the battlefield after my duel with Demarr.'

'Yes, I was going to ask you about him. It was the strangest sensation. I was watching everything that was going on, but I seemed to be completely unable to move when he appeared. It was really most unusual,' the King said thoughtfully.

'The reason that you could not move, your Majesty, was that you were under a magical spell which Selkor had cast over everyone in both of the armies. He is a very powerful Magician from Shandar. I have met him before.'

'A Magician you say. From Shandar. Hmm... that would certainly explain it. However, I am not sure that I can believe that a silver trinket, even one made by Darkweaver, could cause an invasion.'

'I'm not certain that I know the full story, your Majesty, and to tell it would take a long time. However, the unfortunate fact is that Selkor now has the amulet, which he identified as the one created by Derrigan Darkweaver. I have read several texts which suggested that such an artefact had once existed, but none said specifically what powers it had, or indeed whether or not it had actually been destroyed in the battle between Derrigan and the Brotherhood of Magicians all those years ago. What the implications are of Selkor having taken it, I am not yet entirely sure either, but you can be sure of one thing... the evidence points to a disaster that will make this battle look like child's play.'

Here ends Book 1 of *The Darkweaver Legacy*. Book 2 – '*Trail of the Huntress*' will unfold the meaning of the old crone's prediction for Jenna, and see the power and breadth of Calvyn's magical abilities increased by an unlikely source.

For information on future releases, please see our website at www.swordpublishing.co.uk